Further Praise for

THE FUGITIVE WIFE

A *New York Times Book Review* "Editor's Choice"

"An enormously satisfying first novel about the dreamers and schemers who flocked to Alaska at the turn of the 20th century. . . . In the end, Brown's impressive debut is less about the search for gold than the search for self."

—Gregory Cowles, *New York Times Book Review*

"*The Fugitive Wife* is storytelling at its best."

—Sybil Downing, *Denver Post*

"A gripping story about the search for gold, for love; for the discovery of honor and the mysteries of the human heart."

—Paulette Jiles, author of *Enemy Women*

"An ambitious, sweeping view of an unusual place at an unusual moment in history. Brown's prose is extraordinarily confident, his plot finely woven and his characters keenly wrought. Combining facts with a modern-day poetic flare makes his settings melt onto the page. . . . This is not a cannonball blast back in time; it's a seduction into a world . . . of common individuals on a voyage of loss and beginnings."

—Amanda Coyne, *Anchorage Daily News*

"Strikes not one but two rich veins of history. . . . [A] cinematic and artfully braided tale."

—Sarah T. Williams, *Minneapolis Star Tribune*

"This is compelling and entertaining history, a stay-up-all-night read. You'll never forget Essie and her journey to freedom. I haven't rooted this hard for characters since *Cold Mountain*. Peter C. Brown is certainly one of the best new writers of historical fiction on the scene today." —Jonis Agee, author of *The Weight of Dreams*

"An eloquent, memorable first novel, with high-powered characters whose prickly exteriors, created out of the need to survive, hide affectingly yearning and haunted souls." —*Publishers Weekly*

"A cinematic first novel. . . . Brown structures this book like a well-made porch, allowing us a panoramic view. . . . Full of quiet authenticity, sharp observation and wonderful colloquialism."
—Karen R. Long, *Cleveland Plain Dealer*

"In one compelling scene after another, Peter Brown brings the Far North vividly close. His characters, presented with even-handed compassion, face impossible choices and chilling emotional and physical tests as they try to mine and mend a life for themselves. They show that in the harshest of conditions, understanding can grow." —Susan Vreeland, author of *Girl in Hyacinth Blue*

"Eloquent and insightful." —*Historical Novels Review*

"*The Fugitive Wife* is emotionally accurate and filled with splendors. The strong characters remind us that only a hundred years ago we were a nation of adventurers, in love not only with the natural paradise but with the risks and chances of reward. Gold in Alaska, a quest complicated by love? They went for it, just couldn't resist."
—William Kittredge, author of *The Hole in the Sky*

"All about passion, whether for flesh or fortune, romance or adventure, this sweeping debut renders poetically the dynamics of desire. . . . Violent lyricism animates Brown's prose and powerful zest drives his saga. . . . It's as a tale of perennial obsessions—greed, sex, love and fevered need—that the book really works." —*Kirkus Reviews*

"A promising debut." —*Library Journal*

"Peter C. Brown's robust saga of gold prospectors drawn north to Nome is the richest kind of storytelling. You will not forget the lives met here, those thrown-together fortune seekers who left behind marriage, betrothal, family, and ultimately so much else in one of the great American quests."

—Ivan Doig, author of *The Whistling Season* and *The Sea Runners*

"A smooth and interesting read." —*Booklist*

THE FUGITIVE WIFE

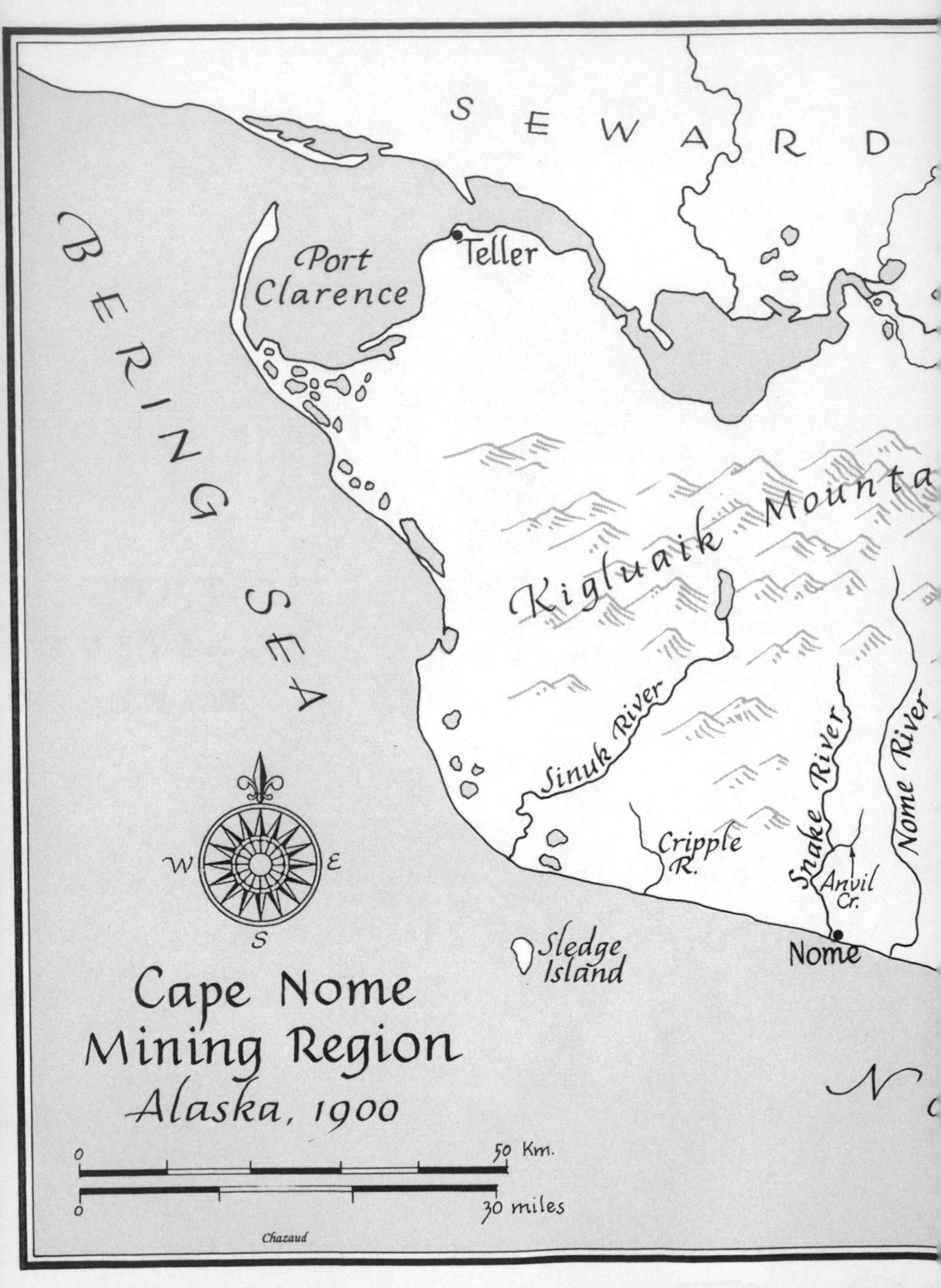

SEWARD
BERING SEA
Port Clarence
Teller
Kigluaik Mounta
Sinuk River
Cripple R.
Snake River
Nome River
Anvil Cr.
Nome
Sledge Island
W
E
S
Cape Nome Mining Region
Alaska, 1900
0
50 Km.
0
30 miles
Chazaud

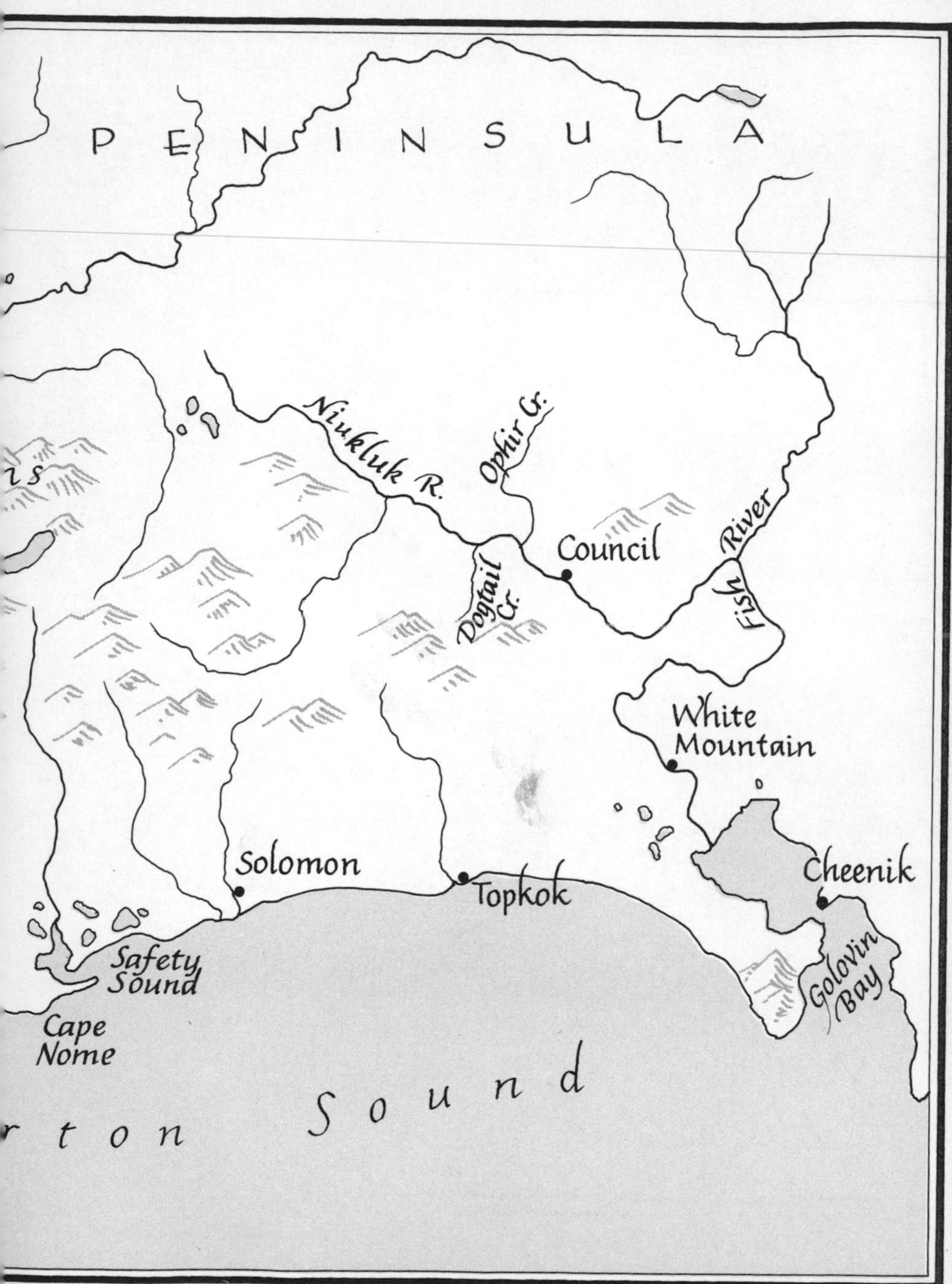

PENINSULA
Niukluk R.
Ophir Cr.
Dogtail Cr.
Council
Fish River
White Mountain
Solomon
Topkok
Cheenik
Safety Sound
Cape Nome
Golovin Bay
rton Sound

PETER C. BROWN

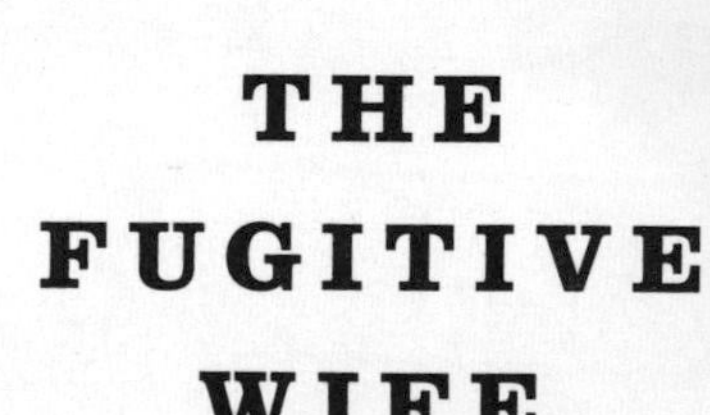

THE FUGITIVE WIFE

A Novel

W. W. NORTON & COMPANY • *New York London*

Two stanzas from Jens Bjorneboe's poem "Siste reis" (in the translation by Solrun Hoaas) from *Aske, vind og jord* are reprinted with the kind permission of Gyldendal Norsk Forlag and the Bjorneboe Estate.

Printed in the United States of America
First published as a Norton paperback 2007

Manufacturing by The Haddon Craftsmen, Inc.
Book design by Chris Welch
Production manager: Anna Oler

Library of Congress Cataloging-in-Publication Data

Brown, Peter C.
The fugitive wife : a novel / Peter C. Brown.—1st ed.
p. cm.
Includes bibliographical references.
ISBN 0-393-06110-8 (hardcover)
1. Triangles (Interpersonal relations)—Fiction. 2. Gold mines and mining—Fiction.
3. Runaway wives—Fiction. 4. Gold miners—Fiction. 5. Prospecting—Fiction.
6. Alaska—Fiction. I. Title.
PS3602.R7225F84 2006
813'.6—dc22

2005024360

ISBN-13: 978-0-393-32975-9 pbk.
ISBN-10: 0-393-32975-5 pbk.

W. W. Norton & Company, Inc., 500 Fifth Avenue, New York, N.Y. 10110
www.wwnorton.com

W. W. Norton & Company Ltd., Castle House, 75/76 Wells Street, London W1T 3QT

1 2 3 4 5 6 7 8 9 0

for Ellen

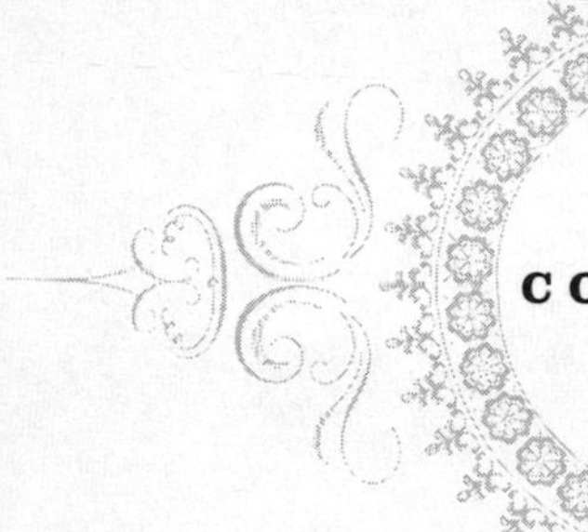

CONTENTS

PART I

1

Seattle, June 7, 1900

Esther Crummey foresaw the accident as it unfolded. "The line!" she cried, waving both arms at the man on the ship's deck who signals the derrick operator, but he and the others nearby were watching the load rise, and Esther's voice was swallowed by the din.

She had tucked herself between a piling and a crate of machinery on the Arlington dock at the foot of Seneca Street, occupying a narrow wedge whitened by gulls, perhaps the last vacant corner in the port, standing resolutely in her faded housedress and thin wrap, a pale blue scarf protecting her head from the weather. The place smelled of wet canvas and hemp and the brine and fetid rot of low tide. She was waiting for a chance to speak with Nate Deaton, to deliver a message from the Major and say goodbye and be off with her own life. Mr. Deaton stood fewer than ten yards across the dock in his campaign hat and oilskins, directing the loading of the company's freight with such importance that she hadn't felt free to approach him through the better part of forty minutes. As she watched him she felt critical of her hesitation and told herself that he wasn't so big a man as she made him—he was two years younger than she (she was twenty-five), and no smarter—but he had an air that made her hold back. It was the smell of an upper-crust education and eastern money.

The docks were a snarl of ropes and cables, men, wagons, horses, and stacked cargo. None of it had to do with her, she felt untouched by the chaos of it, didn't mind standing in excrement. She'd grown up on a farm and knew that it isn't the animals of this world that do you in. All of Seattle was consumed with getting ships loaded and off for the Bering Sea. The hotels and boardinghouses were overrun. The outfitters, teamsters, longshoremen, and stable keepers—the boilermakers, blacksmiths, lumbermen, and ships' crews—all were testy with overcrowded workshops and stores and the teeming gold seekers who had converged in their rush for Nome.

There were twenty or more ships at the piers and more standing off, the owners of each making their best judgment when to sail, late enough to avoid getting caught in the Bering ice pack but early enough to draw the passengers who'd pay a premium to be among the first to land their outfits at Nome.

NATE MOTIONED ACROSS the dock to Hanson at the Northern Pacific warehouse to bring out the next crate. Overseeing the loading of the Cape Nome Company's gear and supplies was Nate's responsibility in his capacity as company foreman. There were seven men in the company: Major Palmer, who was general manager; William Sprague, treasurer; himself, Nate Deaton, foreman and chief engineer; Lars Sunderhauf, consulting engineer; Gus Hanson, shops steward; Walter Steale, master mechanic; and Angus Donaldson, surgeon. They'd left New York on May nineteenth on the Pennsylvania Railroad, changed in Chicago to the Chicago and Northwestern, and changed at Minneapolis to the Great Northern, arriving Seattle on the twenty-fourth after a spectacular ride over the Rockies and then, finally, by switchback, over the Cascades.

Nate and Donaldson had ridden down in the rain to Tacoma the next day to meet the SS *Miss Madden* when she docked from Japan, to get the lay of the ship and confirm arrangements with the Captain, a short, unhappy man named Osborne who smelled of whiskey. His officers bore a sullen demeanor and the crew, some 150 Chinese from the tea trade, had the gaunt, sallow-skinned look of men who spent too much time belowdecks. The vessel sailed for the Northern Pacific Company. She was 360 feet long and iron-hulled, with three masts rigged for sail and a single steam-powered screw. The rigging and mechanicals aft of the stack were black with soot. Her hull was rust-streaked and scarred the length of her port flank, but she was the ship they had booked, and there were fifty men eager to take every one of their berths if the Chinese wished to forgo them. They didn't. New ship or old, if she struck nothing but salt water she would be all right, and if she struck anything else, she would be all wrong.

The subsequent days had been long ones rounding out the company's supplies, receiving the heavy machinery shipped by James Beggs & Company, New York, off-loading the railcars, and getting the freight down to the dock before the *Madden* arrived on the fifth. On the advice of the Northern Pacific agent they'd kept a man on watch twenty-four hours.

While Nate and the other Cape Nome Company men staged the company's freight, the Major and Sprague were holed up in their room at the Hotel Northern consumed with the shareholder solicitation that continued in the East, raising the balance of the capital, getting funds wired, and paying freight charges.

A rat-faced man named Pitts had appeared out of the crowd on the Arlington dock twice in two days and asked Nate what he was needing; there was nothing Pitts and his men could not provide for a price. Heavy on Nate's mind was the absence of their ten-inch centrifugal pump, overdue from the manufacturer, a company associated with Mr. Sprague. Without it, their big dredge would be useless. Pitts wore a dirty longshoreman's suit and billed cap. He came and went with the ease of someone in possession of private passageways. When he reappeared yesterday, Nate had reckoned aloud despite himself that Pitts would surely be hard-pressed to supply a ten-inch centrifugal pump. Pitts had touched his bill and melted away. Yesterday evening, when Nate stepped out of the Northern Pacific warehouse, Pitts was on the dock.

"What you asked for's far from common," he said, shaking his head and sucking his teeth. "Fella'd need a thousand dollars. Deliver it on two hours' notice."

Nate scoffed. The price was double the pump's value, no surprise in that, but he doubted the man could truly produce it. "How do I know it's right?"

"Fairbanks Morse number ten, five thousand gallons a minute, eleven hundred pounds in the crate." Pitts sucked his teeth.

It was precisely what Nate needed. He supposed it would be coming right off another company's railcar, and the idea made him flinch. He was not a man to trade in swag, but their Mr. Sprague had him in a tight damned corner, sure enough, insisting they buy from his brother in Chicago. Ship their entire outfit to some barren strip of sand under the Arctic Circle without a pump to make it work—a picture that made a thousand dollars look like cheap insurance.

Facts as they stood, Nate was more or less forced to do it, meaning it was a thing to settle more on Sprague's conscience than his own.

"Might take it. Tell you tomorrow." The words had come out with an eagerness he disliked himself for.

Pitts looked up the dock. He sniffed and then looked back at Nate. "Pumps is getting scarcer by the hour. This one'll be twelve hundred by tomorrow, supposing I haven't sold it already."

"Forget it, then," Nate snipped, and he turned away from the suck-tooth rotter. The city was lousy with extortionists.

"Tomorrow," Pitts said, and when Nate turned back he was gone.

THE NEW DAY had dawned bright but quickly faded to gray, offering no sign of Sprague's shipment. A woolen sky rode low over the water on a fine mist and West Seattle faded in and out of view across the bay. The docks were slick and anything not covered by tarpaulins grew sodden and heavy. Captain Osborne planned to sail at seven P.M. Nate had posted Sunderhauf above, on the ship's deck, overseeing the stowage of the company's plant and equipment. He had Hanson staging the freight below the ship's forward derrick, some from where it lay in the Northern Pacific warehouse, and the rest from adjacent railcars. He was rapt and failed to see Miss Crummey where she watched him from the edge of the pier.

"The stores?" Sunderhauf called down.

"Six crates!" Nate called back. They communicated through handheld speaking trumpets. The day was still shy of noon, and Nate judged better than half of their outfit was already secure in the ship's hold—the steam dredge, piping and hoses, the machine shop and forge, lumber, half mile of rail with switching and siding, the flatcars, the mining tools. Pitts had made himself visible, propped against the freight agent's office with a cigarette. Nate was in no hurry to confront his decision, preferred to lose himself in the loading, but he watched the time just the same. They had yet to load the company's tents and two portable houses, their kitchen outfit, hospital outfit, Studebaker wagon, seven hundred tons of coal, six months of foodstuffs, and horses.

Nate had put Steale in charge of the horses—five in all—but the man, reed-thin and putty-faced, was a mechanic to the soles of his boots. He'd been positively jumpy over this responsibility and stupidly appeared with three of the animals in a fit of curses and balking long before the ship was ready for them. The man was nearly as provoked as the horses, and the prospect of their getting off the docks and back on again struck Nate as a greater difficulty than working around them, so he had Steale crowd the edge of the dock under the ship's starboard rail, the halters tied off to a stanchion, and the crew proceeded apace to hoist the cargo over them.

It was an animal of some kind skittering under the horses that caught Esther's eye. No, a coil of line. She'd no sooner sorted out what she saw than the rope curled up the horse's leg and pulled tight as the freight net ascended the ship's side. "The line!" she cried, jumping from her nook and gesturing frantically. The horse, a buck-kneed bay gelding, was swept right off its hind legs. Steale jumped clear and the bay let loose a scream of terror that snatched every man's attention across the docks. The horse rose into the air at the rump with its head fast to the stanchion and its neck seeming to lengthen. The caught leg wrenched back and up, up, until she heard the dull thunk of its right hip breaking, and then the tight, high snap of the halter giving way. The horse swung free.

Men were crowding and shouting now. The signalman flailed his arms at the motorman, and the hoist stopped with a jolt and a sharp hiss of steam. The horse hung eight feet off the dock. Its black mane was pitched into the air. Its every muscle was taut, nostrils flared, eyes black sockets of fear. Below it, the two remaining horses screamed and bolted against their harnesses, their ears flattened against their heads. The motorman danced back and forth above, not knowing what to do, then threw the hoist in reverse, but there was a crowd below now and the signalman bade the motorman, "For God's sake, stop!"

"Do him in the head!" Esther called. All eyes turned to her. She had grabbed the speaking trumpet from Mr. Deaton. Her scarf had fallen to her neck and her wet hair shot out from the temples. She was waving toward a crewman on the ship with a sledgehammer in his hands, a fat Chinese boy, and then she drove a fist against her forehead.

"For God's sake, man!" she cried through the trumpet. "Do him in the head!"

Shouts went up from the crowd of men, "Give him a blow!" "Do 'at the lady said!"

The boy with the sledgehammer looked to the signalman. The signalman nodded and called for the horse to be raised a few feet so that the boy with the hammer could do it. The horse was jerked up, frozen in terror, its lips pulled back. The boy hefted the sledge over his shoulder and hauled off in a fluid arc. He planted the hammerhead square between its eyes, forcing gobbets of blood into the air and spattering several of the men below, who cursed and leapt back as the horse went slack and more blood trickled from its nostrils.

A hush fell, and it magnified a contagion of terror that had gripped the two other horses. The Chinese boy shot an insolent look to Esther as if to say are you satisfied, but she was already off to the side of the ship untethering the horses and pulling them out through the crowd with a stern cry, "Step aside!" leading the skittering horses urgently down the dock, exhorting the longshoremen to one side and the teamsters to move their wagons, help her pass.

Steale looked dumbstruck. He wiped a wet sleeve across his brow and approached Nate, shaking his head and throwing up his arms. "Touchy sons of bitches, horses," he said. He was breathing hard and sweating. "Full fuckin' head of steam and no way to bleed it off! Don't trust 'em one inch. Brother got hisself a broke neck by a horse saw a pissant snake, was all she wrote. And who's that woman think she is, run off with the two other'n?"

For the love of Christ, Nate thought. He'd put the wrong man in charge. They were still getting to know each other. Steale, with the reputation of a watchmaker to engines, was wholly beyond his element. How godforsaken hard can it be to stand in one place and stay out of harm's way for an hour? The thing now was, they had to adjust. Not lose momentum in the face of it. Keep the men focused. Nate was breathing hard himself.

"It was an accident, Mr. Steale," he said, shaking his head. "Completely unforeseeable. Don't go blaming yourself. A horse can be replaced."

Steale simply stared at his feet, and in the small silence that gathered he seemed to collect himself.

"If you could see about clearing away the carcass," Nate said. A half beat's hesitation betrayed a note of uncertain authority, but he pushed it back. "I will go after Miss Crummey. Maybe you can get one of the drivers who's unloaded to haul the damned thing straight to the shambles in exchange for what they'll give him for it. When the crew's ready to resume, here's the list of what's left to load. Check it off as it goes up, see? Sundy will tell you what he wants next; you give the word to Hanson. He'll get it staged."

Steale wiped his forehead again. He took a hitch in his trousers, accepted the speaking trumpet and freight manifest, and set off for a driver with an empty wagon.

ESTHER LED THE horses between the railcars where they had been uncoupled at Seneca, and up to the first stables she found on Western, a shabby place called Tilton Boarding and Livery. The horses' eyes were big and one of them snorted at Nate and jerked at the halter rope as he caught up. Esther was faced off with the stableboy.

"Stalls are full," the boy was saying. "Try Waterman's."

"Thank you for intervening, Miss Crummey," Nate said. At this, she wheeled to face him. "And for knowing what to do," he added, forcing a smile of gratitude.

"None of my business, Mr. Deaton, but a man oughtn't to have animals who doesn't know how to keep 'em." There was a defensive cast to her eyes and her chin was set.

"Well, ma'am, it was an accident. That's why we have the word. It means a thing unintended. A bad thing that could as like come to you or to this stableboy here as quick as it did to that horse." He reached for the halters, which she was unwilling to yield.

"It was recklessness," she said. "I don't like thinking how these animals will keep on that ship. Or at Cape Nome, if they live that long."

Nate took a breath. "What happened falls to me and cannot be undone, but certainly we can avoid similar misfortunes." He reached for the horse halters again, and she let them go reluctantly.

"And how will you do that? I mean, who will be looking after them? You, sir?"

"They will be in the ship's stables, Miss Crummey."

"Two and a half thousand miles naked to the elements above deck, Mr. Deaton—or will they be packed away in the dead air of the hold? Have you thought to put somebody in charge of them? A person whose bowels don't flutter in the company of a skittish horse? Have you even noticed that this mare here favors her left foreleg?"

It was a sorrel mare, and it certainly hadn't been lame yesterday when he bought it, nor could he perceive lameness now, although as it stood there, truly, the damnable thing pointed both forelegs. Nor had Nate thought to post somebody with the animals during the passage. Yet the accident unnerved him. Seeing the company's freight safely onto the beaches at Nome, a coast without harbor or wharves, was possibly the most perilous part of the venture, and having noted the caliber of men who constituted the ship's crew and passengers, he saw the woman's point. A point that might have occurred to a more experienced man without prompting. He planned to hire laborers at Nome after the offices and operations were established; there were no ready candidates to play nursemaid to the horses. Should one of their animals perish in the journey, the cost of replacing it would be five or ten times what they were paying in Seattle.

She was a farm girl, the kind who seemed more comfortable with animals than people. He took a risk. "Perhaps you are thinking of yourself in this capacity, Miss Crummey?"

"Not at all, sir. I am traveling to my sister in Ballard, as you know."

"You could return directly with the ship." The particulars of her circumstances were unknown to him. They had met on the Great Northern out of Moorhead, after Esther had been befriended by the Major's assistant, the Negress, Lena Walton. Lena and Esther had been seatmates and had fallen into a quick intimacy as strangers sometimes will. Lena had passed along little—Esther wore a wedding band, but Nate had it that she was leaving difficult circumstances in Minnesota to find her way to her sister's family, that she and her sister were not close, and that when offered a brief stint of employment in Seattle by the Major to help the company provision itself, she had not seemed the least reluctant to postpone her short connection for Ballard.

A breeze blew up, driving the mist before it. Esther retied her scarf and tried to tuck loose strands of hair beneath it. "Actually, I was on the dock to deliver a message. The Major bought a piano and will be grateful for your help in seeing it loaded."

"Surely you have misunderstood," Nate replied.

"For a friend. A Mrs. Trumble, whose husband is a deacon. They will be getting up a ministry to the miners, the Major said. He wants you to keep it from dampness."

As if anything could be kept dry aboard ship. Here was another of the Major's favors, dispensed like Christmas candies.

"Where would I sleep?" she asked.

He had no idea. "You would berth with Miss Walton, I suppose."

The notion of sailing for Alaska was beyond anything Esther could have imagined, yet it was no more so than the circumstance in which she found herself. The moment they had pulled out of Moorhead she had felt weightless—the headlong rush into foreign territory, her sudden ignorance of geography. She was a prairie cottonwood bowled over, the head struggling to get its bearings as the roots lay exposed: her clothing, her speech, the emptiness of her purse. In the course of her journey she had been unable to give herself up to hard sleep, containing her limbs to the seat she had rented so as not to be caught in error or to seem presumptuous or lax or disrespectful of the fare she had paid. Nor had she slept honestly since arriving in Seattle, where she shared a bed at the Hotel Northern with a hardware man's sister from Cleveland. She ached for the comforts of her own privy, the chair by the stove in her kitchen with the bean-husk pillow in the small of her back, her tea steeping at the fire. Above all, she missed her boy, but she barred the door against that part of her grief and salved herself with longings for the smaller comforts. The nicker of Mister Jones when she put the saddle on him. The broody cluck of her old Buff Orpington. The western landscape suffocated her; she could no longer see where the weather came from or where she stood in relation to things. Ballard would be so as well, choking with trees and pushed hard against the edge of the land by the frowning mountains, as suffocating in its landscape as was her sister Constance in her smart commanding of a household.

Nate tried to read her hesitation. The company was prepared for contingencies, but he would not be fleeced. "I can pay one hundred fifty. In addition to your board and passage, of course."

The figure stole her breath. So, he was free with money, as well.

He had a young face, and the front brim of his hat rode upward in the breeze. It was a felt campaign hat that looked impressive at a distance but at close range was seen to be a bit too large. Only moments earlier she had found the same costume daunting—the scarf about his neck, the double-breasted oilskin jacket with bone buttons, leather boots laced to his knee, the laces crisscrossing like so much riprap shoring up the foundation of a great enterprise. Close up, she saw none of it bore the weathering that speaks for experience.

She tugged at the hem of her wrap, a gesture that may have been guileless but was not lost on him. She had, so far as he'd noticed, one change of clothes. "You may need to supplement your wardrobe," he said.

"I hadn't planned on a sea voyage."

"A business expense, Miss Crummey. I will ask Miss Walton to draw an allowance immediately, as there are only a few hours before we sail."

2

Nate paid the stableboy a quarter to hold the horses for an hour and hiked up to the Hotel Northern. He climbed the front stairs to the third floor, where he passed word to Miss Walton and then looked in on the Major and Sprague.

"Better than half loaded, one horse on its way to the shambles," he said. He leaned against the doorjamb. "What about your pump, Mr. Sprague?"

"Ah, Nate!" the Major said. The two men worked across a small table, each with a traveling secretary open beside him on a trunk. A layer of cigar smoke hung in the room. The Major sat erect behind his drooping moustache, while Sprague, a swollen, perspiring man with wattles, gazed over his paunch at a ledger that lay on the table between a pile of invoices and several telegrams.

Sprague waved a wire between two fingers without troubling

himself to look up from his work. "It ships tomorrow, to arrive Seattle Wednesday and follow on the first steamer available."

He was a horse's ass. "In any case, I have bought a replacement," Nate said.

"You bought yourself a replacement," Sprague said. "At what price, pray tell?" He held Nate's gaze squarely now, as did Palmer.

Nate tried to speak matter-of-factly. "It's every man for himself down there on the docks, and a good chance yours will never arrive in Nome, at least not with our name on it. I felt need of insurance, and for that I must have twelve hundred to settle up with the fellow."

"Goddamn it, Major," Sprague said, "our foreman's a chump."

The Major waved off Sprague's invective, but Nate rose to it.

"If the Chicago pump shows up when we need it at Nome, I will sell the other and make up any difference out of my own share of the profits."

"Not necessary, Nate," Palmer said. "You're our man on the front lines. It is not for us to second-guess your decisions. I have the funds in my cash box."

Mollified, Nate changed the subject by lobbing the Major a heavy frown. "And so you've gone and bought yourself a piano."

The Major looked puzzled a moment, and then threw up his hands as if helpless. "Trumble's father married Mother."

Nate listened for more of an explanation. He couldn't immediately take the Major's meaning.

"Damn fortunate for me, I suppose you could say," the Major offered.

Apparently the senior Trumble had performed the sacrament of marriage for the Major's mother and father, the father, in this reference, being imputed. This was an idiosyncrasy Nate had noticed before—that the Major spoke of his mother as if she had formed the entire complement of his parentage and the infant Major had been the product of a latter-day virgin birth. One day when Nate had asked about the father, the Major said the fellow had come into a sizable inheritance when the Major was ten, and succumbed to the muddles, finding sudden wealth incapacitating, whereupon the Major had stepped into the role of head of the family. The point now, Nate gathered, was that the Major bore a debt to the Trumble lineage for his conception, which fact should help Nate come to terms with the Major's impetuous, last-minute purchase of the instrument.

"It's a hulking beast of a thing, Nate," the Major grinned. "A grand piano big as our Studebaker and three times as heavy. I bought it right out of the ballroom downstairs. Mrs. Trumble was so excited we couldn't shut her up."

"And you will be an elder in the Deacon's little church on the tundra," Nate ventured, which raised a snicker from Sprague.

Palmer cleared his throat. "No call for a smart-mouth. Wiser to take your money and run along."

Nate doffed his hat and took his leave, heading up to the sale and feed stables at Fourth and Jackson to replace the destroyed horse.

He found the proprietor eating cabbage soup by a woodstove in his little office. He was a lumbering, ham-handed man who had sold Nate three horses just yesterday and seemed already to have heard about the accident. "Very sad," he said, wiping his mouth and rising to conduct business. He had two geldings and a black mare. Nate had considered and rejected the same horses the day before. Now he walked among them again. The geldings were old and tired, one with cloudy eyes and the other with cracked hooves. He quickly discovered that the mare was a biter and a kicker, but she had muscular legs and fire in her eye, so he bought her. He hired the proprietor's son to fetch her down to the livery on Western, then to check with Sunderhauf and bring all five horses to the docks when Sunderhauf was ready for them.

On his way back to the docks, Nate remembered to post the letter that he had written the evening before.

Hotel Northern
Seattle, Washington
June 6, 1900

Dearest Lily,

I sit at the edge of the continent, willing your hand in mine once more before I steam over the horizon. The pen chases my fingers across the page to you!—perhaps you will trace my words with your own fingers. Three thousand miles from home, and only here does the journey truly begin, west and north into utter wilderness. Now that we are ready to leave, I am stricken by the fiercest of longing: You in the silly (but becoming) yellow hat from your Auntie Nim. You on the bars of my bicycle that day we crashed the boxwoods. You snoozing on the chaise longue and your protestations that you hadn't dozed off while I was talking.

And supposing you were here—I would squire you from merchant to merchant, getting up a lady's outfit in the best Nome fashion: frost extractors, insect masks, Siwash liniment, buckskin suits "for big lunged men and plucky women." I admit I bought for myself a cedar box to keep my bird skins, and my eye wanders to a collapsible skiff that could prove valuable beyond measure at Nome.

In truth, Seattle is a dog's scrape, our machinery arriving piecemeal and my constant badgering of the rail agent, all of us busy to exhaustion eighteen hours a day, stores and stateroom reservations disappearing out from under us except that we have learned to keep a sharp eye and wrestle possession back at any cost to limb or pocketbook. I am sorry you are not here for this adventure, and yet glad you will not be faced with the privation it portends.

Please go by the old Swede and tell him if he feels we should have ordered the larger benches with the built-in vises and the larger lathe and welder, would he please take it upon himself to make the correction? I will stand behind him. I was so overwhelmed by the sums I was committing on behalf of the gold company that when it came to outfitting our own motor-cycle shop I'm afraid I erred in the opposite direction. Now that the Cape Nome Co. is underway I hate the thought of our fledgling company skinning its knees for want of enough fabric to cover them. No money is required beyond what I have pledged until we are ready to take delivery.

Give my love to Mother and to your family, but save the most for yourself, my dear "Dr. F."

Ever your beastly gold hunter,
Nate

The *Miss Madden* was scheduled to board passengers at five o'clock. Esther posted her letter at the front desk at half-past four.

Hotel Northern
Seattle, Washington
June 7, 1900

Dear Sister,

Death took my boy from his burns as our Father most likely sent word to you by now but you may not have learned I left my husband who is living in our barn which is all that stands of our farm. Father went to Stranwold and bought a little white casket—

did you know Stranwold has taken the funeral business from Steen? Then Father paid Fossum's to make our portrait and told Leonard to turn his burn away from the view of the camera. If Father sends it you will see how sweet my boy looked asleep with Jesus. After the portrait I could not bury him in a casket knowing how he liked his Durkee's box so we set him in it on his side curled up with his knees tucked under his chin like he was napping. He is a lamb of God with strong legs running with the boys and girls in Heaven. I can no longer endure Leonard the Lord strike me because as his wedded wife I have forsaken him. Mrs. Loqueshear made me the loan of $80 which I tried but could not deny. I left him what ever did not burn in the house. I did not know where to go. My life being over. I am going aboard ship to earn some money working for some people I met and after to come to you and hope to know what to do. If you write my name general delivery at Nome up in Alaska maybe I will get it. Before the ship turns for Seattle. If Leonard comes do not tell him you have had this from me.

Ever your loving sister,
Esther

She and the Negress, Lena Walton, climbed into a cab and pulled a dirty horse blanket over their knees as the driver steered for the waterfront. A mist that had blown in from the bay that morning hung over the city, putting a chill in the air. Smoke rose from the shops and houses, and Esther found her eyes searching lit windows for a glimpse of a home and a family busy at its own affairs.

When they crossed Railroad Avenue, they arrived at the edge of a large crowd. Smoke boiled from the ship's funnel and electric lights burned extravagantly along her decks though the daylight was still strong. The bay beyond the pier looked cold and uninviting but the port thronged with passengers and well-wishers. Gentlemen and ladies traveling First Cabin had boarded early and now stood at the ship's rails gazing down, the men in crisp suits and fedoras or derbies, the ladies buttoned into tailored jackets and woolen cloaks wearing peach-baskets with spotted nets or flowered bonnets and plumes. Below them, the Second Cabin passengers pressed forward on the pier waiting to board. These were mostly miners with outfits strapped to their backs: packsacks and rifles, tin stoves and wooden mining contraptions, picks, pans, and shovels. The lights and crowds gave the *Madden* a gaiety that overcame her worn looks. There were farm animals penned along her upper decks and enough passengers waiting to board to people a city three times the size of Perley, Esther guessed, all of them gung ho for steaming into the remotest wilderness, confident of their fortune.

She felt herself stepping into a world for which she possessed no fascination or expectations. She carried a new haversack with the clothes that she had bought a few hours earlier, and a worn suitcase she'd taken from her father's attic and filled with the few possessions she had salvaged from the fire and refused to leave behind: the blue shirtwaist with primroses she had sewn to wear for her son's christening, her high-top shoes, the shapeless brown cardigan that she was in the habit of slipping into when the first shadows of evening crept up from Wolf Creek. She'd brought the coat of cream-colored lamb's wool that her mother had given her for her wedding trip; too good to wear, but too good to walk away from, which was more than she could say of the husband. She and Lena Walton set their bags down and watched for some indication of boarding.

THE COLORED GIRL had been a surprise in almost every way from the moment Esther had introduced herself on the train at Moorhead. Esther had come up from the rear of the car and asked a woman whether the aisle seat beside her was taken; only when the woman turned and asked her to sit did she see it was a Colored. Her first thought had been to move on up the aisle, not so much out of distaste as certainty that it would make a Colored very uneasy to share with someone other than her own. But having been invited to sit, she found it awkward to refuse, and so she smiled politely and put her suitcase in the overhead and took the empty seat.

"Miss Lena Walton," the girl said. "Oak Bluffs. Massachusetts." And there was the second surprise, her with an uppity manner of speaking.

Esther smoothed her dress over her knees. "Esther Crummey. Perley."

"Is that North Dakota?"

She wondered was the girl being cheeky. "Minnesota. Other side of the Red."

"I've heard of the Red River," Miss Lena Walton said. "We just crossed it. Drains north."

Esther turned and looked her full in the face to see who she was to know such a thing. She was a young woman, Esther's age or less, slim, high cheekbones. She'd got herself all fixed up, hair under a basket, white gloves on her hands.

"I read the booklet about our route," she was saying. "In Minnesota we crossed three divides. Mississippi flows to the Gulf, Lake Superior goes out the St. Lawrence to the Atlantic, and your Red, being contrary, runs northerly into Hudson's Bay. Nothing for the Pacific until we reach the far side of the Rocky Mountains."

Esther supposed the girl was correct. She had never met a Colored in person. She put her handbag beside her on the seat and thought of the small lunch she had brought and whether she would have to offer the girl some. The first she'd seen were the ones in Chicago. Then, later, she had seen them in the minstrel show at the Fargo Opera House. Not the girls, but the boys. She and Leonard had gone, twice. Leonard had called them coons and said they belonged on the railroad, and in fact she had taken note that the porters on the Great Northern were Coloreds, and she was glad he wasn't along to take satisfaction in it, although she would have enjoyed knowing his reaction on seeing her sitting seatmates with one. Two had come north with the threshing crews once, during the hard times in '94 or '95. She never saw them. There'd been some kind of trouble over in Hillsboro and they were run off.

"Do you live in the city?" the girl asked.

"Farm, Miss Walton." Esther didn't feel like making conversation and opened her handbag and sorted through it. She pulled out the train schedule. Almost sixty hours to Seattle. She hadn't the money for a Pullman berth and planned to sleep in her seat.

"I go by Lena."

"If you like."

Lena smiled, and then she turned to gaze out the window. "Gives me chills thinking of living there," she said. "What's it like?"

Esther looked to see where she meant as the train gathered speed down the rails. Saw she meant the prairie itself. The alders and wild hops greening the ditches. The foxtail and wild tansy, already tall. Redwings swarming in the marshes. The dragging and seeding done, wheat shoots squally as pond water, farmsteads no longer dormant in their windbreaks. It was a question she couldn't answer. "Wind'll knock you flat if that's what you're asking," she said, looking back at her train schedule. "Knock your barn flat, and lay out the nearest town while it's passing through."

"That's what I was thinking," Lena said.

Esther closed the schedule and slipped it back into her bag and found her ticket and slipped it between the leaves of the schedule and closed her bag and worried the fabric where it was frayed at the edge of the clasp. "If it's an electrical storm in August, lightning'll set the fields afire, burn out a whole farmstead." She spoke in a matter-of-fact voice without bothering to regard the girl, but she quickened in a small way to the devastation she described.

"For heaven's sake," Lena said. "I wasn't thinking of that. I was thinking winter would be the worst."

It was true. Winter stole the wind from their lungs. Was how they marked time, winters put behind them, years piling up like snow at the hedgerows and ditches until it was hard to tell one from another except by the tragedies and small excitements that set them apart, landmarks easily cut adrift from their surroundings.

"Winter I was twelve, there was so much snow the wolves came south out of Canada in search of food." Costs nothing to be pleasant. She gave Lena a little smile.

Lena's eyebrows raised.

"Neighbor boy was chased up the road by two of them. Got home by walking backward swinging an ax."

"Go on!"

Esther glanced around, but nobody seemed to be paying any regard. "My brother saw a wolf in the yard one night when we were milking. He yelled and I pushed the barn door shut just in time. Our pa and ma were calling at the neighbors. We didn't know what to do. It began scritch-scratching at the door and chewing the wood. We piled hay bales against the door and then got up into the loft with pitchforks. When our pa and ma returned in the sleigh, the horses scared it off. That winter my brother and I had to climb drifts from the back door of the house and slide down to the door of the barn in order to do the milking. We had a rope. Wind comes up, you can get lost between the house and the barn."

Lena said, "I could tell just looking out this window. Nothing there. 'Trouble likes nothing,' my momma says."

"That spring, the Red rose up and floated half of Perley off to Grand Forks."

Lena shook her head. "I'm thinking you waked up one day when your house was knock-knocking against the front door of city hall, asking for directions home."

Esther laughed. "Not ours. Our place never flooded. When Pa came to homestead in '74, he talked with everyone who knew the area. Walked up and down the whole countryside. Finally picked a quarter section two miles east of Perley, on Wolf Creek. Nothing special to look at, and when others finally knew him well enough they asked him why he picked it, and he knelt down and put his head near the ground and told them to get down and see for themselves. Thing is, if you look two miles west to the Red from our place, you see only the tops of the trees. It's the highest section for miles around. When the spring flood comes, the neighbors bring their livestock up to Pa's place. Ma feeds them all and Pa won't take a nickel for the trouble, says he's blessed just to have such land."

"That's a wonderful story."

"It's no story," Esther said. She watched the prairie go by. It was not only Leonard she was leaving. Let go of the prairie and she was letting go of all that came before him, and what might've been as well.

Her ma, Jessie, always said she'd come into the world with a sea journey in her veins. Had been conceived in the old country but born in the new. Pa had meant to name her Carl Ulverson, but when she surprised them coming out a girl she was given her pa's ma's name, Esther, and her pa, Rugnel, bent to having the son he aimed for, to work beside him on the farm he meant to build, and Carl came in '78, his own tiny veins running with wheat germ and sweat. After Carl, Constance. After Constance, Hjalmer. Then Howard, who perished. Then Arthur, and finally Roy.

Esther was four by the time they'd paid their crossing and broke the sod in Perley, and she was already able to help gather kindling in the woods by the river with her mother and entertain Carl so Jessie could work. The harvest that she was six, her brother was put up top the threshing machine and shown how it worked, where the big chute spilled the river of grain into the wagon, while Esther was made to stay back and put out the food. End of the day, Esther went into the fields on her own. Jess, frantic, sent Rugnel scouring the farm, the haylofts, the breaks, even down the well. It was past sunset when they heard the squeak of her little wagon wheels. She came slowly across the fields, her wagon filled to overflowing with grain she had scavenged a handful at a time from the spillings of the great machine. She had this to show for herself, she who was not invited atop the thresher, and everybody thanked God for the gift of her return. Rugnel wept with relief, and before he remembered to praise her labor, let his fears turn to anger and spoke hard words about a strong-headed girl who failed to think of others. Words that struck like fists, knocked her breathless, and then dissolved her before him. Certain as she had been of earning his praise. Certain to have proved herself worthy alongside any man that threshed.

Her ma came to her in bed that night to say her pa was ashamed at his hard words and didn't know how to show it, but Esther had already collected herself. Did not want the comfort of her mother. Knew she would one day show her pa what she was good for on a farm. Stung with resolve from the age of six.

"It's good land," was all she could find to say in defense of it.

"Momma says, 'Love the dirt you come from,'" Lena said.

They fell silent. When the wooden elevator of a town shot past, Lena asked, "What are the neighbors' names?"

"Strand. Oftedahl. Rustvold. Hjelmquist."

"All Norwegians, then," she said, tugging at one of her gloves.

"Mostly, and a few Germans."

"You ever been where the people are different?"

"Through Minneapolis, once, with my ma, and on to see my aunt in Chicago."

Lena grew animated. "Wasn't it a shock?"

"I guess it was," Esther said, but in truth she had been dumbfounded. Chicago had been her first and only experience seeing entire neighborhoods of Coloreds. Nobody had prepared her for it.

"The different kinds of people were a shock to me," Lena said, "when I left Martha's Vineyard for the university. Boston University . . ." that fact tossed out plain and simple. Soon other facts were coming so fast that Esther had to work at not staring but watched from the corner of an eye to gauge was the girl exaggerating or was she trying to prove something or chivvy Esther out of something, but plainly she wasn't, she was excited about where her life was going and what it might mean, and she wasn't prying, nor was she a gossip, but wasn't it fascinating how, once you leave home, any little thing, even picking a train seat, might end up changing your life somehow. She was twenty-two, she said.

Esther stretched her feet forward. She didn't mind listening.

Lena said she was the daughter of a scratch farmer, boatbuilder, and handyman to the summer people on Martha's Vineyard. She had gone on to university, against all odds and by the good graces of a summer family—the Palmer family, in fact—the Major telling her own daddy, "The girl's smart and deserves a proper education, and I am in a position to pay for it, provided I approve the school—no embarrassment on your part, Mr. Walton, as my means came to me without effort or merit, and I am only doing what any man in my position would, endeavoring to put good fortune to good ends."

"Imagine," Esther said softly.

Lena told how, during college, she had worked as a nurse's aide in the New England Hospital for Women and Children, and how she visited patients in their homes, seeing human misery and coarseness she couldn't have imagined, and although it was her nature to be sympathetic with these conditions, she also learned, slowly and with effort, to be detached from them—nursing did not call to her as a life's work, but she was good at it. "That, the Latin declensions, and whupping a mule are pretty much what I know, but the Major was nice enough to hire me on to his gold company, and I said yes. What else is out there for a Negro girl fresh from the university?"

"I have no idea. What will you do?"

"That's just it!" she said, turning to Esther, her face the picture of wonderment. "I will keep the Major's office and make myself useful, for which he will provide lodging and a stipend, but I am free to find whatever paying employment the place offers."

"My goodness! All the way to Alaska and you cannot say why?"

"Shoo. You know the feeling. Wanting to do something you never did? Where you don't know what's going to happen?"

No girl Esther knew felt that way. Likely came from getting more educating than Lena had a use for, or maybe some rootlessness in her race. "Anyway, I didn't know they had Coloreds up there."

Lena shrugged. "Then I will have to meet other people. You sat next to me."

Esther nodded, not saying it was an accident. "Well, what'd your pa say?"

"Daddy said it's the family itch, come back and tell him everything. His daddy was a whaler. Daddy always says you can't fall into it if you don't walk past it."

So that was the daddy. "What kind of a scratch farmer? Name me some crops."

"Oh, well!" the girl said.

And so, over the course of their journey and a week helping the company assemble its outfit in Seattle, Lena had become something to Esther. Esther didn't know what, exactly. The only word she could find was friend.

A BROAD SHOUT went up and the crowd pressed toward the stairs and boarding began. Mr. Deaton's offer of a job brought money with it, and a place to sleep and time to think. In a month Esther would be carried back to this same place. Possibly it was God's hand that had put her on the docks and wrapped a stout line around that horse's leg. Bludgeon a horse and earn the shelter of a homeless woman. Isn't that God's way on earth? The way of waste and despair. The way of impossible contracts. Here was another that she wouldn't have written, but it was one she was willing to accept. She picked up her suitcase. "I am grateful for the company and for the employment," she said, and together she and Lena pushed into the crowd.

They hadn't progressed thirty feet when two women bullied past, calling, "Beg pardon! Step aside!" One of them was nearly six feet tall and slender, with persimmon hair in a thick plait down her back. The second was a foot shorter, dark, fat as a plow horse. Both wore heavy mascara and formal evening dresses and carried painted French umbrellas. As the men gaped, the women thrust notices into their hands and cried, "Take a leaflet and step aside! French sport for gentlemen! One half-dollar to get on the reservations list!" The notices read, *Lady Jane and Mistress Geena, Les Ma'amselles Sportif, Cabin 12, priority to gents with paid reservations.* Catcalls and whistles filled the air as the crowd parted for the women to pass. Two men brought out silver half-dollars and the shorter woman took their names.

"Take an interest in my claim?" hollered a man.

"When you find your nuggets, sir!" replied the taller woman.

"Over here, miss! I've found my nuggets!" hollered another man, and the crowd roared.

A man in front of Esther cried, "My cock's just a chicken around you ladies. What'll I do?"

"Perhaps you've got a *pullet*, sir," the taller woman said. The crowd roared its approval. "Unhand the little fellow and bring him to us. We'll make him crow!"

Esther felt somebody squeeze her rump as a man's voice yelled, "Look here. Got us one in vanilla, t'other in chocolate!" She spun around, flinging her suitcase and catching the man in the gut. He was runtish and unshaven, and Esther's hostility sparked an aggression in him.

"You dog bitch!" he cried, and lunged at her arm. He pulled her off balance, and as she tumbled onto her suitcase he raised a fist.

She cringed to absorb the blow, but before the man could strike, his raised arm was caught by another, a man who pulled the runt backward a step, jerked his arm around his backside, saying in an urgent, settle-down voice, "Hey, pardner! Lay off, there, pardner!" As quickly as he'd raised his arm, her aggressor had been immobilized.

Lena and a stranger gave Esther a hand to her feet. Esther's knees felt weak and uncertain.

"Look here," the short man's captor was saying, cooler now. "Pays to know a trollop from a lady. Them two as came by are trollops, good and dandy. I believe these two are *ladies*. Don't have to look too close to see a difference, now, do you?"

Esther's rescuer was a long-legged old-timer with a scarred face, tufts of gray hair on either side of a narrow-brimmed felt cap, and a miner's outfit that he'd let fall to the pier in the commotion. The other man was breathing heavily. His eyes darted left and right, sizing up the crowd. He tugged at his captured arm, but the tall fellow cinched it tighter and said, "Your mistake, sir?"

The crowd fell silent to hear the man's response.

Nothing for the longest time, and then, all eyes upon him, the man stuck out his chin and muttered, "You say."

The tall fellow slowly let go of the arm and the runt picked up his outfit and pushed past Esther and Lena toward the ship.

Esther quietly thanked her rescuer.

"Ever' kind of vermin's drawn to gold," he said. "Though not all's ornery as that one." His teeth were brown and a crater on his face gave the impression he'd been shot through the cheek. Esther wouldn't have wagered him for the strength to stop a man in a fit of rage, but he'd been quick and sure. She counted herself lucky.

THE WINDOWLESS ROOM that Esther was to share with Lena Walton in Second Cabin lay deep within the ship, lit by a dim electrical bulb that flickered unaccountably. The space beside their stacked bunks was barely wide enough for the two of them both to stand, and the faint light failed to hide the filth of the place. A ragged pair of men's undershorts lay in a corner like a dead animal. The mattress ticking was stained and the woolen blankets smelled of perspiration. "So long as there's no rats," Lena said, and proceeded to put her things onto a shelf at the end of the upper bunk, but Esther turned her back and stood in the door to the crowded companionway trying to think how she might find something better, knowing there was no chance of it, and when two of the ships' officers appeared in the noisy stream of traffic, she spoke up.

"Our cabin wants linens," she declared.

The men did not stop, but one turned in passing and said, "If it's linens and doilies you're wanting, why, ring for the valet, ma'am." His companion sniggered as they disappeared in the crowd.

Esther thought perhaps to sleep on deck once the ship was making passage, and with that possibility she asked Lena if she wouldn't come up with her to watch the ship pull away from the pier. When they got on deck Esther insinuated herself into a tight space at the railing between a lifeboat davit and a heavyset fellow with the dress and dour look of a banker. She excused herself to the man and he made room for her, and then, seeing Lena, he asked his companions to squeeze over as well, which they did, and the two women looked out at the two or three thousand well-wishers on the docks and along Railroad Avenue. The passengers covered every open inch of the ship's topside, some astride the piles of cargo that hadn't found space in the hold, some sitting in lifeboats, standing on the davits, clinging to the rigging, most waving and shouting to friends and strangers ashore as the *Madden* sounded one long blast on her whistle, followed by three short ones, and slowly backed from her berth, the crowd ashore cheering her off.

Black smoke belched from the ship's funnel. Slowly she turned her stern into the bay, the screw shuddering her deck and railings and churning up the sea. A cloud of gulls swooped at the turbulent water as the ship backed around, and then came a change in the feel, a pause followed by a lesser vibration, and the *Madden* began to draw forward. The gulls fell back into her gathering wake. The ship's smoke organized itself into a plume that failed to rise on the mist but rolled toward the dockland and lost itself against the chimneys and gray hills of the city.

Esther watched the ships and buildings shrink behind them. The low skyline flattened out and grew dim in the mist. Although she had never been aboard a proper ship, the sense of it was oddly familiar, a memory woven by the account that her ma liked telling of the newly minted family crossing an ocean from Norway to make a fresh life in America. Esther was the seed that had already been planted and was growing inside of Jess. The rhythms of the *Madden* brought up with a startling vividness the stories of their immigration, people and ways left behind, kindred souls sailing into the unknown, the kindnesses of strangers, the utter exhaustion exacted by a foreign place. Shipboard passage was ever thus, a voyage of loss and beginning. Now, at twenty-five, in fading daylight, she felt herself pulled into a passage of her own, the sea a veil drawn open by the ship.

As the crowd thinned, she thought to explore the deck for a little hole or nook among the piled cargo where she might make a nest, but there was no such place, and the open air was cold and damp. She investigated the Dining Saloon and Social Hall Lounge on the second deck and the Smoking Room Bar below, thinking she might find a chaise or an upholstered chair, but the public rooms were already populated by a drinking and gambling crowd. The men were rough, and she realized that if she was to find sleep, she required both the lock on their stateroom door and the warmth of the sour blankets, and so she reconciled herself to a night in the squalor of their cabin. First, however, she meant to have a bite of the cheese and apples she had brought in her bag, and to establish her authority in the stables.

3

A "chump" the preening ass had said. Nate couldn't put the word out of mind. He was standing forward to inspect where they'd stowed the pump on the spar deck. There'd been no room for it in the hold with the company's freight allowance because of the goddamned Trumble piano, and because the hold was already filled and the hatches sealed by the time Pitts had shown up with the crate.

The ship rose and fell on the first suggestion of swells, and he glanced out to find that she'd rounded toward the Strait of Juan de Fuca. He pulled at the lashings. They seemed secure but to his thinking it was a heavy damned machine to be carried so high on the ship, and at the foredeck where there'd be the greatest movement.

The word galled. He was a chump indeed. Not for paying Pitts's extortion but for letting Sprague claw his way into the venture and start calling the tune. It was going to stop right there. His deal with Pitts was notice.

He turned to walk aft. He spotted Miss Crummey with the horses and touched his brim to her. She made a motion as if to speak but he pretended not to catch it. She was a noticer of little problems and he had problems enough. She would have to handle it. That's what she'd been hired for. He proceeded through the gauntlet of animals. The *Madden* carried her livestock along the rails of her top deck, from the anchor winch back to the wheelhouse. Two cow houses on the starboard bow and a small service closet opposite. Aft of these, eighteen horses in temporary stalls, nine to either side of the ship. Next, the kennels and pens containing a hundred sixty-three dogs, fifty each of pigs and sheep, and three hundred chickens and rabbits. The noise and smell were an assault on the senses—the kennels stacked four high, the fowl coops and rabbit hutches stacked over the pens of the sheep and pigs. At the center of the foredeck stood the ship's little Post Office, backed up to the forward derrick, where it formed an island in an assortment of freight that had been deemed more or less impervious to the weather—two large stacks of lumber, several crated boilers, Nate's centrifugal pump, and a sizable pile of sacked coal, all strapped down between the rows of horse stalls and bordered by bales of hay and straw kept dry under tarpaulins.

His boot had picked up something foul. He stopped to scrape it on the edge of the ship, trusting the substance to fall clear of the deck below. If he were Miss Crummey, he would be rather grateful for the fresh breeze among the pens. He thought to remark on it to her sometime over the next day or two, an opportunity to warm her up a little. Rather more of a chore than the Trumble girl, he guessed. The Deacon and Mrs. Trumble, he'd noted, were traveling with their daughter Grace, who looked to be twenty or so and was more than a little obvious in her glances. She was a definite possibility, ministers' children being notorious that way. In fact, the only possibility he'd picked out of the crowd so far, discounting the sporting girls.

And suppose by the lowering hand of Mary Mother of Christ the Chicago pump were to present a timely appearance at Nome? He could good and damn well sell the spare. Get at least double what he'd paid for it, possibly triple. Who would be the chump then?

He stepped over a cordon that separated the animals from the public deck. His presence was required in the Captain's cabin again, or so he'd been informed. He walked through the throng of passengers. Every Tom, Dick, and Harry felt qualified to be a mining millionaire at Nome. He pulled at the cuffs of his jacket. The suits had been prescribed by the Major; Nate had thought the man's preoccupation with clothing bordered on the frivolous, but now he was grateful for the oilskin and woolens against the bite of the sea air.

Captain Osborne had invited Major Palmer to share his quarters, two-thirds aft on the spar deck. The invitation had set in motion a chain of inconveniences, moving the Major's baggage out of the First Cabin stateroom he shared with Sprague, bumping Donaldson into the Major's berth, accommodating a stranger in the cabin shared by Nate and Sunderhauf, all of this despite a predictable sullenness from Sprague, who felt by all rights he should quarter alone.

Nate dug at the welt of his left boot with a handkerchief and then knocked.

"Enter! Oh, Nate. Come in and shut the door, man." The Major was in his underwear rearranging the cabin's furnishings. "The man invites me to live with him, and damned if I can find the space to breathe." Palmer struggled to situate his bulky wardrobe and traveling secretary within the pinched quarters, which consisted of a private toilet and two wood-paneled cubbies. The room even smelled close. Osborne's laundry, perhaps, and whatever was rising from Nate's boot.

"You won't believe this, but my other trunk was sent down with the cargo. No room here, of course, but get a man to go after my dinner jacket, will you, that's a fellow."

Nate went in search of the First Mate. How the Major had got as far as he had in life was a question that had come to him more than once over the last few months. The world apparently unfolded before him according to a great plan known exclusively to himself and his God. Eight months earlier Nate had never heard of him and now he was ferreting the man's clothing out of a ship's hold.

FITCH S. PALMER, MAJOR, U.S. CAVALRY (ret.), known for his "stirring account of the battle for San Juan Hill," had been booked by the Quinsigamond Club of Worcester, Massachusetts, to speak at their November meeting of his exploits in the Spanish War. (Just last fall, and how much water over the dam!) Nate wouldn't have bothered with it except that he'd skipped the prior two meetings and risked a blot on his standing. The speaker turned out to be tall and gallant, with a dark hairpiece making him look world-wise beyond his thirty-six years. From the fervor of his account he seemed very much the adventuresome type. The very next day Nate dropped him a note of congratulations, asking whether the Major would have any interest whatsoever in hearing a modest proposal concerning the recent gold strikes on the Seward Peninsula of Alaska. Palmer's prompt invitation to tea was the reply.

He had gone by bicycle to save the trolley fare, pushing along against a fresh breeze that was laced with flurries and threatening real snow. He'd found the large, vine-covered cottage on Harrington

Avenue and stood in the stingy afternoon light for half a minute with his drawings under his arm, wiping his hopeless nose and trying to decipher the house number where it was half hidden by dry vegetation.

The porch light came on.

He rang the bell as the door swung open. "You're Deaton, then," the Major said amiably. He was a good bit taller than Nate, better than six feet, with a crisp bearing that was softened by the informality of his smoking jacket and by a drooping walrus moustache and the wavy toupee. The house was filled with a heady aroma of cinnamon cakes, and Nate heard the strains of opera.

"I hope you don't mind, but I have invited my banker to join us." Palmer led the way to his sitting room.

The fellow stood before a fire and extended his hand. "Bill Sprague."

Palmer said, "I had the vague sense you might be looking for partners in your scheme, Mr. Deaton, so I took the liberty of inviting Bill. My family's assets are under management, and we do not sneeze without first soliciting the opinion of our friends at Worcester National."

Palmer raised the stylus on the Edison, silencing the music. "Verdi, and the sordid business of revenge." He motioned toward a leather sofa and chairs, and the three men took seats across a low table as a maid brought tea service. The room's walls were lined with books and artworks on the theme of the American empire. A ranch house was shaded by large cottonwoods in a draw below looming foothills. A bronze mountain lion rode the flank of a fleeing buffalo. A life-sized portrait of the Major in his cavalry uniform and sword surmounted the fireplace.

"We have all read the banner headlines from Nome," Palmer said. "Perhaps before you relate your idea, you could tell us something of your background. I confess to having asked at the club after I received your note. You are a teacher of physics?"

"I am a master of mechanical engineering, and also something of a fanatic for motors, but, yes, to make ends meet I have taken a stipend imparting the principles of elementary physics at my alma mater." His students were the slack-jawed sons of bankers and merchants who needed only to graduate so they could settle into the sinecures their fathers had established for them. For the science of energy and matter, the joys of invention and creation, his students cared nothing; the class was one more tedious interlude in their passage through a forgettable adolescence.

Sprague glanced at his watch. "So, you plan to strike it rich by digging gold during your summer vacation."

"You find the idea simplistic?"

"Unoriginal."

Nate slid a cinnamon cake onto a plate, and then put before them a newspaper drawing. "This is the coastal area of Nome. The ore is in these creeks, here. The fact has been known for two years, although the richness of the deposits was news last year, and the creeks and streams have been rapidly staked. The ore is also in the beach sands, as you and I have read. I believe the stampeders came out last fall with something like two million dollars dug from the beach, no deeper than a foot or two."

"Yes, yes," Sprague said.

"The one area to my knowledge that has not been touched are the sands below the tide line."

The men gazed at his map without expression.

"My idea is to mine offshore. Erect a sort of factory that would enable us to do it in large volume. A hydraulic dredge."

"Hydraulic?" Palmer asked. Sprague pulled at his ear.

"Placer mining needs a lot of water. Shoveling your paying gravels into a sluice and then pumping water through them to separate out the gold. With hydraulics you could gather the gravel and the water in the same operation."

"Suck up the sea floor with a big pump, you mean?" Sprague said.

"And dump it directly into the sluice boxes," Nate said. The simplicity of it was elegant.

Palmer nodded somewhat vaguely and Sprague stroked his jaw.

"You would need a source of sweet water for the boilers," Nate said.

"What about one of those gas engines?" Sprague asked.

Gas. Nate grinned. He was infatuated with internal combustion. But what gas engine offered the horsepower to run a sizable hydraulic dredge? And there was the question of fuel. "For large-volume hydraulics, you want something tried and true, a big damned high-pressure, reciprocating steam engine, say seventy horsepower, mounted on a lighter or on rails, maybe, that can be run right out into the water."

"Trees for the firebox?" Sprague asked.

Nate shook his head. "Coal. No trees. Tundra."

The men sat silently, seeming to absorb it.

On top of the map, Nate placed several pages of mechanical drawings. "As to the pumps, it's a question of suction or centrifugal. I am thinking centrifugal. Better for volume and depth."

"You have brought your financial pro formas?" Sprague asked.

Nate pulled out his list of machinery and equipment. "One hundred thousand." He passed the figures to Sprague and tried not to sound breathless.

Sprague scanned the page before tossing it to the table. "What are you offering in exchange?"

"Fifty-fifty." It was only fair to give the men putting up the money equal say. Sprague and the Major might think it naïve, but Nate had wanted a genuine collaboration.

Palmer smiled. "All of the financial risk in exchange for half of the reward. Bully for you! I can see you are a first-rate negotiator!"

Sprague lit a cigar. "This sort of thing is always underestimated. Any serious venture's going to need bigger machinery. More men. Capital reserves to give it maneuvering room after you reach the goldfields. Where are your men going to eat and sleep? Where's your doctor? Your hospital outfit? I wouldn't touch it for less than half a million." He turned to Palmer. "Who would you count in?"

"Ned Brown," Palmer said.

"Wilton Wilder," Sprague said. "Pierce Shattuck."

Palmer, nodding, opened his diary and began to jot the names. "Guppy Totman," he said.

Subsequently, Sprague drew up a prospectus calling for the Cape Nome Company to be capitalized at five hundred thousand dollars, and then he went out and raised it. In light of the Major's military experience and equity share, he was to be made general manager; Sprague was to be made treasurer; Nate was invited to serve as foreman and chief engineer, with authority for outfitting the company and for hiring and running the men. One exception: their centrifugal pump was to be purchased from a new metal-castings maker in Chicago, where Sprague's brother held a financial interest. Sprague could not subscribe his funds or the Major's to a company that patronized a competing supplier. Finally, in lieu of wages, Nate was to receive one percent of the company, an equity position equal to five thousand dollars at par.

Nate was dumbstruck. Walk into a man's office and show him how to pull a fortune out of the sea, and then walk out with 99 percent of the enterprise in other people's pockets. It took him three days to reconcile himself to the truth of it: if he was to get into the game at Nome with machinery, he had nowhere else to turn.

The silver lining lay in Sprague's prospectus. There he found a financial calculus forecasting annual profits of three hundred percent. Nate would be in line for a $15,000 windfall every December the first that he still held his one percent stake. He studied Sprague's assumptions: the capacity of their machinery times a season of 120 to 150 days, for output of 350,000 tons of sand, each containing gold variously estimated at $5 to $100, the lower figure being used for purposes of the forecast. He could find no fault in it, especially considering his teacher's pittance of $960 a year!

With the help of a crewman Nate found the Major's trunk more easily than he'd feared, and within it the dinner jacket. (Would that the gold of Nome should be as neatly taken.) In accepting Sprague's terms he had become a man of substantial prospects with responsibilities beyond his years. Prospects that he subsequently pledged, for it wasn't the gold that quickened his pulse, but what the gold could buy him.

AFTER DINNER THE men of the Cape Nome Company stood at the aft rail of the *Madden*, gazing over the ship's wake. The dark coast of Cape Flattery faded into night and the crests of the Olympics rose pink in the last light of evening.

"Had my own share of rough crossings," Palmer was saying. "In '95, on the North Atlantic between two hurricanes—now, there's one I'll never forget. But for sheer terror, I give it to Slocum off Cape Horn."

The others grunted emphatically, recalling Slocum's three tries around the Horn in the spring of '96.

"Never heard of it," Steale said.

Steale was the only one among them, apparently, who hadn't devoured Slocum's account, published last year, of his solo voyage around the world in a thirty-seven-foot sloop.

"Had your head in a boiler too long, Steale," Hanson teased. "If you read a newspaper once in the second half of the last decade, you read of the *Spray* sailing in or out of some port down under, Robinson Crusoe's island and places you never heard of."

"Mr. Deaton?"

The men turned to find Esther lingering at the edge of their chatter.

"Miss Crummey?" Nate released an involuntary sigh.

"There is trouble with the sorrel mare." She set her words afloat on a small carpet of exhaustion. She had knocked at his cabin door and then sought him in each of the public rooms before finally spotting the entire group of them at the rail. She had lost her inhibitions to the lateness of the hour, and to peevishness for having been snubbed by him on the foredeck. Beyond exhaustion, her tone carried the slightest whiff of accusation, as if to say he might have expected this development, for certainly she had.

Nate wished above all to put her off. "I'm truly sorry to hear it. We shall have a look bright and early tomorrow."

"The mare I pointed out at the stable this morning."

"As you just said. The sorrel. Thank you." She gave no sign of softening. He reached for something collegial. "You are settled in your cabin, then?"

She did not respond immediately, trying to make out his point. "If you're asking am I prepared to overlook the filth, the answer is no. When we have dealt with the mare, I must be given a pail of boiling water, a box of lye, and a hard brush. That's Second Cabin. Down a level, I believe, from yours."

Nate heard Angus Donaldson snort at her brittleness but he himself found it tedious. "Sundy, if you would ask the First Mate to send somebody to scrub the ladies' cabin, for Lord's sake."

The Major spoke up. "What troubles the horse, Miss Crummey?"

"Founder is my guess."

Now an unhappy grumble came from Donaldson. "Founder's more or less impossible to mitigate, is it not, miss?" The surgeon was a man of forty with large brown eyes and a thick moustache that flared out over his upper lip like the legs of a bullfrog.

"If you catch it early you can sometimes get ahead of it." Esther's eyes were unwilling to meet the doctor's directly and took refuge in his moustache. "Give her alum root and soak the feet in cold water, but I would not be waiting until morning."

There was a brief silence among them. The sunset had seemed to cap off a very long day, but now this.

Steale spat over the rail. "Horses is useless bastards." He offered the insight *sotto voce* so the men could catch it but probably not the lady. "Was a bearing turning red or metal fragments pissing out a your bleed valve, you'd know where you was at. Thing for a horse is a whack on the noggin. Whack 'em all, you'd be done with your trouble."

"If they were yours, sir, this would be the obvious answer." These words from Sprague. "Let's see to it, boys."

The effect was to break up their little gathering. Nate and Esther accompanied Donaldson below to collect his pharmacopoeia and then went forward. Nate decided to have a private correction for Miss Crummey at the first chance—do not present your business in front of the entire damn company if it doesn't concern them.

The *Madden* was well into the open sea under a clear sky, her livestock subdued in the chill of dusk. When they reached the stables, there was Mr. Sprague leaning against the rail before the sorrel. "It is the left foreleg, then?" he asked.

Even in the failing light it was apparent from the animal's stance that she was not right, straight-legged in front, stretching forward, as if she had two legs on a dock and two on a boat. Esther climbed into the stall, followed by the doctor; she put her shoulder to the mare's flank and lifted the foot so Donaldson could have a look. He probed the foot with his fingers but could find no stone or other explanation for the tenderness.

Sprague leaned on the rail, looking every part the banker. "What causes it?"

"At home, usually it's too much sweet spring grass before their stomachs are ready. But I've seen grain founder, too."

"So they get colicky," the doctor said. "But why do you see it in the legs and feet?"

"Pa always said the animal can't feed its leg if its gut's on fire."

"Blood goes to the gut, starves the extremities," Donaldson postulated.

"Bony parts go soft," she said. "You don't catch it the first day or two, she founders in the foot and there's no making it right again. Best you can do then is deaden the feeling." She touched the two points where cuts would be made. "Might get another year or two, but I've seen them, after they lost the feeling, they walk the hoof right off the leg."

"What'd we pay for the animal, Mr. Deaton? Fifty dollars?"

"Not a horse in a hundred miles of Seattle for fifty dollars, Mr. Sprague. I was lucky to find her at seventy-five." Now he knew why.

"Two or three times we had it," Esther said. "Gave alum root for the gut and cleaned out the foot good and bathed the leg in water cold as possible for five, six days. Box-stalled the horse a month to heal up. Twice it worked, once it didn't."

They decided to treat both forelegs. They removed the shoes and pared out the soles, including the bars, making sure the remaining horns were flexible and the heels well opened. Next, Donaldson prepared a fusion of alum root, water, and syrup, which he mixed in the bottom of a pail. When he was satisfied, he looked at Esther expectantly. "As the saying goes, can you make her drink?"

"Reach me that fork, there," she directed Nate. "I will need two of you on either side of the neck to hold her, and one to put the juice in her gullet when I got her open." There was nothing for it but that Sprague and Nate climb into the tight space.

Esther tucked her hair under her scarf. "Wrap both arms around the neck so she knows who's boss." They did this, whereupon Esther passed a loop of rope through the horse's mouth behind the teeth, where a bridle bit sits. The mare shied and made a loud blow through the nostrils but did not fight. Esther picked up the pitchfork. "Here goes." She slipped a tine into the other end of the rope loop and lifted the mare's head neatly. Donaldson applied the tonic. The horse jerked but the men kept her anchored and in a flicker the job was done.

"By God!" Sprague exclaimed.

"A very neat piece of work," Donaldson laughed, slapping the animal on the flank.

Nate felt a small wave of relief at their success, and at having persuaded Miss Crummey to come into their service. The men lent a hand filling two buckets with frigid seawater and setting the mare to standing in them to her fetlocks. When all was done that could be done, they said good night, and Nate and Donaldson promptly turned for their cabins.

Esther glanced at Sprague, who lingered. She put away the pitchfork and rope and tidied up as he walked two stalls forward of the sorrel and stood before his own horse. "Have you met my Savoy, miss?" It was a big chestnut gelding with a white blaze and socks. He reached into his jacket pocket for something and then let the horse nuzzle his closed hand a moment before opening it to a sugar cube.

Esther stepped over and stroked the gelding's blaze. "I have much admired this animal. You know horses, sir."

Sprague shook his head. "My cousin found him for me. I know little about them. Mother is the one who knew horses. She was a smart farm girl, like you."

She took it as a compliment. "I will enjoy looking after him."

"I will appreciate that." He nodded. "If things are not made right with your cabin, you let me know."

WHEN HE WAS gone, she found a place to sit on the bales where they were stacked against the lumber. She was reluctant to abandon the solitude of her post among the animals. She might have gone below to retrieve her blanket if she felt more secure about the ship's crew and passengers, but as it was she contented herself to sit for a few minutes, surveying her realm. The improvised stalls and pens, the tidiness of the stacks of cargo. The steady rise and fall of the ship, and the curious ability of the horses to adapt. The pricks of light in the deepening sky. The emptiness of the sea ahead.

4

The first leg of the ship's course ran eighteen hundred miles west to Unalaska Island in the Aleutian chain, where Captain Osborne would take on coal and water at Dutch Harbor Station and get news of ice conditions in the Bering Sea before setting a northwest course to Nome, another thousand miles distant. Esther and Lena stood at the starboard rail the first morning, half an hour after sunrise, having passed a fitful night. The ship rose on a five-foot swell that had the women holding handrails and peering down at the sea thrown clear by her prow. They went in to breakfast at the second sitting.

The tables in the dining saloon were covered in worn linens. The room was filling rapidly, and as the two women paused a familiar voice said, "Two places here as going begging for female accompaniment." It was the old-timer who had stepped in for Esther on the pier. He was spooning sugar into his coffee, seated at a table with three others, and beckoned them to a pair of empty chairs. He still wore the felt hat, and as the women sat he touched the brim and held out a bony hand.

"Plug Jefferson," he said. "Used to be eponymous for the third president," he added, tucking his napkin into his shirtfront, "but after I was remodeled by a lead slug through the cheek, my friends went to calling me Plug. You can do likewise, seeing as we are already acquainted by happenstance."

Others at the table were a young couple and their school-aged daughter. Esther and Lena answered the husband's question, what brought them aboard the *Madden*, and then learned the young family were traveling to Nome to get up a mortuary business. The husband was an ash-colored man in his twenties who had taken the undertaker's trade from a brother in Seattle.

"Good pickings ahead for you, sir, I'll reckon," Jefferson said brightly.

The undertaker dipped his head in agreement. "They say some sixty or seventy ships of stampeders are expected at Nome."

"Won't all of 'em find their pot of gold buried in the beach, neither," Jefferson said.

"Only two years ago the city did not even exist," the undertaker said, shaking his head. "And this summer it will be a quarter the size of Seattle or bigger! Pardon me for saying so, Mr. Jefferson, but those who stand to strike it rich, for the most part, are surely the merchantmen."

"You'll get no quarrel from me on that," Jefferson said. "I was at the American River. Deadwood. The Klondike. There's few that find a vein, but plenty that bust their picks trying."

The stewards brought bowls of porridge. The undertaker's flame was lit now. "We have studied the situation. What have you got?" He bent back his left thumb with his right. "You have got thousands, perhaps *tens* of thousands of people, not all of them specimens of health and civility." He nodded toward the passengers filling the dining saloon to support the argument, and then pressed back a second finger: "You've got the natural mortality in pioneer settings. Exceeds those in settled areas by wide margins. Accidents, overexertion, disputation." Pressed a third finger: "Here you will have a concentration of people in close quarters with little or no sanitary services, a formula that spells sickness and disease." His head bobbled slightly left and then right, seeming to say what will happen will happen, it was not for him to decide.

"Now," peeling back finger four, "when I say disease, I speak not only of the diseases that we know, but of the unknown alien afflictions introduced by close intercourse with native populations." He paused half a beat for the weight of it to settle on them, and then, finally, called up his littlest finger. "Over all of this, you have what? The human condition: greed, jealousy and desperation." The five erect fingers of mortuary fortune saluted his audience and then retired to his lap as the man turned to his meal.

Jefferson touched his brim. "Hats off to you, sir, and Nome will be a more civilized district for your services. Can I ask a question, sir?"

"Sir."

"At Dawson, why, the ground never thaws below twelve or eighteen inches. If the Seward Peninsula suffers the same predicament, which I am told it does, where would you be planning on storing your clients?"

The man smiled. "How does a miner sink a shaft, sir?"

"He stokes hisself a long-burning fire to thaw things out."

"I have a hundred tons of coal in the hold, Mr. Jefferson."

A silence fell over the table, interrupted finally by Jefferson. "No disrespect, sir, but when I am finished, I would prefer as you lay me out on one of them raised platforms the natives put up and let the crows bicker over the table scraps."

"Not in the Christian tradition, Mr. Jefferson. And cold comfort to your survivors, I should think."

In the lull that followed, the diners concentrated on their porridge, but before they could finish, the stewards set down a platter. The undertaker set to dishing himself a large serving of congealed eggs and biscuits, asking after Esther's particular responsibilities with the Cape Nome Company. She found herself describing her diagnosis of founder in the mare and how she was nursing it.

The undertaker hemmed and grunted, and the moment she finished he spoke of his own interest in the anatomy of the animal form, and then he quizzed her further on the symptoms she had observed. She told him of the horse's pointing and of her having made a close study of the foot and of finding the exceptional tenderness of the mare's frog—

"Begging to differ," he interrupted, "but certainly it sounds like the bog spavin or splints. Lameness, inflammation. I would hazard there is swelling? Possibly an enlargement upon the seat of the spavin?"

"There is not," she said dryly.

They ate on in silence, and when he had cleared his plate of food he said, "A very interesting problem. Unfortunately, I promised the missus a turn on the deck and I hope you will not be offended if we excuse ourselves." The family rose from the table in one motion and took their leave.

"He is in the right profession," Jefferson said. "If you had to keep his company, you would sooner do it dead."

Lena, who had remained silent through most of the meal, laughed outright.

Esther sat back in her seat. It was pure luxury to linger at the table. "What about you, Mr. Jefferson?" she asked.

"I am an old Sourdough and can't stay away, miss. Finding gold makes me feel good. At my age—I am sixty-eight—things that make you feel good are short and few between."

"Hard work, though."

"Don't mind work, cannot abide boredom."

"You weren't one who busted his pick at Dawson?"

"No, ma'am. I got up there early, staked a lucky claim. Panned some pretty colorful flour and small nuggets—Sir?" He crooked a finger at a steward to fill his coffee. "Trouble you for the sugar bowl, miss? Word of advice, my experience, forget the paddle but don't go up a crick without the sugar sack full, makes a very sour camp! So, along comes a fella from Utah, says he surely would like my claim for hisself, would I take ten thousand for it? I looked to see was he serious, and then I laid down my pick and said I supposed I would."

"He paid it?" Lena asked.

Jefferson nodded. "Went home to Arkansas and sat on my behinder until I contracted the fleabitten tediums. No, thank you. And I will tell you something else this old plug learnt. Gold talks. Somebody finds it, try as he like, ain't no way a keepin' it quiet. You get within a hundred miles of gold, you can hear it whisper. Unless you are so enraptured of your own intonations, like our new friend the undertaker."

PLUG JEFFERSON INVITED Esther and Lena to join him at cribbage in the Social Hall Lounge. Lena was willing to amuse him for two or three hands, but Esther excused herself to tend her livestock. She slipped into the First Cabin companionway to avail herself of one of the public toilets. There were four ladies' halfway forward to starboard which she'd noticed the previous evening and found far more to her liking than those in Second Cabin.

It was upon leaving the toilet that she spotted Mr. Steale stepping out of a cabin five or six doors down. A woman was seeing him out—one of the French prostitutes. Esther turned the opposite direction up the companionway. She was not entirely surprised by the sight. Had not cared for the man since she'd watched his ignorant behavior with the horses. So Steale is one that pays for relations. Marked it to herself in the way that her father had marked a neighbor who showed himself to a hired man's wife; in the way that her mother had marked a Moorhead grocer who showed uncommon fondness for her boys. Steale was a coarse, hungry thing lowering his trousers to mount the sporting girls.

Esther slipped beneath the line cordoning off the forward deck and walked between the pens, swept into the noise of the animals, thinking how their different voices were true to their animal personalities, while also pondering the sexual appetites of men, the hunger of such a man as Steale, a gaunt man given to machines, a stranger among humans and animals. Lost to her thoughts, she failed to see Mr. Deaton, who stood ahead of the cow houses near the bow. She drew cold water for the sorrel mare's feet and, despite herself, felt the seat of the spavin for telltale swelling. There was none, as she well knew.

The undertaker. Another such man as violates you and turns away.

She would have liked a shelter. She thought to rearrange some bales of straw in the lee of the Post Office into a half-enclosed roost where she might curl up out of the wind and spray. And so, with the ship heaving to a rising sea, she set to work at this little construction.

Nate had taken a turn forward with seabirds on his mind, notably the red phalarope, which he keenly wished to spot. He stood abreast of the capstan at the rail and buttoned his coat against the wind and spray. The ship was certainly too southerly yet. Nor in all probability was the bird still bobbing about at mid-ocean so far into the season but rather likely to have flown shoreward for breeding. Yet stragglers and accidentals are always possible and it was in his nature to look. He conned the swells for something that, from the height of the ship's bow, would be barely perceptible, a bushel of corks washed overboard, and what hope of finding a thing so insubstantial on such an expanse of open sea. Like hunting gold, nine parts luck to every part perseverance. Like him in this venture, at sea with responsibilities far beyond his experience. Not, he hoped, beyond his ability to learn. Not beyond his skills. Equipped as few gold hunters ever have been.

The bow fell into a deep trough and he was forced to grip the railing. He tried on the rise to scan with his binoculars, but the ship's motion rendered them useless. And what if they were heading home just now rather than outbound? There'd be something in the papers certainly. Many calls and well-wishers. Remarks before the Quinsigamond Club with his cronies in the audience, everyone asking after his plans now that he was returned and a man of means. There would be firing up the motor-cycle business in earnest. Possibly a little something extra for the old Swede, a new motor of some kind. They could research it together—Nate would set it up as an outing, no hint of his intentions, they would scour the catalogues and showrooms of all the reliable makers for the latest products, and when something caught the old Swede's eye, Nate would slip into the back office and buy the thing right on the spot, a finger to his lips and no word of the purchase until the delivery could be—

The ship's bow dropped from a height into a surprisingly deep trough and threw up a wall of water. Nate's stomach plummeted. The frigid seas shot aft in a stunning blast as the bow shuddered and bullied into the next rise. The swell had been growing all morning and he turned to make his way amidships without delay. It was now that he spotted Miss Crummey. She had caught her balance leaning over a straw bale, her hair flown back, coat billowing open, dress wetted and flattened against her body by the wind, her slim waist, the neat division of her torso into thighs outlined perfectly. She was too busy to notice him, pushing the bale across the deck now. He was about to call out to her but paused, still twenty feet distant. Something in the unguarded way she moved, her dampened breasts.

"Miss Crummey!" He raised his voice over the wind and proceeded in her direction, his hand on the rail and then against the cow house. Younger than he had taken her for. Gone to dishevelment in service to her project, a sight that suddenly tugged at him, so unlike his careful Lily, laced securely fore and aft.

"Miss Crummey!" He was all but on her now, and she started. She pulled her coat closed and steadied herself against the stack of bales.

"Mr. Deaton?"

"What are you doing? I mean, can I help you at all?"

"Surprised me!"

"I called from back there but you did not hear me."

"Well, then." She brushed straw from her coat and wiped the moisture from her forehead. "You look half frozen." She wondered what was he doing, sneaking around the stables on her. "You could lift this bale up for me." She pointed where she wanted it.

He set the bale in place and saw she was organizing a bit of a shelter. "Very clever. Quite inviting, really."

"And what about you?"

The invitation caught him off guard. "Ah—" He pulled at his coat. "Well, I'm afraid I am wet inside and out!"

"So I see, but what I meant was you have come to check on the animals? Is that it?"

"Oh. No. Not at all. I have been on the lookout for birds. I am something of a collector. Strictly amateur."

"At sea?"

"In fact I may have spotted a Wilson's petrel earlier. White rump, black tail, no fork. And I have talked myself into believing that between here and Nome may be the red phalarope."

She squinted at him.

"Not the one they call the red-*necked*," he said, "but the red. You know it?"

"A kind of bird? I know only the common ones. Barn swallows."

He gestured toward the rolling swells. "Just a slip of a thing. Little more than a sparrow. Deep chestnut breast and white face are the giveaway. It's not even a seabird but a wader, and that's the puzzle. Sailors sometimes see it far out on the open ocean, spinning in tight little circles atop the water. Something I should love to see."

"What is it doing?" she asked.

He hesitated a moment and then cocked an eyebrow and gave a stage whisper, "If we find it, we shall ask."

There was a boyish quality she had not noticed before. He looked slightly flushed, and his excitement for the birds made her wish for something to give him. "They flock up the Red in spring." She tried to think of some but she could not. She had forgotten about birds. In truth, she had never bothered herself to learn them, but when her life was simpler she did enjoy seeing them. "I have always liked the singing ones." She felt his eyes on her and pulled a comb from her pocket and gathered her hair at the back of her head and fastened it, and as she did this the breeze played at one edge of her coat and fluttered it open.

Her nipple was hard against her wet dress and he willed his eyes not to stare. Beads of water ran from her temple into the down of her jaw.

"The bright little ones that winter over," she was saying, and then she laughed at her inability to think of the names. Birds had been wholly unexpected between them. The ship's bow plunged again, lofting a heavy spray.

"The cardinals and goldfinches," he offered, and he gave her a handkerchief.

"Yes." She patted the spray from her forehead and where it ran off her nose and chin, and then blew her nose gently and they smiled a bit self-consciously and he asked if she needed any further help with her refuge and she said she thought not, but if he was in the way of bird-watching again he was welcome to borrow it.

He hadn't been gone a minute when they began coming to her, their names rising from the thickets of her embarrassment. Meadowlarks and flycatchers. Chickadees. Orioles. Grosbeaks and buntings. The great blue herons and red-tailed hawks. There were so many. She would tell him. The next time she saw him, on deck or perhaps in the Dining Saloon, she would pick some of her favorites and make a private sort of gift of their names to him.

BY AFTERNOON, THE seas ran a twenty-foot swell before a thirty-knot headwind. Esther found Lena and Mr. Jefferson still at cards in the Social Hall Lounge, now in a foursome of whist, a game foreign to Esther. She went around behind Mr. Jefferson, who had just made book and now led the eight of hearts. Lena capped it with the queen to take command of the lead, but the fourth player laid trump and swept up the trick.

"That's a revoke! That's a revoke!" cried Lena.

"It is a renounce!" replied the fellow, who looked startled by the charge and examined the cards in his hand. "Oh, criminy, I take it back!" he said, slapping down a four of hearts. He plucked his trump from the table and pushed the trick to Lena.

"A revoke nonetheless! Three points!" Jefferson announced.

"Blast your revoke! I have withdrawn it!"

"Watch your language sir," Jefferson said. "You pulled in the trick. Three points fair and square, and start digging for your dollars while we take in the rest of 'em."

With that Lena began a run from the king of spades that finished the hand for a total of nine tricks.

"Game and a point to spare!" Jefferson said, "giving us the rubber, thank you, gents, and put your chips on the table!"

Esther left them to their cards, taking a turn around the ship to walk off her lunch, and then repaired to her new retreat. Building hidey-holes in the hay had been a favorite game of hers in the cool fall nights after the wheat harvest, and it pleased her in a childish way to do so aboard ship and settle herself into the welcoming shelter. The animals were hunkered down in their pens and kennels. The horses all pitched against the aft sides of their stalls on the rise, and against the forward sides on the fall. Below, in her cabin in the night, Esther had slept intermittently, listening to the throb of the engine and groan of the hull and bulkheads against the sea, but on deck the noise of the wind in the rigging and of the tops breaking on the passing combers swept away the ship's complaints and soon also the clutter of animal voices, the chickens and sheep and pigs, leaving only the intermittent wail of the dogs. Occasionally she drifted off, and the smell of straw took her home to summer in the wheat fields of the Ulverson farm at Perley.

5

The *Madden* forged ahead of a black swath of smoke, its bow burrowing through the crests and then dropping into the troughs with great show before rising again to the oncoming sea. Passengers who weren't laid low by seasickness moved through the ship with difficulty or anchored themselves to a rail or post to watch the ship's progress. Major Palmer retired to his berth in the Captain's quarters, eating little of the food that the Captain's steward brought him, despite the urgings of Donaldson, who advised him to eat and gave him hartshorn in water and applied a spinal ice bag to ease his discomfort.

Nate, who fared better out of doors than in, had established a regular roost in the shelter of a davit where, on the fifth day of the voyage, he sat with his oilskin pulled close around him and one eye glued to the horizon. Fighting queasiness, he turned his mind in reverse order through his favorite preoccupations, starting with his motors. He and the school janitor, an old Swede, had tinkered in the shops at Thornton Hall, where Nate had done his preparatory schooling. The old Swede had taken Nate under his wing after the death of his father, teaching him the names and uses of tools and providing an ear when one was needed. The friendship endured.

Lately the two men had been overtaken by the new internal combustion engines, with their loud spark and pop, their tidy dimensions, and absence of boilers. The Otto engines. Nate's pride and joy was a one-and-three-quarter-horse single-piston gasoline motor that they had mounted to the frame of a bicycle. They'd had to rebuild the bike twice to reinforce it against weight and vibration. Then again to lower the center of gravity, and once more to add a clutch and a brake, whereupon the machine had performed exquisitely. The old Swede tore down Barn Road in the dark at better than twenty-five miles per hour, raising half a dozen neighbors from their evening torpor before making the turn at the far end and roaring back. The Otto bike formed the germ of their newest idea, the Worcester Motor-Cycle Shops. A company to be established directly after payout of the Cape Nome Company's dividend on the first of December next. What a year!

When he could, Nate balanced his hours bent over motors by chasing after birds, a union of opposites. Motors controlled your world, while birds had an evanescence—"the little birds that fly / with careless ease from tree to tree." He found an invigorating solitude in the outings, a fellow alone with his shotgun, though just now he admitted to feeling profligate for what he'd spent on the cedar collecting box at Seattle. He'd been seduced by the brass hinges and filigree of inlaid mahogany. And yet, he argued, he was about to set foot upon the subarctic coast with all its exotic species, and wouldn't he be glad of that extravagant little box then.

Next his mind went to Lily Wilder and matters of a romantic

nature. Although Nate had experienced the usual taunting and experimentation of a boys' school, his education about sex was sorely limited until a traveling carnival brought to Worcester a dark-haired gypsy who rode a dolphin in a canvas tank. She turned out to be a Catholic girl from Vermont named Colleen whose appetite for sea life was second to her taste for fifteen-year-old schoolboys needing help over the tricky bridge into manhood. His tutoring was given after closing on each of the five evenings of the carnival's engagement, and refreshed for good measure on successive summers until he was eighteen, when his gypsy failed to return.

At twenty he'd gotten to know Lily Wilder in a group of Saturday regulars at the rink behind Baily's Hotel and had learned to watch for her so they could skate as partners. Soon he asked her to an oration by William Jennings Bryan at the Schubert; she invited him to hear Liszt in her father's music room; he took her to watch the quail dogs compete at the county fairgrounds.

Lily was blond and sunny and loved to read, bringing a favorite book to the Wilder parlor or garden whenever he came, passing along the Brontë sisters, Jane Austen, and Thomas Hardy, while he loaned her Cooper, Conrad, Twain. She fancied herself a renegade, and she believed that those who possess money were required to give it to those in need. She and Nate, like the Romantic poets, should become anarchists and lovers, or so she'd said one day in the garden. "You will be my Percy."

"To me," he said, "you have more of Dr. Frankenstein than Mary Shelley."

"Well, then," she retorted, "that would make you my beast."

He took to calling her My Dear Doctor and he was her Beastly Thing. That he came from modest means and she from affluence was about as much anarchy as her watchful father had appetite for. Saturdays they played whist with her parents or she took him off to a friend's wedding. She loved the pomp and pageantry and being squired by Nate when he was fully rigged out in a rented tuxedo, but she scoffed at the notion of a grand wedding for herself. The fact that Lily considered elopement daring enabled them to sidestep the delicate topic of future intentions.

She accompanied him to the train to see him off for Nome. He had given her a map of Alaska and a framed letter written on the Cape Nome Company stationery, hiring her for purposes as might benefit the company foreman in the performance of his duties, remuneration to be paid in kind and in person upon conclusion of the mining season.

When he kissed her goodbye, he said, "I will write to tell you how my fortune is piling up, and if Nome is a fit place for elopement."

THE SHIP'S ANGLE to the seas was unfortunate and the urgency of Nate's queasiness called for a new venue. He visited the wheelhouse, where he tried to peruse the ship's copy of *North Pacific and Arctic Pilot,* but reading proved ill-advised and he quickly gave it up in favor of conversation. The SS *Miss Madden* was thirty years old, the Captain told him, built at Dumbarton for the immigrant trade. She saw service as a British troop ship during the Egyptian campaign and then was put in service to Australia, the Hebrides, and South America. Nowadays she carried lumber, coal, wheat, and steel to the Far East and ran back with tea, silk, ginger, and straw matting. Like most of the trans-Pacific fleet, she had been pressed into service for the race to Nome, carrying nearly five hundred passengers and fifteen hundred tons of cargo.

"A lucrative run at gold-rush fares," Nate observed.

"And what about your Major Palmer?" the Captain said. "His stores and equipment fill the better part of my hold. By the way, I have invited a passenger named McKenzie to join us at dinner this evening. He is a like-minded capitalist, representing investors from New York."

"The Major begs your pardon in advance for his absence," Nate said. "But I will enjoy making the acquaintance of a tycoon, and watching Mr. Sprague put him through his paces."

ALEXANDER MCKENZIE SAT opposite Nate at the Captain's table. He was a close-shorn man in his early forties with a Van Dyke beard and an appraising eye that reminded Nate of somebody well known to him, somebody Nate could not bring clearly to mind. The Captain expressed his regret at the Major's indisposition and introduced the others around the table—William Sprague, Nate Deaton, the Deacon Trumble, Mrs. Trumble, and daughter Grace. Pleasantries passed among them as Nate tried to think of a topic to engage Grace, but McKenzie asked after the Cape Nome Company, and Sprague set to regaling the table in exquisite detail about the company's intention to establish the largest steam dredge in the history of mining on the entire Seward Peninsula. This through the soup, the salad, and the roast beef and mashed potatoes, with little grunts of encouragement from McKenzie and, in the early stages of the treatise, from the Deacon. Nate would have liked to stuff a hen in Sprague. There were no breaks for air, no openings through which conversation might spread around the table or turn to the affairs of the other guests, and finally Mrs. Trumble and Grace excused themselves, pleading discomfort of the sea.

"You already have claims, of course," McKenzie said to Sprague, declining dessert when it was offered.

Sprague regarded McKenzie as he might a schoolboy. "You do not raise half a million dollars in capital on a lick and a promise, sir."

"On the beach, I presume," McKenzie went on, "for such a machine would be difficult to mount along a creek bed, would it not?"

"We are well prepared for sluicing stream claims, Mr. McKenzie. High-duty pumps and hoses enough to change the course of half a dozen creeks if there's gold to be had. The beach itself cannot be staked, as surely you know. It's every man for himself, wherever he manages to sink his shovel. We shall go as far up the shore as necessary to establish our beach operations." With this, as if the line of inquiry had grown tedious, Sprague pulled a cigar from his jacket pocket, struck a match, and endeavored to redirect the conversation. "And your concern, sir?"

"The Alaska Gold Mining Company," McKenzie said with a deferential nod. "But you sound thoroughly versed in these matters. I had taken you for the Worcester banker of the same name."

Sprague pursed his lips, clearly gratified to be known and not wishing to seem so. "One and the same." The cigar had now caught, and he rolled it in his mouth and chuffed at it to even out the coal.

"Of the Cape Nome Company, your Major Palmer holding controlling interest, if I am to understand correctly?"

"Oh, I should say the shares are held by several of the more prominent men of Worcester. And New York, as a matter of fact. I myself holding not an inconsiderable interest."

Of course, Nate thought, McKenzie was like his Wheeler cousins, they of the casualty insurance business, sharp-beaked men who, in ordinary conversation, seemed always to be gleaning hidden meanings, appraising the speaker, sizing up risks and benefits—at the same time taking care to withhold their own opinions.

With the coffee gone and the dessert plates cleared, McKenzie pushed back his chair and rose.

"Your own plans, sir," Nate asked, "are they principally beach or creek?"

"I will know better when we have been in country a week or two, Mr. Deaton. My company has raised its share of capital as well—some five million, in fact—on a somewhat different strategy than yours."

Five million? That this figure should surface so late in the conversation, after such grand claims for the Cape Nome Company, knocked Nate completely off balance. McKenzie's statement seemed to have the same effect on Sprague, who stabbed his cigar in the ashtray.

McKenzie was saying, "Our strategy is to see where the gold has been found, and then strike an advantageous cash offer for equity interest in the company that has found it. We already own quite a number of claims through our agents in Nome. This will explain the absence of a management complement and our lack of the usual folderol filling the ship's hold. How many tons do you pay the good Captain here to carry north, sir?" he asked Sprague.

"Well, that's a damned fool's game," Sprague responded. "Wait until the gold's been found and then try to buy it for a song. Who'll be fool enough to sell then? You pull my leg, sir. Come to me in a month's time and see what I will settle my claims for then."

McKenzie smiled slightly. "That is my plan precisely. Assuming you find anything more than sand."

After the group adjourned, the Captain invited Nate and Sprague to look in on Palmer. The Major, still pale but now dressed, roused himself into a chair, and the Captain offered a round of port. Soon Sprague was rendering the post-dinner episode with McKenzie for Palmer's benefit.

"The man is a snoop and an ass. 'Where are your claims, sir? Who are your investors, sir? What have you packed into the ship's hold, sir?' He is a jackanapes posing as a company man with nothing to show for it but a bald-ass lie about five million dollars going looking for cheap gold. I am surprised you would have him to table, Captain."

"Pays his First Cabin passage, Mr. Sprague, and is, I am told, particularly well connected in the East."

"Truly?" said Palmer.

The Captain dug a knife from his pocket and began to whittle at the nail of his left thumb, which was thick and misshapen. "Word from Northern Pacific management."

Palmer said, "If the fellow has five million dollars, he might in the end prove useful."

FINDING NOME'S GOLD in one form or another was the favorite subject of each meal in every corner of the dining saloon. Among Esther, Lena, and Plug Jefferson, table talk followed that and other strands: whether a prairie wheat town like Perley was as much an island in its way as a place like Martha's Vineyard; possible retorts to shipmates who inveighed against a woman or a Colored sitting to cards in the ship's lounge; whether prevailing at whist suggested moral or merely intellectual keenness; and what opportunities for employment at Nome a young colored woman should decline out of hand. Depending upon how his cards had run, Plug would dispense the milk of human kindness or rail against humanity, but even the blackest mood would lift with gentle coaxing from Lena. He called her his little caramel.

At Dutch Harbor, where the passengers were let ashore, the three friends hiked up a hill behind town to have a look north over the Bering Sea. Esther had thought to go easy for Jefferson's sake, but he went at the slope full throttle, the gray tufts jutting from under his cap like competent puffs of steam. Afterward they took lunch in the village.

"I still say doctoring's big in a gold camp," Plug declared over boiled halibut. "Lawyering's big if there's any kind of rich claims around, and a lawyer cannot get from his breakfast whiskey to his bedtime brandy without a secretary to type it down and submit it to the court. Of course, the recorder's office is one of the busiest storefronts, second to the bars and sporting girls, which brings me back to doctoring. Oh, and card sharking. I would lay money on you for sharking, Miss Lena."

Dutch Harbor, Alaska
June 14, 1900

Dearest Lily,

Salutations from the coaling station of Dutch Harbor, the compass point from which we finally turn north into the Bering Sea. We stopped to take on coal and learned that the ships departing Seattle ahead of us were forced to lay over here until receiving word of the ice pack's break-up, which word came only two days ago, so we are not so far behind in the stampede as we had feared!

I enclose my diary entries from Seattle to here. I believe that Mr. Sprague wired your father of our success in fully collecting all the capital pledged by shareholders before our departure. A bit of tycoonery that has swelled the man to the point of insufferability. If I could buy him for what he is worth and sell him for what he thinks he is worth, we would have no need of looking for gold.

I must post this and board, as we sail in a few minutes. Dear Lily, I fell at the last for the little folding rowboat at Schwabacher's. It is made of wood and canvas, functional beyond *question, possibly a necessity and yet totally overlooked in all of my planning, something I would have no hope of obtaining after we set sail. The cost was $10. It will be the envy of the company at Nome.*

I think of you always, and when sleep comes, finally, I hold you again.

Your lonely beast of a gold hunter,

Nate

They were out of Dutch Harbor by noon of the fourteenth of June, a week and eighteen hundred miles into their voyage. Captain Osborne set the *Madden* on a north-by-northwest heading, ten degrees off its course for Nome to quarter the heavy swell, but even so the lively roll of the ship subdued the travelers and she steamed into the Bering Sea with her bar closed and most passengers battened into their cabins. The ship's freight strained at its moorings. The crew worked among the narrow alleys, cinching their straps and lines. Esther bade them make doubly secure a pile of timbers on the foredeck she feared could topple, but it wasn't the timbers that cut loose in the night, it was the Cape Nome Company's big pump, a half ton of cast iron three and a half feet in diameter that chafed through its ropes and slammed against the stables and then charged back against the freight, gutting fifty sacks of coal, and then rolled hard against the stables and back, then hard against the stables again. It took the crew half an hour to get lines around the beast and truss it, but not before it had crushed a crewman's leg and pinned two horses under the collapsed walls of their stalls.

Donaldson was called up to doctor the injured man, and he woke Esther to come to the aid of the horses.

Chaos greeted her on deck. The wreckage was scattered from side to side, fore and aft, the injured horses struggling to stand, the heaving of the ship thwarting attempts at order. The ship's crew shoveled coal and restacked and lashed cargo. A knot of company men whose property was damaged were arguing with a ship's officer over the fault and losses. Esther went from animal to animal. Sprague's chestnut gelding, Savoy, was lame. Horses belonging to other companies were worse damaged. One, a roan mare, sustained deep cuts in her hind legs. The other was a brown colt; it showed no broken bones but was unable to stand and Esther suspected damage to the ligaments.

"Step back, miss," the ship's officer said. "The wounded horses are to be destroyed and put over."

"I should say not! These horses can be saved!"

"Captain's order. Steamship's got no provisions for doctoring them."

"Hold off until I've spoken to the Captain." Esther left immediately to rouse Mr. Sprague, with whom she felt a faint kinship in the matter of horses. If his own horse had not been among the injured, she might have been reluctant to wake him, but as it was, she rapped on the cabin door without hesitation.

Sprague dressed quickly and met her on deck.

"Please instruct the Captain that the injured animals be turned over to my care," Esther said. "The next couple of days will tell whether they can be mended. When we reach Nome I will find a stableman willing to let them heal up. He can sell them into service when they are recovered, and pocket the proceeds for his trouble." As for Sprague's Savoy, she thought the injury might be no worse than a mild sprain she could nurse it through.

Sprague intervened, and Esther settled into her expanded duties, calling on Donaldson when he was free to consult with her.

On June seventeenth they encountered their first ice, enormous floes riding the currents south from the pack ice, and despite the long hours of twilight the ship was forced to cut her progress to half speed. When the first seals were spotted on the floes, passengers rushed the rails, and three men pulled out revolvers, taking potshots, succeeding in killing two.

On the eighteenth, more ice and tedious going. On the nineteenth, fog, and the *Madden* inched along at three knots all day.

The twentieth dawned clear and she was back to half speed through wide leads in a heavy pack. She entered Norton Sound with her passengers crowding the starboard deck, scanning the horizon for landfall, finally raising the Kigluaik Mountains and then a stretch of stunning white coastline, a dazzling brilliance that suggested a remarkable surf, or perhaps ice driven against the shore. Nate scanned with his glasses: a jumble of white rectangles spilled down the coast like cubed sugar, crawling with life.

"Tents!" he cried.

It was Nome.

6

A dozen ships already swung at anchor in the Nome roadstead. The *Madden* hove to near the *Tacoma*, two miles offshore, and at six o'clock the following morning Captain Osborne sent a delegation ashore in his launch—the First Mate and the Major to arrange barging services, and Miss Crummey to find a stables willing to accept her goddamn lame horses. There was room aboard for Mr. Deaton and Mr. McKenzie as well.

They rowed in on a moderate swell, sharing few words, intent on the scene they were entering, wrapped in their coats against a damp forty-eight degrees. The beach was hardly visible for the turmoil, and the mate, at the rudder, picked an opening a quarter mile or so west of the town and ran in with the surf. Nate, who had pulled on high rubber boots, jumped over at the last and pulled them up.

Every manner of barge and boat was busy off-loading the ships. Tugs drew the barges to within thirty feet of shore and cut them loose. Lines of men waded out and back carrying freight ashore, piling it wherever there was a patch of sand, not always beyond the lip of the surf. Other men hunted out their scattered belongings among the piles and dragged them farther from the water's edge. Miners worked the beach with pans and shovels and wooden rockers. Men bent over timbers hammering up boats. Men in makeshift booths hawked drinking water, whiskey, cigars, sandwiches, coal, nails, and kerosene. The freight piles extended back forty or fifty yards toward the tundra, and at the high-tide line tents had been pitched among the piles and the proprietors of these camps squatted before low fires cooking breakfast. The beach smelled of damp canvas, smoke, and frying meat.

Nate bribed a miner to keep an eye on the launch, but before the little delegation could set off down the shore they were set upon by a pack of yelping dogs that chased down from somewhere, swarming around the freight piles, tearing at duffels and bundles until one of them snatched a prize of some sort and they set to ripping and scrapping over it. Men whose possessions were at stake ran over and kicked the dogs, yelling and striking them with boards. At the crack of a gunshot a dog fell out, squealing and dragging its hindquarters toward Esther.

"Steady!" the Major cried, and he pulled a pistol from his belt and shot the animal dead. The other dogs scattered.

"Oh, hell. I'd a got him with the second shot," a man said from above. They looked up at a gent in a woolen suit standing atop a mountain of bagged coal, putting his own pistol away.

The fellow said he'd come off the *Roanoke* the prior evening with his company's outfit, which was now interspersed with the freight of half a dozen other companies, so that he, keeping the whoresons and rotters away from his coal stores, was charged as well with guarding the food crates, gasoline barrels, lumber, tools, and machinery scattered over a hundred yards of beach while his associates went in search of drayage and a site to make camp. He gestured toward the top of the beach, where the tent city formed and stretched back on the tundra, a sea of whitecaps claiming a mile or more of the plain before it rose into the foothills.

The *Madden* delegation went on toward town, finding a path that they shared with horse teams and dog teams laboring ahead of loaded freight wagons. There were eight or ten dogs to a wagon, hitched in tandem, their drivers urging them on with cries of "Mush!"

"What are the haulage rates?" Nate asked one of them.

"Two dollars a trunk or ten dollars an hour."

Palmer whistled at such tariffs. It would cost a fortune to move the Cape Nome Company's outfit overland. Better to prospect a place for the company's big machinery, and then hope to barge it directly to the site. They troubled another driver about water transport, and were told to ask at the steamship companies. Lightering was going for ten dollars a ton and the services of the few flat steam scows and tugboats with lighters were long since committed, their captains gaily minting money at the rate of a thousand dollars a day while most of the fleet rode at anchor, unable to empty its holds.

A sluggish river called the Snake issued from the tundra flats and ran east a quarter mile or so between the beach and the western edge of town, forming a sand spit where it emptied into the sea. A family of natives camped on the spit under a skin boat, cooking fish over an oily fire. The slack waters of the river passed for a shallow harbor, busy with dories, skiffs, and small steamboats. Three sternwheelers were moored on the opposite bank, including the *Excelsior*, pressed into service as a hotel. The Major hired a rowboat ferry and the little group was taken across to disembark on River Street, a rather grand name for a crowded strip of dirt separating a string of saloons and attorneys' offices from the river's edge. Here the delegation agreed to part ways, Palmer and Deaton to establish the Cape Nome Company with a bank, and McKenzie to meet an associate who was to have preceded him to Nome.

Esther went in search of a stables. River Street rose up an incline to become Front Street east of the Snake, where the buildings on her right backed hard against the beach. Front Street wasn't thirty feet across in some places. She tried to push her way up a wooden sidewalk but it was stopped solid with men haggling, smoking, and drinking. She joined the river of humanity and animals shouldering up the street, swept along in clouds of dust. The storefronts and hotels were every kind of quickly-thrown-up thing, tents and pole buildings, lean-tos, frame buildings. Anywhere there was a gap, there was a man at work to fill it with a building, going to make his fortune in cigars and patent medicines, mine brokering, tooth extraction, or salooning. The whiteness and shimmer seen from a distance dissolved into filth, grasping, and mongering, a place unlike any Esther could have imagined. She counted as many dance halls and gambling houses as restaurants and grocers. A pair of Coloreds shared a beer in an alley, a relief to see that Lena's would not be the only dark face in the place. The narrow ways between buildings gave off the stench of human waste and rotting garbage. Two miners pushed past her, and as she tried to catch the drift of their talk the hair stood up on her neck; they were not men at all but women who had cut their hair and pulled on men's trousers.

She turned in at Thurl's Livery & Sale, a stables constructed of a tent. The stableman was shoeing a mule. There were only four horses in stalls, and they were being looked over by two men who behaved like prospective buyers.

"Are you selling horses?" she asked.

"First come, first served," he said without looking up. "More when I can get 'em off the ship."

She found them reasonably clean and healthy. There were stalls enough for ten more horses.

"Which do you want?" the stableman asked.

"I have two horses for you, sir," she said, looking him square in the eye.

He glanced out the door to see them.

"Still aboard ship."

"If they're healthy, I'll pay two hundred dollars each. Bring 'em in." He turned away and began to heft hay bales.

"Not asking to be paid," she said.

He turned back to see what she was after. He was tall and hunched at the shoulders. His hands and forearms looked as strong as a smithy's but his face was risen bread, pocked and puffy-like.

"The horses got hurt at sea. I'm looking for a stables to keep them until they're fit to be worked."

"Ten dollars a day until I need the space. Then you clear 'em out of here."

"Need to be fed and let to heal another three weeks. You do that, then sell 'em for what you like, and the money's yours. I'm not asking for anything but what's right for the animals."

The fellow wiped an arm across his face. "Lady, I can sell every blamed horse I can lay hands on three times over. Your horses can't walk, I'll sell 'em for meat, give you half. What works gets fed. What can't work goes for feed." He watched her just long enough to see that she savvied, and then he went back to his work.

"Wait," she said. "Those people on the ships. They'll need horses.

I was at the docks in Seattle. They were loading people and machines and stores, not horses. In three or four weeks, you'll get double what a horse gets now."

"Maybe. Every one of them as gettin' off ships is your next millionaire. Ain't no horse priced too high for a man headin' out to make his fortune. But them as come back, most will be busted. Ain't no horse priced low enough for a man's been busted. A month from now's a long time in a gold town."

She read the truth of it in his voice and sighed.

"If I was you," he said, "I would go to one of them big mining concerns that's scattering its fancy machinery to hell over the beach out there. Ask 'em where they're going to be settin' theirselves up, and see if they haven't got sick services for livestock and maybe even a horse's nursemaid on their payroll, but us independents, all we can do is give you top dollar for what you got today. Nobody knows until tomorrow who's wakin' up fat and who's wakin' up calling Jesus to carry him home."

She tried to find more argument but couldn't.

"You go ask the company men," he said, not so much denying her now as urging her. "Afterward, if you still want me to sell 'em, I'll be here. Name is Thurl."

She took comfort over coffee and eggs at the El Dorado Diner. It was a place of unpainted walls and rough board flooring with benches and makeshift plank tables, the menu written with a pencil on a board nailed to the doorframe. She shared a table with seven other diners but was unto herself in her head, hearing only snippets of their talk: two nuggets big as acorns dug out of the beach east of Lane's Derrick, cost of a lay above Discovery on Anvil Creek and what you could get for it this time next week, price that a Nome city lot commanded that morning. The eggs came with two slices of bread. She parked half a slice at the edge of her plate in reserve and centered the rest, a raft of white on a china sea, then carefully raised the eggs, which had been fried, onto the platform and punctured the yolks so the yellow could swamp its foundation. She took each bite slowly and thought about Lena and hoped Plug wouldn't steer her into getting up a card room or something. Not that she held Lena in such low regard, but how well do you know a person? Put yourself in the path of temptation, how well do you know your own self? Plug Jefferson, for instance. Gold prospector or just a good-time fella?

When the eggs were eaten she mopped the residue of yolk with the last of her bread. Then contented herself to sit a few minutes, erect, unable to lean back, for the benches had no backs. Sat with her hands in her lap, satisfied to let the world spin of its own momentum, without her contribution. Her mind fell silent, and in the silence she felt her stomach wishing for something more. Instead of denying herself, she begged pardon to those beside her, stepped to the door to look at the menu, and then sat again and treated herself to a dish of prune cobbler.

For some reason her thoughts turned to her friend the baker's wife, Mrs. Loqueshear, and her wisdom and her generosity, paying once for Esther's eggs with money and again in kind, with iced buns and coffee cakes.

From the beginning she had taken home to Leonard the bakery goods her eggs had earned her but not the coins, which she kept to herself. The arrangement eased and troubled her. The falseness had not been a thing she planned, but once committed, it was a thing she'd kept at. The lost pastries did not show up in Mrs. L's books, and the coins did not show up in Esther's accounting of her egg sales to her husband. Was an unspoken understanding with Mrs. Loqueshear, who knew something of Esther's marriage before Esther saw it for herself, and who had no shame in the small evening of accounts for two women who should have got far more from the unequal contract of marriage than they did. Mrs. L's friendship had been what she needed, but she could see now that the part of herself she gave to it was a thing she held back from Leonard. She must have known that at the time, she supposed, her spoon scraping the bowl for the last of the cobbler, or why would so small a betrayal have troubled her as it had?

Sweet was gone already and she could hardly remember eating it. She swallowed the remains of her coffee. Bitter and fortifying in the way that bitterness raises the grain of resolve. Folded her napkin, running a nail down the crease, and set it beside her plate. Fished from her purse the unholy charge of $1.45. Alaska was something to see but no place an ordinary person could afford. Nor had she found anything in these past hours that she liked or approved of. Nor did that signify. Wasn't to like or dislike; sole purpose was a place a person came to get rich so you could afford to go back to live what kind of a life you could not see clear to getting otherwise. Wasn't anybody here for any other reason. She had never been in such a place, but here she was, $150 wages in her pocket. The mood of it was catching.

THE BREEZE HAD freshened as the day unfolded, and by the time they were rowed back to the ship the launch was taking spray over her bow. The men had been unsuccessful in opening accounts and depositing their money, as the Bank of Cape Nome consisted of a manager in a storefront with neither vaults nor money. But in the more pressing matter of conveying passengers and cargo ashore they had met with better success. For a premium of a dollar a ton over going rates they had contracted the services of the steam tug *Rebecca* to barge their cargo, commencing two days hence and continuing uninterrupted until completed, location to be determined, such premium offered on the condition that the *Rebecca* transport the *Madden*'s passengers and baggage ashore that very night. While the notion of bidding up prices was anathema to Palmer, Nate had argued that time lost in getting into production would likely cost them far more in unmined ore. The deal was neat, and Palmer took evident pleasure in outlining its terms to Captain Osborne.

For his part, their terse shipmate McKenzie had returned to the ship looking privately satisfied, saying nothing about his day except that he had met his party and transacted his business as planned.

"And what about Miss Crummey's horses?" the Captain asked.

"She tells us she secured an offer," Nate said. "I do not know the specifics. However, she is not certain it is on the very best terms, and tomorrow she intends to approach three or four mining companies directly to be certain of her ground."

Shortly after ten o'clock that evening the men of the Cape Nome Company stood at the rail with their fellow passengers and watched the sturdy tug *Rebecca* steam into the ship's lee on a rising sea, her barge in tow. An odd hour to put ashore, but they had come to an odd place, a place where the sun refused to sink, a place where no tree softened the horizon, a place where little wagers could turn coarse men to millionaires. The passengers were eager, whatever the hour, and so, with the ship wallowing on the swell, they filed down the port gangway to be helped onto the skittish barge, eighty or more passengers a load. Nate and Palmer went on the first run with their horses and a large tent that they could pitch to help hold their claim, leaving the others behind under Sprague's care to secure the company's baggage. The *Rebecca* motored to within fifty yards of the beach, and they were all put off in the surf, everything getting soaked in the bargain.

Nate and the Major worked haltingly up the beach to the west, marking the sheer variety of outfits and machines—hand pumps, all manner of steam engines, gasoline engines, oil engines, even windmills. More often than Nate would have predicted, the air was pocked by the firing of Crosley two-stroke gasoline engines powering pumps and launches. A serviceable little motor that had come into its own. As he watched the launches ply back and forth to the fleet, Nate remembered his collapsible boat. The recollection brought a moment of satisfaction. He had gotten that right. The congested coast of the Seward Peninsula was no place to slog along on foot if a man had a choice to travel by water.

7

Nate nodded to his man Hanson and they bent to a heavy pile of canvas, the folded dining tent, and began to drag it across the beach into position beside the wooden frame they had hammered up.

Esther followed. "Fifteen dollars a week wages, come and go as I please, and you let me sit to table at meals."

After the dining hall they had the men's sleeping quarters to pitch, the infirmary, the stables, the storage and drying houses, and the workshops. He'd put Sunderhauf and the doctor to work building the frames and pitching the Major's and Sprague's quarters. He had Steale and a new man staging the material for the dredge, but there was little that could be done toward erecting machinery before they were encamped and the shops built, and the balance of their outfit off-loaded and safely ashore from the *Madden*.

"What of the mare's founder?" he said over his shoulder. "I need a horse I can put in the traces, saddle, or lead with a packsaddle. It seems the Studebaker wagon will be of little use." A furry thing had got onto her lapel and he looked to see if it was plant or animal, but it was just something blown off the tundra. He and Hanson each took a hem of the tent and backed apart, unfolding the canvas along its length.

"Oh, and I meant to add: fodder for my horse in the company stables," she said. "The one is healing faster than I expected, and in a day or two I will be able to use him myself. The other I will dispose." Of the two damaged animals she had spoken for on ship, the gelding was now possessed of the shivering palsy. Coughed, breathed from the belly, and no longer took food. Not a condition she was going to cure it of. For dirt, wet, wind, and crowds, Nome was not a place to nursemaid hopeless causes.

"What about your return passage?" He had foreseen it would come to this with her horses. As if he had nothing better to worry about than finding accommodations for a woman in this free-for-all. Nor was he entirely put out.

"Your sorrel's gaining but the leg shouldn't be worked for another two weeks is my guess. I will see her through, keep the stables, and take care of whatever the company needs in the animal way," she said. "I will be in service a month's time at the longest. More like three weeks." By then she would have set herself up with something or be off.

She reached over and tugged at the canvas, helped peel open its width where the waterproofing had stuck the material to itself. "I've checked the later ships. Fare's the same everywhere; you'll be out nothing more."

"We've got no ladies' tent," he said. "I suppose you could share with Miss Walton, but she's lodging near the office, which would mean your having to negotiate the shoreline from town every day."

This was the rub. She had been sleeping aboard ship as the unloading continued. She gazed at the small community of wood frames awaiting their canvas skins. Was going to propose he let her camp in the infirmary, but she did not see how to have her privacy there and decided against it.

He stopped working, took off his hat, and had a long drink from a canteen. "Something on you, there."

She looked down. "Oh, that." She tried to straighten it a little but she had it pinned crooked. "Know what it's called?"

A piece of bark would've been one guess. "Got no idea, honestly."

"Man up the beach told me it is called reindeer moss. Isn't that perfect?"

"I'll be." He gave it a closer look for her benefit, then took another drink and offered her the water out of politeness, thinking she would decline it for sanitary reasons, but she took the can gladly and had a long drink of it.

"Fifteen dollars is two days' wages for a hired man," he said. "Stables is less than two hours a day, would you guess? Let's say eight dollars the week plus your meals, and maybe I can spare one of the small field tents for that long."

"Suits me," she said. A tent of her own was better than she'd let herself hope for. She looked around to see where she might want to have it set.

Hanson had cast three stout lines over the roof beam and waited to hoist the canvas while Nate opened his money belt and picked out several banknotes. "Sunderhauf will get you pitched tomorrow. Would like to put you in the infirmary tonight. Now, as you are in the firm's employ again, perhaps you could find your way to town and act as our agent in securing something to replace the mare."

"What you need is a good all-around horse," she said.

He handed her three hundred-dollar bills and five twenties. "Perhaps you won't need to spend it all."

"I will haggle them down the best I can." It was more currency than she had ever been responsible for, and the moment she was in the stables she went behind the door and unlaced her shoe and tucked the banknotes inside it.

SHE CHOSE NATE'S Gunga Din for the five-mile ride to town. He was a black stallion with a deep chest and strong legs. She worked him slowly through the beach congestion. Guylines strung from tents and poles would easily trip a horse, and holes from fresh diggings would break a leg. Where no other way could be made she steered him into the shallows. She delighted to hear his feet splash, feel his power between her knees. He was built for swiftness and she yearned to canter him, but there was no open stretch. Men with machines had dug trenches the entire width of the beach in three places, and here she had to dismount and walk the horse or coax it up the steep bluff onto the tundra to the far side of the works.

When she reached the sand spit at the mouth of the Snake River she stabled him, crossed to River Street on the rowboat ferry for a nickel, and proceeded afoot. She asked directions for Steadman Avenue and found where it opened at Front Street opposite the Headquarters Saloon. Steadman was barely fifteen feet wide and choked with merchants.

She was searching street numbers when somebody caught her arm and she turned to find Lena, dressed in her traveling hat and gloves.

"Why, Essie! I have just been to the doctor's office and gotten a nursing job! We're over here." She led to the door at Number Ten, under a new sign, Cape Nome Mining Company. "Mornings I do the Major's office work."

Inside, the offices were compact, with bare plank walls and floors and a corrugated iron roof. The lumber still smelled piney. A table in the front room served as Lena's desk, and shelves above a sink along the back wall were stacked with supplies. The Major had his private office in the next room: Persian rug, leather wing chairs, and a big desk. Esther stole a peek at his sleeping quarters and out a back door to see their privy and a covered horse stall. "You have set yourselves up in a regular business way."

Lena pulled off her gloves and unpinned her hat, revealing her perfect hair set in a bun. "You couldn't guess the rent. Nome lots are being jumped worse than gold claims. Five hundred a month. They're getting sixty for an office the size of a closet!"

"For goodness' sake. Costs a dollar to look a man in the eye at Nome."

"You visited the public toilets?"

Esther made a face and they both laughed. The toilets were hung over the beach on pilings and flushed by the sea when the tide came in, the filth carried downshore on the riptide.

"So, you will be nursing after all."

"Half days for Jolly Irvine, Irish doctor up the street. Mornings he waits on the sporting girls. Line of misery forms outside his office every day at noon."

They tried the leather chairs in the Major's office. A set of gold scales and a retorting pot on either corner of the Major's desk gave the room a prosperous feeling.

"I believe you have bought yourself a new dress."

Lena shook her head. "Just something out of my trunk. Like it?"

"Very much." There was a slight ribbing down the bodice that slimmed her and gave the dress a crispness Esther liked. "You ought to come on out to the beach camp and see how we are getting set up. You'll want to change your shoes first."

"You say 'we' like you're one of the men now."

"I have taken over the stables for Mr. Deaton. For a month."

"Essie!"

"Thought maybe I could find work and put more in my pocket before I leave."

"What'll you do? Oh, let's see, let's think about it. This place is wide open. What about a shop of some kind?"

"I could clerk."

"I mean opening your own."

"Takes money for stock," Esther said. "No, has to be labor. Cooking, clerking, laundering, maiding."

Lena grinned. "Plug says the sporting girls are made of gold."

"Well, that's a labor I *wasn't* thinking of. Where's he keeping at?"

"Gone prospecting up the creeks!"

"I was afraid he'd talk you into opening a card room."

Lena laughed. "Oh, Plug's been all about gold from the moment we landed."

"Goodbye Lena, hello shovel."

"He's a sweet old thing. Said if I came along, he'd show me where the real money's at."

"Oh, ha! I can see you and your white gloves at the business end of a shovel!"

"Go on! Truth is, I have worked myself sore getting the Major set up here while he noses out who's meat and who's sauce at Nome. I put those shelves up all by myself. And what about your beach camp, then?"

"Beach camp is all sand, dogs, and piles of junk waiting to be built into a steam digger. At night we sit around trading rumors and what's been learned about the contraptions the other companies are setting up. Mr. Deaton's going to pitch me my own tent."

"I believe he is happy to have you stay!"

"Didn't give him a choice. It was either my own tent or let me squat forever in his precious infirmary."

"You'd have to start doctoring the men."

"Lord save me!"

"First patient, Mr. Steale."

Esther rolled her eyes. "Imagine!"

"No, no! First patient, Mr. Deaton!"

"Now you're gone to drink and loose ideas!"

Lena clapped her hands and jumped to her feet. "Come on! Let's go and show you what kind of a room I have got myself!"

She marched Esther up to Third Street, and a boardinghouse. The sign over the entrance said "*The Le George*, A Residence for Ladies." Lena's room was a cubbyhole upstairs at the back, as tight as the cabin they'd shared on ship, but with a ten-inch window opening over the lots, tents, and rooftops of Fourth Street.

"I am not the only colored tenant, either," Lena said. "There's a Negro seamstress named Miss Robertson, came down from Dawson."

The chamber was a little sanctuary. Esther loved it. "Cleanest room west of Seattle."

Lena took Esther's hand. "You stay anytime you come to town."

The invitation, and the warmth with which it was extended, pleased Esther inordinately. "Shared a bed with my sister," she said. "Would be the same."

SHE WENT ON to find the Post Office, which turned out to be a shack on the west end of town, just up from River Street. A double line ran around the block. Esther took her place at the end and was roped into talk by a weedy boy from Ohio who had waxy skin and brown stains on his teeth. Name was Bjorkman.

"The line today's normal and will take two hours." Bjorkman held a thumb to his cheek and worried a scab on the side of his nose with his forefinger. "You can pick up the mail for one addressee only, so there's no use trying to sweet-talk somebody at the front of the line into asking for yours unless you hired him for that purpose, because he'll need to get his own."

"What's it pay?" she asked.

"What?"

"Standing in line for somebody."

"Two dollars."

She could make six dollars a day if she hired out three times and stood the fourth for herself. Doubted her feet and legs were good for more than that, plus her work at camp and the time it took to travel back and forth.

"Few know it, but some people are getting their mail delivered," Bjorkman said. "No charge."

Several people turned to hear more. "Fellow I met carries it. He and his partner came up to dig beach gold. Mailmen from someplace, Oregon. Brought their wore-out uniforms to dig in. Weren't making wages, so they decided to get a job and marched up to Inspector Crum and said he should hire 'em to start free mail service to businesses with fixed addresses. Crum gives 'em this little test to see if they know the head of the alphabet from its arse, and then he hires 'em. The one of 'em I know told me, when they first went around, the business owners didn't believe it was free. 'Yes, sir,' he says to 'em. 'Courtesy of your Uncle Sam.'"

"Free delivery," said a woman behind Esther. "Don't that beat all to pieces!"

"However," Bjorkman said, "seeing that most miners can't light in one place more 'n a few days, most of the population gets their mail addressed general delivery and calls for it in person at the Post Office. And here we stand."

"Them businesses ain't so all-fired fixed, neither," said the woman behind Esther. "Feller bought a lot next to the repair shop on West D, set up a grocery in a tent. Three days later that feller's sold out and the new owner's throwed up a wooden lean-to doing blacksmithing. Week later *he's* rented out the lot and carried his house on his back up to a place on Second Street, and the new guy on D's put up a cigar store and fruit stand, and the blacksmith up there on Second's making more in a month on rent from the cigar man than he could make shoeing all the horses in Nome." She turned to Esther. "Mrs. A. A. Nichols." She pressed a calling card on Esther that read "Dogs. Mrs. A. A. Nichols. Leave message at Robert's Repair All, West D St."

Bjorkman himself had a tent and a rocker half a mile east of town; used to be west of the sand spit, then up on Dry Creek, and now back on the beach working his way east toward the Nome River. His mailman acquaintance told him Nome had the largest general delivery service in the United States. Took seventy boxes just to sort the letter *B*, the eighteen Bjorkmans fell in the twenty-second *B* box, and if he had a mother at all, she was smart to write his middle initial in his address if she wanted her letters read by him in particular.

Esther turned to Mrs. A. A. Nichols. The woman was square-bodied with a large head. "You have dogs?"

"Buy 'em, sell 'em. Need one?"

"What kind?"

"Dogs is dogs," the woman said. "Takes five or six to make a team.

Made fifty dollars profit in four days on a bunch of mongrels. In this country, come winter, any four-legged mutt is worth fifty, seventy-five dollars, you can believe it. Good lead dog'll bring a hunnert, hunnert fifty."

"Where do you get them?"

"Tell ya story. True story. I kept seein' this Eskimo on the sand spit, pack a malamutes, and finally I asks him what's he want for one of 'em, and he says, 'Hunnert dollars or a bottle of whiskey,' so I guv him the whiskey. Purebred malamute. Got a hunnert twenty-five for it same day."

"Buy and sell horses at all?"

"Horse is worse 'n a husband. Costs a fortune in spring, can't give it away in the fall. Few as can afford to feed and water it over winter. Any horse you met pulled a sled up a creek on deep snow? Me neither. Think dogs. Another month and a half, you'll see."

Esther waited two hours, as Bjorkman had said, thinking to get a letter from her sister, but there was none.

She went on to Thurl's Livery & Sale and negotiated the purchase of a six-year-old horse named Ben that looked strong and not too greedy of food, and then the sale of her animal with the palsy.

"Buy and sell dogs at all?" she asked. She counted payment for the horse into Thurl's open hand.

"Strictly a horse man," Thurl said.

"Ever met a horse pulled a sled up a creek in deep snow?"

"Never gave it a thought."

"Come fall, you might want to change over to dogs, is all I'm saying. A dog'll pull a sled all day on a fish. Think about it."

"All right."

"I bring you some dogs, you sell them, we each take our costs, split the difference."

Thurl looked her up and down. "Ask me again in a couple a months."

"In a couple of months a dog'll cost you a small fortune, don't you see. People are thinking horses now, you're skinning them alive at these prices, dogs are running on the beach in packs free for the taking. We get us some dogs now, sell them when the horses are low and dogs are high, is all I'm saying. I can get them all right, got no place to keep them."

Thurl looked at his stable, hitched his trousers, and said he would think about it. "Won't have room for three or four weeks yet."

"I will keep an eye out." She held out her hand so he could count out his payment for the ailing gelding, twenty dollars. Thurl's meat horses were sold to a man named Eskimo Tom.

CNCo. Beach Camp
Nome, Alaska
June 30, 1900

Dearest Lily,
Six letters from you fresh off the SS Wisconsin*! Your hand and scent: such comfort they bring to an old walrus where he has washed up against remotest Alaska! I am sorry for your loneliness, but dearly thankful for it.*

We are keeping house on the sand and continuing to barge our freight ashore, a job with no end in sight. Companies are set up all down the beach bolting together digging contraptions, and every inch between is taken by men shoveling sand into rockers and long toms. Up and down the coast pass steam scows, dories, sloops, tugs, and skin boats filled with stores, miners, and entire families of Eskimos. Dogs roam wild, stealing a man's dinner right out of his campfire. We have left night somewhere in the southerly latitudes, and with no end to the work or the daylight one is tempted to go at it 'til breakfast. Having done so once teaches a fellow the purpose of clocks.

I have hired a cook and several laborers. The Major has set up in Nome to make a base for the company. He has kindly left us the companionship of Mr. Sprague. The fellow decks himself out in one of his worn banker's suits every day and wanders around tut-tutting, "I am capital." He helped himself to one of my hired men and a pump yesterday, going up a hundred yards to try his hand at sluicing but managing only to foul the pipes and fittings by using seawater for boiler feed. Today I hear he is wandering east, poking his nose into the works of other companies. Perhaps he will find a concern he prefers to ours!

When will I have a moment for birds?

I do not understand what you write of the old Swede ordering tubing and motor parts. Better to apply what little goodwill we possess to laying in the lathe and welder and postpone inventory until there is need and money. I thought to have made that clear in my recent letter. Poor fellow is more shopsman than financier. He adores you and will do anything you say.

Give my love to Mother and to your family and save the most for yourself.

Ever your damp and sandy Beast,

Nate

Eskimo Tom showed up at the beach camp the next morning in a large boat with his family: three men, two women, four children, and three dogs. Esther climbed in and sat quietly on a wooden seat beside the children. The boat was just a hide stretched over thin poles, nothing for riding out to sea in, but before she could organize her argument the men were paddling hard for the *Madden*. A boy of ten or twelve sat up straight against the edge of the boat with a paddle in his hands and dug the water in pace with the men. She could not keep her eye from this boy and his young manliness. When the father happened to glance back he saw her studying the boy. "Eskimo Boy Tom," he said proudly, and Boy Tom turned at the sound of his name and grinned at Esther.

"Boy Tom," Esther said approvingly.

"Boy Tom," the mother said, pointing to the son.

Esther nodded and forced a gay smile, this strong little black-haired savage. Berries in cream were his eyes. And she squeezed the edge of the boat, fought off a wave of emotion that swept up inside her for this brown-skinned family at work together with their son. She stiffened and looked away, having seen how it pleased the boy to be noticed, how he paddled like the devil in her presence. She put her mind on her business. On the tattered dogs and the high-cheeked mothers that smelled of smoke and fish oil, on the thickness of their words, grunts that fell like thumps of blubber or the webbed feet of beached sea mammals. She held herself with a parson's correctness, barely breathing, until the boat of sticks and skin drew under the side of the hulking steamship, back to a world she felt she could manage.

She said her goodbye to the gelding with a pat on its neck and no thought of tears, and then stood back and watched. Two of the women stepped forward with skin bags. Eskimo Tom stood before the horse with a club and a sharpened bone. He set the bone against the animal's neck vein, drove it in with the club, and worked it sideways. The blood pulsed out and one of the women caught it neatly in the sack. When she could hold no more, Eskimo Tom stanched the flow until the second woman was in position, and then he filled her bag. Life drained from the horse. The women moved in with knives and opened the belly and gutted it, saving the organs and throwing scraps to the dogs, emptying the intestines and washing them in seawater.

The sight of it took Esther back to the accident on the docks in Seattle that got her into this. She had thought she was going to her sister's, but Ballard, when she conjured it now, was a place that came to her as a vague dampness perched on the remotest edge of her former life. A life that had run its course. Like a bled horse, she was gone on to another use.

The motorman hoisted the carcass by the hindquarters and the men skinned it, then quartered and sectioned the meat, packing it into the boat, leaving nothing behind, head, hooves, and all stacked neat between the seats, the whole job completed inside of forty minutes. The dogs were in a froth, darting hither and back through the boat. The Eskimos chattered and passed a bottle as they shoved off. They paddled Esther back to shore and let her out in the surf (she took off her shoes and stockings and held up her dress), and then went back up the coast they'd come down from.

She walked up the beach to the infirmary. The tent was warm from the heat of the morning sun. She hung up her cloak and found a cloth to wipe her feet and legs. She stepped into her shoes again, and then reached for her cardigan where it was draped on a chair back and pulled it around her shoulders. Sat herself onto the wooden floor at the front of the tent, planting her feet on the gray sand, and looked out to the *Madden* in the distance. She didn't trouble herself over a horse's quick death. The meat was going to use. What more can you ask of a death? The twenty dollars in her purse—you could ask that and get it.

"THERE YOU ARE!"

Mr. Deaton's voice came from behind. She looked around the side of the tent. He was striding up with his coat off and his sleeves rolled back.

"I was looking for you earlier. You are well ahead of us in meeting the natives, I notice."

"I have been to sea in a walrus and stick boat," she said, hardly believing it herself. "Was at the task of horse butchering, doing it the Eskimo way. Quick and happy."

"Your gelding?"

She nodded and looked back to sea. Tugged at the shoulders of her sweater. "Had the palsy."

"Well. I'm sorry." Came as no surprise. He pushed a knot of seaweed aside with his boot. "I guess there's worse. Klondike stampede, you know, they had to pass horses piled one atop the other."

She looked at him, hoping it wasn't true.

"Two or three thousand."

"I never heard of such disease!"

"No, the trail is what I read. Fell off it. Got swallowed between boulders. Dropped dead of sheer work."

"You mean their owners knew? Led them to it?"

He instantly regretted mentioning it. He let a decent interval pass, and then got to his point: "Sundy has hammered a floor for you, but Mr. Sprague kidnapped him before he got your tent pitched. If you are free, we could string it up now."

"That was near here, where they did that?" She could not get rid of the picture, horses piling up.

"Way over in the Yukon. Twelve hundred miles east of here." In God's name, what had he been thinking? He took her to see where Sunderhauf had set an eight-by-ten-foot plank floor onto wooden blocks between the dining hall and the camp office. The tent was a bundle beside it.

"Oh," she said, clearly unhappy.

"Will it suit you, then?" He had expected her to be well more than satisfied.

"I was thinking to have it over thataway." She pointed to a nook between the shops and the stables. She had picked it because it was a good distance from the men's tents for privacy, more to the edge of things, and she would still have the stables separating her from the want and misery drifting past. Annoyed her that he had not bothered to ask.

"Truly? We thought you would want to be more inside the camp." Beach trouble was on the rise. The latest game was to slit a man's tent while he slept and poke a wad of cotton through on a stick, knock him out with chloroform, then go in for his poke. Nate knew better than to tell her this. Just gave her a minute to come around.

She had her jaw set.

He let out a sigh. "Maybe tomorrow Sundy and I can carry the floor over there and you can find a moment in your schedule to tell us exactly how you want it set."

She made a little sound, let him know his tone did not sit well. "Why don't you and I just do it now?"

"Well, I doubt that we can. Very seriously. The lumber's kind of wet. The thing's heavier than it looks."

She reached down and tugged at a corner and it came up off the wooden footing a few inches. "Not so bad as you are thinking, or am I stronger than your eastern ladies?"

"We can certainly try," he said, knowing it was folly.

She went around opposite him and they bent for it. He got his end up, but hers felt positively nailed down. "Hold your horses!" she said. "You should've let me lift first."

He set his down. "Spread your feet and get lower to it."

She bent down and gave it a pull. It came up off the ground this time and she tried to get under it better, but as soon as he raised his end she knew that she wasn't going to hang on and better set it down quick. Before she could manage it the thing pulled out of her grip and fell catawampus, one corner unsupported, and the whole structure twisted and made a cracking sound.

"Not going to work, Mr. Deaton," she said snappishly, as if it had been his idea. "Better if you lift your end and I come around and help you drag it, if you want to try that."

He kept his thoughts to himself. Got his end up again and she came around and backed up to it, and then he got himself turned around, and by this method, two oxen in yoke, they set to pulling it out from between the tents and turned to the right, dragging it across the beach past the dining tent. The trailing edge worked like a grader, scraping up six or eight inches of wet sand, and made for hard going.

"Heavier than I gave it credit for," she admitted. "I want you to know that I am not ungrateful."

"Tell it to Sundy. He was over an hour on his knees setting the blocks and trenching around the backside to keep you good and dry."

"You needn't instruct me, Mr. Deaton. Of course I will express myself to him. As soon as he finds where we've pitched it he will see the logic of it."

They had to work around the guylines of the shops, and then Nate stopped pulling, saying, "Here is good until we level the site. On the count of three." It hit the beach hard.

She sat herself down to catch her breath and he took a seat beside her, rubbing the circulation back into the meat of his fingers.

"You did it different," she said. "I congratulate you for that."

"I would have been a sight happier to carry it than drag it if you had been Sundy or Hanson at the other end."

"I was meaning the horses, Mr. Deaton. You did not bring them to pile up like firewood. You hired me to see them here safe and well used. Not every man would do that."

"Oh, Nome's a different kettle of fish from the Klondike."

"Maybe so, but you did hire me."

"True enough." He wiped the sweat off his forehead with a handkerchief and looked at the slope of the site to see how much digging was needed to set the floor. "But the decision was yours, and the health of a few horses is not the best reason for a single woman such as yourself to stay on."

She did not remark.

"Nome's a rougher place than maybe you know." He would have liked some explanation. He felt he deserved one. By staying on, she was making herself in some measure his responsibility.

"I have left my husband, Mr. Deaton."

There it was. Flushed her right out of the weeds. Well, he was glad of it. The words were stark, but did not catch him much by surprise. There was a fury to her that he aimed to get ahold of if she was going to stay. "I am twice sorry to hear it. Once for your loss, and once for the cause of it, for I am certain you had reason."

"It's my own business and nobody else's."

"Unless you walk around with your chin out like you have been, in which case you kind of make it other people's business. Seeing as how you are joining the camp, I believe it would be civil of you to get a little friendlier about it." He got up to let her chew this over. Went to the shops for a couple of shovels, and when he returned he put one in her hands without asking and the two of them set to digging out the back of the site and throwing the dirt forward.

"Didn't mean to be a burr," she said.

"All right."

She helped him set one of the footings. "Have never been in this situation before."

"I believe you."

They set the other footings and worked the platform onto them. Carried the tent over. Raised the two ridgepoles, pitched out the ends, and then pitched out the four lines on either side. It was a two-man wall tent. While she went to the infirmary for her bags, he went to the stores and found her a folding cot and a pair of blankets. He brought a scrap of canvas from the shops that he thought would do for a rug to cut the breeze that blew up through the floorboards. Found her an empty packing crate for a small table. Strung a spare line between the ridgepoles so she had a place to air her bedding or damp clothes. When they were done, there was nothing more to do, and yet he wished to give her something further. "You could call me Nate, then," he said.

"All right."

He held out his hand, make a fresh start, and she took it.

"We will all of us keep an eye on you," he said.

FROM HER FRONT door she looked out on the sea. The ships rode at anchor like homesteads across the prairie, but the beach was barren soil and she did not feel at home upon it. Would have preferred to be on the tundra, among the living earth. She scaled the dirt behind the tent to stand calf-deep in the greenery. She gathered up mosses, grasses, and lichens and brought them back and arranged them on the sand, a bit of a greengarden before the entrance to her billowy little home. We will all of us keep an eye on you. Nobody'd ever said that to her. She saw now she could've thanked him. Wondered why she did not.

PART II

8

Near Perley, Minnesota, August 1895

Tall, slender, and soaked in bloody filth was the first memory Esther had of Leonard Crummey, which was thirty or forty minutes (she was never clear about the sequence) after he, or he and Aagot Norgaard, had pulled Aagot's brother Halvor off of the thresher pulley. This was in '95, a bumper crop in a depression year when grain prices were low and men were hungry and moving north with the harvest in search of work. It was the second week of August, after the barley had been threshed, after her pa had gone down to Moorhead to hire help because the wheat had dried in only a few days' time and they could get a badly needed jump on the threshing and plowing.

The weather had been scorching. It was partly to beat the heat and partly because they had two hundred acres to thresh that the men had started into the fields with the teams and bundle wagons so early, at five o'clock, and begun working their way up the endless rows of shocks, pitching the bundles into the wagons until the loads towered and threatened to fall over, an acre of wheat to the wagon. They drove their loads in across the stubble to the thresher where it was set up at the edge of the field south of the farmyard, waited their turn to unload, and then went out again. By ten o'clock the heat was up. Heavy to breathe and an effort to work, their clothes wrung with sweat, their hands slippery on the forks and levers.

At the separator, the men stood atop their wagons two at a time and forked the bundles in fast, setting them straight, tip to butt. A living drive belt spun around the pulley of the steam tractor, which they'd set well back to reduce the chance of sparking the straw afire, and then ran to the separator, a wondrous machine, all belts and pulleys spinning and vibrating, disgorging a torrent into the straw pile, making its own weather, a blizzard of dust and straw bits that billowed and mixed with the engine's wood smoke and fouled their eyes and mixed with their sweat to form a paste on the backs of their arms and necks. Some men worked with kerchiefs tied over their mouths and noses and sucked for air. All of this for one sound, the rhythmic click of the tip that gathered and counted pure grain by the half bushel before giving it up to the sack men.

They'd had the usual trouble with the drive belt, but nothing out of the ordinary except that young Norgaard had reached in. Reached in, it seemed, of all damnable things, to free his oil rag where it was wrapped on the main shaft. Caught his sleeve quick, and in three or four turns got his arm took off.

Or nearly off. Esther didn't know. Someone said that Leonard Crummey had separated young Norgaard from his arm to free him from the pulley, but there was disagreement about this as they had tried to reconstruct it, Leonard puzzling over it himself, saying maybe he just caught the boy the moment his arm had come apart at the shoulder. This they agreed on: that they had struggled with the drive belt, which was repeatedly coming off the pulley. That they had stopped to line up the engine straighter and to pitch the belt. That the Norgaard boy, whose pa owned the rig, had squirted some oil on the bearing and wiped the excess with the rag he kept in his hind pocket. The boy's father, Anders, who saw it all at a distance from his seat on the engine, said that Halvor gave him the sign and he put her in gear and the belt started and by the looks of it the separator went into action normally, shaking and blowing, the elevator feeding the wheat into the knives. Aagot, who was up on the one hayrack, recommenced to pitching in the bundles, and that's when Halvor must have seen the rag wrap into the thing and reached between the belts to snatch it out. Leonard, who was setting the pitch bucket back of the engine, saw Halvor thrown over twice and dashed to help him. Aagot jumped from the hayrack. The blood had been shocking, how it had caught Leonard in the face and hair and soaked his shirt and overalls and grown matted as he and Aagot worked to cinch it off with Aagot's rope belt. There had been nothing to get a purchase on. And then the father came running with a burning log out of the firebox and they jammed the coal end against the mess, but there wasn't enough fire to sear shut the flesh, and in another minute or less the boy was gone.

LIKE BEES SPILLING from a ripped hive. All shouting and running. Esther had heard it in the kitchen with the other women, and they ran out to see what. And then nothing to be done, just the struggling to tell it, to make sense of it.

Halvor knew these machines inside and out, the father said in a voice that was high and insistent, shaking his head. He knew don't you go fiddling at a live shaft, the father cried.

They lifted the boy into a wagon. The father and the brother named Aagot went and picked the arm free of the thresher pulley and set it beside the boy, and then, ashen, they giddyapped the team out the driveway for home. Rugnel Ulverson sent his son Carl along to help somehow, and told his daughter Esther to find fresh clothes for the boy who'd tried to help. Then he drove himself to Perley for the pastor.

She got a shirt and trousers of her father's and went out to find the Crummey boy.

LEONARD HAD COME north with the transients who poured into Fargo to work the bonanza farms west of the Red. He'd got hired as part of a gang to work shocking near Mooreton, but the crew boss was all rules and don't-evers that didn't sit with Leonard and inside of a week he got himself fired for cussedness. He had never been a place as pan flat and stretched out as the valley of the Red. There was no valley to it. Just grain and prairie weeds running to the edge where the sky took up, and a line of trees where the river went. He walked to Fargo and found the whores on Third Street, and when the whores kicked him out he walked over the river to the labor agents in Moorhead, where Rugnel Ulverson found him.

Leonard was strong and knew how to look willing. The rest of the men working the Ulverson wheat were part of Norgaard's threshing crew or neighbors helping neighbors. Leonard knew none of them, and in the carrying-on over the accident, he'd left the crowd and gone back of the barn. Peeled off the bloody shirt and sat down in the shade with his eyes shut against the outfall. They would have preferred it was him. Will say he could've prevented it, or stopped it. Something. That it was his pitch laid too thick on the belt caught the rag into the shaft. He was done here, anyway, and if he was fit for it he'd strike out now while they were distracted.

She choked back a retch at the sight of him.

He stood up out of showing respect and struggled to pull on the sticky shirt.

"Pa said bring you something clean to wear."

"All right. You can just leave it."

She wondered how he would wash it all away. Out of his thick hair. "Fill you a bath from the cistern?"

It would take two or three baths. "Easier I use the hose behind the tanker. If they won't mind." He gestured across the field at the wagon that carried creek water to the boiler on the engine.

He was taller than she, maybe six feet, with tanned leather for skin. "Everybody appreciates what you did."

He wondered was that true. What he did was nothing but reflex. Try and stop a death. A death that clamped on fast and certain, no chance of prying loose. "Who was he, then?"

"Halvor Norgaard. Farm boy over at Perley."

Leonard saw that her eyes were red, and he supposed she'd been one of the women crying. "Married boy?" He wondered if there was going to be a widow.

She shook her head.

He nodded. Felt a chill against his skin even in the heat, and forgot himself a moment, asking, "What'd he want, you think?"

She didn't comprehend the question.

"Out of his life, now he won't get it." Who gets what the boy had coming, is what he meant. Try to save a dying man, oughtn't you get paid what the fellow lost. He knew it didn't work like that, he just wondered what it was.

She looked at him, tried to see what he was driving toward, but couldn't make it out. His eyes were two gray stones. She thought about Halvor, but didn't know what was in his dreams. They'd been sweet once as children. "What we all want, I think. His own farm. A son to pass it to." She set the clothes in the grass and left him, pondering how she'd found him, sitting with his back against the barn and his eyes shut to something that gripped him. What he'd seen, she supposed.

When Rugnel returned with Pastor Torvald they all gathered silently under the pooled shade of the sugar maple out back of the house. The droning of the cicadas pinned their ears to their heads, and the heat rising off the land turned the stubble fields of their labor to liquid. Leonard had shrunk back at the fringe, but they parted and pressed him forward, two or three hands touching his shoulder as he passed, and there he stood, washed of one man's blood and clothed in the starched shirt and trousers of another, looked at by the men and women alike, none of whom had paused to notice him until he'd bloodied himself on behalf of their neighbor.

Pastor Torvald prayed aloud in Norwegian. He commended to God the soul of Halvor Einar Norgaard. The strange words washed over Leonard, who held his ground dumbly, staring at his feet, wetting the fresh shirt through its collar and down the sternum.

"In the Book of Luke we have prayed, 'Lord of the harvest, send forth laborers.' Lord, You have answered our prayer in sending forth Your son Halvor. We ask that You help us to become better servants of Your word. We pray for acceptance of Your mystery. That the boys who have struggled to save a life will find peace with their failure. That we who are gathered here will be forgiven our sins and blessed in our labors, for we have worked hard and achieved much, the glory be to God. With Your blessing, we will honor our brother Halvor by returning to the fields, for certainly it is a greater sin to turn our backs on Your bounty than to bend ourselves to its harvest and the nourishment of our bodies."

When they had said what could be said, they put out the noon dinner at the long table on the back porch, and sat to eat. Rugnel seated the pastor and the Crummey boy near him at the head. Leonard gave polite but short replies to their questions. Ashland, Wisconsin, by way of Winona and La Crosse. Lumber milling and fieldwork, mostly. No, his people had all passed. Follow the harvest into Manitoba, he reckoned. Soon the talk turned elsewhere, to the Norgaard family and its many difficulties, to the tragedies the valley had known, and to friends and neighbors whose farms had succumbed to the droughts of '88 and '89, or had been lost in the panic of '93, or carried off in the current depression. Farmers who had homesteaded wet land, spent too dearly on machinery, borrowed too eagerly from the St. Paul banks, lacked storage to carry their grain, or simply failed to put aside their own seed. The conversation flowed in circles of failure that came back, time and again, to poor Halvor. When a silence settled over the table the women began to clear. The men pushed back and finished their coffee and got up in threes and fours and slipped behind the hog barn to piss. Slowly, they returned to the field.

Arne Sevre, who ran the tanker, hosed the Norgaard boy's blood into the soil and forked a layer of straw over the wet ground. Hans Gaare stoked the firebox and Peder Jensen, who was familiar with the engine, climbed up to Anders Norgaard's post at the controls. Smoke rose from the engine's stack. The boys climbed back onto the bundle wagons. The Oftedahl boy filled in at Halvor's post on the separator, and when he raised his arm Jensen released the clutch, the drive belt came alive, and soon they were lost in the familiar rhythms of threshing.

The funeral was conducted the next day out of concern for the heat. The Bethania church rose from the fields to a great height, a ship of the faithful on the ruffling prairie sea. Leonard was ushered in and asked to sit immediately back of the family, in honor of his efforts. After the service, they buried the boy in the little cemetery behind the church in the shelter of the cottonwood breaks that shaded the flanks of Wolf Creek. Mrs. Norgaard took Leonard's hand and thanked him personally. She had laid four boys under the prairie. Each time she saw the sod cut for another one, she wished to lie in the wound herself and pull the earth shut against the struggle.

THEY THRESHED THE Ulverson wheat in two and a half days' time and would have moved along to the next farm but for allowing the Norgaard family a few days' mourning. In the lull, they cut and threshed the Ulverson oats and flax. They worked from half-six in the morning until six in the evening. Esther, who was twenty that year, and her sister Constance, sixteen, rose at five-thirty, lit the stove, collected the eggs, and served breakfast. They carried sandwiches, coffee, and cookies into the field for morning lunch at half-nine. They returned to the house to help their mother, Jess, and two neighbor women prepare dinner. They put out washbasins and towels in the yard for the men, and at noon they put dinner on the long table on the back porch. They washed up from dinner and set the clean dishes back on the table for supper. They carried afternoon lunch to the field at three-thirty, freshened the basins and towels, and served supper on the porch at half past six. Except for care of the animals and men, the work of the farm was suspended.

LEONARD, SEEING THEY meant to have him stay when he'd thought to be run off, kept his hands busy with the work of the place. Had lived at the edges of other well-off families and knew how they liked a hired man. They liked a man who did not figure to piss in their same hole. Who could smell an act of Christian charity when it was pushed in his face, didn't turn away but didn't either take it for friendship, the one having an odor to it, and you'd better know the difference. He was hungry for the work and contented himself to watch and fall in step behind the sons of Perley. He saw they worked hard enough, but that kind of work was not so all-fired hard. When the land was yours, he meant. For every spunk of sweat that fell there would come up a stalk of wheat to call your own. But work another man's dirt without the promise of his working yours in return, certain only of a few dollars and a handshake at the end of harvest. And do it agreeably. And then move along. That was hard work. These boys were stupid of the difference, while at the same time thinking they had earned it.

He watched Esther, too. The easy way she sat a horse and carried her duties. How she provided at mealtime. The steel glint she showed for farming, reaching her hand into the stream from the straw blower to feel for grain that missed the chute and then telling the separator man didn't he think he ought to reset the baffle over the sieves, lose less of the crop. Bullying the sack men to guess the bushels per acre before they had a count from the tip. She was lanky and practical, with slim hips and that fair Norse hair gathered up onto her head in a loose coil. He watched her with the boys in the field to see which one she favored, thinking to himself she could make the worst of them turn to account for himself, but Esther did not show herself in that way. She was not a flirting one. He liked that about her. That and her cock-certainty. Would like to prick her certainty hard between the legs.

INSIDE THE WALLS of his house Rugnel Ulverson was heard to say of the Crummey boy, "He's a hard worker and keeps to himself. An asset to the farm beyond what a man might expect of an itinerant."

"But a rootless boy," his wife, Jess, was heard to reply.

"The fact his people are all passed would explain why," Rugnel said. "That and the depression. But he is a boy who is looking to latch on someplace. You can see it in him."

After Saturday supper, Rugnel turned to Leonard privately. "You'll be wanting to join us to worship tomorrow, which will be fine."

"Am a stranger to it," Leonard began, but he caught an eagerness in Ulverson's eye that brought his thinking around even as he spoke. "A stranger to the Lutheranism and the Norse," he said. "But I would be grateful for sitting at the back of any church, in the privacy of my own thoughts, if it would not trouble." He was amused by Rugnel's churchiness, for the man gave no outward appearance of needing such a thing. He sensed in Rugnel an appraising eye, and Leonard wished to appraise well, for he had not yet run out the possibilities of this place.

Later the same evening Leonard looked in at the barn for Esther and found her grooming her horse, a big red roan stallion she called Mister Jones, and humming to herself a tune he could not make out.

"You always hum to your horses?" he asked her.

Esther looked up, startled. She had not heard him approach. "Was I humming, then?" Had been lost in thought. She turned back to her work, neither welcoming nor cool. Humming was a habit people told her she had, but she was not herself usually aware of doing it.

He entered and closed the door. "Likes what you are doing," he said of the stallion.

"Of course he does," she said.

"No," he teased. "There." He pointed beneath, and she bent to look and saw it was the horse's extended penis he meant.

"Yes," she said curtly, and resumed her combing. "You think I've never seen such a thing?"

Tried a different approach. "I am to have more of your religion in the morning."

"You have need of it, is my guess," she answered.

"If I had more need of it, time'd be better spent."

She said nothing.

"What about you?" he said.

She remained silent, but still she combed the horse.

"You pray every week?" he said.

"You are a fan of regular prayer, Mr. Crummey?"

"I am a fan of thrift. Why run up extra if you have no need to draw against it?"

She stopped combing. "We are all sinners," she said.

"They say. But all sins're not equal."

"Some are worse," she agreed.

"Some're more worth the bother of a church bench and a lecture," he corrected.

"Of that I am ignorant," she said.

"Maybe you need some help in that matter."

"You want to be a help, take that other curry comb off the nail."

To her surprise, he did as told, helping as she moved on to groom the Percherons. Nor did she altogether mind the company.

He had dark hair curling over his ears, and a small mole at the back of his neck that rose and fell behind his collar as he stroked the horses' flanks.

AT TWENTY-FIVE, Leonard was seven years older than the eldest Ulverson boy, the one they called Carl, and five years Esther's senior, and though he trailed behind as they entered the church, he felt the others' eyes on him, and he tugged self-consciously at his sleeves. He was taller than any Ulverson, feeling too long in the limb for his worn clothes and naked in his poverty among the others, who were all in their Sunday best and full of themselves and their godliness.

He was ignorant of the traditions, and yet events had made him known to them and they greeted him with a nod or a handshake that made it impossible for him to hang back. Rugnel showed him into a pew after Esther. Leonard sat down beside her uneasily and kept his hands on his knees and looked ahead at the pastor as the service began. The congregation stood for a hymn and Leonard was surprised at the strength of Esther's singing. The windows stood open to the drone of the prairie, the heat of the morning beginning to rise where the sun pooled on the plank flooring, the close spaces of the little church amplifying their voices. They sang and prayed as one, calling their god down from heaven with a conviction that felt superior to Leonard. He sat rigid in their midst, his ignorance announced by his inability to join in. Rugnel reached across his wife to hand Leonard the family Bible. Leonard took it and opened it randomly and stared at its Norse pages, feeling his face flush. He was trapped at the center of their excitement and felt his devil stir. He would have welcomed a pull of whiskey. Them and their smug farms and rich Norwegian god. Maybe Ulverson brought him into this church service for a reason, which would be what, except to drive home to him his strangeness? The longer he sat, the more certain of it he grew, and the more agitated.

He clenched his jaw and looked for a thing to bleed off his steam. He pulled himself into the swell of Esther's risen voice, willed himself to become the hot blood in the veins of her neck. He filled his head with the odor of her, bleach and starch and the female smell, a smell that reached down to his gut, and in the midst of "Holy Be Our Father" he put his mouth behind her ear and whispered coarsely, "I am like your horse." She turned quizzically and he gestured with his chin and eyes toward his lap.

She did not catch his meaning and looked down. He lifted the Bible to one side and showed her his tenting trousers. The sight stole her breath. She jerked away and turned her back to him, feeling her face burn. She had never entertained a sexual thought in the house of God, and what kind of an animal was he, make a mockery of her, show himself? She could not sing for fury, nor for the vision that forced itself upon her, Leonard naked in the barn with the organ of a workhorse.

IN THE DAYS that followed, Leonard made himself helpful in unexpected ways. He rose early and collected the eggs from the henhouse and had them there in the basket for Esther when she came out to do it. At the end of the day, while everyone else was fading into bed, Leonard went to the woodshed and spent twenty minutes splitting kindling and carrying it into the kitchen for the morning fire. Esther avoided him as best she could, but watched what he did. He was a brooding one, lacked a god. He had learned his way among them quickly, though, and he was strong. He was different from the local boys in a way she liked and disliked. Hard and watchful. She judged his watchfulness to be half eagerness to do right, and half suspicion not to be done wrong. Her pa had taken a liking to him. He would be a strong puller in the harness. She felt him watching her and she did not mind it.

LEONARD MOVED ON with the Norgaard threshing crew, keeping to himself, sleeping in hay mows on the farms they worked. Some of the men he threshed alongside were also transients, and one of them let Leonard take a pull of whiskey from a jug one night. Fire spread through his gut and set his hand to shaking. He dug a coin out of his pocket to pay to have another slug, but the fellow said, Go ahead and take another, so Leonard helped himself to a long one. It torched a craving he knew he could not subdue. The fellow had got it down on the Red River from off the back of a barge by Perley, and the next night under darkness Leonard took himself a Norgaard horse and rode it into the village, past the dark houses and stores to the water's edge, where he tied it and then felt his way on foot by the light of the moon until he found the thread of a path running through the trees along the top of the bank.

The barge was two hundred yards downstream, tied to a tree, riding the current ten or twelve feet out from shore. There was a shanty at the close end, and beyond that, in the glow of a lantern near the stern, two figures sat on deck. They were smoking and arguing over something in hushed grunts. Leonard lowered himself down the bank and held his breath to make out the gist of it, but the noise of current riffling under the hull covered their words.

"There, on the boat, sirs!" he called.

The men snuffed their lantern and peered into the trees. "Says who?" one of them answered. The voice was younger than Leonard expected.

"A friend in need." The moon lay in the west and silhouetted their figures. One of them limped forward along the rail to a pivot pole, which he swung out to shore, offering a pouch at its end.

"What's the fare, then?"

"Big's yer jug?" came the young voice from the stern.

"Got none."

"Nickel for a empty pint jar 'n fifteen cents for what he puts in it," the voice said.

"You give a sample, then, or how I know it's fit?"

The gimp at the pole, who had left the talking to the boy, turned and ducked into the shanty now, and then came out again with a burning lantern and a glistening pint jar. He hung the lantern and then struck a match and touched it to the mouth of the jar. Blue flame leapt up.

"Pure enough," the boy's voice said from aft.

"Lord, that stuff there'll dissolve flesh you leave something soak in it." These words came from hard behind Leonard, and he started and turned, unaware he was followed. A man about his own age held up an empty jar. "Waitin' after you. But lookee, see, here's a bell," the man said, and gave a light clang against a small brass tied to a branch to their left. "Once and the old guy swings the pole. Twice fer the boy. Aldritt don't like hollerin'. Raises curiosity."

Was as smart a setup as Leonard'd seen for months. The portability of it struck him. Get run off one place, you just haul up- or downriver and reopen pretty much wherever you damn like, and never bother to roll up your bedding. "Here's a half dollar, friend," he called. "Name's Crummey. You keep the difference." He'd barely dropped the coin into the pouch before the gimp swung it aboard and pulled it out and held it to the light to make sure of it, and then banked it in his pocket.

The boy showed a sudden interest in their new customer, sidling up the railing to stand across from Leonard. "A gentleman!" he said to Leonard, acknowledging the gratuity. "You, ah, want a come aboard, if you like, 'n have a sip with us, you are welcome."

The voice had a sweetness to it made Leonard faintly uneasy, but the large tip had brought the result he'd wanted. "Wouldn't say no, friend," and he found a fallen log to step onto and work out toward the boat.

The boy pulled on the mooring line. As the barge edged closer he dropped a ladder over. Leonard caught the bottom of it and climbed up. The pivot pole swung out to collect coin and jar from the man that was waiting behind, and Leonard watched while the gimp swung out a fresh jar, and then the two bargemen walked him aft and they took seats together on crates and relit the lantern, which stood on the engine box with a deck of cards. The boy set a third glass on the box and poured whiskey from a jug.

"Leonard Crummey. Representing interests in St. Paul." Leonard offered the second statement unimportantly, almost apologetically, and followed it with a sniff and a little settling-in sigh, to say his affairs were of no account to men with a thriving business like theirs. He took the glass with a nod. He hacked the clabber from the back of his throat and spit it over the rail behind, as if to cleanse himself of a long stretch of distaste, and then smelled the glass of whiskey and drank deeply of it. The blue fire rekindled the furnace in his gut. It ran to the tips of his limbs and clarified his mind in a surge of rightness. He settled back against the rail, stretched his legs.

"Daigneault," the boy said, and stuck out a hand.

Leonard took it. Boy's stringy black hair hung over his shoulders and he had a soft, Indian face, maybe seventeen.

"This here's Anson Aldritt," the boy said, gesturing at the gimp, who busied himself packing his cheek with tobacco. He was a chaw-stained man with matted hair and one side of his face droopy; looked to be running hard toward sixty.

"Got his tongue took off," Daigneault said, and laughed. "I'm the only friend that hears what he's saying. Ain't it so, chief?"

Aldritt opened his mouth and honked and quacked angrily at the boy, including a word Leonard thought might have been bitch.

"I say his words for him," the boy said, looking at Aldritt. "'Less he gets ugly at me, 'n then he can piss in a wicker basket all I care." Boy turned back to Leonard. "Clerks at the Perley Store, which belongs his brother, Jonas Aldritt, big shot in town, you may know him."

Leonard did not.

"Clerks days. Nights, has his whiskey-selling. But don't never open it until after darkfall, anybody comes before that looking for drink, we don't know 'em, we don't know what they are talkin' about. First time. Second time, we give 'em a taste of Miss Sap, shut 'em up."

Leonard saw the butt of a pistol in the old man's pocket. "Oughta be so. A business needs its rules," Leonard said.

"Thank you," the boy said on Aldritt's behalf. He struck a match and picked up one of the half-smoked cigars. Leonard watched the flame draw into the coal until the boy's eyes rose to meet his, and then he looked down quick, at his glass, and took a swig. "What's your part, then?"

"Partner," the boy said.

Aldritt uttered something sharp at the boy, who shook his head briefly in disagreement.

"Look after the boat during the day. Night, when the moon's growing, I run my trapline."

"For what?"

"Mink. Skunk. Fox. Otter. Depending on the season." He pulled at his cigar, and then, suggestive of something, he added, "Or whatever."

Leonard wasn't certain what.

"Whatever's got certain appetites," the boy said, giving Leonard a long look, and then Leonard thought he understood well enough. Supposed the boy had a sweet ass got hard-used.

Aldritt blurted again, angrily, and the boy smiled and asked Leonard, "Yourself, sir?"

Leonard cleared his throat in the manner of a man organizing his thoughts. "Size things up hereabouts for a party with financial interests." He pulled on his nose briefly and rubbed his palm over his mouth. "Hired myself to a thresher, as not to raise eyebrows. Would appreciate this not going beyond us three. Curdle the cream before pulling the teat, know what I'm saying."

The boy drew on the cigar again and nodded. Aldritt, possessed of a sudden charity, reached the jug and helped Leonard to a refill. With the other hand he made a slight signal, possibly, Leonard couldn't say for certain.

They all three sipped whiskey, listened to the river go by.

"Fact is, good you come by," the boy said, "or the old man like to have kilt me over these goddamned cards."

"No percentage getting nasty at cards," Leonard said. "Is all in sport, far as I'm concerned."

"I was saying that myself!"

"Feller pays to win or lose, counts the cost against the pleasure of another man's company." Leonard supposed he could afford to run into them for two dollars, provided they didn't give him all the good cards.

A solitary clink of the brass came out of the woods and the gimp bothered himself to his feet and limped up the railing. He served two customers, came back and sat down again, said something at the boy. The boy said, "He asks what's your game, then."

"You say. Five-card draw?"

The gimp gathered up the cards and shuffled and dealt around. Cool of night settled slowly into the woods and pushed out the last warmth of day, air currents bearing the smell of stagnant water and dead fish. Made the lantern flicker.

"Five cents to see your cards is how we play it, all right with you," the boy said.

Leonard put a nickel on the engine box and the boy and the gimp did likewise. They picked up their cards and sorted them in silence. Leonard had nothing.

"Cost you a nickel to stay in," the boy said, putting his bet into the pot. Leonard put in, as did the gimp, and the boy picked up the deck and asked Leonard, "Cards?"

Leonard kept an ace and a jack, traded in three cards, found himself looking at a pair of smiling jacks, making three in all.

"Another five cents," the boy said.

Leonard ordinarily would have worked the stakes upward, but knew better and pulled a long face and allowed as how he'd see the boy's bet on principle. The gimp raised him five cents. Leonard and the boy saw him. The gimp put two pair down, queens and nines. Leonard hated like hell to do it but tossed in, and the gimp half rose out of his seat to sweep up the money. He stuffed most of it in his pocket except what he needed to keep seeding the pot. Leonard knew the type. The gimp passed the cards to the boy. Tapped his fingers on the box and made little satisfied grunts while the boy shuffled.

"Who's buying the whiskey, then?" Leonard said. Put out his coin for the next hand.

"Métis, mostly," the boy said, dealing.

"Half-breeds," Leonard said matter-of-factly, a piece of the puzzle in place. Every enterprise is a puzzle with its own necessary pieces, any piece of it missing, you have no business. Selling to half-breeds was good, famous taste for drink, not welcome in the bars, had ways of getting money.

"Thieving Frenchie half-breeds like me," the boy said. "Some whites, sure, who'd knife an Indian to get 'im out a the way if he's waiting on Mr. Aldritt's pole, there, but we won't serve 'em if they knife somebody."

"Ten cents," Leonard said on a pair of tens. "And some freebooter tries to climb aboard, you do him with the old man's pistol."

The boy laughed. "Sharp eyes, sir. No, Miss Sap. Quieter." He rose and stepped lightly toward the back wall of their shanty and returned with a leather sack hung from a short rope. "Eight pounds of lead shot. Feel it."

Leonard hefted the sap approvingly.

"Why, we put Miss Sap to work two nights ago, fella tried to climb up and help himself to the product. Mr. Aldritt put him out with one swing. Fella come to in the water, I says to him, looking over, I says, 'Appears you had a little mishap, sir!'" and the boy and the gimp burst into titters at the boy's cleverness. "Ain't no report like you get with a pistol, neither, 'n no poking around afterward for who done it."

The gimp grinned and put in twenty cents. The boy raised his eyebrows, grinned at Leonard, put his money in. Leonard put in, and when the boy asked him, Leonard drew three cards, not a one of them doing him a lick of good. Gimp put in two bits. The boy folded. Gimp grinned and stared at Leonard, was he in or out?

Leonard had two tens, meaning nothing. "See your twenty-five, raise you ten," he said. The gimp was the kind of drooling pigstink of humanity Leonard was comfortable dealing with.

The gimp put in the ten and then raised it fifteen, stared at Leonard, was he still in or out?

Leonard put in and waited on the gimp to lay down. The gimp honked and quacked and showed his hand, full house, eights and sixes.

"Son of a bitch," Leonard said amiably, and tossed his cards in. The gimp swept up the money, poured some whiskey.

"Luck'll turn, you give her a few hands," the boy said, and passed the cards to Leonard.

"Where's the whiskey from, then?"

The boy looked at Aldritt, who grunted and waved his hands impatiently.

"Moorhead."

Aldritt batted his hand for the boy to go on, tell.

"In kerosene drums," the boy said. "Shipped to the Perley Store. Mister high-boots brother of his don't know the difference."

The gimp's face, turned to Leonard's to read his reaction, was lit with joy at the simplicity of it.

"Who's the bootlegger, then?" Leonard tried, but with that the gimp just shut his trap and grinned.

Didn't matter. Maggots'd already given him the key, if he wanted to worm into it.

It took little over an hour to lose the two dollars, and Leonard rose to say good night.

"Come back tomorrow," the boy said, "you get a chance."

LEONARD WARMED TO the habit of a pint sipped in the woods downstream of the barge, where he took off his overalls and soaked his feet and thought of nothing or of women. When he thought of women, he thought often of Esther. Some nights his imagination wallowed in lust and lewdness, but other nights he spit at her high and almighty bearing and what he took to be her grasping hunger for a farm of her own. One night he bellowed into the darkness, "Ain't a man's prick she wants the length of, but his fucking fields," and laughed at his wit and heard his own animal sounds echoed back from the opposite bank.

"Whyn't you fuck her, then!" came a holler.

Leonard climbed to his feet to locate the scab-tongued bastard that hollered it, but found he was fairly drunk and couldn't say where the voice had come from.

He clutched a sapling. "Come again?" he hollered, and listened for where the voice was at but the woods were silent. He knew what he'd heard, son of a bitch didn't want to repeat himself. He wiped spittle from his chin and looked for the way out. The goddamned path. The woods were changed around, and he could not get oriented. He found a trail that went away from the river. It was unfamiliar but he followed it, stumbling over roots and scraping his face on branches, and he came out in a field like the one where he'd left the horse. He looked up the field but it was too dark to see any horse. Stars spun above him. He walked up the edge of the woods in the soft dirt, whistling for the horse. Heard a whinny and found where he'd tied it and managed to heave up onto its back. The horse took him across the fields a mile to the barn where his blanket was.

The Red flowed north. Leonard would do the same. No use trying for the Ulverson girl unless you had half a section of dirt and six plow teams to make good on it.

LEONARD'S PEOPLE HAD been lumberjacks and sawyers, starting in the North Carolina hill country and moving west with the timber cutting. In the '40s they sawed the Tennessee valley, moved on in the '60s to the bluffs and coulees of southeastern Minnesota to work the hardwood stands along the Mississippi and its tributaries. Leonard's father and uncles worked north into the stands of white pine, maple, and birch where they clearcut under the south rim of Lake Superior, booming their logs into Chequamegon Bay for the mills at Ashland or sluicing them down the Namekagon and St. Croix for the mills at Stillwater. The Crummeys were hired labor who never had a thought for getting up a stake or starting their own business but were satisfied to follow orders, pocket wages, move on when the work moved on.

Leonard came in '69, born in a tenement in Ashland. His daddy was Jack, who lived in the camps, and his mother was Glennis, who lodged in Ashland and worked at the Cushing mill on the sawdust burner, sending forth a plume of nicotine-yellow that settled over the town with the chronic smell of a bar at six o'clock on a Sunday morning. Glennis was a dark and pretty girl who kept boyfriends while Jack sawed trees. She stayed out late and made talk of dumping Ashland for a real city somewhere, but with a husband and a boy on the line there wasn't one of her men would take her up on it.

A winter night when Leonard was eight he answered the door to a pair of lumbermen asking for Glennis, who was not at home. They had his daddy's body outside in the company wagon and thought it probably oughtn't to be let freeze. Wasn't killed in a felling accident like so many were, but over in Brule behind the Snow Goose Tavern in a knife fight.

Glennis buried her husband in two days and bought train tickets for her and the boy to La Crosse. It was dusk on a frozen Sunday in February when she found the simple house of Jack's cousin Willa up a narrow coulee on the south side of town. Glennis banged on the worn wooden door, and asked to stay the night.

Willa put Glennis and Leonard in her own bed and tucked herself in with her three shy boys.

Next morning Glennis was gone. The boy, Leonard, sat to breakfast without eating or speaking. No, he didn't know where she went. She does that. Then she comes back. He said he would wait.

Auntie Willa let him stay. She was a large, turnip-colored woman who smelled of poultry and lye soap. The husband traveled for the railroad. She made the boys' clothes, worked two jobs, raised turkeys for meat and cash. She told Leonard what she expected of him, and when he did it, she did for him like she promised. He studied her ways and how to be pleasing. Fed mash to her turkeys and brought them in out of the lightning. Swept the house. Learned to read her moods, signs written in air. Filled the wood box. Washed the dishes after their meals. When he began to work for wages doing cleanup at the rendering plant, he put his earnings in the household kitty. Strand by strand he tied himself to his new Auntie Willa.

She did not scold him or show him up before the other boys but liked to say they could learn how to be useful watching Leonard. She told him what a strong young man he was. One day when he was twelve, she saw his thing go hard inside his pants. Said, "Lenny, come here!" with a laugh and squeezed it and laughed and said, "So strong! Makin' me weak." Startled him, her reaching to grab his thing like that.

Next day, they were alone, there it was again, pushing his pants, and he let her see. How she squeezed it and hugged him. Made her feel weak and strong both at the same time, she said, did he feel that way, too, and he said he did. Made him dizzy.

That night she called him to her little room, would he please look at her lantern by the bed, see did it need trimming. There she was, in her gown with her hair unfastened and her titties hard as acorns against the inside of it, smelling of soap. His power came on him. She reached out and felt of it.

"I open the buttons?"

He nodded, so she did and reached down and wrapped her hand around it and ran her fingers up and down, made the skin slide on and off the end of it and made him so dizzy he could not stand.

"It's all right you get on the bed." She said it nicely, patted him to sit up at the pillow, lean his back on the headrail.

"Know what it's for?"

Shook his head.

"Make a woman strong. You make me strong?"

He nodded.

She kissed it. Hair fell onto his stomach and tops of his legs and hid her face and what she did with her hands and all of a sudden his body buckled and shuddered and he squirted the juice of strength upon her face, her hair, the power leaving him, his knees bucking, making her strong.

He had a power inside him and never before knew it.

"Make me strong today!" she would ask on the days the other three boys went out before him. He made her strong in her hand, in her wet crack, her mouth. His power spurting out, leaving him weak, but how she smiled to be so strong from his gift. And then, wait a little, didn't he fill right up with it again, wasn't he the strongest boy. Make a bull of a man. His Auntie Willa the strongest woman. Until he slipped and let her down, let the pneumonia take her.

The rains had come and they'd all five caught the same spring cold, one that carried with it a hard cough. The simplest chore triggered spasms of hawking and wheezing, and when she asked him one morning about the turkeys, he said he was in the grip of the cold sweats and could not go out, make one of the other boys go. It was Willa that went out and got herself drenched. She came all over feverish by evening and the next day she wouldn't get up off the bed. He stood beside her, frightened, asking should he make her strong, but she hardly found the wind to speak. In a week she was gone.

He was thirteen. Fell in a hole had no bottom.

He was sent to a boys' home in La Crosse, but he knew before they did that nobody could stand him long, and by fourteen he lived on his own. He walked his life along a narrow ridge, telling himself, "Work hard, get along quiet." He was let in at the rendering plant to wheel pig offal in a barrow to the sausage station. Hauled it for two years before getting himself raised up to one of the casing stuffers; two days later, the foreman fired him for rat feet in the product. It was not Leonard's sausages had the rats, but the others on the line made sure it was Leonard that got the ax for it.

He began stealing food to eat. He stole liquor to sell, and then stole some to drink and took to it. Got work for a hardware man who showed him how to fit pipe, bend tin, hang a door, hone a scythe. The man paid in money and praise, words that Leonard drew in like pure water. The harder he worked, the more the man gave him to do. Before long Leonard could not sleep for worry and it was the whiskey he took to calm himself that turned the man black on him, got him fired. What calmed him was whiskey. He took it for nerves, took it for rage, took it for courage to lift himself up and move down the road, find work and rooms where people didn't know him.

He'd turned out tall with his mother's dark looks and the Crummey capacity for hard work. He could get on to the next county. He could talk his way into a new situation. When a job hit trouble, he picked up the bottle knowing the storm would take its course. He got hired off the street in Winona to fill in for a drowned deckhand on a working boat headed north; got fired when they docked at St. Paul. Scrounged work at the sawmills, stockyards, and switch yards; got himself fired from more trades than he could count working at. The panic of '93 forced him out of the city in search of farm work. By the summer of '95 he'd learned to drift south for the start of threshing and work the harvest north. Thinking he might as well follow it all the way into Manitoba, nothing to lose, nobody to stand still for.

Put Willa's face on every woman he went with. Not a one was that strong, until Esther.

9

Rugnel Ulverson had released his hired man two years earlier, when his own son Carl had grown strong enough to do the man's work. With four sons, there was the matter of adding to his patrimony. Rugnel's eye had been focused on the Pederson farm to his north for better than a year. Pederson was a lardish, disorganized man whose wife was two years dead of a horse kick in her thigh that had not healed.

Pederson had let things go, failed to pay on his mortgages. Rugnel watched the opportunity ripen, and then, unknown to Jess, signed a note to buy the place. The bankers agreed to finance it with nothing down and ten percent interest on the condition Rugnel pledge his own acres as added collateral. Spread over both farms, the mortgage added sixty-five cents an acre to his costs. Steep terms, but even at depression prices he figured he could squeak by.

The day after he signed the mortgage, Rugnel was visited by a parade of imagined catastrophes, driving up his costs and savaging his crop. For two days he wasn't himself, possessed with remorse, but he told himself what a hard worker his oldest boy, Carl, was, and how far they'd come since homesteading. How little they'd started with and how they'd built it up. He berated himself for the momentary lapse in courage and determined to get on with the task. There were buildings to repair and Pederson's failed crop to be plowed under.

It was the day after they'd completed threshing that he chose to tell Jess what he'd done. Jess was only thirty-nine, but the exhaustion of the past week and the death of the Norgaard boy had left deep lines in her face. She was in the kitchen pickling beans, and wholly unprepared for Rugnel's announcement. "Who's going to work it, then?" she said.

"Have to hire out the fall work."

She waited for him to say more, but he was done. "And pay a hired man with what?"

"Next year, when Hjalmer's got a man's body on him, we can free up Carl to move over and work the Pederson place. It's how you build up, Jess. You take what you have and you move the pieces to where they do the most good. Then you borrow against them to get some more, and you work that into production and it pays for itself, and the next boy comes along, and you move the pieces around again and make it all bigger. The boys will have farms, Jess, because of what you and I started."

She threw her towel at the floor. "I won't allow it. Not Carl, next year. It would mean his not having college, and my boys will have an education before I will see them lashed to plowshares. It's what we've worked for, Rugnel! To lift them up!" She turned her shoulder to him. "Carl will go to St. Olaf. After a college degree, it's his decision. But not before. You'd better think again."

He had a standing promise to Jess that their boys would get

college-educated if that was what they chose, but you don't let land slip through your hands, you keep your eyes on the horizon and suffer the privations when they're called for. That's how you make a future. The whole family sacrifices.

Rugnel rubbed his forehead and his eyes, which felt tired deep in their sockets. He was right, and he knew well enough that she was, too. He left his wife to her labors without another word. They would find a way to do both things. Possibly he could find the money to run Pederson's for a year or two with a hired man, but unless they could get more for the wheat, probably not. Strand, to the north of Pederson, might pay to plant those fields for a year or two; he'd been eager to buy them but not so quick as Rugnel. In any case, there was time enough to worry about it. The place was his now, and it presented immediate needs. It was already the first of September.

He rode out to the Oftedal farm and found the Crummey boy working there and pulled him aside.

"I have bought my neighbor Pederson's farm," Rugnel said. "The buildings need work and there's a hundred acres in need of the plow, if you're willing to stay on for a month or so after threshing."

Leonard nodded.

"You can sleep in the empty house. Same wages as Norgaard's paying."

Leonard let a small smile of satisfaction show. "Suits me."

"All right, then." Rugnel put out his hand and let a small smile answer.

LEONARD WOULD NEED a bed, and they moved the one from the hired man's room at Ulversons' place. He was given the use of Carl's bicycle to pedal to the Ulverson house for his evening meals, but Rugnel sent Esther to the Pederson place to prepare

Leonard's other meals and to help with the work, and he saw to it that young Hjalmer, who was fourteen, went with her.

The Pederson house was small and hungry-looking, an L-shaped building in flaking clapboard set among a scrub windbreak of red cedar and box elder, taken over by wood spiders and field mice. A pump and sink occupied the six-by-eight-foot back porch. The porch entered into a dark kitchen heavy with trash but empty of furnishings except for a rusting woodstove and a pair of shallow pantry shelves made from a cracker box. Corncobs for stove fuel spilled into the parlor, a room with pale blue walls, two broken chairs, and the glass of a broken window.

The stair to the cellar smelled of mold. The stair to the attic climbed steeply to a bedroom over the parlor with a sloping ceiling too low to stand under except at the center. The room smelled of urine, and on the floor at the back of a narrow dormer closet lay the dead wife's things. It was a small pile.

Esther clucked her tongue at the filth.

"Doesn't bother me," Leonard said.

They cleared the house out with a shovel and broom and wet mop. Esther found a patch of late-blooming white asters on the sheltered side of the barn and made a small bouquet of them in a bottle which she hung from a nail beside the kitchen door.

Rugnel had bought Pederson's two draft horses and implements. Esther and Hjalmer picked through a tangle of harnesses and fittings on the floor of the barn and sorted out what was serviceable. She adjusted the cutter and gauge wheel on the plow. It was a single walking plow, to Rugnel's pair of two-bottom gangplows. Leonard would be doing well to cut two acres a day.

Esther instructed him on the lay of Pederson's fields. "Lower the ring in the clevis if the heel wants to rise in the heavier soil near the creek." She read his face to see if he was getting it. He had a thin face with a hard jaw.

"I have walked behind a plow before," he said.

His eyes looked less certain than his words. She asked, "You want me to cut the first furrow, then?"

"If you are offering."

She hitched up the horses and cut him a good straight line. She could do that better than her brothers, and liked a man that was willing to let her.

After that, he plowed, and in the days that followed, while he was in the fields, she and Hjalmer dug at a three-foot pavement of manure in the barn, reglazed the broken windows, burned piles of refuse, and repaired some of the fences and gates. They cleaned the chicken house, and she brought twenty hens over from home to populate it, and then bought a rooster for a dollar. Esther and Hjalmer cleaned the stovepipe, which leaked and was caked with creosote, and then, over four days, they laid up firewood—enough to see the house into November, when frost would end the fieldwork and her pa would let Leonard go.

THE BREAKFASTS SHE cooked him were coffee, eggs, cured sausage, fried potatoes, ham, and bread—all of it but the coffee being fruit of the Ulverson farm. The milk and butter from Constance's cows, the honey from Esther's bees. Hjalmer sat to eat with Leonard at a table they had fashioned from boards. Hjalmer was blond and gangly and friendly toward Leonard. Ulversons' hired man had been like family, welcomed into the home and given to tutoring the children in the mechanical arts, and when he was let go to save wages and board, it was a sad day. At any amusing or unsettling turn, they still spoke of their hired man and what declamation he might have offered on the events of the moment.

Leonard stepped unknowingly into the hole the man's absence had opened. Esther felt it. She thought that Hjalmer did, too, judging by his animation. He asked Leonard questions freely, questions about his travels and different jobs, the farms he worked, his experiences on the big rivers on the far side of Minnesota. Leonard unfurled his tales stintingly at first, but as Hjalmer pressed for details the stories began to come, some drawn from a strand of truth, like working the loading derricks in the big sawmills at Stillwater, and how, in the slaughterhouses of St. Paul, he had inked the tattoo hammer, salted the hides, and kept the blood trough flowing. Other stories were woven from whole cloth—working for Mr. Hill's railroad, the people who had come to him for advice or who urged him to help them out. Esther listened from her post at the rusting stove, picturing the sights as he described them and thinking how wide the world stretches. She cooked until they were satisfied, and then, while they harnessed the horses and got down to work at their separate duties, she fed herself and thought about the Pederson place and what needed doing in their own little world.

The quality of the farm was all in the soil. The buildings didn't count for anything; time and effort would make them what you needed, but if the soil was too heavy or wet or alkaline, no amount of work would make you money. This land, worked right with good seed, would produce. Granted normal weather. Barring fire, infestation, and the wheat rust. Produce as good as her pa's, she was certain.

And such was the drift of her mind again two days later, a sunny morning as she propped open the windows and hung Leonard's bedding out in the sun to air. Brushed something off the back of her arm and tarnation if it didn't sting her. She wheeled in pain. Saw a wasp on the wing. Later, when she went around the end of the barn after a wood stake or something to tie back the grapevine, she saw where the wasps were entering through a knothole.

The nest was a large one, hung from the ridgeboard over the

hayloft. Come frost, the wasps would leave it to find winter crevices, get into the house. It was better to kill them off while they were gathered, which meant doing it at night.

At dinner, Rugnel asked Carl to go back with Leonard and take it down.

"I will go with," Esther said. "Got a hen that's going broody I want to check on."

"No need of Carl, then," Leonard said. "If she holds the lantern, I'll go up the ladder with the hoe and cut it off."

It was well after sunset when they went back, him on the bicycle and her beside on her horse, Mister Jones, the air cool and autumny. The sweet smell of the straw burn off somebody's farm caught Esther by surprise and flushed fall memories like a flock of chicks out of the garden, vivid sensations that disappeared as fast as pullets after grasshoppers, no particular story so much as the feeling of busyness, of putting by for winter, of hard sleep. Nothing between the two of them as they traveled the road but the early stars and night crickets, the shirr of his tires in the gravel and dishclop of the horse hooves. The immense sky going to ink.

THEY BUILT A fire in the driveway to burn up the nest once they got it out, and then went in to look.

The barn was pitch-dark. They lit a lantern and climbed up into the hayloft by the ladder that was nailed against the wall of the grain room.

She held the light up and looked to see were they busy outside the nest or gone in, and decided they were gone in.

"Ladder won't reach it, though," Leonard said.

"We stack some bales it will."

He moved four bales, stacking two on two.

"Make it five below, three on top," she said.

"Two and two's good," he said, disliking her bossing him and going ahead, hoisting the pole-wood ladder up, see if it reached the ridgeboard, which it did.

"Loosey-goosey at the bottom, Mr. Crummey. You get up ten feet, you get a good sting and a jerk, this thing's coming down and I will not feel sorry for you, you don't put more to it."

He saw it was true and pulled four more bales over, saying nothing.

She found two boards. "Set the feet of the ladder on these. Spread the weight."

He never knew a woman to boss a man like she did, like she put on pants when she got up in the morning. "If you want to do this yourself, I will hold the light," he said.

"Don't get uppity, put the boards under the ladder, save yourself a broke neck and me having to put a foot on it, finish you off."

She sniffed like her nose was wet or get on with it, so he put the boards under, knowing he would have thought of it himself if she didn't make him so damn jumpy telling him what to do, make sure the lantern's plenty full, hoist up that ladder, want to make a quick job of it and not chop them into a fury, as if he never once'd met or used a garden hoe.

He put a foot on the ladder to check its stability before going up—

"Wait," she said. "You cut it off and then what? If it falls down, they will spill out."

He sighed heavily. "Goin' to cut and grab it," he said, his words exaggerated for clarity. "Let the hoe drop. Carry the nest down." He gave her a long look that said, *If it please your lady paramount.*

She stared up at the nest and pictured what might work and couldn't think of a better way. "It's your skin."

"You hold the damn light up."

"No need to get peevish, Mr. Crummey."

He went up the ladder, a strap of leather in wore-out overalls, the ladder swaying, and she held the lantern as high as she could reach. Had a set to his jaw like a jackass sometimes but it didn't stop her taking a good long look of him. He stuck his face right up there and swiped the blade through in one stroke, and then he had the nest against his chest and the hoe fell into the hay and he was already coming down so quick she could have lit up his pants with the lantern. The two of them clambered down from the loft and she followed him out and he threw the nest onto the fire. She put a log over it, made sure it didn't roll out. The wasps teemed out of the hive and curled up and fell into the flames and the hive began to burn away in layers and turn to paper ash that rose on the currents, large flakes lighter than air, drifting into the sky. The stars had come out. It was the kind of night when she was a girl she sailed at sea under, to the place where the horses began. She felt a chill even while the fire warmed her.

"Thank you," she said, and she moved to stand close beside him.

Her words made him feel capable. Doing this chore together, and then her thanking him this way. The two of them standing there felt like they already belonged to this place, and he asked himself how was he going to make her feel it, too. He did not have an idea on that. He watched the fire burn and felt her silence. Wanted it to be them, together, more than anything.

"Remember this one? 'Out of the eater came something to eat, and out of the strong came something sweet,'" she said.

"No. What is it?"

"You don't know it? Samson's riddle, from the Bible?"

"I forgot. Give me a clue." He did not know the Bible.

"What we just did." She could not believe she had stumped him with it. She waited a few moments for him to think, but then she was afraid he'd guess it, so she said, "The answer's a bee."

"Oh, darn it," he said, and he laughed at his own stupidity.

It was one of her favorites: out of the strong something sweet.

"All right. Why'd the policeman arrest the bird?" he asked.

"Never heard about it."

"You don't know? It's in the Bible."

"Go away!"

"He was a robin."

"Oh, fiddle." She would try to remember that one.

He said, "What starts with an *e* and ends with an *e* but only has one letter?"

"Hold your horses! I believe it's my turn!"

"Give me one, then," he said.

"Well, just a minute." She had a dozen riddles. "Oh! My house has no door. What am I?"

"Egg."

"You heard it before."

"No, I just guessed it."

"I think you heard it before," she said. "I'm taking my turn over: You must keep this thing, for once yours is lost, it will soon be lost by others. What is it?"

He was stumped.

"Give you a clue: This is especially important for yourself when you happen to be putting ladders up to wasp nests."

"Got no idea."

It was so perfect she danced a little jig before she told. "Your temper, Mr. Crummey."

He laughed outright at seeing her girlish like this.

"I am surprised you did not figure it out. I know the answer to yours, by the way."

"Well, say it, then."

"So easy, anybody could guess. It's an envelope." She had heard it before, but she wasn't about to tell him that.

TOWARD THE END of the second week of their occupation, the Pederson place was habitable and Jess kept Hjalmer to stay and dig potatoes. Esther trotted up the road bareback on Mister Jones. Goldenrod scumbled the ditches and verges and the sky was the tinny blue of autumn with a briskness that elevated her spirits. She loved the season of harvest, the land slowly shorn and plowed, a tidiness and abundance that made her feel affluent in the face of the long nights soon coming. The sky had showered before dawn and the soil was freshened without being sodden. As she turned into the Pederson driveway she saw Leonard step onto the porch half naked, and she raised a hand to wave, but he turned inside the house. A shyness had grown between them, their conversation mostly said toward Hjalmer. She put Mister Jones in the corral and went into the kitchen and lit the fire in the stove and then went out to the henhouse and picked the eggs. He was leaning against the kitchen doorway when she returned. He'd put on his shirt.

"You are still here, then," she said, teasing him a little.

"Where's your shadow?"

"Working for Mother."

His eyes were sunken and he looked wasted. She wondered was he working too hard. She pushed past and set her eggs on the table. He was unshaved and smelled sour. She added fuel to the fire, put beans in the grinder, and turned the crank. She stepped out to the pump and filled the coffeepot, put it on the stove, added the grounds. He is maybe one of them that don't sleep, she thought. She lit the lamp. Even in the light of day, the kitchen's window cast a stingy beam into the room that was absorbed by the smoked-up walls.

"Heat you some wash water?"

"Um." He pulled an overall strap over his shoulder and sat.

She filled the enamel ewer and put it on a back burner. She put the skillet on the stove and scooped a plug of lard into it. She found the knife and picked two potatoes from the bin and steadied them on the table and started chopping.

"Water's come in at the chimney," he said. He rubbed his hand back and forth over his mouth.

"Was going to flash it this morning," she replied, not looking up or missing a chop. She'd thought of it as she laid in bed hearing rain. The leak already rusted the stove and kept the floor wet to the point of going punky.

"That fella could've woke up to his stove disappeared through to the cellar, never figured out where it got to," he said. "Is there a name to that tune?"

"What tune?"

"What you are humming."

She turned to see if he was joking. "Was I doing that?"

He nodded.

"I never know," she said. She poked more wood in the firebox.

He sat without speaking. Watched her work. She scooped the potato pieces into the pan and reached for a string of sausage links hung from the ceiling and cut off two and added them in. The room filled with the sound of fry sizzle. The smell of hot oil on wood smoke.

"Any part of farming you don't know?" he asked.

She looked him straight on again. "Can't think what."

"Me neither," he said. He scratched the back of his head and then held his cup out for coffee.

"Wait," she said. "Settle the grounds first." She cracked an egg and dropped it into the pot with the shell. She gave it a minute to sink and then poured his cup.

"You like it here?" she asked him.

"I like sleeping indoors," he said.

"I was meaning, with all you have done, you like this kind of life. Prairie wheat farm."

His tired eyes went out the window for a few moments and then looked back at her. "Man likes what's his. This was mine, sure. Otherwise—" He made a dimissive gesture. "It's work for wages. Don't pay to be liking a place. See what I mean?"

She supposed she did see.

"Reckon same goes for you." He almost said, *you, Esther,* but they were not on first names. "Miss," he said.

She gave him a quizzical look.

"All itch and nothing to scratch. Or am I wrong?"

She gave him a small scowl to say what could he mean by that, and turned back to the stove and fussed the potatoes and cracked five eggs into a bowl and beat them with a fork and watched the potatoes fry.

She served the food onto his plate and set it before him. "You can leave the nose cups off of the horses, as the flies will not be out in this cool of weather."

SHE GOT HIM into the fields, and then she went back in and cut herself two thick slices from the bread loaf and toasted them over an open burner. She set one in the center of her plate and the other to one side. She fried two eggs easy and placed them onto the one slice and sat down with her coffee. She broke the yolks and let the yellow run in, thinking that he somehow saw what she was feeling about the Pederson place. That the two of them had something unspoken between them.

After she washed, she went out behind the barn and rummaged in the dump to find some scraps of sheet tin. Ordinarily she wouldn't go on a roof, it was a job for one of the boys, but she wanted the satisfaction for herself. She got the ladder down from the loft and set it against the eaves and climbed onto the roof. From the height she could see beyond the breaks of the Red to the Nora church in Dakota and the farms beyond. From horizon to horizon. Men in their fields plowing the wheat stubble under, haystacks like new barns, straw piles waiting to be burned. She watched the black earth curl away from the moldboard of Leonard's plow. He had a relaxed, rolling gait and an easy way with the horses. And what of his sexual advances? Maybe he had more need in that area than some men. She tried to picture Rugnel showing himself to her mother and could not. She did not know if she was in some way responsible. She heard his words, "Man likes what's his." She would talk with her friend Mrs. Loqueshear. She should list the questions to remember to ask. Like why was Leonard so much on her mind.

The stovepipe was six or eight feet to one side of where she'd been able to prop the ladder and she had to scuttle over to it. She tucked her scraps of tin under the lip of a shingle and inspected the leak. She cut one of the metal scraps to size with a snips and then tried to slide an edge of it up beneath the shingles, but it was blocked by something, a knot or a nail head. Later she would say this was when she should have quit and gone for a saw blade to cut through the obstacle, but she had no patience for climbing down and chasing after tools. She braced and—once, twice—pounded her palm against the edge of the metal. On the third blow she really gave it what for, and the butt of her palm caught a burr and she sliced herself good and deep into the meat of her hand.

"The devil!" she yelped.

She looked to see how bad and saw the blood well out of it. It trickled down her wrist. "Oh, the devil!" she said again, berating her own bullheadedness. She pulled a rag from her pocket and wrapped the hand. The wound throbbed and the rag hardly slowed the seepage. She had better get down before she grew faint. She backed very slowly down toward the eaves, jutting a foot in the air to locate the top rung of the ladder, and before she could orient her final retreat she knocked the ladder to one side and it skittered along the eaves and crashed to the ground.

"Hell and damnation!" She turned and sat square on her rump and studied the fix she'd got herself in. There'd be nobody to halloo to until Leonard came in for dinner. She would not hold her water until dinner, and as she pondered how in heaven's name she could discreetly pass it, she caught sight of Leonard coming into the yard holding something. "Halloo," she called.

He saw her from a distance, sitting on the roof. He held up the strap. "Broken tug!" he said.

She raised her swaddled limb. "Gone and hurt myself," she said, shaking her head in disgust.

He set the ladder up and climbed to her and helped her back herself between its poles and get a foot on the top rung, and then he stood below and looked up her dress as she climbed down, shaking.

"Let me see it," she said, picking up the tug.

"Better we doctor you up."

She sat at the kitchen table. He put the pitcher on the stove, urged a flame from the coals, added some sticks. Peeled off his shirt and stepped out to the pump and washed himself. Then he poured a basin of warm water and unwrapped the dirty cloth from her hand and slowly immersed the wound.

She sucked in air, sharply. The water stung.

He washed the hand with soap.

She leaned against his bare side and looked away. She smelled the fields on him and the horses and his work. She felt the certain movements of his body as he pressed his fingertips to either side of the cut and urged the flesh gently to give up blood and clean the wound. A wave of heat swept up inside her with a rush that caught her unprepared and made her damp and caused her to sit upright in the chair and lightly tug at her hand to pull it free of his. "Thank you," she said, not wanting his kindness to be thought unwelcome, but the surprise of the unbidden feeling had alarmed her, and she wished to push it away.

"A clean rag now," he said, wiping his hands on his overalls. "Your pa'll think I come after you with the ax."

She smiled at his joke but felt light-headed. "Rag sack's on the pantry shelf," she said, and she crossed her ankles and wiped a forearm across her forehead while he went looking.

When he had wrapped the wound he admired his handiwork. "You look like a one-armed boxer now."

The coffeepot had been left on the stove and he poured himself what was left, then thought to offer it to her, but she shook her head no so he sat and drank it himself.

"I want to thank you," she said.

"Glad I came to find you."

"Hate to think if the tug didn't break. I'd be a pigeon by now."

"Any of your chores you can't do while that heals up, you holler at me and I will fill in," he said.

"I am supposed to be keeping you too busy for extra chores," she said. "Pa's orders."

"He don't have to know everything," Leonard said. "We make a good team."

His words gave her a touch of the butterflies. "That's the truth."

He liked that she cut her hand. Needed pulling off the roof. Owed him something. He felt the day was coming. That certain things were expected of him to reach it, things he could not see but would know when they came up. Like today: the wound, the touching. What was expected now? He asked himself this question, and in the silence of their sitting together the only answer he found was this: You are still the hired man.

"Find me a new tug, I will get back to work," he said.

As Leonard walked behind the plow, his mind turned over the problem of Esther. The accident had been a gift. Made her weak and needful. The moment he stepped in, a warmth came from her he had not felt before. Then it passed, and she was all raised grain again. But he'd felt it. He'd made her weak. Wanted to get that feeling back.

He worked to the creaking of the plow and harnesses, under the full sun in the growing heat of the afternoon. He knew it was her strength that drew him. They were alike that way. Seeing her in the fields with the local boys, it was her knowing more and not caring what they thought that put her above them. He was like that. Strong to the kernel of his core. He had to show it to her, in a way she would admire. Other women wanted a man to hold them down, but Esther did not. She wanted one that was as strong as she was. Leonard was strong in ways she would not imagine.

The team shied suddenly, flicker of something in the field ahead. He jerked the reins and whoaed them and went to see. There was a huge snake, nearly four feet long, the biggest goddamned hognose he'd ever seen, winding out of the grain into the woods of the creek, but slowed by heat and by a lump, something it had swallowed, fat as a small rabbit or a gopher, maybe. He loved to see a big snake like that. When it had pulled free of the field he stepped over to see where it went, but it was right there, just reached the shade of the woods and stopped. He could catch it easy if he wanted, and with that thought came the idea he'd been hunting.

He unwrapped a sack he carried around the plow handle. He walked a few yards down the edge of the field and broke himself off a stout sapling and stomped across the top end where it branched and broke it off to make a short fork. He picked off the rough ends as he walked back to the snake. It was still there, asleep in the grass. He wiped his sweating hand on his pants for a better grip. Took off his hat. Pushed the stick through some leaves. Lined up the fork, and then, at the last, thrust down, but the snake had sensed him, turned its head to look, and Leonard sank his fork in the dirt. "The hell," he muttered. The snake raced forward through the grass, Leonard after it. The snake went under a log; he kicked the log over; it went under leaves; he beat the leaves with the stick and looked where he thought it would come out. It didn't come out, but turned on its back, posing dead. "Ha!" Leonard cried, dropping beside it. He grasped the fat neck back of the head and scrambled to his feet before it could wrap on a log or tree, holding the snake at arm's length, the snake coiling in air and gaping at the mouth and hissing to kill.

It coiled up his arm as he carried it back to where he'd left the sack. It was surprisingly powerful. He grabbed the sack and laid it open on the ground, then peeled the coils off himself and raised the sack and dropped it in. The big snake went wild inside the sack, writhing and striking at the gathered neck, trying for his hand. "You devil!" he cried, and laughed, and put a quick twist in the top of the sack and then knotted it and fastened it to the tie bar that ran between the plow handles. He didn't guess a hognose was poisonous, but wasn't this one a mean cuss. Raised a sweat on him, and he had half a mind to whack off its head, but he would bide it. He had other plans for it.

"YOU DON'T KNOW who his people are," Mrs. Loqueshear said, pulling an almond cake from the back of the cooling rack.

"All are passed," Esther said. She thumbed through the pages of the magazine she had brought with her, the *Century Quarterly* of May 1890. It had been in a box of yellowing periodicals her aunt had mailed from Boston ("I have cleaned the cellar and thought you might use some news to pass the winter or kindle your stove!"), and within it she had discovered a rather riveting piece called "Chickens for Use and Beauty" by H. S. Babcock.

The bakery was a storefront in the center of Perley on Second Street, and Esther had stopped in early with her eggs, as she did on Mondays and Fridays. The rooms were still warm from the ovens. Mrs. Loqueshear's husband baked at night, and then while he slept Mrs. L got up and opened the store by six o'clock and cleaned and stood behind the counter until eleven-thirty. Then she closed for the day, ate her dinner, and went up to the Perley Millinery and Dry Goods where she worked afternoons clerking and arranging displays.

"So you said." Mrs. L tore a length of paper off a roll beneath the counter. "Sara Bjorndahl over Hillsboro married one, come up with the transients. Next spring comes up this sorry bedraggle of a female asking has anybody seen her mister, one Harold Entwhistle. Same name as Sara's husband. Turns out this slip of dog's breakfast is Harold's other wife and the mother of his three boogery children down in Alexandria. Essie, his people may be dead and sure enough gone, but every man with a trout between his legs has a past." She arched an eyebrow at Esther and wrapped the cake and tied it with a string and attached a tag on which she had written "Alrick."

Perhaps because she worked in ladies' dry goods Mrs. Loqueshear felt an obligation to her appearance. Her tastes ran to the blush tones ("colors of the heart") and to ruffles and silk flowers, which she ordered from the wholesalers in the East and demonstrated to the women of Perley and surrounding towns with many feminizing touches, stitching moss roses or pink carnations on the sleeve or the shoulder, replacing a humdrum sash with a gauzy print or adding a ruffle at the bosom. She urged the women to see themselves as bouquets and to arrange their stems with flair and imagination. For this she had earned something of a following. Mrs. L was herself a heavy woman with darkly furred cheeks and dewlaps at the neck, and her gift with fashion showed others, including Esther, how far good taste and attention to appearance could go toward softening the female form. She was the top clerk at the store, selling even to mistresses of sod houses, for whom the significance of a special-order dress Mrs. Loqueshear grasped instinctively, fulfillment of repressed longing, color and joy against darkness and silt, her women emerging from their sod hovels like posies from the prairie grave.

On this day, beneath an apron of flour sacking, Mrs. L worked in a simple mauve day dress with skirt that flared smoothly over the hips and balanced rather grand leg-of-mutton sleeves. Her hat was a boater with cream gardenias, and while it was more style than Esther would be comfortable wearing, on Mrs. L the effect was undeniably handsome. At forty, she was twice Esther's age, and, in Esther's esteem, twice the woman.

Mrs. L had removed the hat and raised the sleeves while she worked. She wrapped another almond cake and set a plate of sandkaker on the counter for Esther and herself.

Esther took a cookie and ran her finger down the text of the poultry article. "No difference in any case. He will be let go when freeze-up ends fieldwork. Pa will winter the animals over to our place— Here," she said. "The Andalusian." She commenced to read:

> Plumage of a slaty blue, each feather having around the outer edge a delicate lacing of a darker shade of blue, sometimes nearly or quite black. The hackle and saddle feathers are usu-

> ally darker than the under parts, and often show purple reflections in the sunlight.

She looked to Mrs. L for her reaction.

"Layers or eaters?" Mrs. L asked over her shoulder from the sink.

"Related to Leghorns, so layers I would guess. Do you think that sounds pretty, or too dark?"

"Too dark."

"Um-hmm." She flipped ahead two pages. "Listen to this one, the Turkish cock."

> His whole body is exquisitely adorned with lines that are sometimes golden, sometimes silver, and it is wonderful how beautiful an effect this produces. His legs and feet are tinged with blue. Presents a union of Hamburg characteristics—the lines of penciling, the spots or spangles, the silver or golden colors, the blue legs, the projecting spike or point of the rose comb.

Mrs. L leaned over her shoulder for a look at the drawing. "Florid little things, prancing around like it's the Queen's birthday. What would you do with them?"

Esther hummed a little noncommittal note of possibility: Who's to say what a person might do with such birds? She had a hundred and fifty Barred Rocks and Rhode Island Reds, and before meeting Mr. Babcock in the *Century Quarterly* she had never given a thought to owning a chicken because of its showiness, but the way he described them had caused her to want. Purely frivolous, but no law says you can't read about them.

> There is no breed that possesses more admirers, and upon which more thought, time, and money have been lavished, than the Games. *Hundreds* of dollars have, time and again,

> been paid for a *single* remarkably perfect specimen [emphasis Esther's, followed by a glance at her friend, who did not turn around to remark]. The hackle of the male Black-breasted Red Game looks almost like *spun silk* of an orange or light-red hue. The back is of a rich red, the breast is jet black, and the wings are dark red, traversed by an iridescent bar of black.

She sucked her lower lip and looked at the drawing. It was an erect bird in its little vest strutting around with its hands folded behind its back.

"Does this look like someone to you?"

Mrs. L turned from the sink and gave it a quick look. "Mr. Flint at the feed store?"

"That's what I thought!" They had a good laugh at Flint's expense, and then Esther pressed the pages open against the table. Of the odd-looking Houdan she read, "hardy, well formed, an excellent layer of remarkably large white eggs, and very quaint in appearance from the large size of its crest and muff of feathers," and she thought she would ask Flint the cost of special-ordering five or six of these or the Turkish from St. Paul.

"Did you see the Steen girl's baby, then?" Mrs. L said, as if suddenly remembering to ask.

"Not due for close on a month, yet," Esther corrected. Kari Steen's father was the Perley undertaker. Kari was eighteen, a friend of Esther's sister Constance, and had been married by young Stranwold last winter more or less at the point of her father's shotgun.

"Yes! It came! Poor scrawny squirrel, gray and shrinking in its skin already."

"It came?"

"Two days ago. Tries to eat but does not get her milk. Won't Steen look the fool if the baby dies and there's his precious Kari tied to that lout Stranwold."

"That happened to Nilla Carlson with Lars," Esther said. "They put a balm there to numb it and let the nipple open and the baby began to grow like chickweed. Have they tried that?"

"I will ask Agnes."

"Stranwold's a worker," Esther said. "They will do fine."

"And of your Constance and young Heiberg?"

Esther sighed. "Father will not let them marry until she is eighteen. Two more years. And then she will follow him to Ballard, where his people have a mill and more work than men." It seemed to Esther that Constance couldn't get away from Perley fast enough, was set on becoming something superior to the rest of them. Heiberg had promised her they would come into an ownership share at the Ballard Mill through the offices of his uncle, and so Constance had set her designs on becoming the wife of a Puget Sound industrialist. It would probably come to pass, and where was the justice in that, when all Esther wanted was to cut her own piece of the prairie without answering to a husband who thought he knew better than she did. A partner, yes, but no Perley boy. There was no Perley boy that didn't know it all. Plow a field in his own daddy's image.

"Them as went to Ballard have prospered," Mrs. L said factually.

Esther picked at her sandkaker, making crumbs but not eating. Mrs. L held her tongue, and eventually Esther came to what was weighing on her. "He shows himself to me. Through his trousers." She said it without looking up.

"What do you do?" Mrs. L asked.

"Turn away, of course."

Mrs. L swilled the water around the pot she was cleaning. "He's showing you he's a man, like any. When he is alone, he will bring himself to relief."

Esther felt her face grow warm and let the silence return.

"If he asks, you must not let him enter you."

"Of course not," she said softly.

"You know nothing about him."

"He is a worker," she said in Leonard's defense. "He's not always trying to show off how smart he is. Wants something to call his own."

Mrs. L turned. Her eyebrow was arched again. "Abbott Torvald told Gladys Meekins that if she didn't let him have his way with her he would go on and have one of the girls in Fargo."

"Well, she has been with Abbott a good long while," Esther said, trying to see Gladys's point of view.

"Don't no woman owe any man to spread her legs."

"So you say, but a man's going to have what God made him to need." Esther felt her heart race slightly. "What are we underneath but animals?"

"Underneath, Essie, of course. But we elevate ourselves above it. We become the person we fashion after. How we dress. What we *let* ourselves hunger for. The animal we keep hid is the one that will not hurt us."

"I know," Esther said, but she did not see it so plainly herself. She wouldn't do what Gladys Meekins did for Abbott, but if they were intended, where was the true harm in it, except they might make a child early, and then there was the public shame of that, but a child they wanted, after all. She had no intention of cheapening herself or of marrying badly, but where the animal act was concerned, she was not put off. A man who was respectful of his wife and wanted frequent relations was better than one who didn't, and a wife who denied him and got a wandering husband got what she asked for. Thoughts that were better left unsaid to Mrs. Loqueshear, whose fashions nor labors were sufficient to keep her man where he belonged.

SHE TROTTED MISTER Jones up the driveway the next morning, Hjalmer still choring for their mother. Leonard's face appeared and disappeared in the upper window. A spare-looking window that needed dressing. If it was her place, she would spend the winter to spread paint, sew curtains, go to Moorhead for a wall-paper border for the parlor.

Leonard was slow coming down. She stood at the stove thinking were they married she would be doing this very thing. Wondering why she wanted it (for she did want it, she was willing to admit that to herself). How much of the wanting was of the animal kind (for there was that, she could feel it), and how much was wanting to yoke in with a man to possess and green her own soil, a man who did not put himself above her but saw through to what she was capable of, a partner to show her papa proud. She liked being with him, liked doing for him. How was it Leonard and the Pederson place had come into her life the same month if not for a reason? The Lord opens a righteous path before you, turn not your back upon it. Heard the noise of paper blowing across the floor, and she turned to look, but saw nothing there.

"Ready if I put on the potatoes?" she called up the stair.

"Yep," he called down, still not coming.

She reached beneath the table for the potato bin, but did not feel it in the usual place. She leaned down to look and saw it was slid back out of reach, a nuisance. She muttered, "Uh, uh, uh," disapprovingly and hitched her dress and got on a knee and yanked it forward, and the bin scraping across the wood raised a hiss she could not account for. The sound came again, and she turned the bin to look behind. There, backed into the corner, it rose up, mouth wide, neck all puffed out, hissing to beat hell.

"Mother of God!" she screamed, and cracked her head on the table. She scrambled to her feet.

"What?" Leonard called down the stair.

"Snake!" She was backing away. "Big one! Mad as a hornet!"

She got ahold of the broom and backed out the kitchen to the parlor. "Get quick and chase it out." She had never seen one so big. Gray with black splotches, she didn't know what kind but it liked to have bitten her if she gave it the chance. There must be mice or rats in the house—dear God, in the potato bin, maybe, and her reaching in there day after day, not so much as a thought to look what else might be in it.

Leonard came down the stair loosely, his face lit with a grin. "Where?"

She thought he was making fun of her. "Go poke your nose hind of the potatoes," she said, annoyed.

Leonard made a show of peering at the snake. "Well, well," he said. "Wait'n I'll get me a stick'n take off its head."

"No."

Leonard turned, questioning.

"Just get him out. If he's here for rats, better he's alive. Find the hole he snuck in and stuff it shut is all." She handed him the broom, thinking she would step outside until he had rid of it, but then changing, not knowing which way it would choose to vamoose.

Leonard opened the door and pulled the table and chairs away. He prodded it, making a show, but the snake turned over and posed dead.

"Think I killed it," he joked, although he knew the snake's behaviors now. He reached down slowly, slowly, then quick grabbed it back of the head and lifted it up for her, a trophy.

"Devil in it!" she said, gesturing him to put it out. The snake hissed and coiled around his arm and settled. He had fed and handled it for two days. It calmed in the warmth of his arms. He reached a forefinger between the eyes and stroked its head. The hissing ceased and the snake did not struggle, but flicked its tongue and looked toward Esther. He held it toward her for a good look.

She stood back. "You have tamed it, just like that," she said, gazing as much upon his hands and their strength as upon the creature itself.

There. He heard it in her voice. It was the moment he had longed for. "Touch it," he said.

She glanced in Leonard's eyes to read if he was in earnest. She was frightened of it and yet drawn. It was magnificent. It recalled to her the serpent in the Tree of Knowledge. It was coiled at the head and neck, watchful, beckoning. She reached around behind and touched it far from the head, and when it did not seem to mind she put her whole hand on it and let her fingers curl around its thickness. She felt of the surprising silkiness, the skin a sheath over its living power and wildness. "Put it out, then," she said softly. She felt herself perspiring, short of breath.

"Yes'm," he said, grinning like a boy. He pulled at a coil to disengage it, but the tail flicked up and grazed his eyes, and when he threw his hand up the snake sprang at Esther and struck her in the breast. She yelped and jerked backward but the snake had lodged in her breast and would not release.

"It has got me!" she said, stunned. Her eyes were enormous, disbelieving.

In his fleeting blindness, Leonard had not seen it. He squeezed the jaws but the snake would not open or be pulled free.

"Get him off!"

Leonard glanced desperately about the room for something,

reached the dipper in the bucket, and poured water on it. The snake snatched its head free and dropped itself to the floor and slid off in a lick down the cellar stair.

She turned away and unfastened the top of her dress and looked at her left breast and saw the two wounds an inch above the nipple. Its hind teeth had been the biggest, and these were what had pierced her flesh. Twin bee stings, turning red and proud.

"My Lord, what now?" She tried to calm herself.

He cast his eyes downward and shook his head. His elation had run out with the snake and rendered him empty and bewildered. "I should've kilt it right off, is what."

"It's not your fault. I am the one asked you let it live."

What she said was true and he looked up with gratitude. "Milk of a hognose'll not kill you," he said by way of offering comfort. He wiped his arm over his face, uncertain what to do. "It'll make you good and sore, though."

"Should we suck it out?" She was direct and matter-of-fact.

He dodged her eyes and dipped his chin slowly. "Whatever you think."

She exposed the wound, keeping the nipple covered, and turned her head against their shared embarrassment. Leonard bent and put his lips to the bite marks and sucked and spit into a cloth. He looked at the growing redness. He bent and sucked again. Spit.

"Done." He was not wanting to say it was just his own spit he'd got, for the wound had given up almost nothing.

"Thank you," she said softly. She turned from him and refastened her buttons.

"It'll be no worse than mighty sore, I think. Watch it for streaks."

"I keep getting myself in trouble and owing you thanks, don't I?"

"Maybe I'm the trouble," he said, knowing he was.

"It wasn't you that bit me," she said, and then could not hide a smile at what she'd asked him to do. "Was it?"

She turned to the stove and pulled the pan off the burner, thankful the fire had dwindled. "You go in the cellar and catch it out and then you come and eat your breakfast. Hard as tack by now. I will go home and see what Mother says. A hognose?"

He nodded.

"If I am not feeling the effects, I will come back and fix your dinner, otherwise you come over to the house."

He nodded and walked her out to Mister Jones. Then he went down in the cellar to find the snake. No sign, and no shortage of holes and cracks a snake might lodge up in, either.

JESS SENT HJALMER for the doctor, but before he'd gotten out of the yard she hollered after him, "You make it your business to be at the Pederson place anytime your sister is there." She was near sick having kept Hjalmer for chores, no matter how the accident with the snake happened. Esther's explanation, which was vague, had made her uncomfortable.

She put her daughter to bed and applied what she knew for stings, a touch of arnica and a poultice of wood ash with white oak bark and leaves. Esther had a mild fever by the time Doc Alnes arrived, and the breast had gone to swelling. He was a humorless, thin-lipped man given to coarse talk but possessed of a gift for salvaging the hapless. He looked at the breast, felt the heat and tenderness, and asked two or three questions. "Least she had sense to ask the fella to suck her titty, draw out the poison."

Jess coughed.

He wished to see the snake. Hjalmer was sent to find what the

Crummey boy had done with it, a journey that proved fruitless. While he was gone the doctor prescribed Fowler's solution internally, twenty drops every two hours in a little water, and, externally, a dressing of permanganate of potassium. "She'll have one hell of a mule kick but no worse."

The breast swelled prodigiously over the next hours.

Leonard came at suppertime to eat and he gave the mother a small bundle of coneflowers. "Good for bites."

By the following day the puffiness had advanced up into her shoulder and neck and around her side, the wound glowing red with fire. Late in the second day it came on to itching, and in the fullness of its swelling it came on to weeping a colorless milk. Esther drifted in and out of feverish sleep. Her wakeful thoughts were tainted by her dreams. She was swept into the Red and gasping for breath, her legs and arms dead weights she could not command, weighed by a force she could not see or overpower. Every few hours she found herself in her own bed in the room under the eaves that she shared with Constance, and in these moments the lunging of the snake came back to her, but in a confusion, struck by a water serpent and pulled into the suffocating darkness again, the drowning sweeping her downriver past muted fields of shriveled crops she could not rise to see, a suffocation of three days' duration.

Leonard pedaled to their place for his meals and was slow to leave. Hjalmer was helping him again, but the Pederson farm was not so lively without her there fussing over things. Leonard told Rugnel, "You know she's under the weather if she does not go out to spoil that horse of hers." Twice he surprised himself, going across to the Ulverson barn to curry Mister Jones.

On the fourth day the fever and swelling subsided, leaving behind a hard knot, fiery to the touch. Jess put her hand on it, felt the hardness and the fire inside it. She let Esther dress and come down and sit under a blanket by the kitchen stove, and it was another two days before she was allowed to gather the eggs and help with light work, asking Leonard at the noon meal how was he getting on in the field and if the tug was still good where she'd mended it.

THE FIRST TIME he entered her was six weeks before the wedding.

They were putting the hay up in the loft when she got a speck in her eye. "Drat!" she cursed.

He turned to see what bothered her. She'd wiped her fingers on her blouse and was trying to pick something from her eye.

"Drat, drat, drat! See if you can get it," she said, urgent.

"Hold still, then." He leaned her back on a bale and pulled the bottom part of her eye down with his thumb on her cheek. "Bit a stem," he said, and pulled the tail of her blouse out of her skirt to brush it with something clean, and the back of his hand touched her bare skin and her hand gripped the muscle of his arm and next he was over on top of her, a hand all over her titties and then shimmying out of his overall straps and hitching up her dress, pressing himself between her legs, just that fast, no words but animal grunts coming from somewhere, out of both of them, her trying to say would be better to wait but no words formed, and she didn't either want to wait and slid herself up fully onto the bales and let him find her. Felt his strapping sides and tried to wrap around him but he was all breathless to get in her and jerking at her so quick and hard, three times, made her eyes tear all over again and then was out and panting and wiping his forehead, strapping up his pants again, the semen everywhere inside and out of her and his sweat and her own pasted with hay, the prickles and bits in her hair and her blouse, her skin raw.

She sniffed and picked at her hair and gave him a smile to say it was all right, not to feel dirty by it. It was the moment of her betrothal. Not what she had expected but the animal thing she knew it for. She had to tame him was all, and she would, give her time. "Reckon we will be married, then," she said softly.

He looked out of the window, got his bearings, and then gave a short laugh. "Means you will make me a farmer, I guess."

She looked at him with steady eyes that said she would.

"You better get your clothes straight 'fore that brother of yours shows up," he said.

The air was a chill against the wetness but she felt no hurry to pull herself together. "Big thing a yours. Maybe already makin' a baby in me, what do you think?" She couldn't help herself. She would've liked it better if he was naked before her so she could see him fully. She was her own person.

10

"He'll need a .22," Leonard said.

Esther looked up from her list. "What makes you so sure it's a boy?"

They were sitting at the kitchen table. He bobbed his head to one side, trying to squelch a smile. "Just a feeling. Go ahead"—he waved his fingers at her—"write it down."

"A .22-gauge is not a baby thing. List is for baby things."

"I know, just put it down to one side so we don't forget."

"Pig'd be more useful." She wrote down the rifle, and after it she wrote "Age 10" and underlined it, a date that wouldn't come until 1906. "How much?"

Leonard considered. "Three or four dollars."

She gave him a doubting look.

"Secondhand."

She put down five. "Got a few years to work our way up to that one. I'm going to put down 'Pig, age 6.'"

"No fooling?"

"My brothers each got one. A boy learns how to keep it and raise it up, and then what kind of food it makes into. One day he sees his pork on the cutting board and he sits to table a foot taller than before, knowing he is a farmer now. Grows him up."

"Pig's a good idea," he said. "Write it down." She was smart about this business. He lifted his coffee for a sip, but stopped. "What if it's a girl?"

"Oh, pig's still very good, but a chicken or lamb is just as good."

"Put down pig, then."

"Did already."

"What all have we got?"

She looked at her notes. "Just a second." She scratched something off of one list and added it to another.

He looked out the window. The drippy eaves had gone to steady trickles over the last two hours. The fire in the cookstove liked to melt the snow over the kitchen, which ran down to puddle behind the ice on the porch roof. It worked up under the shingles, and every half hour or forty minutes they got a good dose of it out of the ceiling where he punched a drain hole and set down a catch bucket. Took her a while not to jump at the sudden noise every time it decided to pour out, which he teased her for, but not meanly. March was a do-nothing month. He should've been in the barn finishing with the harnesses but the mud was as much excuse as they needed to stay at the table after breakfast, making a list of stuff to do or buy, thinking mostly of two things, what they needed to turn the Pederson place into a going farm, and what to have on hand when the baby came, most of which they could get from her ma's attic.

They were only three or four weeks away from seeding and dragging the fields. A farm's a business. He'd never had charge of a business, but when they'd gone down to make the transfer, it was his name that went on the deed. Puffed him up and set a question in his mind over what might be expected and required of the responsibility. Husband, father, farmer. The changes put him above the Ulverson boys. Put him above the Perley merchants, nothing but shopkeepers. Put him above any farm's hired man or son of Perley who did not have a place to call his own. Thought he wouldn't mind to strut a little if the worry of it didn't make him feel some like he was asking for trouble the way a chicken's neck does.

He reached over to the cookstove and turned down the damper and cracked the door to the porch, let out some heat, but she looked up and shook her head no, so he pushed the door to again and took off his outer shirt.

When they'd spoken to Jess and Rugnel of their intention to marry, her pa had said that if they meant to live in the Pederson place, the way he saw it they ought to take over the mortgage and make it theirs. Which was what Esther had wanted, though she'd thought Jess would need to bring him around on it, but her pa'd said it himself: Take it and go make your own place, daughter.

She'd been excited the day they went for Leonard to sign the papers. She had her own life, all in the tumble of a few months. It was like the hand of Providence reaching down upon her, so right and natural, she remembered thinking, that she could hardly stand back far enough to see it all. How they had met and she had witnessed his difference. How he'd showed her his want.

They got married without a dollar in their pocket, her carrying the child and growing fat by the week, feeling like it had a hunger inside of her she could not appease. They carried her things over to the Pederson place and warmed the rooms with the few gifts from the wedding: two blankets, a rug for the parlor, an oil lamp, a spool rocker. They worked their way through the winter fixing Pederson's implements and re-sewing harnesses, cutting firewood, and doing a hundred small repairs. Leonard got work in Perley building the new elevator by the railroad. It paid him fifteen dollars every Friday. He came home with frostbit ears but it was money they could use to pay on the mortgage, buy groceries, and put down for seed. Evenings they ate what she cooked and then let the fire die and went up to bed early, shucking their clothes and crawling under the lowering roof and four woolen blankets, pressing into each other naked until she could thaw out the core of him frozen from a day hanging off the side of a grain elevator thirty feet in the air. When their heat came up they made love. He called it "doing farming," saying he was a farmer now and he was counting on her to teach him the business; they had their first crop planted and it was coming up inside a her like a big ol' sugar beet and he was the man to cultivate or weed or baste it, whatever kind of farming she was wanting or open to in her condition. If she was feeling too big or uneasy for it, he made himself be content just to lie together in the minutes before sleep, feeling their chests rise and fall and knowing the baby felt it, too.

Morning, when he went off to work, he told her what he expected done that day. She knew what needed doing, and not always what he thought, so she learned to steer their supper talk indirectly to what was on her private list, and come morning when he went out the door, often it was those same tasks that he said he wanted done when he came home at the end of the day. Sometimes she got Hjalmer to help lay in supplies beforehand, so when her husband told her to fix where the snow's blowing in under the eaves she had what she needed stacked in the corner of the barn.

By March the elevator work was done and he was unable to find anything else.

She held the list up. "What we've got so far is, under 'Crops,' sixty acres of wheat this year and next, carry over next year's seed, and use the money we save to pay down on a two-bottom sulky plow, which is under 'Tools and machines.' Mow the other forty for hay this year, and plant five in oats and five in barley next year." She looked up. "I wish Pa had bought the whole hundred and sixty."

"You got big eyes. We can't use all hunnert we got. No need of the worry over another sixty. Go on down your list. You'll be surprised how much we already wrote that needs doing."

"I have: 'Trade Leonard in Pa's fields for Hjalmer's help seeding and raking while I'm big.'" She looked up again. "Hjalmer goes at food like a freight train, but you can eat at Ma's while you're working there. Try to eat a lot."

"Fix him extra potatoes."

"Oh, and while we have him, you two help me put in the garden." She added that.

"Let's see. Under 'Animals' I have 'Two cows this summer, double the henhouse, and get up an egg route. Next year start pigs or sheep and maybe bees.'"

"Whoa. Startin' a family, Essie. Don't you go startin' pigs and sheep on me now."

She let loose a chuckle.

"Under 'Tools and machines' I have the sulky plow and the cultivator and I don't think we should add anything else except the hand tools for the garden, or what we'll need if we start bees. A proper laundry tub. Canning pot." She went down the list. "Under 'Baby,' I have diaper cloth, some toys, rifle, pig, and you are going to make a crib out of something or he'll have to sleep in a drawer."

He laughed. "Yes, ma'am."

"You got three months to get it done."

"Same as you." He pressed the back of his hand against her belly and stuck his nose in the air like he was feeling to see was she keeping up with the schedule. A boy was something he'd never let himself hope for, and now it was happening, even odds, boy or a girl. Most likely a boy.

IT WAS A PERIOD he was off his drink. He was too busy, or did not feel the need of it, knowing his life was now in a whole new direction. Some days it surprised him to wake up lying in his own house on one hundred acres of dirt that wanted only sunshine and seed to grow him a crop that would pay him the money to do whatever he saw fit. The kind of good fortune that gives a man the nerves—if something can go wrong, it will. But then, he told himself, his side of things was different for a change: he had Essie.

He started to talk around the edges of it to her one evening before they quit the kitchen for bed. "No shame that we come from different people," was how he said it, meaning to get at the fact that she held the key to it for both of them, but just as easily could have been him.

He had stoked the fire to warm the room a little so she could undress and wash out of a pan of warm water. She had draped her things on the back of a chair and stood naked on a towel in the buttery lantern light, soaping her cloth. His eyes lingered on her ivory belly that had a part of him inside it. She had let her hair down and the ends had got wet and were stuck to her shoulders.

He said, "If you told me one day you wanted to go live in a log camp, it would be me showing the ropes to you."

"You have already showed me some farming ropes I never learned from Pa," she said slyly. "Hate to think what your logging would involve."

That was one of the nights they melted into each other. Leonard let it go, what had been on his mind.

THE BABY GREW uneasy in her and she should've guessed he wasn't right entirely. June was the month he came. He came with the buttercups and the prairie roses, but he came out scrawny and wanting for baby fat, stunted on one side, his right arm and leg runty, with the other side bony but fully developed. Wary eyes and cheeks drawn like an old man, half of him stubbly, like one side of her womb had gone droughty.

She had the baby at her mother's house and Jess helped the delivery. When Jess saw the boy was afflicted she went downstairs for Leonard. "Best you go up. It's a boy, slow on the left side and maybe won't make it. Don't go and name him for a few days if I was you."

Leonard did not understand what she meant, slow on one side. He went up, feeling light in the head. Esther was in her old bedroom, lying with her bundle beneath a framed Bible print, Noah calling the Lord's creatures to his Ark.

Hearing his step, she looked up with a smile and a tear.

"Got a boy?" he asked.

"Guess he is still coming along on the one side," she said, her voice empty of all feeling but exhaustion. She unwrapped it and showed him what had come out of her. Looked like a peeled squirrel, raw and all over shivery, its head too big for the rest of it, the stunty limbs poking out of the one side useless and surprising. She wrapped it up again. "Handsome, though," she said, and smiled at Leonard, but he was feeling dazed, uncertain what it meant, how it could've happened.

"Your ma says let's don't name it yet."

She looked confused. "We said a boy's going to be called after you."

He squatted low to be near her. "If he might not make it, we can save the name." His voice had a quaver.

She shook her head, her eyes glistening. "He isn't finished, is all. For heaven's sake, Leonard, he only just got here. Give him half a chance!"

He put his face into the pillow next to her temple and hot tears came out his eyes. He tried to catch himself but could not. She put her hand in his hair and held his head and let him have his minute, and when he was finished she knew he was embarrassed by it and she found some thread of a sunny voice inside herself and said, "You know what I want?"

He sat up and shook his head.

"If you would go to town and tell Mrs. L we have a boy now, and wouldn't it please me for her to come let me show him off."

HE WENT TO Perley and gave the message and then went on down to the river and found the barge and put himself into whiskey, wondering why he'd ever let it alone. Put himself into drink deep enough that he could not say what it was that ate at him or why he cared. By the second day the Indian boy made a fire and cooked him a rabbit and cornbread and refused him drink if he wouldn't eat. He ate the food, and then he drowned it. Had the damaged seed of his daddy, and where'd he get the idea he was better? Got his wife a cripply scrap of a thing ought to be tied in a sack and sunk in a bucket.

Her ma was quiet about it. Rugnel invited the preacher to come, but nobody said a thing outright about the baby's being off or the daddy gone missing. After three days Esther took the boy home, saying Leonard would pull himself together and she wanted to be there so they could start their new life as close to what they'd planned as possible. Hjalmer took her in the sulky.

The house was empty. She lit a fire and lined a pan with rags and put the boy in it and set him on the warming shelf. There was no time to ask herself was this the child she wanted. If Leonard was weak, she would be twice as strong. Their boy needed to be fed and cradled and cleaned and kept warm. That he was afflicted didn't mean you could not love him just as much, and maybe more. He would have need of it.

The first she knew of Leonard's return was catching sight of him at work in the barn the next morning. She put the skillet on, fried up some hash and beans, and called across the yard, "Got breakfast here."

He washed at the pump and came in and sat himself at the table, looking like barrel dregs, wet with the smell of whiskey and sweat, his eyes red and baggy and his hands shaky. He'd been gone four days.

She dished the meal and sat across the table with her coffee. "Not going to ask where you been."

He nodded.

She waited for him to say.

He forked in the hash, not returning her gaze and not saying.

"Well, where in blue blazes you been, then?" She hadn't meant to raise her voice. "And then come back and sit to breakfast like it was Sunday morning and no chores before noon, thank you, ma'am. I had a baby, Leonard! You are my husband!"

He wiped the back of his hand over his mouth and looked at her. He was not a fit man for her, and now she knew it. "He still breathing?"

"Go look!" She pointed to where the boy was asleep in his pan.

He just nodded, staying put. "Didn't think he was going to make it."

"Leonard, he wasn't what we planned, but he's what we got. He's our boy to raise up."

He sniffed and tried to clear his vision. He had meant to apologize, but he would come apart if he tried it. Didn't know how to raise up a cripply boy, either, but didn't know how to say it.

She stood up. She wasn't some kind of diviner, see into a man's mind. "Did you think I was going to throw him away and start over?" She shook her head.

"Just didn't think he was going to make it."

"Of course he's making it. Comes out of you and me. Couldn't be any other way but strong." She gave him a hard look, make it sink in.

He nodded.

"Got to believe it," she said.

"All right." He reached his hands across the table for hers.

She sat down. Would like to have strangled him, but tried to let it go. She gave up a long breath. "I was thinking we could name him Gabriel. After the archangel."

He wiped his eyes on his sleeve. "Gabriel's all right, if that's what you want."

For the county record, without telling her husband, she had them write the name in full, Leonard Gabriel Crummey. The boy had a father, and she meant to see it written so.

FOR THE FIRST two months, he made her keep the boy wrapped in a blanket, just his face showing. She bathed him alone, kneaded his stubbly limbs, and soaped them and urged him to make them grow. When she put a mirror against his middle, she could see him whole. It was a trick. She did it once to show Leonard, "Will you look at that!" but he left the room. She did it for herself, anyway. She told the little one, "Look at the boy!" She showed her ma and pa, saying, "If we all think it will happen, it can." And if the parts didn't grow out completely, maybe they would grow enough for him to be a tough little banty.

What she had not told Leonard, or even Mrs. L, was nothing had come out of her left breast. It swelled up with milk like the right one, but was blocked and ungiving, the flesh around the nipple just a hard knot left by the hognose. The baby suckled only from one side of her, and in this way the truth of his stunting seeped into her, that it was her own blemished hardness that refused to make him whole in the womb, and she could not forgive herself the failure, or say it aloud to her own husband or best friend.

11

February 20, 1899

"Better if you stayed home," she said. "Going to snow again." A stiff wind that blew out of the north all night and drove the mercury under minus twenty had swung around to push up from the southwest and she could smell the moisture on it.

"Hell with the snow, then." He laced up his boots, not bothering to look at her.

"Traps'll still be there tomorrow." If it was truly his traps he was after, not some neighbor's livestock pen.

He pulled on his overcoat. He knew what she was thinking, but there was something he needed to do she did not know about. Even so, he would've gone in to Perley or to see the Indian boy, Daigneault, before holing up in the goddamned house through another blizzard.

He let the door slam and went to the barn and saddled the horse and tied on his rifle and a shovel, going to see about the thing that was busy on his mind, and it wasn't his muskrats. He turned the horse north toward where his trapline was set a couple of miles away on Wolf Creek, past the roller mill and dam. Pulled his scarf over his face. No snow flying, but all signs it was coming on to.

SHE TOOK THE flatiron off the stove and held it close to the glass in the parlor window, working its heat slowly over the sheet of ice that had built up from their breathing and cooking. It turned liquidy and ran down to thicken at the sill, and she could see out again. She sat herself beside the fire and watched the storm move in, a dark wall that swept across the fields and swallowed the house, snow heavy as wool. The boy lay on the floor in the corner, absorbed by four chicks, taking turns putting them inside of a cigar box and telling them to nap. He was already two and a half and busy as a pullet. His own napping box was a Durkee's spice crate. It had been his baby crib and wagon, both. They had put wheels on it and she toted him around at the end of a rope. The sons of city mothers were pushed down paved walks in perambulators. The son of a Perley mother rode in a yellow spice crate and didn't know the difference. He was too big for it now and slept nights on a tick on the floor of his cubby, but for naps he wanted the spice crate and had to curl up to fit.

Esther had steeped tea and laid out her boxes of horsehair on the parlor floor and settled in to making up her eight-strand pulls, picking the hairs according to the colors she needed. The winter before, she'd hitched three hatbands for a man in Fargo who Mrs. L knew of had a haberdashery, and when he received them he sent back what payment she had asked for, along with a friendly note that said he could sell as many as she could make, so last spring and summer she'd gone after it in earnest, cutting clumps from the undersides of her neighbors' horses' tails as well as from Rugnel's horses and her own, combing them out, washing and sorting them into bundles, putting them aside for winter work, which she was glad of having now.

She was as ready to be rid of Leonard for a few hours as he was bent on going. She thought his thieving livestock from the neighbors was ended, but she could not be certain. Plenty of wolf-kill this winter, which is how he had disguised it. He had something gnawing at him today besides getting at his whiskey.

She favored the hairs of her Mister Jones and of a sorrel gelding of Soren Strand's for their rich red, and of her pa's old Joe for its ebony black. Joe had a bushy tail she could take from twice what she got off the others. She sorted her colors. Black, mixed dark browns, reds, mixed light browns, yellows, white. She kept each pull to eight hairs to get a nice, delicate knotwork, and put a hair of Mister Jones somewhere in every hatband, just liking the idea of him getting around so.

She had braided herself mecates and hackamores, too. To make a horsehair rope you spin mane hair into strings one way, twist the strings into strands the opposite, and the opposing twists hold the finished rope from unwinding. Forces against each other get you a thing both of beauty and utility. What she had once thought to find in marriage was nonetheless true in the matter of horsehair rope. A little wear takes off the prickles and you get a soft rein that lies easy on a horse. Hitching was finer work, each knot like a decision you made that cinched into place and added to a pattern you could see only gradually, looking back over the lay of it. The boy's conception. Her marriage. Taking the Pederson place for their own. She watched her fingers form the loops and snug the knots, the diamond pattern slowly widening.

You could say she'd had a pattern in mind but it turned out otherwise. For one, the house was coming apart. The studs were rotted inside the walls. Mold filled the races between them. Moisture softened the plaster in the corners of the parlor and mildew blackened the painted surface like a fever bloom. She'd tried to beat it back, got on her knees with a bucket of bleach and a stiff brush, but the plaster crumbled away under her brush. In the little dormer closet, where the dead wife's things had laid and their boy slept nights, she'd discovered a settling crack wide enough to stick a hand out of doors. Pederson had framed with cottonwood. He'd been stingy with nails and roofing felt, and didn't bother himself to flash sills. She and Leonard could not keep the house warm. Snow and grit blew in through the walls. They banked the foundation with horse manure. She got Leonard to help her shore up a corner post of the porch, and then the cellar stairs, but the decay ran ahead, and they could no sooner catch it than they could catch the rain where it blew in through the sash or the mice that fled the straw tick when they lay down to sleep at night.

She put her work aside, added wood to the fire. Poured a hot cup and watched the storm, which had not let up. She had been lost in her knots; the snow was easily six inches already. She sat down and stretched the piece of work and picked out a red pull to put a line inside the diamond. A thin line of red, not so much for show as conviction.

Leonard was more than a fit farmer when he was willing to work it her way. That first year they got sixteen bushels an acre of wheat, thinking it was their own cleverness that did it. They put the earnings down on a plow and five acres each of barley and oats, but '97 was a letdown, twelve bushels. 'Ninety-eight was worse yet. When they sat down and subtracted their costs, they had lost money. Leonard pushed the paper off the table in disgust.

"Farming's walking backward up a hill when you could a gone around it if you'd turned and opened your eyes."

"There's good years and bad," she said.

"That's what I'm saying. We get one penny extra, we shove it back in the dirt, meaning we got to worry over it all year and hope it comes up again so we can do the same next year, when like as not it won't. Why bother?"

Tell the truth, he had become a hard husband. Never approached a thing head-on, and was something of a conniver. She did not begrudge his name on the deed to the farm, but his private thought and twist of mind was a knot between them. More since their boy was born, he was all to himself, his jug, and his friend the Indian boy, setting her apart with her own want for companionship, a thing that had grown into a longing. Longing for a communion was how she put it, and when she'd confessed it to Mrs. L, Mrs. L had said, "Looking for the part of us that's missing. Woman looks at a man and thinks she sees herself. Can no man crawl inside a your skin and be for you. Not capable of it. God hung a trowel on a man, don't care what furrow he digs, while a woman's looking for him to crawl inside a her like the Holy Ghost into the Virgin, fill her up. Complete her. Kindred soul. Kindred soul of a woman can only be another woman, is the Maker's little joke. You want to get past it."

SHE WAS CAUGHT short by a shriek from the boy, who set into wailing.

"What is it, honey?" She went to him and found one of the chicks had fallen into a crack of the floor and was cheeping frantically. "For heaven's sake." She knelt and tried to pry it out with her finger.

Gabe put his head in her way, trying to help and suggesting, "Stick, stick, stick!"

She went into the kitchen and took one from the kindling. She poked it into the crack and the chick came free and began to run across the floor, but Gabe snatched it and rolled over to his cigar box with it and popped it inside, gleeful.

The boy had been a surprise in every way. He had a mop of blond curls and a quick smile and never fussed unless he was hungry or had the croup. Mrs. L had said, Wait until he gets to be two, he'll be a regular little tyrant by two, but it wasn't so at all. From the minute he could sit up, whenever she toted him in his spice box he threw his head back to laugh and make faces at strangers. At home, he scootched through the kitchen and parlor sidewise on his normal hand and foot. She would watch him, feeling proud and uneasy both, because it was such a cripply way of moving he had invented. Leonard's eyes were opened one day when the boy turned his Durkee's box over in the kitchen, climbed atop of it, and from there finagled himself up onto his daddy's chair where he could reach his hand up to the table and snitch a piece of bread.

"Did you see that?" Leonard said. "We got us a little thief!"

"Wonder who he takes after."

Leonard started bringing the boy found things when he came indoors, coon's skull or a beetle off the stoop. The boy squealed at each new thing and made up how to play with it, which got Leonard down on his knees, telling what the thing was and how it worked. When he noticed her grinning at seeing him sprawled on the floor one day, he snapped, "Boy's smarter than you take him for."

"I see that," she said.

SHE FELT THE wind beat against the house. Time to carry water, but she made no move to do it. A horse will not drink in a storm. The chickens would keep another hour.

Her chickens were her solace and amusement. Amusement she justified by the sorely needed earnings from eggs she sold to the baker and traded at the mercantile, and, in the wintertime, sold to her neighbors whose hens were in molt. She'd spent some of her egg money to make a proper chicken house, getting Hjalmer to help her adapt a pattern she found in an old magazine. It was ten feet by twenty-six, set over a dug floor which they layered with gravel and clay to absorb the stink of the droppings. She cleaned and tarred the roosts, dusted the broody hens for insects, spread lime wash and creosote to keep out the red mites, and threw her excess cockerels into the pot the end of May.

She read what she could find about chickens and asked the rest of Flint at the feed store. She learned to overlap her new chicks with the older hens to get a steady supply of eggs. August was critical that the pullets come along at a pace but not too fast, Flint said. Feed hard grain to slow them down or ground bone to push them ahead, get them all laying in late September if she could, and sure enough, last year by October, when prices began to rise, they were into the full swing. In December, Esther's eggs brought three times what they fetched in April and she had plenty to sell.

She was not one to name the chickens, but her tiny General was the exception, a runt cockerel she named for the "Little General," Tom Thumb. He was out of one of the Silver Spangled Hamburgs' eggs she'd had Flint order, the last to pip. She'd watched the egg, finally saw the little beak poke through. Not so strong as the others, and she watched it get two-thirds around the shell, losing ground, the little yellow beak pecking air, gasping. She should have thrown it out. She was not against killing, but she found it very hard to kill an egg. It was too tired to turn its head and peck at the shell. She knew better than try and help. Break him out, and he will bleed to death. The little thing rested and tried again, and finally she could no longer help herself, went and found a small scissors and a pair of tweezers and began to pick away the tiniest bits of shell and cut away the membrane for him. She could see he was a small one. Each time a spot of blood appeared she quit, gave it time to dry up. It took her half of the morning, and what came out when she was done! The neck was crooked like a finger so its head looked sideways, too weak to stand, just laid on its side peeping faintly and looking up at her. She tried twice inside of an hour to throw it away but could not bring herself to do it.

The chick was able to stand that afternoon and walked in little circles that slowly grew wider until he bumped into the feed and water she had put down. He ate twice what she expected, and slowly got his head straighter.

Her little General grew to have fat wattles and an ermine coat studded with black spangles. She put him out with the others, but he watched for her, followed her around the house and yard, nudged her to scruffle his cowl with her fingers. If she set a fork against the garden fence, he flew up to sit on the handle, full of himself as the governor. If she sat, he flew up to her head and tried to crow. "Look at him," she would call to Leonard, who shrugged his shoulders so-what.

"Cupboard love," Mrs. L had said dismissively. "Not good for the animal not to know it's a chicken," she said, as if to say Esther was going soft on her flock, where in fact she culled and tended them scrupulously, making producers of all her keepers—

With a start she realized she had forgotten their water. She glanced at the clock—ten-thirty. She pulled on her boots and jacket and opened the door to the storm. The wind slammed the door open against the wall, nearly threw her off balance. She set the water bucket at the pump and looked out at the yard while she sawed at the handle. The barn was a vague darkness, and she could not even make out the chicken house; she wondered where Leonard was holed up at. It had been a blizzardy February. The storm of the week before had piled the drifts so deep some of the neighbors went in and out of their upstairs windows. Beyond their own barn a drift had crested twenty-five or thirty feet high. She took the bucket in one hand, stepped off the porch into ten inches of fresh snow, and shuffled to make a little trail to the corner of the barn. The sawbuck was fattened with batting, the privy wore a fleece hat, the raspberry canes swooned. In some places the new snow added on to the old deep enough to swallow a well house or hog barn. Would be a floody April, certain.

LEONARD HAD JUST reached the edge of the woods by the creek when the snow struck. He worked his way down the fields, watching through the storm for the opening in the trees where he liked to tie the horse. He and the horse had a trail they kept more or less passable along a line fronting the big drifts piled up in the lee of the woods. His snares had given mostly disappointment, the muskrats few and Leonard's snares crude, but several weeks earlier he'd spotted two sets of dog tracks crossing the creek ice. He guessed they were brush wolves. It had been a winter of wolving at the chickens and sheep around Perley and maybe this was the pair responsible. Maybe the reason for the muskrats being scarce. The bounty was a full fifteen dollars the female, a price that gripped a man's attention. Male or a pup would still get you five.

The day that he first spotted the tracks he had followed them downstream until he found the den burrowed into the bank, and then he was patient a full week until he got a clear look at them and saw she was a bitch in whelp. Answer to his prayers. He came back the next day before dawn and laid behind a deadfall alongside of the creek where the male liked to cross. He'd wanted to kill it away from the den, make it easier to go at the whelps when she finally gave them. He did not wait a half hour, the dog came at a trot. Leonard was not yet into his jug that day. He took a bead, pulled the trigger, got off a clean shot, and dropped it dead at fifty feet. He lugged it home across his horse, and it must've weighed fifty, fifty-five pounds. He skinned it out that night, his mind full of the she-wolf and the litter inside her belly.

The bounty agent had whistled. "Where'd you get him at?"

"South of Kirkebo a half a mile," Leonard had said, lying comfortably. Where's its bitch was what the man wanted to ask. Leonard did not intend anyone else to get her. Took his five dollars and gave it to his wife, proof his fur trade was providing, but all the while he was thinking that to earn as much with the snares would have taken a month of muskrats and a lot of fooling with wire in the snow.

He had kept to himself about the female, going back every few days. Today, once again, despite the snow falling heavy now, he came at the den from above and behind, and when he got close, he finally heard the sound he had been listening for, the squeal of new pups. From the noise, he guessed there might be five or six. He wiped his nose on his sleeve and felt the delicious predicament before him. Should he shoot the bitch in the den or wait for her to come out? For one thing, he did not know how deep she was. He knelt in the snow and hung his face over the hole's edge very quiet. Blood rushed to his face as he lowered his head for a view. For the effort he got himself a world of stink and nothing to see but frost from their breathing and a tunnel of darkness. Say he took a shot blind and did not kill her, would she come after him? Or, come to think of it, would she have another way out of the hole? He was not about to risk it. Better to shoot her in daylight. He looked around for a perch, and decided to have a sip and wait awhile. She would come out when she was hungry.

He set himself onto a low tree limb with his rifle across his lap. Ordinarily he made himself wait on the jug until ten o'clock, but not under present conditions. He took a long pull to help keep warm sitting still.

HIS WOLVING HAD probably started with the first animal he took, which was one of Oftedahl's chickens. That was well after his wife had given him the damaged boy; after the letdown crop of '98 and Rugnel instructing him to pay on the mortgage first before anything, hunger's the human condition, God forbid you lose the land; it was about the time that he saw the truth of his situation, that he was not working for himself, and the harder he did it, borrowing for seed, working to plant more of his land, the poorer and more stretched he got, tight as a fence wire.

This was just last fall. Seemed longer ago by how it soured things between them and Essie's father.

After the piss-poor harvest and the plowing, on the first day they could take the time, he and Esther had driven the buckboard to Perley to lay in some of what they could not provide on their own. They were the only customers in the mercantile, but the missus at the till did not lift a finger to help them find what they needed. She just stood there with her lips clamped, waiting to take their money. After a while, they put their things on the counter and Leonard said, "We'll take it on credit again."

The missus gave them a look like wouldn't-you-just-know-it and trotted into the back for her mister. When they came out the mister looked a long time at Esther, not unfriendly. He was one she traded her eggs with. The missus stood beside him with a face like Leonard had asked did she mind if he dropped his drawers and took his ease onto the floor in front of her glass display. The mister said, "We can take credit again today, but we will need to see some cash next time." He raised his eyebrow to make sure they heard. They heard.

It would've been one thing if he'd said it to Leonard, what did Leonard care, but he did not. Had raised his eyebrow and said it straight to Essie. It was not Essie's fault they were in need any more than Essie had control of the weather or the price of wheat. Leonard liked to have poked a fist across and emptied the bastard's mouth of his teeth.

They'd got in the wagon and giddyapped the horse toward home. A silence sat between them like a bad smell, and when some of Oftedahl's Plymouth Rocks fluttered out onto the road Leonard stopped and reached down quick and grabbed himself one, knocked its head on the wheel rim. "Oh, damn!" he said. "Just run over a hen. Better cook chicken tonight."

Esther rode over the next day to give one of her best hens in payment, saying they'd hit the Oftedahl bird with the wagon, a lie to cover for her husband, whose behavior she decided not to think about.

That, and drinking with the half-breed Daigneault one day in October while Daigneault was fixing up his traps for winter, was what gave Leonard the idea. The Indian was saying you got to check your traps every two or three days, or the brush wolves'll clean them out for you. That was the exact moment the idea hit him. He got himself a stick and drove four nails through the end to imitate a wolf's claw. He sneaked into Soren Strand's sheep pen that night, knocked one of the ewes cold, and then mauled her open with his claw. He clubbed another and dragged it away, leaving the first to bleed itself empty there in the pen. From that night, once or twice a week, he was into the yard or barn or stock pen at a different farm, helping himself to a pig or what was available. He skinned them out and sold them to Daigneault, who had a butcher in Georgetown who wasn't particular where his meat came from and sold the hides with his furs to whichever company gave him the best price, which was lately Northwestern Hide.

Word of the wolving spread through the valley like worry through wheat. It was uncommon early for wolves, before snow drove them south, but everybody said they were getting to be a problem, the taste of easy meat.

He should have been more careful, but it was the first successful business he had ever set up. One night, in his jug and feeling full of his cleverness, he slipped back of Strand's sheep pen again, could not help himself, it was too damned easy, but this time Strand's dogs caught scent of him and raised the roof. It was Leonard's bad luck that Strand happened to be coming up the road. When Leonard fled the sheep pen and ran smack into him, Strand had a stick raised to clobber whatever came out.

"Whoa, Soren," Leonard said, out of breath.

"Leonard? What the hell?"

"Chased in here on the trail of a wolf," Leonard said. "It was going for your sheep, I think."

Strand lowered his stick, studied Leonard in the darkness. Strand was the kind of man that got Leonard's back up. He ran a successful operation and was always happy to tell you how he did it.

"What's that in your hand?"

Leonard held the claw of nails. "Nothing," he said. "Something I made to protect myself."

Strand spit in disgust. "I ain't a fool, Leonard. If you're short of meat, say so and we will give you some. But you come poaching my animals again, I will be laying for you. You will be lucky if you can tell your name to the sheriff after I'm done."

The next day before noon Rugnel hollered into the front door of the Crummey house. "Where's Leonard at?"

"Barn," Esther said. "Why?" Her pa was not in the habit of coming by.

Rugnel strode to the barn, Esther chasing behind.

"Strand says you've been stealing livestock," he said.

"Pa!" Esther said.

"Strand's a liar," Leonard said. "I tried to save a sheep of his, so he calls me a thief. That what you think I am?"

Esther got between them, turned on her father, red-faced and shaking. "Shame on you! My husband!"

Rugnel looked down at his daughter, his face tight. "Your husband's a drunk, Essie." He looked hard at Leonard. "Strand's a sackload of talk but he's no liar. Do it again, I will be the first to turn you in." He turned and walked out of the barn.

"Strand's a bastard!" Leonard hollered. "He wants this farm is all. Trying to set you against me."

Rugnel mounted his horse and cantered out the drive.

Leonard slammed his fist against the stable wall. Why'd he ever go back to Strand's place? It was his rule: you don't go back where they'll be on the lookout. Such a sweet goddamned business he had himself, and now this.

Esther grabbed Leonard's wrist. "What are you at? Say it. Have you been taking Strand's animals?"

"What I am at is my owned damned business. Am at trying to make a living. Am at trying to pay on the land so your pa won't chew my head off. Am at trying to keep the house dry, feed the boy. What are you at, you and your little runt cockerel and fancy chickens, so special they got to have their own tickets to ride up on the train from St. Paul?"

"You want to think about it, Leonard," she said. "Because I will not abide it. Any number of things you and I can do to keep above water, and I am not above the meanest, if it's honest. And if in one year or another we cannot manage, my family will see us through. But we are not thieves, and if that does not sit with you, it was my mistake. The boy and I'll go to my mother's and you thieve until they catch you. I will not be a part of it."

"Don't be stupid," he said. "Ain't a thief." He sniffed, wishing to make it so. "Don't talk that way."

She turned and ran back to the house, let the door slam.

After that, it settled down, but cool and uneasy. Why is it I never hear you hum anymore? is the question that slowly formed, the question Leonard would have asked if it didn't sound so simple-minded, because the fact had been on his mind a good deal. How things were sitting between them. Cool and uneasy.

THE POACHING HAD been a good sideline, but he'd had to give it up then. The Indian boy set him to laying muskrat snares. The same team of oxen that pulled the Minnesota end of the Perley bridge up to high ground before spring breakup pulled Daigneault's barge out of the river for the winter, and the boy lived on it in the woods where it sat across log skids. The boy had set up a little lean-to out of scrap wood beside the boat where he skinned out and stretched and salted his pelts and hung them to dry. "Small sac a yellowish juice near the sex part a the female," the boy said. "You squeeze it into a little jar or whatever you got, and after you have set your snare, sprinkle it all over. Brings the old chief in right where you want him." Snaring turned out to be fussy work, though, and Leonard was not good at it. The best winter rat pelts paid thirteen cents. He could be catching more with a line of number one spring traps, but it took three pelts to buy one, and he'd want a dozen at least.

THE SNOW DID not let up. He brushed it off his legs and shook his feet to try and warm up. He was a man in need of an idea, married to a woman who would not sit still for failure. The strong ones move along, was his sense of women. Felt her slipping through his fingers. He'd done roadwork to pay his poll tax. He asked after work in the harness shop, the mortuary, and the hotel. Stopped at the blacksmith, who was known in three counties for his knives. No extra hands required. One day he got the idea to cut firewood for sale and he set himself to sawing trees at an empty lot along the Red, but the railroad section boss heard about it, came by to tell him it was company property and get the hell off it.

Daigneault had said why didn't the two of them expand the whiskey business with three or four barges parked near to some of the other towns, and Leonard was not sure it was a bad idea if he had the money for it, which he did not. Since the train had come up the valley in the eighties and the farmers quit barging their grain you could have yourself any number of boats cheap enough, but cheap wasn't free, and it cost money to run them. He and the boy had spun it out in their talk, how they would set up and run it, who they might have live on the boats and sell the product.

Daigneault had managed his own business all right since the gimp had been killed. The gimp had been strangulated. Daigneault came back one night, found him blue-faced on the floor of the hut with a wire around his neck. The gimp had gotten free with some of the local women and the boy had himself a short list of suspects, but could not say which one it was. The boy had wanted to talk about it, and it was during the next couple of months they had got to enjoy each other's conversation so much, even stripping naked together one steamy night and holding hands to pick their way through the silt and deadfalls of the shallows into the current of the river to cool down, just their heads above water and the flash of their limbs. That was the night that the boy'd offered his ass, and Leonard had said, "No, thank you," taking care to do so politely. Boy's ass did not interest him. Boy's whiskey did, however. Whiskey trade had fallen off for a week after word of the gimp's murder, but then resumed. The boy made arrangements with the supplier and no longer took it through the Perley store, which meant it cost him more, he said, but with the gimp dead he did not require as much profit on the business. The boy was free with it for the pleasure of Leonard's company.

It was the evening that they swam and afterward lay on the deck of the boat to dry off that Leonard had come to see his situation in a new light. The boy had a few yards of cheesecloth that he pitched when the mosquitoes were out. They lay close beneath, Leonard's manhood was restless, and the boy repeated his offer.

Leonard said, "Matter of fact, I was thinking, I am naked as a bone on your little floating whorehouse and not a woman in a half a mile."

"Might like it better," the boy said. A little curl had come into his voice like the creeper on a bittersweet.

"Would be easier if I did," Leonard said, thinking his life had worked into a snag somehow, enjoying the boy as easily as he did but caught by a hunger for Essie he could not satisfy. "Cannot say why I don't. Am your old bull muskrat still nosing the bank for cunt when he's blind and half dead. Do not understand it, though. More you try, harder it is to keep it. Essie's going to slip away, and I cannot say why or know how to stop it."

Daigneault lay silent a minute. "Female of any animal wants the same thing," he said. "A nest to suckle her young in is all," and Leonard was struck by the truth of it—he had never thought of it this way, as the animal part that she was powerless over. The key to the riddle of his satisfying her, that she needed him to be her provider when all along she'd acted otherwise, and the starkness of this understanding, taken with whiskey, circled the conversation back to Leonard's money problem and ways to solve it, most ideas lying out of reach for lack of capital.

IT TOOK THE bitch wolf almost four hours to show herself, too hungry to be careful, and when Leonard saw her nose poke out he fumbled for his gun. His hands were too cold to follow orders. She saw him and lit out. His shot went wide, knocked her head over heels but she was up and disappeared by the time he got down off of the tree limb.

Shit and goddamned son of a bitch! His own legs gave out after so long in the tree, and the whiskey made his head cottony. He stumbled in the deepening snow a couple of minutes to get his balance and feel the truth of it sink in. She'd got away.

He emptied his bladder against the tree and shook his sorry head. Chrissake! Got his shovel and went over to the hole and commenced a fury of digging. The hole was lined with white from their breath. The first parts came out in big chunks where the earth was frozen, but the freeze did not penetrate far on account of the heavy blanket of snow, and maybe from the heat of the animals themselves. The deeper he got the easier it went and the more noise and stench the whelps raised, the dirt flying off his shovel, the work of it warming him up so that he got to sweating from the labor of it, wet through. He set the shovel down to rest a minute, heard something on the bank above him. He glanced up at precisely the moment to catch a sight wholly unexpected: the bitch was lunging from above, throwing herself down upon him, her jaws wide and her lips drawn back. He dodged to the side, grabbed for the shovel, but she caught him at the shoulder and they tumbled over. Mother of Jesus! He twisted, figuring himself for a goner, but damned if he didn't scramble away and turn himself around and get an angle with the shovel. He walloped her as hard as he could up side the head with the flat of the blade and then rolled and reached for his gun. She backed into the hole snarling and barking, like she would drive him off, but he had the gun now. Took his aim, let a beat pass to steady his hands, and shot her square in the face. She rose up and fell back. Collapsed into the mouth of the hole, her head slumped into the snow, just a trickle of blood. Leonard allowed himself to breathe. He walked over and kicked her to make good and sure, then pulled her out of the hole by the front legs. His first shot had taken a piece of her haunch, and lucky for him. Would have been touch and go, she'd had all her strength.

Well. He straightened out his clothes and wiped his nose on his sleeve. He had him the she-wolf after all. He felt light-headed, all that effort on top of the whiskey. Wasn't she a sneaking bitch to come down from the top of the bank like that, take him by surprise from his own trail.

The day was growing dark. Midafternoon, he guessed. He went up the creek to where he'd left the horse, surprised at how deep the snow was, even on the trail. He led the horse down and hefted the she-wolf up onto it behind the saddle, guessing her at forty pounds, and roped her good. Then he set to finish digging out the nest. It didn't take him but two minutes and he turned up a whole pile of furry gray pups. He could not believe his luck. He grabbed for two or three, but they were squirmy and shitted his hands, so he took one, knocked its head good on the flat of the shovel, and tossed it into the gunnysack. Grab, knock, toss. When he was done, he washed his hands in the snow, feeling giddy with fortune. He put his gun and shovel up and held the neck of the gunnysack as he climbed into the saddle. He settled it safe between his legs and felt the dead pups' warmth spread across his lap. He had not told Esther what he was up to. He wanted to surprise her with it if he was successful, and save having to explain if he was not. Felt like a man bringing home salvation.

Outside the woods, no landmarks were visible. He steered the horse left where he reckoned the trail should be, keeping the darkness of the woods over his shoulder so as to follow the creek; follow the creek, you cannot get lost. When the horse stumbled in deeper snow he reined it right a little to stay out of the drifts. The horse knew the way. It was the kind of blizzard'll take a man out of sheer meanness. After twenty-five minutes the darkness of the woods fell away and different shadows loomed. He'd reached the mill and dam. He stopped to read the wind and decide should he hole up in the mill or turn away from the creek and chance it. He was glad of the warmth of the whelps. He felt at peace with the inconvenience of the storm, with the rawness of his wet clothing and the chill that had started to shake him at his sides. None of it counted. He could see the disbelief in her face over what he'd managed to do, and he turned south where the road should be, wanting to get there and show her. It was a godforsaken flat damn country. He could be anywhere and nowhere. He goaded the horse with his heels. Out of the shelter of the woods the wind bit against his right side, crusted his eyebrows with ice and made his forehead ache.

TWICE SHE THOUGHT she heard him and she stepped out the front door, but it was the noise of the wind. She picked up a shovel and cleared a path from the porch to keep busy, thinking he might appear, but he did not come and she went inside and dabbled at her hitching and imagined if he got lost and froze in a ditch and she woke up a widow what would she and the boy do. Rugnel was set against Leonard like lodged wheat, how could she ask his help?

She put the hitching down; the light had grown too dim for it.

If Leonard were dead, she supposed, one, Rugnel would apologize, and two, Jess would ask her and the boy to move home. But Esther was not sure she could do it. In the house of her father, it was her own failure she would daily be reminded of.

The boy fussed in his crate where he napped. She checked his diaper and changed it for a fresh one. She took off his shoes. Her mother and she had secretly bought two matching pairs of red buckskin shoes by mail order, so that he had one that fit each foot. Esther threw away the extra small shoe and wrapped the extra full-sized one in a neckerchief and hid it in a drawer for when he grew to fit it.

She tickled his bare feet, first his normal side to make him laugh and then his shrunken side to help make it grow, although he lacked touch on that side. She talked to him about his five strong horses, a little game she played with his fingers and toes, made him smile. She had a liniment of eucalyptus that Mrs. L had found out about and got for her, and she rubbed some into his stubbly limbs, singing:

Row, row to fishing-reef
All little children sleep.
No one knows where Daddy lies
Below the billows deep.

Row, row to fishing reef
Old Daddy's fast asleep.
Among the many fish they took
From the salty deep.

She tucked his feet back into his perfect shoes and wrapped him in his blanket and put away the liniment and pulled his little wagon cradle into the kitchen. She added wood to the fire and set to heating water to boil potatoes for supper, and that's when she finally heard it for certain. Leonard's holler from the yard.

"Come out 'n see what I brought you."

She caught her breath and pulled on her coat and stepped out the door. He was on his horse, whitened with snow and ice, sack in his lap and an animal tied on behind.

"Was worried you might be getting lost."

He pulled loose a rope and let the mother slide off the horse to the ground. "There's fifteen dollars," he said.

Her eyes were big. "Where'd you kill a wolf?"

"Bitch to the dog I took two weeks ago at the creek," he said, reaching into the sack.

"Oh—she must a had little ones!" Esther said with alarm, seeing the bitch's loose belly and swollen teats.

"They's what I've been waiting for. Look here." Leonard pulled out a pup. "Plus five dollars for each whelp! This one makes twenty," he said. The pup landed against the belly of its mother.

"Oh!" Esther cried in distress.

He tossed another, "Twenty-five." Another, "Thirty." The pups piled up against their mother.

"Stop it!" She crouched and gathered up the limp pups.

"Thirty-five." Was more money than they had seen in months. "Forty." He ran the addition forward and backward in his head, see if he was making a mistake.

"Leonard!" she screamed from where she was picking them up.

He gave her a look of surprise and his hand stopped where it was drawing another from the sack.

She tried to reach up for it but could not do it without spilling the five others from her arms.

He saw her eyes were wet. He was confused by what she was saying.

"No need to throw them is all," she was able to say at last.

"Oh." He looked into the sack. "There's four more, making nine in all. Guess what it adds to."

She shook her head, the tears streaming now. Whelps become wolves, it is certain, but tell me who have they harmed? They are but pups at the teat!

"Sixty dollars." It was a sum he himself could not believe. It seemed wholly correct that she was overcome, and her tears filled him up: to see in her eyes a gratitude for his accomplishment beyond any words she could find.

12

The big flood hit at the last of March. A hot south wind caught late winter still heavy on the land, a winter of such snows as to collapse roofs, strand travelers, and suffocate livestock. It was the winter of Leonard's getting paid to dig out the train at Lamb's Siding, the winter of his uncommon luck with wolves, all of it ended by an untimely blast of summer that rushed the snowmelt ahead of the thaw, swelling Wolf Creek and breaking the ice into floes as wide as two or three hayracks, the ice and water piling downstream, uprooting trees and bullying on into the Red. The melt happened in the space of two days, a surge of water and ice the Red could not carry off to Manitoba, which was still locked in winter. The ice jammed sometime the evening of the twenty-ninth south of Grand Forks and piled itself into a mile-long dam. The blocked river rose four feet in less than an hour, overflowing the banks to race across the darkened fields and farmsteads.

They had slept with the window open that night for the first time in months, and thank God, because it was the horses that woke Esther at four in the morning, whinnying and kicking their stalls. There was a roar from somewhere that she'd been hearing in her sleep, and now she knew what: Wolf Creek storming out of its cut. The smell of meltwater poured through the window, drove out six months' stink of chimney weep.

"Git quick!" She pushed Leonard awake. "It's the water!"

They scrambled out.

"You drive the horses to Pa's while I move the chickens."

He pulled on his pants but she didn't take time to dress, ran down the stairs and pulled on her boots and banged out the door in her nightgown, stepping off the porch into inky water above her ankles, the night sky shining off much of the farmyard already in flood, the water swirling around the corners of the buildings, making a truckly sound like a living thing, carrying along bits of straw and ice.

The birds were in a fright, squawking from the roosts. Her General raced back and forth above the door, flapping at the water to scare it back. She got a flame to the lantern and tried to calm them with talk while she reached here and there for them, catching their legs and ferrying them two and three at a time across the yard, the birds hanging upside down, flapping their wings, her feet blind in the water, the yard still frozen beneath it. Inside the barn she climbed the ladder high enough to toss the birds into the loft, where they skittered free, squawking and acting dazed. She went back and forth to the chickens while he hitched the plow horses into the wagon and tied Mister Jones behind.

"Wait and see what we can salvage," she hollered.

"Was going to," he said. "Don't see me pulling away, do you?"

They loaded up tools, grain sacks, anything lying around the barn that was too good to let soak, which was not a lot. When he was ready, the horses refused to git until he slapped them hard, and then he was off, the end of the driveway swallowed up already, the roadway outlined by low walls of crusted snow that still stuck above the water but would not last for long. They were lucky not to have sheep, pigs, or cattle to move. They were lucky to have waked up, rate the water was coming.

Esther waded around the yard in the dawning light tying up anything that looked like it might wash away. The big drifts were gone gray and shrunken away from the buildings, dead swans settling into the flood. She had to hunt up twine and tie some scrap wood into a floating fence to corral what was left of their firewood pile. Leonard got back shortly after six A.M., brought by Hjalmer in the undertaker's rowboat. "Thirty pigs drowned in Jensen's barn," Hjalmer said. "Ma says you three come stay at our place. Here." He held out a sack.

She pulled the boat to the porch, looked in the sack. It was bread and cheese. "Coffee's just come at a boil," she said. The water was more than calf deep.

"Need you to row me down at the crossing, Hjalmer," Leonard said.

"No, sir. Steen'll have a conniption if I don't get the boat right back. Ma made him let me take it to collect Essie and Gabe. Sis, Steen says the main channel's choked with whatever you can name. Half of Fargo's come to Perley, including the paving blocks off the streets!"

"Can all float to purgatory," Leonard said. He climbed out but Hjalmer stayed put in the boat while Esther poured him a coffee to warm his hands. The three of them looked out at the world unveiled by daybreak. Cottonwoods the size of locomotives pushed into the fields. Was unnatural.

"Tell Ma we'll be all right here." She didn't speak her mind, which

Hjalmer and Leonard knew anyway. It was not her pa's invitation. Her pa would not have Leonard under his roof. Esther wouldn't have wanted it, anyway. Leonard was no longer secretive about his whiskey.

"Hell's bells. You and the boy go on," Leonard said. "I'll keep the chickens."

"Not likely. If a chicken was a jug, you would," she said. "Take some eggs, though," she said to her brother.

"I'll come back soon's there's a boat free, see what you need, or if you change your mind, bring you home."

They watched him row off. The current past the corner of the barn nosed the rowboat north, but he got it straight and lifted a hand goodbye and was over the road and into the next field, pulling strong.

They went inside, cooked up eggs and porridge. They were hungry from the night and she cut a thick slab of ham into a fry pan. "May have to move into the barn," she said. They had been stretching her egg money and his wolving bounty and muskrats and whatever her mother gave them out of her cellar, like the ham. Hadn't seen a red cent for the hatbands she'd mailed off to Fargo.

"No way to cook in the barn."

"It makes no difference, if the kitchen's swimming," she said. "Going to come right on up inside here, is my guess."

After breakfast he would've liked to spend a while in the shitter with his thoughts, but it was flooded. He used the pot and dumped his business out the parlor window, looking down to make sure it swept north, which it did, then he brought a chair out of the kitchen to the porch and sat down and tipped back against the kitchen wall to watch the show. There wasn't anything going to be the same after this. Rules would all be different. Some high and mighty folk were going to come down a notch. There was going to be a chance at something, if only a man could see what.

Gabe woke up and she brought him out to see. The water spread out westward past Perley and the tree line of the channel, clear to the horizon. The hot wind had come up again while they ate and now waves spooled down with the current, made it seem like the buildings were all steaming south on a big open lake.

"That wind feels like something's wrong," she said.

"Something is."

They sat in their shirtsleeves and listened to the water lick at the house and marked the line of wet as it crept upward. They chewed at the bread that Jess had sent, not hungry so much as all-overish, nothing to be done. Gabe scuttled inside and came back on his wooden horse to watch and fiddle with the horse's reins.

"Looks like we're sinking," she said.

"It's the water is rising."

"Oh, hell, I know that. I'm just saying it feels like we're going down."

"S'pose we are in a way, seeing whatever we do makes no difference."

The bitterness in his voice turned her head. She saw he was at it already. The day was early, but then they had been up for hours. "What we do is the only thing makes any difference at all."

He turned and looked her square. "If this is farming, I ain't in favor."

She did not reply. He looked back at the situation. "You cannot plow a river bottom, Essie!" His voice was up. "We go to the Cities, we can sign on at the mills or slaughterhouses or get some other kind of business. Everbody who lives in the city has a line of some kind. We would, too, you know sure as I do." Something caught his eye way across onto Oftedahl's fields. "What'n the Sam Hill's that?" Maybe a floating hog house.

She looked but could not tell. "Flood's a thing you live through, Leonard."

"Eating what? Won't be any fields dry enough to plant before harvest." The thing was coming at an angle to the current.

"Pish. Quick spring flood improves the land better than a whole fallow summer. This'll drain off, we'll get seed set before the end of April, you watch."

He pushed off the wall and brought his chair legs down with a bang, threw his bread at the water and shook his head.

"Meanwhile, there'll be cleanup work," she said.

"Shout hallelujah."

"No need to get short with me. It's not my personal flood, Leonard. I am not the one made this land flat or piled the snow up to the eave and put the winds of Hades to it."

"No, but you are the one in this family who requires farming."

Now she turned and looked at him. "You say that once more, I'm going to clobber you." She felt her eyes burn. "I am full up to here of you putting the blame for all your troubles in my lap."

"You let go of farming, you let go of the chief trouble, is what I'm saying."

"A farm gives back what you put in it. If it don't go right for you, maybe you want to look for the answer, and I would suggest you look in the same place you turn for everything else."

He spat over the rail. "I'm only pointing at the truth." If it was grit under her eyelid, all the better he had the nerve to say it. Since she mentioned it, he felt the need of a swallow and took one. He gave her a false grin. He was not going to be shamed by his own wife.

She said, "If you want to acknowledge the kernel of it, anything goes right, it's how clever you are. Anything goes wrong, it's Essie's got her head so deep in the dirt she can't pull it out."

He half laughed, like her getting her hair up made no difference to his day.

This made her want to strangle him. "If you don't want to put in, don't go and marry yourself a farmwife. A little late in your case."

"The farm's a sinkhole, Essie. No end to the mortgage. No end to the work. Prices that don't pay the cost of seed. Your drought. Your flood. God's truth, we would be money ahead empty-handed."

"Don't you think it," she snapped. "Without this farm we have exactly nothing." She wiped her eyes with her sleeve. Tried to get past how he stung her.

They didn't either of them talk.

"Land's the only certain thing you can pass," she said softly.

He said nothing.

"Leonard, if you don't bait trouble it runs off of its own, like floodwater."

"Trouble piles up, Essie. Got to cut it away and run clear before it takes you over."

Shook her head slowly. "There'll be jobs for the Great Northern to clear track. The county's got to grade the roads and clear the ditches. I guess somebody's going to pay for that work."

"Ever farmer in the valley's going to be full of the same ideas this morning. Won't be enough work for all those wanting it. When all creation's trying to sell, there's nobody to buy. That is how it works. Why we aren't making it. We gotta break out of what everbody else is doing."

"We just need to be quicker 'n them is all."

It was a goddamned barge chugging along, a plume of smoke pouring out of a short stack and plucked flat by the breeze.

"I believe it is your friend."

"No fooling!" He got right up out of his chair.

Daigneault stood at the rudder, his boat moving slower than walking speed, and when he got to the crossroad he steered for their place, came right around the windbreak into the Crummey farmyard, the entire Crummey family perched on their porch with their jaws down.

"Here's hoping this water holds," the Indian hollered, "or I will be a cow up to her bag in gumbo." The barge came alongside the porch and the Indian threw a line. Leonard hauled on it until the front end swung around and then he tied on to the porch post, hoping the boat wouldn't pull it off the house.

"It's some excitement out there this morning," Daigneault said. "I brought you this." He picked something raw off the deck, held it up, a skinned carcass that still glistened. "Fat mama coon! Anything 'at climbs trees is settin' in one this morning, free for a potshot. Hello, missus. That's your boy, there, Leonard?" Daigneault reached across and tugged playfully on the reins of the boy's horsey. "Where'd you get them fancy red moccasins?"

Leonard took the coon.

Daigneault said, "Leonard, I come for your help. River's bringing down a wealth a material you could build a small city out of. Roofs. Walls. Timbers. Whole chicken houses. We get out there with some ropes and lay on to it, we'll have us a pile a goods people're going to be needing."

Leonard felt his mood lift at once. "Why didn't you say so?" He untied the line and got aboard. "The coon won't keep, you want to get it in the pot," he said to Esther, and then to Daigneault, "Drive me over to the barn there for my gloves."

SHE MADE THE boy a raft in a basket and floated him like the baby Moses over to the barn when she went to do her chickens. The waters came up inside the house fourteen inches, a lick below the firebox, and she set the boy on the stair and stepped across chairs in the kitchen and did her cooking crouched down before the stove.

Whatever was living in the basement drowned or moved up into the wood-frame walls.

Over the next week the three of them kept to their little room under the eaves unless they were in the barn, or Leonard was off with the Indian, or she and the boy were rowed by Hjalmer over to her ma's for a meal or buckets of drinking water and stories of the flood. Seventy-five houses were swept away at Moorhead. Ole Tangen over in Kragnes lost two horses, seven cattle, all his hogs and chickens, all his seed wheat, and most of his seed oats. At Fargo the Northern Pacific stopped a train over the Red to weight the trestle on its bearings and the structure stayed. All the bridges over the Buffalo were swept away but for one. At Georgetown, the Great Northern agent stepped out onto the river with a maul as the bridge timbers groaned and the pilings cracked and single-handedly broke up the floes that were holding back the water. Saved the bridge. At Perley the station agent was running a dock for the convenience of the few locals with boats. There was not a dry house or business in Perley. Andrew Gunning herded his pigs into the barley bin of his granary and got his horses onto a low straw stack, but when the straw began to give way he took the big doors off his machine shed and set them onto stumps on the granary floor and got the horses up onto that. Oftedahl got his horses onto the manure pile. Others got their animals onto the platforms of the Perley grain elevators. Aldritt moved the entire contents of the Perley store upstairs into the living quarters. Plenty were too stubborn to get their stocks up and paid for it, losing potatoes, oats, flax, wheat, hay, barley, and more. Flint at the feed store lost three thousand bushels of oats and three hundred bushels of seed wheat for want of a place to get it up onto. Loqueshear, the baker, removed himself and his wife to his brother's at Halstad, but the Red simply followed them there. The Ulverson farm stood dry, but you could cast off from the back of the sheds and sail fifteen miles west with no risk of grounding. It was an ocean that could not run off until the river broke up at Pembina, which was always ten or twelve days after the ice was gone at Moorhead.

They laid themselves in under the eaves at night like stowaways, their ship smelling of damp plaster and soot, of sodden clothes. Even the moldering straw of their tick smelled damp. The nights were silent but for scratching and gnawing from inside the walls and ceiling, a hunger sound that might as well have been inside of their heads for how loud it came in the small hours.

"Sounds like rats come up inside of our walls," she said warily.

By the second night the agitation inside of the north wall had been stilled. Night following that, the noise overhead had been stilled. When they searched for sleep on the fifth night there was nothing but a heavy rasp that moved slowly through the walls. Esther said, "By God and Jesus, sounds like a snake through the plaster."

"Snake's a good thing, Essie. Eats the vermin."

Took most of a minute for the snake's length to pass from one cavity into another. "I won't have it in my house. Tomorrow, you find it and get it out."

"I will have a look."

"After that, you go see Soren Strand about the fields by the creek." She had been figuring their situation. "We either need a four-bottom plow or a hired man to put that forty into wheat with the rest, not to mention a loan on the seed. If we take the rent from Strand and put it into seed for the other sixty instead of taking a loan, we can make enough to plant the whole hundred next year."

"What about Oftedahl?" Leonard did not want to sit across from Strand on any kind of business.

"It lies up against Strand's fields, and he's the one who was interested."

Next day, Leonard took a board off the underside of the eaves to look up between a section of rafters, but there was no way to see inside of the walls without tearing them open. They talked about putting in poison or trapping it out with some kind of bait, but thought maybe they ought to wait until after the water so there was someplace for it to go away to. She did not want to drive it out of the walls into the room.

Made her ornery trying to sleep on the other side of a nest of snakes, added to the general exhaustion of the flood.

Each of the next three evenings she asked Leonard, You talk to Strand?, and he said, Been too occupied. In truth, his going to ask something out of Soren Strand was no more likely than a snake leaving warm walls for ice water, but the way she picked at it he had to do something, so on the fourth day he had the Indian boy drive him in search of Strand, but to go it slow so he could get the strength of his jug in him first.

That night when she asked again, he said, "I talked to him."

"And?"

"We're going to work something out."

"When?"

"Tuesday."

"All right, then. He say how much?"

"Needed to talk to his banker. Tuesday he will have a proposal."

"Don't give it to him for nothing, Leonard. Don't hold him up, though, because every dollar he pays is one we won't otherwise have, and we got no use for the acres this year."

"I know."

The flood was already two weeks old by Tuesday and beginning to drain. He left early and she waited all day, but it was midnight before she heard him stumble up the stairs; he could hardly make it. It was a wonder he did not drown himself. He was a dark shape standing over her.

"Well?"

"He's going to plant our lower forty." His tongue was thick. He sniffed and pushed his fingers through his matted hair. There was more to say, but he could not make himself do it. "Hell. He's going to cut up them cottonwoods and drag 'em to the edge of the fields, soon's the ground dries out." He snickered. "Which could be next Christmas, look a things."

"What's he paying?"

"Creek bottom is worthless, Essie."

She felt her stomach clutch, thinking he got nothing for the rent, but then he pulled a piece of paper out of his pocket and gave it to her.

"It's a check, Essie. Sixty dollars."

Not likely. She groped for a match and lit the lantern. She looked at the check and could not believe it. A dollar and a half an acre. They could hardly make that on farming wheat. "Maybe you should've rent the whole blame farm!"

"Exactly what I was thinking."

Even so, after the flood was gone and the prairie hens and meadowlarks came, it was an odd feeling to stand at her window to look for the wind quivering the cottonwoods at the creek and see Soren Strand riding up and down the fields there, having his way with them, cool and businesslike. The idea of renting another man your own soil sat funny with her. She liked the money, but would not do it again. This time next year it would be Leonard and her.

It was her pa who tumbled to the truth, one day toward the middle of May. Esther was in the garden, looked up, and her pa did not so much as say hello but asked her, "Why's Strand fertilizing Leonard's north forty?"

"Rented it."

"Strand says Leonard sold it to him."

Esther laughed. "Strand's too big for his britches," but there was no joke in Rugnel's eye. "Hell and damnation!" she said. "I will find out."

Leonard came in to eat. She put dinner on the table, one of her Barred Rocks, and he went at it before she pulled up her chair. She felt her stomach in a twist and could not think of eating.

"Did you rent that land or something else?"

He ate like he'd missed his last two meals. "What else?" Had his mouth full of potato and his fork shoveling at the beans.

"Sell it off?" The question came out a whisper.

He slammed his fist so hard the plates jumped. "Goddamn it! Ask me! Did I sell off that piece a sump-hole river bottom that's sucking us under? You're goddamned right I did. I dumped it onto Strand fast as I could, and could not believe he was fool enough to take it, under ten feet of water. The dog's ass laughed at me when I asked did he want to rent it, Essie. He said I could sell it to him or shit on it, my choice, and it came to me clear, then, Essie. Take the bastard's money but make him pay dear, and by God I did! I got more for it than your God Almighty pa paid for it, yes I did—you look at me!—I got seventeen-fifty an acre, so don't you say one goddamned word at me, Essie." He was out of his chair, pointing his finger in her face. "Not one goddamned word! Paid off the bank for what we owed on that piece and gave you every cent that was left. We are free of forty acres. Sixty to go. Oh, I chopped a big hunk off the mortgage, you bet. Paid cash for our seed. We can almost goddamned breathe now. Was not an easy thing, you think it was easy. It was not. Was the fit thing. Did it for you and the boy. Here's my goddamned thank-you!"

He was out the door and across the yard and into the barn.

The boy was squalling. She could not breathe. She could not have been weaker if he'd hauled back and planted a fist in her stomach. She had no comfort left inside of her to give the boy and left him wail. She joined him, too. Her own husband had killed the thing even as it was growing inside of her. For sixty dollars. Then he let her be the fool over his dirty money. How she'd gloried over it, taking it for a small fortune of rent when he knew the truth of it, that it was no more than the ash residue of a thing she'd worked for and nursed and prayed after and he could not wait to shed them of. You got to grow into your land. It only wanted faith. How hard is that?

PART III

13

Ballard, Last of June 1900

The sister had been all business when he finally found her place. Showed no surprise at his standing there on her stoop two thousand miles from his home, new suit of clothes. Just pulled open her door and saw it was him and shook her head.

"Your wife's gone to Nome up in Alaska. Spend the night here if you like, and then you are on your own, unless you want to work for Gunnar in the mill and go get yourself a room at the boardinghouse over on Tenth. I am not running a hotel."

After he got off the freight, Leonard had eased himself through the window of a mortuary, thinking to make himself look better before he went for his wife. Had to sit down and cut the old pants off his burnt leg so he could pull the new ones over the piece that had become a part of the barky scab. The fever and pus had turned it hot and the scab was weepy at the edges where the flesh was proud and at the places where it cracked open when he bent his leg, which he tried not to do.

Now he studied the sister a minute, trying to make sense of what she'd said. Essie wasn't there after all. She had gone to fat in the neck, Constance, and her face flushed and jiggled as she shook her head. He did not know if he believed her and asked could he just come in and see for himself, which he did, and then he passed the night lying awake on the bed he supposed she must have slept in when she knew she would be going on up in Alaska. She would have laid there with that idea, knowing he would be coming to find her. Gone with the stampeders. That was another thing he never would have guessed. Was not normal in her, but then neither was leaving Perley. A hurt dog goes into the woods to die was the closest he could figure it.

He went down to Seattle and passed six days pilfering food and sniffing around the docks and bars along Railroad Avenue. Asked to hire on at six or eight ships, but his bad leg worked against him, no surprise. He figured to stow away somewhere and nosed around among the pikers and muffs likely to know how that works. There was a weasel in a docks uniform and billed cap that caught him by the arm one day.

"Heard what you been askin'," the weasel said.

For a split second Leonard thought he'd got himself in trouble, but the voice was not so hard as inviting.

"No kidding. What'd you hear?"

Weasel gave him a long look-over. "One hand washes t'other."

"Like to think so, friend."

"Friend a mine's captain a the *Skookum*. Can get you on, if you are feeling helpful."

"Friend of yours'll see I got a problem with my leg."

Weasel said, "Not if I tell him, he don't."

"What kind of help you needing, then?"

The fella sucked his teeth. "Furs."

"Kind of furs, then?"

"What the fancy men're buying for Alaska. Polar bear, otter, beaver, wolverine."

Leonard laughed in the man's face. "Where am I going to turn up truck like that?"

"Was me, I would look in a warehouse. But maybe I made a mistake." Weasel turned to go.

"Hold on," Leonard said. "Suppose I get lucky?"

"Name is Pitts. You tell anybody you're looking for me, I will hear about it."

Leonard passed the next three nights snooping around trains and storehouses. He got friendly with one of the boys watching the Northern Pacific freight house on Marion Street, bought him a quart of beer, jawboned awhile, and then asked did the boy mind if he went inside just to have a look-see. The boy said all right, but if Leonard come out carrying anything but his clothes and his pecker, the boy would whistle up the alarm so fast Leonard'd be cooked stew before he was skinned meat. It took Leonard an hour inside but he found what he was after in a couple of crates outside of the strong room. He dumped out a rubbish barrel, stuffed the furs inside it, covered them with the rubbish. Then he stepped outside barehanded and had himself a smoke with his new friend and said his thank-yous and good-nights and crawled into the coal shed he'd been sleeping in behind the boxcars at the foot of Pike Street. First light of morning he went over, borrowed a dolly, rolled the rubbish out the door, calling hi-ya-fellas and whistling a tune. Nobody bothered him.

THE *SKOOKUM* WAS a red giant of a cargo barge wearing the stink of urine and the bellowing of cattle that were penned too close to move or lie down. Captain Folsom had a full crew already, but an hour before sailing two Seattle constables came down and carried away one of his deckhands. Leonard was on the dock when it happened, right where Pitts had told him to stand. Folsom called him out—"You! If you can be ready within the half hour, you're hired." Leonard climbed aboard on the spot. Got himself a mile-long stare from each of the other deckhands until a sailor named Billy came over, shook his hand, and took him to see where his bunk and locker stood.

"How d'you know the Cap'n, then?" Billy said pleasantly. He was a short and powerful-looking man a couple of years younger than Leonard.

"Don't."

Billy regarded Leonard. "You got kin at the barge company, eh?"

Leonard shook his head. Billy wore a knit cap, and when he packed chaw into his cheek, Leonard saw he was missing the middle fingers of his left hand.

"You don't know the Cap'n, you ain't kin, you walk like you got a pole up your backside. Guess you are one long-lost bastard brother to the Pope himself to get yourself hired on here, but I ain't going to piss barnacles down my leg tryin' to figure it out." He set his jaw.

Leonard calculated Billy. "Stole some furs for it."

Billy relaxed into a wide grin. "And the leg?"

Leonard fought the urge to turn and spit. "Burnt it climbing out my own damned house afire."

"All right, then," Billy said agreeably. "I'll tell you how it works here. You stay off the joy juice or Cap'n'll put you ashore. If you go over the side, you swim home. And my day with Cook's wife is Thursday, you work out your own deal." He hooked his head for Leonard to follow, and set off to show him around.

Skookum was bigger than a thing should float, Leonard thought.

"No wooden vessel ever put into American Pacific waters was bigger," Billy said. She was two hundred fifty feet in length and fifty-four feet in the beam, had a covered deck and eight cargo holds. She was loaded heavy with cattle, sheet iron, whiskey, lumber, and general hardware, which Billy moved over and through with the ease of a chimpanzee. When Leonard could not keep up, Billy said, "Never had a cripple for a deckhand before. Must've been Mr. Astor's own furs you stoled."

The passage was going to take two months, up through the sheltered waters of the southern coasts, westering to the Aleutian chain, and then northering along the exposed rim of the Bering Sea to Norton Sound. The last leg was against open seas, Billy said, sure death for a motorless barge sitting heavy in the water, but he said Folsom wasn't one to be giving her up to Davy Jones. "Don't matter, though." Billy counted eight dories lashed along the awning deck. "Them is paid cargo doubling as lifeboats."

SKOOKUM WAS UNDER tow of the ocean tug *Holyoke*. The first day out, over dinner in the cabin, the Captain's English bulldog wrapped itself around Leonard's gimpy leg and set to humping, chuffing, and wheezing like a worn-out locomotive. Nobody paid notice, so Leonard put his other boot against the dog's face and scraped it off.

The Captain slipped a piece of meat to the dog and turned to Leonard. "Didn't see you was lame until after we slipped our lines or I wouldn't have took you." He did not say it meanly, more like

Leonard had pulled one over on him and the Captain was willing to own up to it, but was Leonard? As if to say the once had better be the start and end of it, a cunning man was not a welcome man in a ship's crew.

There were eight of them aboard, and everybody but the cook and the man on watch sat to dinner, and every one of that number looked to Leonard.

Took him by surprise. "The leg don't slow me down any."

The dog was retching now.

Captain held Leonard's gaze.

Leonard felt his heat get up. "If you think I am not carrying my load, put me off at the first stop. Got more work in me than any man here." He sent a good-natured look around the table at each of them. The cook's wife sneaked him a grin.

Captain nodded. "First stop's Ketchikan."

The sweet stink of the dog's mess rose from under the table.

"Heffala, Billy!" the Captain said irritably, and Billy went and got a rag and ducked under the table with it.

Heffala was what the dog went by. It was fourteen years old and both eyes were grown over with cloudy skin so it got around following its nose. Leonard learned it mostly kept the company of the cook's wife, Suzy, but it liked a leg any chance it got. He could stand to throw the dog over the side and thought somebody else maybe had the same idea once, because the dog had a cork float the size of a gallon jug tied to its neck.

Leonard took a break after that first meal, getting Billy to roll him a cigarette and then going forward alone on the awning deck to lean against the derrick mast and smoke in privacy, feeling uncommonly exhausted by the events of the day and all the strangeness of his new situation.

"He don't mean it."

Leonard turned, and there was Suzy. He judged her to be fifty or older. She had coal-black bangs and friendly eyes that looked out from dark pools of extra skin.

"About Ketchikan?"

"Captain's never put anybody ashore in his life. But what about that leg of yourn, sweetie?"

IF THERE WAS squatting he got Billy to do it, and made up for it in kind. It was Billy and him on all animal chores, twelve hours a day. Milking in the morning and again at night he could sit the stool and keep the one leg stiff. Carry the bales and cut the wire and fork the hay into the bins. Clear the drains. Shovel the manure over the side. They lost one or two beeves a day in the first week from sickness or overcrowding, and Leonard or Billy had to work his way in with the animals to the carcass and latch on a chain so they could winch it to the side and slide it over. All the while, Leonard feeling dog-weak for whiskey.

The tug *Holyoke* led them by two hundred yards. At that distance there was no sound of her engines, just the stream of soot out her stack and the smell of her coal sometimes and the foam off the *Skookum*'s pointy bow as she split the sea into a pair of waves that rode out to either shore behind them. Billy said Folsom was a washed-up captain who lost his ship on a rock off Tatoosh Island and no barge towed by a tug needed a captain except for legal and insurance reasons. But Leonard thought otherwise. Captain had eyes that looked inside a man.

Nights Leonard lay on his cot and thought of his jug rat. Reached into his bag to see it was still there, and then let it be. One morning he thought to bring it out, show Billy.

"What in the hell?" Billy said.

"Indian friend made it for me. Skinned this big bull muskrat and stitched him into a sack just right for a fruit jar. Put it on this length of rawhide so I could wear it around my neck."

"Looks alive."

The rat sat on its ass with its tail tucked up along its backside and its forelegs reaching around its belly.

"Tip the head back, and lookee, there's the jug!"

Billy whistled, charmed past speaking.

Leonard passed it over for inspection.

"Whiskey'll get us put off," Billy said, looking over his shoulder.

"I am not saying drink it, just go ahead and have a peek, though." Thought he would have some good-natured fun.

Billy unscrewed the metal lid, took a whiff, and then gazed deep into it. "Mothering God! What is it?" He clapped the lid back on.

Leonard gave a nod and accepted it back. "My secret recipe," he said, enjoying his little joke. Would have given his right arm for a couple of long pulls, but made himself sit back and think of something else.

It was a fact he was weakened by the sores. He came up short of his duties and Billy covered for him. One day Billy showed him a place you could crawl through the cargo on the aft deck and come out in a small clear area on the port side where nobody could see you. Billy had a water pipe and opium that he'd got off a Chinee that drowned on their last run up to Skagway, and he lit the pipe and gave it to Leonard. The smoke eased the leg and filled Leonard with a calm. The day was a rare one of full sun, and Leonard lay in its light and felt the warmth soak into his wasting body.

"Hold on," Billy said, and disappeared through the cargo. He returned with Suzy.

"Going to look at your sore now," Billy said.

The dog came chuffing out of the cargo and got onto his good leg, but the cook's wife dug her fingers into the soft flesh behind its ears and gave it a deep scratching that distracted the slathering wretch from its frigging, turning now to arch its neck into her ministrations. Thus Suzy pulled the dog off of Leonard and told it to sit aside for now, and it settled down quiet but for the wheezing.

She gave Leonard a friendly smile and said, "Better unhitch those pants." She tugged them off and sat beside the leg and studied the wound with her fingers, pressing at the festering edges. "That hurt, sweetie?" She had a gravelly voice and a way of laughing when she talked. He felt a sharp pain where she squeezed his burn and he turned to the pipe and inhaled deeply from it and laid back and watched the shore slip past. The strait they ran up was like a fine river blooming with life. The air was piney and damp. Trees and mosses made a solid wall right where the rocks quit at the high tide line and hid whatever lay in the land beyond and who might be watching them pass.

"You just wait here," Suzy said. "Going to get a few things."

"She's a randy bitch," Billy said, "and Cook don't mind, so long's you don't screw her under his nose." Billy gave Leonard a grin like they were in cahoots. Which they were, Leonard supposed.

She returned with a pail of warm water and washed the leg and cleaned the wound, taking the better part of half an hour just to pick out bits of the old cloth where it festered under the new skin.

"Going to prop it up on my lap now, hold your breath," she said. She lit a piece of birch bark afire and got it flaming good and then blew it out and moved it slowly along the underside of the leg, letting the pitch smoke swirl over the damaged flesh.

"Made you a poultice, sweetie." She had a sack full of something and put it on the sore and tied strips of cloth around the leg to keep it there. "We're going to wash it once a day, now, hear? Freshen my herbs and repack the poultice." She and Billy helped him pull up his pants. She gave him a little pat on the inside of his thigh for good measure, and then she left. The dog got to its feet and chuffed into the cargo behind her.

The heat drained out of Leonard's leg and the puffy redness quieted and the weeping ceased and it began to heal. Suzy was sweet-faced with thighs like cork oaks. She told him sex was the life force and anybody that preached against it preached against the temple of God. He gave it to her on Saturdays, there in the secret place, the dog lying beside them, wheezing and rattling like the sound of death.

14

Beach Camp, July 1900

The wind blew in from the sea, driving its dampness deep into the tents and bedding and forcing the men to stoke their stoves to beat back the moisture. On days that the weather swung around to the north and blew down out of the Kougarok, spilling the arctic chill over the lip of the tundra, the camp swirled with eddy currents of grit and smoke. The coal stoves balked and puffed from every joint, and the fires heated poorly. The soot burned their eyes and the backs of their throats and they rousted out testily and set about their work with headaches and the sensation of oncoming colds.

Without a proper night, each day melted into the next with a sameness that wore on them. The hour before bed was passed in petty arguments or speculation over failures elsewhere on the beach. Angus Donaldson, company surgeon, suggested a series of orations to lift the mood, going first with remarks on "Bacteria Which Assist in the Making of Cheese and Butter." The next night Gus Hanson, the quiet shops steward, surprised them by passing an entire ninety minutes with "Reminiscences of an Undertaker's Assistant," a topic that was notably successful. Nate gave "Sex Differences in the Northern Avifauna" with a digression on the mid-ocean proclivities of the red phalarope, but birds did not stir the men particularly, and the next morning young Lars Sunderhauf, their consulting engineer, scratched "Beware the Phalarope" on a broken oar blade and hung it over the sleeping tent. Within days the sleeping tent was known simply as the Phalarope.

Sunderhauf was a short man who preferred a fleece pixie cap to the broad campaign hat he'd been issued. For all his twenty years, he was a sprite, up to unseen mischief, hanging scavenged treasures over the entrances to the other tents, each inscribed as struck his fancy, so that the infirmary came to be known by the men as "Soul's Harbor," the office tent as "City Hall," the dining tent "Cook's Plea," the toilet "Cook's Jury," the workshops "Hit or Miss," and the stables "Crummey Acres." Not everybody embraced his wit. Mechanic Steale read "Hit or Miss" as an indictment and removed the sign, but the name stuck, the others seeming to enjoy it, and Steale took to baiting Sunderhauf, who was half his size and age and the least likely to offend of the group, his cheery disposition itself working like a thorn in Steale's side. When the flue in the Phalarope fouled the air, Steale accused Sunderhauf of pissing the coals. When a wrench went missing, Steale supposed aloud, "Young Lars has hid it up his arse to give himself starch and pity it ain't working."

It took them six days to build the dredge platform, an immense flatcar eighteen feet wide by thirty-five long, set on wheels and track so it could be run down to the sea to do its work and then winched clear of the surge in big weather. The seventy-five-horsepower engine was a son of a bitch, weighing almost five thousand pounds.

They'd had to contract a barge with a derrick that could be run against the beach at high tide, simply to get the main casting ashore and hoisted into place.

They riveted the boiler sections together, put up the connections, and ran the piping. They bricked in the firebox and erected the stack. They raised the A-frame and put out the big suction pipe. They cut fifty-four six-foot lengths of steel to build the grizzly that would keep bigger rocks from clogging the sluices. They set to digging a six-by-eight-foot well behind the camp, seeking feedwater, but as the hole grew the walls thawed and sagged and they were forced to buttress the shaft with timber and lagging fit for a quartz mine. Two days later, at fourteen feet, they were still in blue clay with no sign of water.

While the men were thus engaged, Nate and Steale prepared the engine. Steale, it was reported by Donaldson, suffered from weeping sores on his genitals of such alarming scope and repugnance that it was a wonder he didn't amputate his own manhood. Yet, when addressing the machine, if left unmolested, the man was a model of patient industry. He placed the centrifugal pump, set the crankshaft in the journals, and aligned the crankshaft with the cylinder. Finding the slightest play in the fit of the piston, he removed the rings and peened evenly along the inside of their circumference until they fit the bore precisely. He cleaned the gland and cut new packing for the stuffing box. He reassembled the linkages, connected the shaft couplings, and adjusted the eccentric for valve lead.

Major Palmer made it a point to visit the beach camp twice a week to rally the men and report on recent events in Nome. Usually he sat to the evening meal, taking his place at the head of the long table, with Nate to his left and Sprague, if he was present, to his right. All told they numbered sixteen now, including Esther, who chose to sit among the laborers toward the table's lower end.

A typical accounting from the Major covered recent ship arrivals, gold strikes, and the failure of one or another company on the beach. He closed with any diverting fatalities, such as the two he recounted on July the fifteenth: One resulted from the near-decapitation of the dance-hall girl known as Fay the Fairy of Nome, whose launch was driven beneath the mooring line of the sternwheeler *Excelsior* on the Snake River. The other resulted from strangulation sometime following the city's Fourth of July parade (when the victim was last seen about), but not discovered until nine days later. This was the suicide of a broken miner who for want of a tree limb had strung a rope from his windlass and hung himself in the shaft of his own drift mine, a feat that the editor of the *Daily News* lauded as civic-minded in the extreme and worthy of broad emulation, as the city would not be out of pocket to bury the feller, nor the Revenue Service taxed to ship him Outside, which was not the case with the four or five thousand beggared indigents still remaining who lacked this man's imagination.

ESTHER WAS FINISHED in the stables by ten and got in the habit of riding to town. There were things the men hadn't thought to bring but found they needed and were glad of getting without having to put down their work to go after themselves. One day she rode in through the light and shadow of a furrowing sky for a box of bearing grease to replace theirs that had been ruined by sand, and, since she was going, they'd sketched a pair of iron brackets that would be more easily got at a hardware than smithed in camp. Another day, when a storm sea hardened the sky to bluestone and the air smelled of salt spray, she made the journey to stand in line at the Post Office and submit all of their names to the postmaster for free mail delivery to the Steadman address. After that she went daily to Steadman to check for mail and bring it out to camp. Delivery was intermittent, depending upon shipping. The first bundle she carried smelled of toilet water. She dug through in search of the culprit and found three lavender envelopes addressed in great swirls from a Lily Wilder of Beauxchamps Road, Worcester. She marked the name, not surprised so much as let down to imagine Mr. Deaton gone slack in the knees over one so florid and patently eager.

Some of her errands were of a personal nature, requested quietly and with shyness—only if she had the room and the time, nothing they couldn't make do without or go to get for themselves—a tin of Prince Albert for the doctor, chocolate for Sunderhauf, socks and underwear for Hanson, who had shorted himself rather badly in this department. She carried saddlebags, but if the return load was cumbersome she looked for Eskimo Tom or hired a gig to take her back by water, stabling the horse in town overnight. The next day she walked in and rode the horse back.

Inside of a week she knew many of the miners by sight, passing through their camps and diggings twice a day. There was one she called Pickerel, an English sir who wore green and had liver spots on his hands and face. There were brothers she called the Pickaxers, who used the same tool for every purpose, including the pitching of their laundry line. There was a miner named Isaacs of the Brooklyn Gold Company who had a crew of men putting together some kind of a motorized digging machine. He was a pale, Jewish-looking doodle with a scraggly beard who took the liberty of introducing himself and always tipped his hat when she passed and gripped her horse below the bridle to walk it through their works on sure footing. The second time she came, his crew was venting steam from a boiler. "A pleasure to see the female form!" he shouted over the noise.

It was a gray goose of a day, a spit of rain in the wind, and she had been mulling over the problem of boots, particularly a pair of rubber ones she had seen at the Alaska Commercial Company store for ten dollars, studying the men to see how many had rubber or leather, and thinking she would get ten dollars' wear out of them on the days she went by boat, but would find them heavy and hot on horseback, and if she rode in shoes and carried the boots in her bag they would take up space and require that she return by boat more often—in which case she would be glad of having them for keeping dry. She forced herself to push boots aside for the moment, smiling pleasantly but not inviting forwardness.

"You are here with your husband?" he hollered.

She opened her mouth to speak, but the noise was too much, so she nodded and pointed up the shore toward the beach camp.

Isaacs stuck two fingers in his mouth and whistled over his shoulder. A coot at the boiler shut the steam cock and raised his face in question. "Mothering Christendom, Douglas, lay off a minute 'n give a man to speak! That thing'll wake snakes!" and then for good measure he hollered to a man bent over a winch: "Frankie! You push them bolts through and nut 'em down before tipping her up or you'll strip her out from pickle to Balzac!" He turned back to Esther. "Couple of monkeys can't find their own banana if you don't put it in their hand for 'em. Your fella's up the beach, then?"

"I am in service to the Cape Nome Company, who are putting up a big contraption like your own, all soon to be millionaires, sir."

"Jim-dandy," he said gaily, although his eyes looked tired at the corners. "Well, I have left my wife at home." He led her through the disorder of his camp, its crates and machinery scattered in the sand. "Sits on her spreading hinder all day and barks like a seal. I came up to this frozen desert just for the quiet of it." At the far side he said, "You come back when the pot's on, we'll have a cup."

"Might do," she said.

He nodded her off. His boots were leather and looked wet through. She giddyapped the horse, settling on rubber. Behind her the Jew cried, "Party's over! Pile on the agony, there, Douglas!"

She took her noon meals with Lena before Lena went to her nursing. They sat across the reception desk at Ten Steadman, or, if the Major was away, took the side table in his office near the stove, sharing a dinner that Esther carried in from a small kitchen she'd found on Second Street called Mrs. Powell's. There was a colored dining room in town, but Esther wasn't sure of her welcome in it. They chanced the dining room at the Hotel Baltimore one day but the dogsbottom johnny standing door duty received them with, "Welcome, ma'am, and cook will feed your nigger in the kitchen," so they preferred the privacy of the company offices.

Esther spent five dollars of her own money at the Alaska Commercial Company store for a Yukon stove to heat her tent. At camp she helped herself to the company's coal and kept more or less to her lodgings or the stables, joining the men at breakfast and the evening meal, sitting in on the evening's oration. She would have parted with five dollars to put a rug on her floor if Nate hadn't already laid canvas, which did little to cozy up the space but was too good to go spending money covering over. A tent was no real kind of a home, but it did make her feel good to nicen it with a piece of muslin for the entrance, which she stretched across at the height of a Dutch door's bottom for days when the weather was warm and she could sit indoors with the flaps pitched open. She missed having a piece of hardanger to dress her packing crate table. If she thought she was going to stay she would go after the linen to make one, though her evenings were better used extending the life of her wardrobe, patching the elbows of a work dress, reversing the cuffs, and repairing the seams of her shoes. Ladies' fashions in the Nome shops came from

Chicago, New York, and Paris. She would love to see Mrs. Loquesbear walk up Front Street with a peplum on her jacket and flounces under her skirt, but they were nothing Esther could carry. She had two work dresses, which she wore in camp on alternate days, and the blue shirtwaist with primroses from her son's christening, which she often pulled on for town with a darker blue skirt that Lena had picked out for her in Seattle. The skirt fell in a straight line from her hips and flared at the hem with a cheek that belonged on some other woman, a woman whose reflection she watched in the shop windows she passed, hardly believing it was her own.

She stopped at the Laird's Provisioner after a tin of shortbread for Nate one day, and returned to camp to find a small pile of boards beside her tent.

"Ready to put up the shelves," Nate said, coming up behind her.

"Oh, good! Had no idea you remembered. I just left off your cookies and more sniffy mail inside the door of your tent. Maybe you want to go read your letters first."

"My head's full of our little shelf project, might as well do it."

She opened the door and stepped in, plucking her nightie off the rope and tucking it beneath her pillow.

"You have made a very homey nest." Everything was folded and orderly, a hairbrush and hand mirror on the little crate of a table, the bedding without a wrinkle.

"It will be a boost to have shelves and unpack my things. I want two boards, maybe yea high, and pegs beneath."

He put himself to measuring and setting his boards over the edge of the flooring to saw. She held the canvas aside.

"Another company's calling it quits. Phillips. Dredging with an old-fashioned scraper dragged by horses. They have gotten nothing."

"You could never go deep enough with a scraper," he said. "Sundy saw them at it the other day, said they'd have better luck mining the

Pope's privy with teaspoons. Hold these now while I knock some nails into the braces."

"Very quick piece of work," she said. "I was thinking we'd have to set big posts or something."

He turned the shelves upright and ran a rope around one of the ridgepoles for stability, then he went for a bit and brace. When he came back she was moving the little table aside and pulling her suitcase out from under the bed. He drilled holes and tapped in dowels.

"I am more grateful than I seem," she said.

"Tell you the honest truth, you are a bright spot among a sack of gloomy faces," he said, and then, "I was thinking, sometime we could look at the birds through my binoculars."

She raised her eyebrows to see what he had in mind.

"Just up behind the tents here you can see a fair stretch of beach. There's more different kinds than you would guess. After supper?"

THERE WERE BANDS of kittiwakes marauding the surf for herring, and glaucous gulls wheeling and fighting over scraps of trash. He'd brought a blanket, and they sat with their legs hanging over the bluff, fifteen feet above camp. She had seen such birds every day on her way to and from town. Not that she had known their names.

"A very skimpy showing this evening," he admitted. "Perhaps inland a ways I could find us a lark or something. A snow bunting."

She didn't have on the boots for it even if she meant to traipse off toward the hills with him. It was a mild evening, and it restored her to sit among the greenery.

"Yesterday from the platform I saw a pomarine jaeger steal a gull's lunch." He'd also helped himself to an eyeful of Esther where she was bent over something by the stables, him thinking what he wouldn't mind doing. "You know, there's not one in a hundred women would come to Alaska on her own."

"It's hardly a fit place," she said.

"Go so far from home, things are going to be different."

"I know that."

He smiled. "I just mean there's no shame in finding comfort in the company of a like-minded person."

She put the lenses back to her eyes and studied the comings and goings below. "I have seen you up there on that barge platform with your spyglasses."

"Oh, and I suppose you yourself are nothing but work?"

"Work's not a sin, last I heard. I will have to look up about spyglasses, though. Hardly like-minded, in any case, you being in the business line of thinking or whatever you call it." A swarm of little waders charged the lip of the surf and turned back in unison. "Tell me, why do those bitty gray ones go at the beach like they had a club?"

"Good question! And why are all those miners going at the beach right where others are digging?"

She shook her head. "Got no idea of their own, maybe."

"See, that's what I'm saying."

She handed back the lenses and gave him a good looking-over. "What?"

"Most people don't have their own idea. You do."

BEFORE BED, SHE unpacked her things and put them up. At the bottom of her suitcase, folded with moth crystals, lay her wedding coat. She had bought a gray cloth cloak for the voyage, but it was nothing to the lamb's wool. She lifted the coat out and laid it on her bed, smoothing the fabric and beating gently at the creases. She unfastened the buttons and held it up. Looked like new. She slid her arms into the sleeves just to feel the lining against her skin. It felt like she was pulling on a life she'd never let herself have the joy of. She stepped out the front of the tent and made two circles in case anybody wanted to see what she looked like dressed up, and that's when she saw where it had a hole in it the size of an apple seed in the right sleeve near the cuff. She couldn't believe it! Clear through to the lining! She would get herself a thread and fix it.

She turned the sleeve so as not to see the flaw, and then, still in the coat, sat on her stoop and crossed her ankles and watched out to sea, picked at her garden mosses and rearranged them. The smell of the lamb's wool and moth crystals brought her Jess and Rugnel's attic where she used to play with Carl and Constance and Hjalmer on a winter afternoon. She ran a hand down the outside of her leg to feel the wool's softness. She had no desire to take it off. If it was going to be ruined by moths anyway, better to ruin it by wear. So she would. She held her left arm out and tilted her hand up in a certain way one last time before she took it off, and saw what the problem was going to be. Her wedding band. It did not feel right to wear the wedding coat and her wedding band together. She pulled the ring off. She turned it between her thumb and forefinger a minute. Maybe she could get a fine ribbon and wear it on her neck.

The next day she wore the coat to town. She let her hair down and brushed it out and cleaned her shoes and put on her shirtwaist and blue skirt and then slid her arms in the coat's silk sleeves and pulled her hair up so it billowed a little out the back but did not fly loose, and it was so that she set off for Nome City, sitting tall, clad in pure cream.

The beach was a dog's tail overrun by fleas. Where one man dumped his slop into a hole, the next man cursed to find he'd dug it up and sluiced it through his rocker. Men who'd gone bust squatted in wait for the government to take them home. The newspaper said a man got a nugget worth fourteen dollars just a foot deep and seven miles toward Penny River, and suddenly everybody that was east worked their way west. Those that were already west and none the richer worked their way east or up into the creeks. All was in contagious migration except for the company camps where men hurried to get their big machines built, but even these men paused in their work that morning to watch Esther and her fine coat pass. Isaacs, the Jew from Brooklyn, spotted her from a distance and watched her advance, not seeing it was herself until she was almost among them, and then hurried over to give her a hand.

"I knew it was you from way up the beach," he lied, taking her reins and pulling the horse into the debris of the camp. The place looked wet and forlorn, the tents sagging, the tools lying out in the weather. Isaacs pinched the hem of her coat, feeling of its thickness. "Lady such as yourself seems to be doing very well!"

"It's nothing new," she said, but it made her feel above him in a way, like she had earned something that he had not and was his better for it and entitled to the feeling, given the slack he was running, the untidiness.

The camp lay idle. "Your men're not working?"

He wiped his mouth with the back of his hand. "Today's an argument. Some woke up excitable and said the beach is bunkum. This whole outfit cost me thirty thousand dollars. Haven't seen a penny on it yet!" He turned his shame away from her a minute as he led the horse. At the far side of the camp he stumbled slightly and smiled sheepishly, wishing her the blessings of her day.

She gave him thanks and rode on. There'd been a look in his face that brought her Constance's Gunnar. Gunnar was not Jewish, of course, but when you glimpsed him unawares he had the same motherless look, a foundling in want of a woman's breast. Not that

Constance was one to suckle, she was a grasper who drove her man. Esther pulled her coat close and asked herself were suckling and being driven two sides of the same coin to a man, and was she herself such a woman, was it a thing the Ulverson girls took from their mother, a way of driving their men hard such that a man without an iron core, a man like Leonard, could be somehow damaged by it instead of called to a higher purpose? Meaning was it her driving him that got their lower forty sold.

TWO DAYS LATER, it was the Jew who put her into the line of making money. She had been paying him only half of her mind when she reached his camp and he took her reins. The engine of the Brooklyn Gold Company had been set up onto stilts as if it had only to wake up and walk itself into the sea. He said, "Miss, if you are going for the mail, I would thank you to ask after mine while you're there."

She hadn't been expecting a business proposition. The horse tried to find something in the Jew's jacket worth eating while he held the bridle.

"Postal line costs two dollars if I had the time to stand for it, which I do not today, but maybe tomorrow I would." She took a long look of him to judge would he pay if she stood for him and found there was no mail.

"Tomorrow, then," he said. He smiled pleasantly and stepped back to let her go. She started ahead but stopped and looked back. "Could set you up for delivery. Don't see why not."

"Delivery?" He stepped forward.

"Number Ten Steadman," she said. She looked around at his men. She knew by now they were nine or more. "Say you gave me every man's name here, and I told the postmaster they are under the wing of the Cape Nome Company and please deliver to Steadman. Then I will bring it out. Or you could pick it up yourselves at Number Ten, for that matter."

Isaacs screwed up one eye and drilled his ear with a finger. "Just like that?"

She sucked in her cheeks. "Twenty-five cents a letter that I carry, ten cents a letter you collect yourselves."

He turned away, stepped over to a tent, and disappeared inside. She thought she'd seen his true stripe at the mention of money, but he popped out again with a scrap of paper and a pencil and wrote out their names for her, eleven in all.

She hardly noticed the rest of her ride to Nome for thinking how easy the terms had come to her. When she arrived at Ten Steadman she had another pleasant surprise, finding Plug calling from the creeks. The three of them went around to Mrs. Powell's Kitchen, where they put in for hot ham and pecan pie.

"You are a happy sight," Esther said. "We have been wondering if you got your fill of gold and went home or got swallowed by a polar bear."

"I wouldn't've knowed you to tell you about it anyhow, in that wool."

"My wedding coat," she said. She made a little turn and then took it off and hung it on the wall. They were lucky to get one of the few tables.

"You want to be careful parading like sheep past some of these boys with their big guns," he teased.

Wasn't enough meat on him to fill out his clothes, which hung like loose skin, but his eyes were bright. "So, you're back?" Esther said.

"I have come to lose at cards to Miss Lena, and then I'm off to prospect in the Council District. The creeks hereabouts are all staked. You look full of beans."

"Well, I would say. I have just put Lena and me into the postal business."

She told the story of Mr. Isaacs, and how the idea had struck her out of nowhere. The conversation wandered to other beach diggers she'd met, then to the pie-eyed idiots Plug found burrowing away in the interior, kindred spirits. Plug excused himself to call next door at the tobacconist.

"He's plenty sparkly for being skunked," Esther said.

"Plug's not skunked so much as choosy. Said I ought to go to Council with him, make myself a stake."

"He's supposable, isn't he? In a nice kind of a way. How'd he take it?"

Lena did not reply.

"Well, certainly you're not going."

"Where's to go? He doesn't have a claim or anyplace to live."

"You wouldn't do it."

Lena shook her head no but said, "Can you see why not?"

"Other than he is not colored, he is older than your father, and what do you know about him?"

"Besides that, I mean."

"Plug'll have a history, Lena. You want to know what the story is before you make yourself a part of it. I know what I'm saying." She had been going to gossip about Mr. Deaton's birds, but certainly not now.

AS SHE BEGAN to carry mail for the Brooklyn Gold Company, the men would spot her coming up the shore from town and lay off work and crowd around the horse or gig until she handed it out and collected payment. There was such a hunger for it that she didn't see why other companies wouldn't want delivery, too. She stopped at some to ask, showing them that she was already in service to two of the big beach enterprises. All of them wanted it. Within a few days she and Lena made $18.75 between them on the mail service and had six companies signed up.

She had sundries and provisions in the boat for the Cape Nome Company when she came up the coast the next Wednesday. The oarsman nudged ashore so she could deliver the mail of Behring Ore Extraction. She stood in the bow of the gig and let the men come around.

"Four letters," she said, holding them up. "Linehan, Ferrell, Temple, Brown."

The mail was snatched up and paid for in a lick, and as she turned to step aft so the oarsman could push off, one of the miners who got nothing said, "What're you asking for that box of cigars?"

"Spoken for, sir, but I can bring you one out tomorrow. Three-fifty."

"Three-fifty!" he snorted. "Can get 'em myself less than three!"

"Yes, sir," she said.

The oarsman made to push off, but the miner gripped the gig's bow and held it. "Pay you three dollars for 'em, fair and square."

"The three-dollar boxes are sold in Nome City, sir, and enjoy your walk. Up at our camp the men're taking a dollar an hour in wages; that'd be three dollars' walking to save your fifty cents, but good exercise climbing around all the beach diggings, no argument there."

"Three-fifty, then. Got no time to be walking to hell and damnation." He dug in his pocket.

She waved him off. "Sit on your money until I bring 'em, so I don't have to."

Another miner stepped up. "Mind if I put in for a canned ham?"

"Don't see why not. I can have it on the boat tomorrow, let you know the price when I bring it. Anybody else?"

Two others put in for cigars, and one put in for stationery and stamps to write his ma, now they had mail service.

Her trade up the beach grew like wheat afire. She was walking to town and boating back. It would have worked better to take a boat both ways, giving her more time to do her buying and delivering, and for what she was paying to hire the gig she could afford to buy one, but she was no rower. She left word for Eskimo Tom at Thurl's on a Sunday to see if he would be interested in steady work twice a day. Next morning, eight A.M., she saw a small skin boat coming down the shore, pulled by a pair of dogs that ran at the water's edge, the boatman steering through the surf. It was Boy Tom in a small umiak. Esther made him wait until she was done with her stable work. At 10:20 she put on her high rubber boots and her coat and climbed into the skin boat. It was a brisk morning, clouds herding upshore on a west wind like a mirror to the surf. Boy Tom mushed and the dogs sprang down the beach, the two of them in the middle of the little craft, him with one hand on the rudder and her in her lamb's wool with clenched teeth and a grip on the seat. Boy Tom steered through the long reach of the broken swells. The boat was little more than a shell skittering over the foaming water. The miners looked up and some had to step quick to stay clear of the traces, and where congestion blocked the beach the dogs had to be hauled into the boat so the boy could hoist a sail.

It became a daily journey. Esther paid the boy twenty-five cents for the ride in and half a dollar out, loading and stops included. The miners had an appetite for fresh fruits and greens. She kept an eye on the cargo of arriving ships, sometimes bringing a case of oranges or potatoes or eggs, peddling them one and two at a time and selling out before she reached camp. She was making thirty-five to fifty dollars a week. More than she'd ever seen. Would have liked to tell Leonard. He would not have believed her.

After dinner on the twenty-first the Major quietly asked Nate to join him for a smoke in the office tent with Mr. Sprague and give them the benefit of his current thinking on how soon they might be pumping gravel.

"Comes a time you're better off to shoot the engineers and fire up the goddamn machine," Sprague said. He sat at the table they used as a camp desk. He'd shoved aside the inkwell and papers and spread his arms across the top. "Engineer wants his digger to run like fucking clockworks." He banged the tabletop with the flat of his hand. "Tinkers away at the goddamned thing, no thought to the money that got him here, come the middle of August we got our plant tuned up sweet as a quivering schoolgirl and the season's good as over." He turned away in disgust.

For a man of position, he lacked so much as a whiff of common civility. They'd put in long damned days, weeks strung together without break, the men getting testy, Nate coaxing them on. "Sluice boxes in place by week's end," he said, addressing himself to Palmer and trying to sound conversational. "Then the riffles and plates."

"Feedwater?" Sprague again, chipping away.

The failure of Nate's well couldn't have been more apparent. "We'll be transporting a pump out to a pothole the boys found half a mile back on the tundra. Float two or three thousand feet of pine stock from town for the flume. Use the well for a cistern."

"There it is," Sprague said to the Major. He raised his palms, as if the added delay confirmed what they had already discussed.

The Major said, "Bill, here, rightly thinks we ought to double down our bet."

Nate didn't take his meaning.

"Plain English," Sprague said, "while we're sucking hind tit down here on the beach, the smart money's up in the creeks digging gold."

"Bill's idea is even while we're getting the big plant up, let's not wait on prospecting the creeks. Get up there now, lock up a claim, show some gold before freeze-up."

Nate shook his head, disbelieving. "We'll be running in a week, nine days at the outside, but not if you siphon off the men to wander up creeks. We're on the brink of it, right here."

Palmer sat back. "Bill's going to Solomon River. If we had two of you, we'd send one up on Anvil today, start prospecting lays." He turned to Sprague. "Quicker we see it through, the better." Then back at Nate. "Get it running. Show some gold or not. Then we'll know."

CNCo. Beach Camp
Nome, Alaska
July 26, 1900

Dearest Lily,

Two of your letters today! To think the Swede has laid in such a quantity of inventory and motor parts! By now you will have persuaded him to undo some of this business. What will be his tune when the invoices appear?

Here, we are approaching the moment of truth, while many companies about us are giving up the ghost. Tomorrow we will load a boiler and pump into a flatcar and make a railroad of timbers that we can leapfrog across the tundra to a lake we have found. The men argued against it, complaining of the suckholes and niggerheads, but I said if we've got water by Wednesday evening we'll take a holiday Thursday. Our first pause, and likely our last, once we see fortune mounting by the hour.

How many nights I have dreamed of squiring you off to the theater, dinner afterward at Baily's, gazing out on that great lawn where we have skated so gloriously! Instead I wax poetic on birds to the men, and none has come down with my enthusiasm, at least not so winningly as you, my dear Dr. F.

Ever your lonely gold hunter,

Nate

Construction of Nate's flume proved harder than he expected. It was late on the third day that the water finally began to flow. Half the men lit out for town right after dinner, getting a start on their holiday. Thank the Lord that Sprague was still at Solomon, ignorant of the scheme. For his own respite, Nate decided to sail his skiff up the coast six or seven miles with his bird gun, bringing his pan and calling in at Cripple River by way of justification. The moment he was committed to it, his thoughts lit on Esther for companionship, but it seemed she had persuaded Sunderhauf to take her berry picking. The farther from Nome the less molested the berry patch, Nate argued, and in the end they agreed to make it a threesome.

15

Nate had proposed to name her the *Pegasus*, but Sunderhauf had called this a horse of a name and christened her *Nate's Misnomer*; from that tendril of wit she had become the *Miss Nomer*. She was a thin-skinned, flat-bottom rowboat, lateen-rigged, with a triangle of tarp pulled between two spars that Nate hauled up a small mast he'd stepped aft of the forward seat.

It was a brilliant day, temperature in the high sixties with moderate seas and a light breeze at a downshore angle that put the skiff and her skipper to task. A small boat quickening to wind in her sail had something of the thrill for Nate of learning to ride bareback, the unexpected surge of a gust, the perilous heeling, the lifesaving turn to the wind.

Sunderhauf slipped off the center seat and used it as a backrest, sitting on a folded jacket and propping his legs on the knapsack that contained their lunches. He pushed his pixie cap over his eyes and folded his hands on his chest like a cat in the sun. Esther hugged the narrow forward seat, facing aft. She felt too big for the boat, sitting high in its pinched front.

"I ask you not to steer deeper than my feet can touch," she said. She might travel daily over the surf, but she did not enjoy a boat.

"Sorry, but it's stay beyond the breakers or be fished," he said. He shot her a grin, which she did not return, and he noticed she clenched the gunwales.

The three of them bounced along, now and again wetted with spray, and the line of beach encampments grew thin as Nome fell farther behind them. The sun warmed their legs even as the damp and breeze chilled their shoulders. Under her dress Esther wore her prized rubber boots, which reached to her thighs. Annoyed to think they would go down with her, she drew her knees to her chest and smoothed the hem of her dress against her boots.

"What kinds of berries were you hoping for?" Nate asked.

"Blueberries and salmonberries."

He glanced at the trim of his sail and then used his teeth to adjust the sheet where it wrapped around his fist. "But instead you find yourself at sea in the company of two walrus baiters, and you wonder where you went wrong."

Esther smiled despite herself.

Cripple River emptied into the same wide coastal plain they knew well from their beach camp, forming a spit at the sea, and when they came abreast of it Nate could see an Eskimo encampment at the mouth and men working the river with nets. He should turn in there, and yet his eye had caught a line of soaring bluffs four or five miles farther west, certainly more propitious for birding. So he let the Cripple pass without comment, thinking to wash out two or three pans on the return.

THE BIRDS LOOKED at first like bits of debris whirling in the updrafts, and then Nate saw that the cliff face, rising a thousand feet or more, was alive with them. A colony. From their thickened shapes and coloring he guessed they were murres and gulls, but then he saw swimmers and divers on the swells, and these would be puffins. He scanned the shore for a landing. There was a narrow ravine between the hills and signs of a creek, and it was toward this that he steered, swinging the rudder hard over.

At the change, Sunderhauf sat upright. "We're nearly opposite Sledge Island."

"I was drawn past the Cripple," Nate said gaily. "Can you see why?"

He alternately slackened sail and filled it, with designs of heading landward at the speed of the swells and finding easy water at the creek's mouth, but as the seas gathered in the shallows he came on too fast. The bow dropped, she dodged broadside, and rolled. The icy water knocked the breath from their lungs. It was chest-deep on the surge, pushing them in, and they struggled for footing. The boat washed up ahead of them, their gear following along, the knapsack, spare oars, and lines, all but the Remington and binoculars, which Nate had grabbed and held aloft.

The two men worked their way ashore, shoving at the boat until they were able to grab and right it and pull it up on the sand. They scuttled back into the surf gathering up their possessions, but Esther stood fifteen yards out, unable to work her way ashore, her boots filled with water.

"I am caught!" she shouted. "Mr. Deaton!"

Suddenly drawn deeper by a retreating swell, Esther found herself swimming but refused to be taken. She tucked to get a grip on the heel of her left boot and pulled the leg free, came up for air, tucked again, and pulled the other leg out. She was tumbled and thrown against something that grappled with her.

He'd found her and clamped an arm across her chest and now he pulled for shore. She pushed against him, trying to twist free, forcing him to tighten his grip.

Esther felt herself overpowered, the breath squeezed from her lungs. When she surfaced and gulped air and heard him breathing beside her she saw finally that she was being saved. Soon she felt the bottom rise. She turned over and gained the beach on her hands and knees. Nate came up beside her and they dropped onto the sand, gulping air and coughing.

She lay on her back and clapped a hand to her chest, trying to get ahold of herself. Every muscle in her body shook. The swells reached up the beach and washed over her feet and she forced herself farther up the slope, and when she could she sat up and wiped the water from her eyes. The sun was warm but her wet clothes clung to her and she shivered from chills as much as fright or exhaustion.

"Oh!" she cried.

"What?"

"My boots!"

He waded into the shallows to search. He was wet through and scrawny. Looked like a boy. One of the boots washed in twenty yards down the beach and when he'd corralled it and plucked it out he struck a pose, standing stock-still for a minute gazing at the surge, then darted his long arm into the water and came up with the other, raising the pair over his head to her. He loped back and offered the prizes.

"Lord above," she said. "I feel like flotsam. Or would it be jetsam?"

"Salvage."

"Then I believe I am yours, Mr. Deaton, and grateful for it."

THEY GATHERED DRIFTWOOD into a pile and Sundy lit it afire with a waxed match. The first curl of smoke gave way to flame. The flame licked up through the abundance of fuel they laid on and grew to a blaze. She would have liked to walk into it, her frigid hair and clothing clinging to her skin, and yet she was strong at the marrow and exhilarated. They draped their jackets and stockings before the flame and settled themselves as best they could on rocks and sticks and likewise perched their legs off the ground with their feet near the fire, and began to recover.

"So far, it's been an outing of the first-rate," Nate declared. He peered through the willow tops in hopes of making out the seabirds. "Kittiwakes, I believe. The big ones are certainly murres."

"A disappointment, then," Sundy said. "Common as your housefly, from what my cousin says."

"Oh! Their colonies are two or three hundred thousand birds! Each on its sliver of ledge with an egg tucked between its knees. Something I have longed to see."

"Every man to his poison," Sundy said. "This same cousin has collected their eggs off Newfoundland, which he says people like better than hens' eggs and will pay a premium for. Two thousand eggs to a man in one day's work. But I believe these were from a low, rocky island, not your soaring precipice. Pink slime to his ankles, and many of the eggs succumbed for having been shat to obscurity—" Here he gave a perfunctory nod of apology: "Ma'am."

Nate craned his head around. From their position below the creek bank the bluffs were hidden. "There's no choice but to climb up. I wouldn't miss it for the world. I wonder if any are the thick-billed ones—if there are, I would happily have swum the distance. You only find them at these rare latitudes. I know no one personally who has a thick-bill."

Sunderhauf winked at Esther. "Certainly it will be slick as the devil."

"We'll eat, and then hike around and come up from behind. You see there," Nate pointed. "Those smaller, stubby fellows. They are the puffins."

THEY FED THE fire and laid out their lunch and ate, for they were ravenous, and then they pulled on their damp socks and boots and set about scavenging among the driftwood and willows for a new mast. Their clothing was still wet, but if they kept moving they stayed warm enough. There was little pole wood, and what they found was too short or partially rotted. The willow saplings were too pliant. And so they decided to fan out in different directions.

As Esther walked along the gravel creek bed, she recalled how she and her mother would go down to the Red in the fall to gather firewood, how the cottonwoods and oaks towered over them and blotted out the sun. She followed the creek up into the ravine between the hills and around a small knoll, where she found a pocket of the hillside that faced south but was sheltered from the wind. There was a flat rock in the sun and she sat on it to rest, surprised at the warmth it gave up. She was perfectly sheltered. She lay back and absorbed the stone's heat.

Her ribs were sore where he'd gripped her. Would bloom into a good-sized mouse. She was not going to ride back by boat, whatever sweet talk they gave her. Could likely get Sundy to go afoot, but she was not afraid to go it alone if he wouldn't. She watched birds wheeling high above, but didn't know if they were the special ones at all. May have dozed a moment, but only briefly, for she heard a noise. She sat upright. It had been an animal voice, just below, an odd bark and rustling in the willows. As she stared through the trees she saw movement and then picked them out. They were large short birds, six or seven, pecking the ground and the low plants. She climbed down and went for Mr. Deaton.

Nate and Sunderhauf had decided to restep the broken mast, which was shorter now by eighteen inches, and were at the task when Esther appeared out of the brush, slightly breathless.

"I have found your birds, Mr. Deaton."

"Which ones?"

"How would I know? Snipes, if you ask me."

"Kind of a round thing with a very long bill?" He cupped his hands to indicate a bird of seven or eight inches.

Esther looked off and pictured them in her mind. "Fat, with a short beak. More like a chicken. Little leggings."

Nate's eyebrows knitted. "Color?"

"They are snipe-colored. If you want more specifics, come and look for yourself."

He and Sundy tied off a lashing. "We shall take the knapsack, in hopes that after you show me your snipes we might hike up the back side of the bluff."

She led them without error to her landmark, but the birds were no longer below it. Nate scouted the bushes and had been at it for less than a minute when—blam! blam!—she was startled by two shots in close succession. Away fifty feet in the willows two birds rose.

"They are ptarmigan, Miss Crummey!" Nate cried. "Willow ptarmigan. A cousin of your prairie chicken." He reloaded, advanced on the spot, and got off two more shots. "I have read about them for years." He took three birds, two of them cleanly. They had rufous heads and necks and white breasts. He held one up for inspection. "See the little leggings you mentioned!" his voice raised in utter delight. He ran his finger up and down the feathered leg. "Even their toes are plumed. It makes a kind of shoe, enabling them to walk on the snow."

"Showy and overdressed," Sundy said, "which I am willing to overlook on the spit."

"I'll save the skins of the two less damaged. How smart of you to find them, Miss C. I have a brand-new collecting box and not a single Seward skin. These are my first specimens."

ESTHER SAW THAT her birds had made a success of the day regardless of what might follow, and the fact pleased her. She tackled the backside of the bluff with a spirit of exploration that had eluded her in the sailboat, and within the hour her clothes had dried. They paused frequently to rest and to look out over the landscape opening around them, hills gathered against more hills, barren of trees and backing up to the Kigluaik Mountains. The hill rounded at its summit, and at its brim over the sea they heard the low roar of the surf far below. They could see the beach and the creek and their tiny boat. Countless large birds wheeled in and out of the cliff immediately below them.

"Kittiwakes," Nate announced. "Oh!" he cried. "They are the horned puffins!" He threw off his knapsack and stepped closer to the edge in hopes of seeing the nests, then fell to his hands and knees and crept nearer. Despite the stiff breeze he could catch the shrill noise of the colonies and the pungent smell. The kittiwakes wheeled on the wind, while the fat murres and implausible-looking puffins darted in and out of the cliffs.

Esther and Sunderhauf stayed back. "They nest on the rock ledges," Nate said. He looked about for a better vantage, perhaps a rock from which he could cantilever himself, but the small outcroppings were not well positioned. He pulled the rope from his pack.

"Certainly not!" said Esther, guessing what he intended. "I must insist. Please don't, Mr. Deaton."

"I won't do what you are thinking, Miss C. I simply wish to climb down a short distance with the rope under tension so as not to lose my balance."

"It can only end badly," she insisted. "We are such a distance from camp. How will we get help? I cannot allow it."

"I am a regular fly, Miss Crummey. Now, Sundy, if you brace yourself behind that little outcropping and take two turns around your waist. And Miss C, if you felt the least insecure you could pass my brief absence standing behind Sundy there, perhaps with the rope around your waist as well."

She stiffened against the both of them, telling herself that she knew well enough how to find the camp by foot, that should Nate fall she would have little to feel in consequence, it was not her place to save a man from his own folly; Nate's loss would not be hers in any case but his own mother's, or the Cape Nome Company's, or somebody else's. Not hers. As he climbed over the edge, which she saw he did rather nimbly, and disappeared from their view, Sundy paid out the line, and an odd thing came to her. Nate, she had just called him to herself.

THE BROW OF the hill disappeared above him. He looked out over a rime of surf that whitened the coastline all the way to Nome and beyond and felt the splendid isolation, far above the ocean's roar, a world of rock and sky. Wheeling birds. Their cries, and the acrid stench.

Immediately below him the soil gave way to rock. He climbed over a small ledge. The next foothold was a bit of a stretch, and he searched for it with the toe of his boot. He kicked two or three loose rocks away. They bounced twice before going airborne, and he leaned out to catch a glimpse of where he thought they might strike the lower cliff, but they disappeared into the vastness.

He found himself at a level with the upper reaches of the colony. It seemed that he could enter into its midst by working onto the ledges to his right, and he gave this a try. The black and white murres sat their eggs, packed along the ledges, their backs to the sea, alternately blackening the cliff in their sheer density and pinking it with dung. By their coloring and semi-prone stance he thought they must be the thick-bills and he so longed for his Remington to take a specimen, but he hadn't chanced it down the cliff. Nor, from such a position, could he possibly have taken a shot except at point-blank, wreaking havoc with the pelt.

He glanced down the cliff and made out the horned puffins where they were flying out of the wall, perhaps two hundred feet below. He could not make their nests, which would be built in burrows. They were plug-shaped and ungainly, and their earnest industry dropping into the sea and rising again beguiled him.

The murres at eye level loomed surprisingly large, fat as thighs in boots. They refused to fly, bowing and growling at him. He mimicked their growl and dared them, working closer, drawing almost within arm's length before they burst away on the wing. Ammonia burned his eyes. Where one ledge ended, he stepped up or down to another. As the birds were flushed, several eggs tumbled into the void but most did not, for they were conical in shape and rolled in circles. His first was a luminous, mottled specimen in cream and brown, still warm from the parent. His second was dappled gray, the third ivory-colored, and thus he went, getting another and two more, working horizontally along the ledges at the height of his knee and his shoulder.

When he had six or seven in his jacket pockets he feared of crushing them and could take no more—and yet he saw now that a mere twenty feet away there was the promise of very easy pickings. He supposed he could take off the jacket and fashion it into a sack. He began working his way toward the place, but he was hindered by the rope, which did not readily slide along the cliff face with him. He tugged it lightly, which sent down a cascade of dirt and small rocks, one striking a surprisingly keen blow above his left temple. A dozen birds exploded from the cliff close beneath his feet and he recoiled instinctively, letting loose a shriek. His fingers went to the wound, finding little blood, but he decided he was done.

He stepped left, but somewhere above his sight line the rope snagged and would not slide left. He shielded his head and tugged at it. Sundy gamely tugged back, keeping it under tension. There was no feasible route upward but the notch Nate had descended. Slack was the answer, but he had no way to call for it. He stood there a moment, resisting the urge to untie. Then he tried pulling steadily, as if descending, and Sundy paid the rope out. Nate gathered a loop while keeping the main line under tension, and before Sundy could draw it back, he swung the loop over the rocks above. As it was drawn snug he pulled from his end and repositioned it. He stepped left along the ledge and the line slid left with him. It was free.

The little crisis had come to nothing. In a few minutes he arrived at the notch, a very welcome sight, and only then did the strength drain from him. He rested a moment and then began to climb, buoyed by his prizes.

Sundy coiled the line and they watched for him to appear, which he did, from out of nowhere.

"See what treasures!" He pulled the eggs from his pockets one at a time, turning over each to show it off and to see it properly himself before setting it gently on the ground, making a row of them, not a one of them cracked. Every egg a different color, every egg a teardrop.

"How perfectly beautiful," Essie said. "And you knew they would be there." She was as taken by his knowledge of them and the lightness of his touch as by the eggs themselves, but the eggs truly captivated her, so much larger and wilder looking than hens' eggs.

"These are for you." He picked one with islands of dark green among oceans of pale blue. "A bird's map of the world," he said, "now that we have made an explorer of you." He paused over the others and then reached for the first he had collected, the luminous cream one with brown mottling. "You, in your wrap of lamb's wool," he said, more than a little pleased with his muse. He put them in her hands and she felt the weight and texture of them. Such wild and perfect things. What had God intended, that such eggs were laid on a rock cliff above the pounding sea?

THEY RETURNED TO the beach, where Nate succeeded in taking a male and female of the thick-billed murres as well as the horned puffins, sturdy specimens that nestled easily among the eggs in his knapsack.

When Essie declared her intention to return to camp overland she did it more tactfully than she had rehearsed, but no less firmly. Sundy declared himself her hiking companion, but Nate questioned the arrangement. He needed to call in at Cripple River, and didn't it thus make more sense for him to go afoot and Sundy by boat?

There were nine or ten miles to cover, most of it by beach or the edge of the tundra, and they walked without difficulty. She was easy company. Something about the day had softened the stiffness between them. She was not in need of constant talk, nor shy of speaking her mind but had a naturalness uncommon to the women he had known.

On the sand spit at the mouth of the Cripple they watched a party of thirty Eskimos pull salmon from the river with a seine. Nate washed out three pans and found a good quantity of fine gold in every one, but the spit had been an Eskimo encampment for so many generations that it was saturated in whale and seal oil and the fine gold floated off and could not be captured. They hiked up onto the open tundra above the river, where he took a solitary yellow wagtail, a male in full mating plumage, so brilliant in its undersides that it almost seemed alive in his bag as he set it among the others. He descended the gravel bank to try his luck with the pan, but she had found her berries and stayed above on the tundra, picking them into a pocket of his knapsack.

When he came for her, he laughed and pointed. "Look at your tongue! You have eaten up half of the tundra!" He helped himself to a small handful from the pocket.

"Keep away from those!" she said. "I am going to make a tart of them."

He made great show of smacking his lips, and then he stuck out his tongue.

He shouldered the knapsack, feeling oddly elated. They walked up the river a mile or so and he panned it twice more, to no effect, and then they returned to the mouth and took a rowboat ferry across and pressed for home. As they walked the beach, his hand found its way into the berry pocket, and as his came out in went hers, not a word said, but every ten or fifteen minutes they turned and showed their tongues.

It was fully eleven P.M. when they paused outside her tent, tired as dogs, but neither of them ready for the day to end.

"You may take the *Miss Nomer* to sea any day you wish," he said.

"You have been properly baptized, and it is only Christians allowed at the helm."

"When you have had your tongue scraped," she said, "you will be allowed in the stables."

He reached for her hand but she turned and went in and wished him good night through the tent flap.

HE BENT OVER his specimens on the dining table until well after three o'clock, skinning and salting the pelts, blowing the eggs, and putting the flesh and the liquid of the eggs into the meat pantry, a tin box dug down to permafrost beneath the kitchen. The eggs he'd given her he borrowed back so as to empty, after which he tied them up in a square of cloth to return. Only that morning he would have guessed that the subtleties of texture and coloration would be lost on her. How wrong he had been. Ruffle the feathers, and there, in the right light, flashes of brilliance.

He climbed into bed but was far from sleep, unable to blot out the events of the day—his descent into the alien world, the utter joy of the unexpected ptarmigans, the puffins' extravagant bills. The surprise in Esther's face as he proffered his gift. He strove to empty his mind that sleep might come. What rushed in, however, wasn't sleep at all but the litany of events to be faced upon rising—the firing of the big plant, the proving up of all their efforts. Everything coming together for them, finally. If the big plant found paydirt, the first luxury he would grant himself would be the charter of a boat to sail him west around Cape Prince of Wales and north to Kotzebue Sound before freeze-up. Fill out his specimens from above the Arctic Circle. He felt a rush of satisfaction. The elevated stature it would lend his collection. And, he couldn't deny it, returning not just as a man of wealth, but, arguably, one of science.

THE LAST IMAGE to visit her in the onrush of sleep was the memory of his fingers around the murres' eggs. Plucking each from his jacket, examining it, and setting it in the moss for their admiration. Leonard and her brothers carried their hands at their sides like blunt instruments, cracked and chipped, but Nate's had a kind of intelligence. Long. Slender and strong. Turning over his prizes with a sureness that seemed to come less from strength than from something else, a kind of confidence. You could read something of a man by his fingers.

16

At five A.M. the Major rousted Nate with a shake. "A word with you."

Nate pulled on his trousers and stepped inside the office tent. The temperature had plummeted twenty degrees from the day before, barely making forty. First week of August, and a touch of fall in the air. The little Yukon stove glowed red and the Major, who was shaved, combed, and dressed in his campaign suit, sat stiffly with his hands folded on the desk. He pointed Nate to sit. He leaned back in his chair and leveled his gaze.

"We brought Charlie Lane out yesterday to show off the big plant and the crew we've fielded."

"Oh, Lord."

"He owns many of the richest claims in the district," Palmer said, as if Nate needed reminding. "Built a town at White Mountain just for staging his outfit upriver to Ophir." He nodded in the direction of Nome. "Lately, built himself an entire railroad just to reach his Anvil Creek claims. You know who I mean."

Nate nodded dolefully.

"Mr. Sprague and I are proposing some business with his Wild Goose Company. Spent two days looking at some of his properties. Sprague's idea, put a steam shovel up one of the creeks and do the work of a hundred men. Brought him by here to meet you."

"Wish I'd known," Nate said.

"I told him you're our man on the ground, the fella who knows his motors, and he was best meeting you and judging for himself."

Nate winced.

"Not a damned fool in the entire camp but the cook."

"I gave the men a holiday," Nate said. "Took my pan up to Cripple River—"

Palmer leaned across the table. "Sure you did. And why not? You run the men. That's our deal. You make the operations decisions. I back you up. So where's the trouble? Trouble's in the fact you didn't tell me. Money doesn't like surprises. I was caught short, Nate, and I told Mr. Sprague and Charlie Lane a little lie. I told them I'd given you leave to shut down camp for a day in the company's interest, preparatory to launching the big plant, for the transition from construction to operation, so to speak."

"In fact, you got it exactly."

"Lane said he'd never heard such a jackaninny thing. He runs men and mules on slim rations to hone the keen edge of appetite. So he says. 'There's no dirt flying, there's no gold to clean up.' Hell, I don't need sermons from Charlie Lane. You put me in a spot, Nate."

"I struck a bargain," Nate said. "Not saying it wasn't my fault. Just that we got in a bit of a box over that flume."

Palmer sighed deeply. He pulled at one end of his moustache.

"Let you in on something. When I was at San Juan Hill?"

"Yes, sir."

"There was every kind of commander, but only one kind the men respected and followed. The one that marched toward the guns, knowing there was a job to be done."

"Yes, sir."

"Never try to buy your men, Nate."

"No, sir." He nodded. "Toward the guns."

"Attaboy." Palmer rose and offered a friendly hand. "We are on course to fire the big plant today?"

"First thing."

Palmer broke into a broad grin. "Lane says your plant looks like a gold-eating son of a bitch, and he was sorry to miss meeting the man who dreamed it up."

NATE CLIMBED UP onto the car, stoked the firebox, and burned it with the dampers open to a roar. He kept an eye out for Esther. In twenty minutes she came across for the dining tent, glancing up to see him there. He smiled and waved but she did not return the smile. If he was not mistaken, she exposed the tip of her tongue as she marched past. Oh, she had a wicked vein, he was seeing that for the first time. He climbed down and went in to breakfast, taking a seat next to her at the bottom end of the table. Dickson, the hired man who normally sat beside Esther, entered late to find his seat occupied. He stopped short.

"Excuse me, Mr. Dickson, if I might have a word with our stables boss. You are welcome to my seat."

Dickson went up the table and settled uneasily between Palmer and Donaldson.

Nate paid no attention to the curiosity that hung in the room, nor to Esther, but merely sat up straight and looked about for his breakfast, finding that all the platters had been set near the head of the table. "Sundy, do us a favor and start the food. Some of us have a busy day." The platters began to circulate and the room slowly filled with conversation.

"Had my hat handed to me for our little expedition," Nate said quietly.

"Whatever for?"

"Absent without leave."

She pursed her lips in general disapproval of naughtiness. "And so you have roosted with us chickens in penance."

"Possibly I should have taken my meal in the stables."

"Not at all. I run a tight ship."

"Well, exactly. I was thinking about a ship. In a week or so, when I am rich as Croesus, let's the two of us hire a sloop and sail up around Cape Prince of Wales."

She saw he was looking for some sort of an answer, and cleared her throat. "Knowing your seamanship, how could a person refuse?"

"Esther, I absolutely mean it. We would hire a sloop. All aboveboard. With a proper captain. Sundy could come if you wish. No impropriety." He was speaking too softly to be overheard, but she saw that the men's eyes were on them, and she wished him to stop but he would not.

"Think," he said. "We are nearly at the end of the world here. A fella's got to do these things when he gets the chance, or admit, 'I am not such a person. I am a person who will be satisfied never to go.' You are a natural explorer. We would get above the Arctic Circle."

"I don't even know where it is," she said. Her heart had quickened, but there was no question of going, certainly. "I have my delivery business. You know, I will have my hat given me today as well, for the same reason as you, but not just once. At every stop I make."

"We'll leave it as an idea, then."

"All right."

THE TEMPERATURE REFUSED to climb as the morning came on, but the wind grew, snatching the tops off the waves and making the air a mist of salt spray and sand that worked into their eyes and teeth and into every part of the machinery. They lowered the car to the water's edge by cable and winch. Sparks blew from the stack in a straight line toward the tundra. When the boiler neared a hundred pounds Steale positioned himself at the controls of the big pump. Sunderhauf stood at the winch that raised and lowered the suction pipe. Hanson took possession of the agitator engine. Steam puffs shot from the vents and vanished on the wind. A crowd of onlookers gathered. Sprague and Palmer, ever the capitalists, appeared in fresh-minted parkas of arctic fox, their faces framed in halos of wolverine. As they climbed the platform and took positions beside the A-frame derrick, Donaldson shot Nate a furtive snicker that seemed to say, *Ain't they grand, our own pair of potentates.*

Nate worked his way out to stand on the end of the suction pipe, just above the auger, taking a firm grip below the lifting cable. He signaled Sundy to lower away, and the auger disappeared in the turbid waters. Steale opened the valve on the pump and the pipe came alive beneath Nate's feet. In a moment a torrent gushed into the sluices, looking every part of full capacity, five thousand gallons a minute! The water dashed out the far end of the sluices and took half a dozen onlookers by surprise, close to drowning them while others hooted and laughed. A man jeered, "Amateurs!" at the men running the machine. Another cried, "King's ransom, what you spent to come piss on the beach!" Two of Nate's hired men set up planks to carry the tailings away, and the big plant ran on, a steady growl of pump, agitator, and gravel, the seabed washing into their boxes. The crew hailed each other over the roar as they shoveled the tailings clear and traded off coaling the firebox and operating the motors.

After six hours they could hold back no longer and agreed to power down and clean up one of the sluices to see how rich it was.

"Company men only!" Sprague cried. He pushed the gawkers back from the left side of the plant to make working room for the cleanup. He held a leather poke and a cigar in one hand, ready for any coarse gold or nuggets, and a whisk broom and dustpan in the other for sweeping up the grains. Palmer had brought quicksilver for amalgamating the gold flour.

Nate and the doctor began by tossing out the larger rocks and gravel that hadn't been flushed through the sluice. They lifted out the riffles, and where these had crossed the bottom of the sluice there remained the small deltas of gravel and dirt in which the heavy gold would be concentrated by the action of the water. The thumb-sized nuggets of their dreams were not there.

"It'll be fine-grained," Sprague said.

"An ounce is an ounce, nugget or dust," Sunderhauf said.

Nate and Donaldson shoveled up the little deltas and dumped them into the top of the box, and then reset the riffles. Sunderhauf had filled a reservoir at the top with water, and now he released a trickle and Nate stirred the dirt to settle any gold against the riffles while the sand and gravel washed out.

There was none.

"It's all washed through," Sundy said.

Sprague snorted. "It's all washed out with the tailings, for Christ's sake."

"Fornicating sluices are too steep," Steale barked.

"Let's look." Nate scooped some of the tailings into a pan. He gently washed it out. There was no gold. He washed out two more pans. He couldn't even get colors.

17

The next morning Nate was late to breakfast. He'd been firmly against a new day, on principle, and had stayed in bed past seven. He found Donaldson alone in the dining tent having a smoke. The man was sitting sideways to his dirty breakfast plate, one leg crossed over the other at the knee, a cigarette in one hand.

The cook put the griddle on the heat and Nate took a chair. The day had come on clear and bright for a change, but the Cape Nome Company's beach camp felt weighted down as if under a heavy stone. "Where's everybody gone?"

The doctor grinned. "Tweedledum and Tweedledee have bustled off to the Steadman office in a fit of wheeling and dealing. See about buying lays on the creeks and look up that judge in town about a receivership on one of them fancy mines that's in dispute. Judge

Noyes. The Major says he is a pal from way back. Sprague has just remembered his close friend with all the money."

Nate gave him a puzzled look.

"That conniving ass, McKenzie."

"Oh, Lord." Nate drank his coffee and rubbed his scalp. "Feels like we've been through the mill."

"I believe we have."

"Sundy and Steale?"

"Sundy's asleep. Steale never came in last night." The doctor pinched a tobacco flake from his tongue and examined it briefly before flicking it away.

"Out spreading the itch," Nate said.

"That boy's cocksmanship is all behind him. Drinking and remembering is my guess." Donaldson made a small circle in the air with the toe of his boot as if he hadn't a care in the world.

"If you don't mind running the men today, Major's got me headed up Anvil Creek."

"All right," the doctor said.

"Rebuild the sluices. Extend the slurry pipe and the track, if you get to it. Whatever you have time for, and I'll pick up tomorrow. We'll need to raise the car on its trucks to clear the water." One last try with the dredge.

The cook put down a plate of pancakes and bacon and Nate dug in.

"I was just thinking," Donaldson said.

"Umm?" The pancakes were cooked through perfectly.

"Miss Crummey."

Nate looked up.

"Wasn't her idea to come up to Nome, and here she's the only one of us making any money at it."

"Good money, too, don't you bet." Nate went back to his meal.

Donaldson took a long drag, finding obvious satisfaction in the irony as he released his smoke. "More to that girl than meets the eye. If I was single and ten years younger—"

"Well, you're not."

"I guess you are, though."

"I guess so, Doc. I guess a fellow can do as he sees fit."

"Free country," Donaldson said noncommittally.

Nate studied the man. "But for what?"

"But for nothing, unless you care what the men are saying."

"Which is?"

"Not enough that you get the best mail in the whole damned camp, but here you've gone and got yourself Miss Crummey on the side."

There it was. "I guess it's none of their damned business, Doc, is it?"

"I already said I wished I was in your shoes. Anyhow," Donaldson said, slowly unfolding himself and standing up, "time to rise and do, I suppose."

Nate pushed his plate away.

ESTHER WAS AT the stables spreading straw.

"I have received marching orders," he said. "I am to get my fanny up the creeks and find out where the gold is."

"Oh?"

"Off to look over some claims on Anvil Creek and Nekula Gulch. I will be taking Mr. Charles D. Lane's new train from the sand spit and I am hoping you will come along for the scenery and maybe see some birds."

"Is this invitation in addition to your yacht around the Arctic Circle, or must I choose?"

"Oh, no, no. You are already booked, paid, and confirmed for the North Pole in my skiff," he said.

"The dandy little collapsing one?"

"Perhaps you've seen her plying the seas hereabouts." He was grinning like a damned fool and tried to sober up.

"I have been wanting to go on the Wild Goose train. I'll ask Boy Tom if he can do the deliveries without me this afternoon."

NATE SHELLED OUT the princely sum of four dollars for two round-trip tickets, and then he and Esther climbed up, him with his knapsack and shotgun, and took seats on plank benches that ran the length of a flatcar at the front of the train. Three more flatcars were loaded with lumber, pilings, and pipe. At the head of the train was a little boxy engine bearing the insignia "W.G.R.R." on its sides, and "NOME 1900." On recent Sundays the train had been crowded with picnickers reveling at the novelty and the chance for a firsthand glimpse of placer mining on the richest claims, but today the passengers were mostly miners and company men.

At one-fifteen sharp the engineer sounded his whistle and they pulled ahead across the flats west of town. The little harbor fell away on their right and the West End Hotel passed on their left, at the edge of the tundra. A low trestle carried them over the Snake River and then they were rolling across the lowland tundra toward the hills. It was a narrow-gauge road and the cars dipped and swayed where the bed sagged in the soft ground, and although the train did not move more than eight miles an hour, Esther felt a thrill and a fright to sit so high and exposed. They gained height, chugging up the lower slopes of Anvil Mountain, bending west and north. The air was uncommonly clear, the sky blue as delft but cool, with a hint of fall giving rise to exhilaration, the harvest season, no such thing at Nome and yet Esther felt something of it in the air, the willows turning gold and the leaves of the blueberry and salmonberry beginning to purple, the daylight wearing thinner. The town fell behind them and the view spread broadly to the sea, the coast stretching east and west, Sledge Island in the distance, the ships in the roadstead, the ponds and potholes on the lowlands glinting like beads, the crooked Snake, the ragtag fleet of skiffs and paddleboats tucked into the sheltering arm of the sand spit. The rails traversed the west side of the hill above Anvil Creek, and now, below them, she saw the digging and sluicing operations—dams holding back the creek, gangs of men shoveling gravel into elevated flumes. The train sounded its whistle and pulled to a stop by a tent saloon and a tent rail station bearing the name "Anvil City."

They climbed down. "This is Anvil Discovery, Essie. It's where the Three Lucky Swedes staked their first claim. All the claims on Anvil are numbered upstream and down from this one. Over there's Number One Below, where you see those stakes. Thirteen hundred and twenty feet beyond it, somewhere in there, will be the corner of Two Below, and so on. Twenty acres each. They're all pretty much tied up by Pioneer Mining or Wild Goose and their friends. Very rich diggings."

"But what're your chances? Seems the whole creek's already spoken for."

"We're interested in Five Above. Owner's offering a lay to Sprague for fifteen thousand dollars on bedrock. A lay is a lease," he explained. "We would bring in the men and all the equipment to build sluices and develop the claim, and when we start cleaning up, the first fifteen thousand dollars' worth of gold goes to pay him for the lay. Next we get our costs back. What's left is profits, two-thirds to him and one-third to us."

"Why doesn't the lout dig his own hole?"

"Two-thirds of the profit's not bad wages for sitting back and letting another man risk his shirt on the operating costs. And if the claim's rich enough, a third's not bad wages for us, coming so late to the party."

"Isn't that dandy," she said. She turned on up the shallow valley. "Let's go see about paying the man a lot of money for watching you and the boys do his work." She strode ahead with a switch in her step it would've pleased him to get ahold of.

They checked stakes as they went along, and when they found Five Above, they saw that a modest earthen impoundment had been built and several men were running short sluices but had not run a cut all the way across the claim. Getting water to process the gravel was a problem nearly everywhere, but Nate reckoned there was head enough to run two or three sluices. He asked a miner where he'd find the fellow named Hultberg and was directed to a shanty with a blanket for a door. Nate knocked on the doorframe.

A man came out wearing a suit and bowler hat and carrying a shotgun in a loose grip, the barrel pointed at the ground. No call for the gun, but then, maybe the fellow had seen Nate's Remington and misread the situation.

"Name's Deaton. Bill Sprague asked me to come up and wash out a few pans, if that sits all right with you, sir." Nate offered his hand.

Hultberg took it. "Help yourself, and I will stay here'n wait on your missus." The man had a thick Swedish accent. He invited Esther into his shanty.

"I prefer to sit in the sun, no offense," she said, "but you do not need to entertain me, sir."

"I am just boiling my afternoon tea," he said. He sniffed like he had a cold. Showed her to a plank bench by a water tank and went back into his shanty while Nate walked among the scrub willows with his pan. Esther was glad for the offer of tea, but Hultberg did not reemerge for ten minutes, and when he did, he was empty-handed except for the gun. He sniffed and took a seat on the plank beside her. "Richest creek in Alaska. You are the fella's wife, then?"

"I run the company's stables," she said, lacking a better explanation.

"Un-hnn," Hultberg said. He lit a cigar and nodded for her to say more. Apparently he had taken his tea alone in the shanty.

She did not know what else to say. She liked being here with Nate and not explaining herself to anyone, and Mr. Hultberg was free to think what he wished. The sun beamed down, warming the place where they sat.

"These boys're too slow making me rich, and too poor to develop the claim properly. Takes pumps and hoses and lumber and men to get the ore out at any volume. Should have thirty-five, forty men on two shifts shoveling into sluices running across the whole claim. Your fella smart about that?"

"Very much so," she said, and she felt it was true enough. She watched Nate crouch with his pan and wash out the gravel. When the pan looked all but empty he sorted the remains with his forefinger. "Looks like he might be finding something."

"Oh, he'll have something, all right," Hultberg said. "Anvil Creek's where the gold's at. Most of us have got forced out, you know." He fiddled with his nose.

"Would you like a handkerchief?"

He shook his head. "Got one."

"How do you mean, forced out?"

"Lindblom, Bryntesen, and Lindeberg. Discovery claim, and four of the others. Richest in the district. You know the talk."

She knew what Lena had told her. "That they staked them illegally, not being Americans."

"No truth in it, but a hungry man'll eat big on wishful thinking. So these other fellas came up and put down their own stakes and then filed with the court. Judge said contested claims have to be put under protection until the mess gets sorted out, which is what he did, last month. Only thing is, he named that shifty fella McKenzie to be the receiver."

"Meaning?"

"The watchdog. McKenzie's a fox in the henhouse."

Esther shook her head politely, then said, "Oh, yes! He was on our ship!"

"Big, blustery son of a gun up from North Dakota with a pile of funny money, going around buying claims from men who don't hold honest title, tying good mines up in legal knots. Struts around telling people how it's going to be, and if they don't like it, well, that's too bad because he's like this with the judge," and he showed her two fingers lying tight together.

"He is all trouble. Trotted up here to Lindeberg's claim with the court order in his hand and a posse of goons and took over the whole blankety thing. Sluices, lines, pumps, shovels. Even the tents and supplies."

Esther had not kept up with it. She watched Nate fuss over the residue in his pan, using a little scale and putting what he'd found into his handkerchief, which he tucked into his pocket. He went over to one of the men working at a sluice and asked him questions and poked his finger in the box, then went to a new part of the stream and squatted with his pan again.

Hultberg said, "If I was Lindeberg, I would've run McKenzie off at the end of a shotgun, but Lindeberg's against guns. Says he will get the claim back in court."

"Better than guns," Esther said, feeling peckish and wishing more than ever she'd had a tea.

"So you say." Hultberg finally fished a dirty rag out of his back pocket and blew his nose. "McKenzie's taking a fortune out of the ground every day. Receivership's not supposed to work that way. Put a mine in receivership, you ought a let it lie fallow, leave the gold in the ground until the ownership's set straight."

"Is that so?" she said. Nate was on to another spot already. Why hadn't she thought to pack a picnic?

"Not according to McKenzie. Season's too short! He's obligated to work it! It is not only Swedes that're getting jumped. Anybody making good cleanups is asking for it. One of the reasons I have not pushed to develop my claim. Brag up what you got, and McKenzie'll get you relocated before breakfast, blessings said by the God-Amighty Judge of the Second Judicial District of the Territory of Alaska, the Honorable Arthur H. Noyes himself.

"I myself got jumped last year, but got it squared by the U.S. Commissioner and have had no trouble since." He lifted his shotgun a few inches to put across his point and leaned it back against the bench.

"I have other interests, you know, oh, yes, I do. I have Number Five on Melsing in the Council District. I have Number Six on Ophir. Going to be a wealthy man, get these parasites, pirates, and blasphemes cleared out, get some crews in here to work the claims properly."

"My people are Norwegian," she said.

He grunted. "They call 'em the Three Lucky Swedes, but Lindeberg's a Norske, you know."

"Worked eight pans," Nate was saying, coming up from the creek. "Got good colors in six, right off the creek bottom." He opened his handkerchief and showed them, then Hultberg opened a poke. Nate spilled the flakes into it with great concentration.

Hultberg tied the poke. "Discovery's cleaning up fifteen thousand dollars a day, and I don't see why this one'd be any less'n that, but I will thank you not to advertise it."

"I will report to Mr. Sprague," Nate said. "I'm sure you will be hearing from him quickly."

"I don't promise to hold it," Hultberg said sternly. "First reputable outfit that meets my price gets the lay."

"As they should, sir. We will not hold you in suspense." He offered his hand, which Hultberg accepted. "Miss Crummey and I have another obligation and must get along."

NEKULA GULCH LAY a mile and a half up the valley, and they went along by foot, in no hurry. The upland tundra made for considerably easier walking than the tussocks and sponge mosses of the flats.

"Was it good?" Esther asked.

"Oh, probably. You can't know without mining it, but what a penny-ante operation. All this manual labor. What these claims up here are begging for is machinery, Essie. What I could do with a big old steam shovel and a gravel elevator! Dig down to bedrock from one end of the claim to the other in a single season. Pull out my gold and go on home and get busy with spending it."

"You are all up on motors, aren't you?"

"Nothing's more useful, and no better place than here on one of these creeks where all you've got is break-your-back shoveling to reach the pay streak. If I had a steam shovel, I wouldn't need a claim, I could make all the money I want hiring out to drive it on another man's claim."

"That Mr. Hultberg was tied up in fits over the man named McKenzie taking over his neighbors' claims."

"I understand there's some dirty dealing," Nate said.

"The judge is a part of it?"

"I would be the last to know. Nekula Gulch is over thataway. Isn't it a grand sight up here, though, high and looking out?" He stopped to take off his mackinaw.

"I am positively kicking myself for not packing a picnic," she said.

"Oh," Nate said. "Hang on. Let's sit a minute." He spread the mackinaw on the ground and they sat down and he loosened a tie on his knapsack and rooted around, pulling out something wrapped in a towel that turned out to be a cornbread cake. "How will this do?"

"Oh!" She threw her arms around his neck to hug him, but he turned and caught her lips with his own. He took her in his arms and kissed her with a heat that drew a squeal from her, sent her hands to the back of his head, her fingers through his hair, he pulling her down to the mackinaw, his hands running up the sides of her, grazing her breasts, cupping the curve of her jaw, and then she turned her head aside and said, "My heavens." She raised up on an elbow, fanning herself to make light of the sudden heat.

He lay back and laughed. "I could no more keep from doing that than keep from breathing. I am feverish around you, Essie. I never met a girl like you. You have more sass and go-do-it than any girl I know."

"I get a kick out of you," she said softly. "Isn't it nice?" She broke off a piece of the cake for him and one for herself and leaned back and looked him in the eyes and told herself not to think or to say anything much, just feel the sun and like the boy and don't make it complicated.

When they had eaten, he laced fingers with her. "You know, if the big plant doesn't find gold in the next few days, we'll be striking the beach camp. Heading up to creek country."

She felt the twinge of disappointment. It was no surprise, but she'd hoped it wouldn't come so soon. "Where will you go?"

"There's rumors coming out of the Bluestone District, northwest of here. Or maybe up to the Council District. Ophir Creek."

She sat up. "Well."

"What?"

"You won't be much around here, then."

"Sure I will. I will go and come back."

"I have liked knowing you."

"Don't say it like that."

"How should I say it?"

"Like you want to keep on knowing me."

"Sure I do, but you're going off, and then the season will be finished."

"Are you going out, then?" he asked.

She thought for a while. "My own business has gone iffy. Three biggest customers quit their beach plants last week. The others might do, too. Luckily, I have Boy Tom getting dogs. I believe Mr. Thurl will move his livery up to Third Street so we have the room for a dog lot. We're going to make good money on them at the first serious snowfall. But I'm going to be rid of my delivery business sooner than I guessed. We are looking at trading in surplus."

"You're not going to sail for the Outside, then?"

She broke off another piece of cake. "Not soon." She watched the wind ruffle the cotton flowers.

He leaned over and kissed her again, and she gave back, letting him explore a little, and when it started to gather steam she broke it off and he pushed his nose against her hairline, her temple, her nape.

"Beginning to wonder what kind of a picnic you have invited me on, Mr. Deaton."

"Another few minutes, it will come clear, I believe."

She adjusted the mackinaw. "See this sleeve? Your side is there, this side is mine."

"You are a hard customer!"

"Yes, sir." She slid the knapsack under her head and reached for his hand and stared into the thin sky. Things had happened so fast, she couldn't see ahead. For the first time in her life she had some money, and for the first time it wasn't money that she thought about, or her old life, or who she used to be. What she thought about was him, and who she was becoming, and she did not have an answer for either. People looked at her differently here. She felt like she had found a part of herself she'd always longed for but never knew how to get, and she didn't know if it was being in Alaska that made her feel this way and it would disappear the minute she went to her sister's, or if she was different for real and she could take it with her. It was a mystery that made her happy and uneasy at the same time. When she thought of going back to the States, there was a reckoning she did not wish for.

"What will you do, Nate?"

"Try to set the company up with three or four solid creek claims. Come back next summer to work like a sorry son of a gun and make 'em pay off." He would have liked more than anything for her to go creek prospecting with him and make an adventure of it, but it was a foolish thought. The two of them gallivanting across the countryside. The going would be rough. It would hardly be proper.

"Who are your people?" she asked.

"Oh, insurance men. The kind who peer over actuarial tables, take checks from young family men, and write checks to their widows."

"Not you, though."

"No, I am a motor man through and through. Getting up a dandy little manufactory, once we make this gold business pay."

"Do you think a person can become something different from what his people are?"

"You should be the last one to ask. Your people are farmers and you are a natural capitalist. You should take what you made here and parlay it into something. I mean it. Not one man in ten has your sense for business."

"Don't be silly," she said, but his words gave her a little thrill, because a part of her thought he was right, she ought to do exactly that. "Most likely I'll go on to Ballard and look for work in a mill."

"I don't like to think of it, Essie."

"When will you be going out, then?"

"Last of September."

She knew he had people waiting for him. One would be the girl who sends the letters. Lily Wilder. Esther felt the air leak out of her and the old flatness come back, for the truth of it was that it would not pay her to be overly fond of him. He came out of a different world, and he would go back to a different world. It was all right to enjoy a walk with him in this place, but she had no business getting ideas he wouldn't fit with.

A silence settled over them, and her disappointment in him made her itchy. She picked up his shotgun where it lay across the mackinaw and put her eye to the sights.

"Where'd you get this, anyhow? Let's shoot something."

"Nothing here but moss and cotton flowers."

She scowled.

"Those barrels are real Damascus steel, by the way," he said. "Made by hand. Remington 82, twelve-bore, choked for small birds. Belonged to my father."

"Let me try it."

"Fine, but what're you going to aim at?"

"Watch me."

He dug a shell out of his pack and cracked the gun and loaded it and gave it back to her. She lay on her stomach, propped the barrel on the knapsack, and sighted for the tops of the cotton flowers.

Blam! "Got it!"

The gun blasted a gully through the flowers and mosses. She sat up and admired the weapon, particularly an engraving on the side of the chamber showing a hound with a cock pheasant in its mouth.

"A beautiful thing," she said. "And your pa gave it to you."

"He was taken by the consumption when I was twelve."

She nodded slowly and handed it back. She gave him a sweet smile, and by some invisible signal they agreed it was time to press on, and so they gathered up their things.

AS THEY AMBLED on toward the head of the valley, they paused frequently to remark the view and point out signs of work below or across the way.

"See those men on the hillsides above the creek? Those are bench claims. The gold's in the ancient streambeds, which ran a different course than the creek you see today. You guess where the old bed's going to lie, then you dig a shaft down to bedrock, tunnel around till you find the pay streak, and then mosey along following the pay. You call them drift mines.

"Those little log cribs built up around the openings? The man above lowers the bucket on the windlass. His partner below fills it and gives a jerk on the line. Up goes the bucket. They'll do that all winter long, make a great big molehill around the crib. Next summer when the creeks thaw they'll shovel their diggings into a rocker or a Long Tom and clean up their fortune."

At Nekula Gulch they met a man named McCormick who had a bench claim a hundred feet on a side and showed Nate an honest-to-God ounce-and-a-half pan. Nome gold brought $16 the ounce, so the fellow had a $24 pan, a thing Nate had heard of hereabouts but never seen. The pay streak was eighteen feet deep. The claims were small and hard going; the men were striking permafrost at ten inches and had to go at it with coal fires and picks. One fellow had a small boiler that ran steam through hoses to metal points he drove into the ice with a wooden hammer. McCormick's pocket was rich but too small for what the company needed.

They headed back down the slope for the train at Anvil, holding hands, in no hurry to get home.

"Plug Jefferson told Lena that Ophir Creek's as rich as Anvil and maybe more."

Nate nodded. "Everybody's heard of Ophir."

On the train they watched the coastal plain slowly rise to meet them. "Sorry you did not see any of your fancy birds," she said.

"Only the one," he said.

"Where?" She hadn't seen any at all.

"Out on the open tundra. I believe you were gazing at the sky."

"Darn it! Why didn't you say?"

But it was her that he meant. A true accidental, blown from her home by the winds of fortune, and it was he who'd spotted her first.

18

The wind roared out of the west that night and raged for the next four days, raising an angry swell that swept the roadstead and thundered against the beach. The big ships sailed to sea rather than drag their anchors. The Cape Nome Company men bit their tongues and winched their car to the top of the beach. They humped their stores to higher ground, double-pegged the tents, and sat by their roaring stoves hearing the guylines sing. Up and down the beach, miners with rockers abandoned their diggings and company men worked to save their plants. Barges and small craft struggled to make the lee of Sledge Island or the shelter of the sand spit.

The gale subsided to a freshening breeze on the fifth day, and the Cape Nome Company men could wait no longer. They lowered the car into the rollicking sea and gave it a hard run. For three days and three nights, uninterrupted, they dredged bottom gravel into their sluices at the rate of five thousand gallons a minute. Nights were dark now, and turned freezing, but the men worked around the clock in shifts, their hands gone numb, their hats pulled down and their wool collars buttoned close. On the morning of the fourth day, the mountains to the north lay white with fresh snow. Exhausted, they blew down the boiler and cleaned up the sluices, but the floor of the Bering Sea gave up no riches.

WORD CAME THAT the strike at Gold Run Creek in the Bluestone District was solid and the stampede was on, sixty miles northwest of Nome. The best route was by sea around Cape Douglas to Teller, at the foot of the broad bay called Port Clarence. A man named Wooley, in possession of inside information at the Pacific Abstract & Title Company, held claims on Farrington and Nickle Creeks in which he offered a half interest to the Major, along with a half interest in Number Three Below on Gold Run.

"I will go, of course," Nate told Palmer. "But the Hultberg lay at Five Above on Anvil is here in our own back yard."

"Hultberg's asking too much. Bill wants to wait him out."

It was the last of August already, and the weather still continued rough. Nate made a pack of a rubber sheet, two woolen blankets, his pan, shovel, shotgun, and personal gear. He abandoned any thought of a tent for the weight, taking a bottle of whiskey for barter instead. He collapsed the *Miss Nomer*, making a bundle of her, rather cumbersome with the sail and spars, and secured passage on the steam schooner *Albion*. The *Albion* burrowed into a westering sea with such a pitch and yaw that not a man aboard her kept his dinner, but they found a camaraderie of misery at the rails.

They steamed into the shelter of Port Clarence late the next afternoon and put ashore at Teller. To their south was a settlement of

Eskimo huts, skin boats, and elevated funerary platforms, but where the *Albion* landed was a city of tents and stampeders in the midst of a great commotion, men staking lots and laying out the coming boomtown. Nate entrusted his pack and boat to the freight depot and went on with twenty or more passengers to the recorder's office in hopes of seeing how the creeks had been staked, but when he got there the place was in hopeless confusion. Ten dollars and earnest pleading rented him a narrow strip of plank flooring in a drafty tent billed as the Kougarok Hotel. Three dollars at a grimy diner called the Republican got him counter space and a plate of boiled mackerel. The company was loud and well aroused by whiskey, and as soon as he'd eaten he walked to the pier to get his pack out of hock and turn in at the hotel.

The next morning it took an hour and a half to find breakfast, but he was shoving off for Gold Run Creek by seven, sheathed in his oilskins, climbing the gentle rise from Teller. There was not a tree in the entire country, nothing but scrub willow on the creeks and tundra up to the tops of the hills. There was no trail, either, and any kind of normal stride proved impossible, the tussocks standing up eighteen inches and rolling the moment he placed his foot. The rain fell in showers off and on, and when it came it drove straight into his face. This gold-hunting business was not as he had imagined it from the hearth of his first-year teacher's apartment at Worcester, an apartment that six months ago had felt like suffocation itself but now struck him as the dearest of refuges, if he could have it without the life that it entailed, which of course he could not.

He stopped to dig for his handkerchief. For more than two weeks he had been derelict in his correspondence with Lily, reluctant to disappoint her with news of the company's fading prospects. Better to say nothing until the outcome was certain, and then present it forthrightly and ask forgiveness for the hiatus. And so in the mindless work of traipsing across the Bluestone he composed some opening lines, looking for the one that would pull him neatly through his little discourse.

> *Dearest Lily, Please do not misconstrue my silence. Nothing is so predictable in the gold hunting business as the unpredictability of it! Duty and distance . . . , we have turned every stone, quite literally . . . , still remains some possibility of the creek claims. . . . For example, when I investigated Anvil Creek . . .*

This brought him to the interlude with Hultberg, which account would require the omission of his travel partner, a fact that caused him to discard this line of explanation altogether and look for something entirely different.

> *Dearest Lily, Please forgive my silence. We have been at our utmost in the gold hunting enterprise. Do not let my epistolary negligence belie the fact. Au contraire. Ever mindful of our first duty, that being the pursuit of our investors' interests. . . .*

He stopped and blew his nose in irritation at himself. Normally he was adept at this. Nothing yet had the simplicity and buoyancy to carry him to the far side of his problem. Which was what?

> *Dearest Lily, I have come to believe that our futures do not belong together.*

Oh, Lord. There it was. Chased into the clear. How could he think it, much less say it?

Dearest Lily, In all seriousness, there is a farm girl among us who deserves a proper rogering, and Doctor Donaldson reports that I am to be the man for the job.

He stopped to rest, letting his pack drop and then sitting himself down heavily upon it. Lily and he were not pledged to each other. That was a point right off. Why did he labor under such a weight of obligation? It was the future that she had constructed for them out of one simple idea. The idea that they were very good together. The unspoken symmetry of it: her picture-book good looks, the Judge's position and means but lack of sons; Nate's brains, his family name but vanished prospects. She would restore to him what had been lost; he would give his name to her and father Judge Wilder's grandchildren. A tidy package. Their suitability had gained a certain currency among their friends, and, by reflection, with Lily. And, by extension, or for lack of objection, with Nate.

He leaned forward, stretching the muscle at the base of his neck that had gone crampy, and massaged his shoulders where the straps had dug in. Other stampeders had walked ahead of him or lagged behind, and he was grateful to be free of the forced cheer of comradeship, mile upon mile.

He hefted the pack and pressed on, feeling very low indeed. None of them had considered the possibility that gold could sit upon the beach in abundance and be wholly absent in the gravels below tide. One day you are a man of expectations. Cock of the walk. All of your ideas are clever ones. Next you're just another long face staring at an empty hole. The difference was entirely of the mind. He sighed and wondered why he could not rise above it. Entirely of the mind, but paralyzing nonetheless.

His mood was elevated briefly by the sounds of bugling, and he looked up to behold a vision that arrested him where he stood: a flight of seventy or eighty little brown cranes passing overhead, making their way east. The migration was on.

Would that he could join their flight. The sodden land stretched before him in a gentle rise for miles. It was a curiosity of the tundra, lacking outcroppings or trees, that a man had no landmarks by which to judge distance or mark his progress. The far mountain seems only a short hike away; a man walks for days in the misapprehension that he is soon to surmount a pass or reach a near-off valley, but every time he lifts his head the view is just as it was the hour before, or even the day before.

After a very long five hours from Teller, it was only just noon. He hadn't the strength to embrace the next hundred yards, much less the four or five miles remaining. He shed his pack and sat down, dug out a loaf of bread and a salami, and unlaced his right boot. His heel stung unmercifully. He'd raised and burst a blister. He doctored the wound with tincture of carbolic acid and covered it with a layer of cotton which he endeavored to keep in place as he pulled up his stocking. A sparrow lit on a mossy hummock and began to search for insects. A Lapland longspur. It pecked in the grass, hopped to a new hummock, pecked twice, then flitted off. A small perfection. Nate felt ever the dull giant.

The miserable sponge of a sky began to shower on him again and he moved on, tucking his thumbs into the pack straps to ease the strain on his hips from favoring the foot. It was a dreary damned empty place with not so much as a solitary tent in sight through all the hours of the afternoon.

The rain gave over to cloaks of mist that masked the hills intermittently. Finally, the strike at Gold Run appeared out of the gloom as two hundred or more white tents marching up both sides of the creek. He limped into the settlement's lower end at a half past four o'clock, already pulling out his whiskey bottle. He was in no mood to fuss over amenities and secured himself squatting rights in the first halfway-commodious tent he reached.

After changing his socks and piling the bulk of his cargo in his corner of the tent, he hiked on up the creek. At Number Nine Above he watched the day's cleanup. It was rich: two men in a two-length sluice box cleaned up more than $1,000. Men were getting pans from 50 cents to $10 right off the creek bottom. But Number Nine proved to be the only place they were taking any significant gold. Claims Five, Seven, and Twelve were prospecting and getting ready to work. He could find no trace of Wooley's Number Three Below. All had been jumped several times within two months and promised a tremendous tangle of litigation.

THE RETURN HIKE to Teller passed more easily than the trip out. He spent another night at the Kougarok Hotel, and at mid-morning the next day he set off from Teller in the *Miss Nomer*, sailing on a close reach fourteen miles south by southwest down the coast of Port Clarence for Nickle Creek. He'd brought his entire kit and prepared to stay the night, using the craft for his shelter. He ran ahead of a dark storm cloud, feeling the thrill of the live rope in his hand, great flights of geese and ducks laboring south in the low sky off his right shoulder. With only himself and his gear for ballast the skiff flew ahead like a trotter, heeled to leeward, dipping into the troughs and slapping the crests. He would far sooner raise a blister on his hands and a sore back from pulling the sheet than repeat his misery over the tundra. The cape sat too low and distant to be seen, and yet he scanned for a dark rim on the horizon that would suggest migratory birds massing against the far shore. Almost certainly they were there. After he'd done with the creeks he would hoist sail and go around to see. Why not? With a hand on his steering oar and another on the sheet, the bay of Port Clarence was his to explore.

He threw his head back and laughed aloud. There was something about the cleverness of what he'd built, the skiff's prevailing against the quick sea despite its crudeness. The remoteness of this wilderness. The crust of salt on his cheek and the implausibility of his being there. He filled his lungs and pitched his voice to the wind and gave out cry. He felt a part of the wildness. He imagined Essie beside him, and in a way she was. She was the wind and he was the dancing skiff: improvising, alert, full-blooded. She was the storm he meant to sail into. Whatever the mess and impossibilities. A married woman. Would you say headstrong? He could not turn away from it, would never be more alive. He hadn't known his mind for certain until he'd struggled for the words to write Lily. In truth he wished the same for Lily: to feel caught by the storm. To hoist her scrap of canvas and be taken.

He reached a sand spit short of Nickle Creek and ran the skiff against the beach. Quickly, he pulled out his gear and raised the leeboard, dragged her over to water, her canvas snapping wildly, and suddenly he saw them: The inlet formed by the sand spit was teeming with sheltering waterfowl.

He ran back for his gear, his heart racing, stowed it and shoved off.

He sailed the last mile on a broad reach, parting rafts of resting northern pintail, eiders, and brants. Scaup, harlequins, and oldsquaw. Pelagic cormorants. A pair of black-throated loons. He could hardly navigate for the distraction.

The gathering storm lowered over him as he nosed into the mouth of the Nickle. He dropped the sail, unstepped the mast, and overturned the boat. He stole two minutes gazing back at the birds before the cloud opened and he was forced to scuttle into his shelter like a hermit crab.

Lord above. He propped himself on his pack, the noise of his own thoughts drowned by the sudden thrum of rain against the hull. The wind licked under the gunwales and pierced him with a chill. He rolled onto his belly and unpacked his rubber sheet and blankets, found his food sack. He wrapped himself against the wind, and when the blankets' warmth seeped through him and stilled the shivering he relaxed and began to eat his dinner. Hardtack, kippers, and cheese. There was never a tastier meal, nor a sanctuary more welcome.

HE DOZED UNTIL the rain cleared, and then forced himself out of his cocoon. See to the business of hunting gold. Nickle Creek yielded nothing that afternoon but the pleasure of prospecting to a backdrop of bugling and honking, thousands of birds on the water and those passing low overhead.

The next day, at Farrington Creek, the willow thickets were alive with sparrows and their like—Lapland longspurs, Wilson's warblers, a gray-cheeked thrush. A wagtail appeared through the willows but left before he could mark it clearly. Probably a juvenile in its first winter plumage, but he was nagged by its overlong tail and decided not to move up the creek for a while, and sure enough, minutes later it lit on a branch not twenty feet away. He took it with a solitary shot. The gun's report cleared the thicket, sending the birds aloft in a whoosh, but he didn't care, for he bent to discover his wagtail was the rarest thing—a white, a denizen of Asia blown across the strait, or perhaps come for better summer forage. A treasure! His collection was truly growing into something.

Farrington Creek was his lucky stop all around. A white wagtail in his pocket and colors in two of the four pans he washed out. He'd do what he could back in Teller to verify Wooley's title at the recorder's office.

Duty performed, he launched the *Miss Nomer* without sail and rowed slowly through the rafting birds toward the base of the cape that formed the bay. The cape itself was low-lying, broad, and marshy. Tundra swans circled and landed by fours and sixes and then took flight again. He nosed the skiff ashore and sat statue-still, letting the birds on the mudflats and in the salt grass draw near. Arctic terns. The long-billed dowitcher. Whimbrels. He thought of his precious wagtail, and a fragment of Shakespeare came to him: *Fortune brings in some boats that are not steered.* That he and the wagtail should meet at the same moment in this remote corner of the world—surely this was the hand of fortune. He was not a deeply religious man, and yet to what can you ascribe it? Fate. Yes, of course. But what is fate? Take Essie, for example. Was her boat steered?

In a moment of lesser wind, a movement in the salt grass caught his eye. Little heads bobbing his way. As they emerged they were unmistakable: *Phalaropus fulicaria*, the red phalarope. Juveniles. Dark cap and eye patch, thick bill, dark back with a hint of buff at the hindneck and breast. They pecked at the ground and moved slowly toward him, four, six, nine, ten, eleven—dear God. Busy at their foraging, unaware of his presence. He forced himself to breathe. Slowly, slowly, he broke open the Remington and fit a shell into the right chamber. He shut the gun and raised it to his eye. They were no bigger than six inches. His finger rested on the trigger. Some would be obliterated at this distance, but three or four would be presentable. They were not so rare as the white wagtail—why did his heart race?—but they were rare enough, more than rare enough. It was their lore and mystery that intrigued him, that he longed to possess. *Phalaropus fulicaria*. (Squeeze off a shot. Where was his shot?) Waders, not true pelagics, and yet they fly impossible distances to sea and spin in mad circles like corks on the surface of the deepest ocean and no man can explain it. No man can explain it.

Blam!

He sniffed and cleared his throat and put down the gun. Wiped his forehead on his sleeve. His trigger finger had nearly betrayed him.

> *Dearest Lily, This separation has revealed my truer nature to me. It is baser by far than you have reason to suspect. I find my attentions drawn afield. I no longer know my own self. Nor can I say that I aspire to the kind of life you and I have spent happy afternoons sketching on air.*
>
> *It pains me to hurt you, but if in doing so I save you from a future humiliation, then it is the pain of needed medicine, and I apologize even as I insist on administering it. I will hardly blame you for feeling a deep anger and resentment.*

Something like that it would have to be.

PART IV

19

Leonard stood at the bow of the *Skookum* as the *Holyoke* hauled her into Norton Sound. The Bering Sea blew up as sharp as shard ice and he longed for the banked fire of whiskey. The towline pulled from a chain shackled into a bridle at the bow, and with the rise of each swell the *Skookum* reined back, sending a shiver through the hawser and forcing a groan from her bones. Leonard stared off where he thought the horizon should lie, hoping for an opening in the weather and a glimpse of shore, but rain squalls shrouded the coast. At twilight half a dozen ships ghosted out of the soup riding at anchor, and it was then he knew they had finally reached the place called Nome.

The *Holyoke* pulled the *Skookum* around to face the wind and then cut her power so they were going neither forward nor back, just holding their position against the storm. At the sound of her whistle Captain Folsom called for the *Skookum*'s anchors. Leonard and the other deckhands lowered away; the *Holyoke* apparently cut her power again, for the *Skookum* slowly backed off her position, unfurling the chains of her anchors. When it was certain she was holding, the Captain called for the towline to be released. The *Holyoke* steamed around beside the barge and the two captains spoke through trumpets before the *Holyoke* went off a thousand feet and set her own anchors. Here the *Skookum* would sit until the seas settled and they could round up the fleet of barges and scows needed to take off her cargo. Leonard paced the long deck, did his work, and kept an eye toward shore. The first place he would look was at all the stables.

ESTHER PUT THE Major's mail on his desk and made a face over his sour ashtray—a man whose stride is not slowed by particulars, sure that others follow with dustpans. She emptied the cigar ends into a wastebasket and carried the ashtray and his dirty coffee cup to the sink, where she rinsed them and caught sight of herself in the mirror. She dabbed cold water on her face and pinned her hair back and tried to give her smile a little starch, but uncertainty pulled at the corners of her eyes and she looked away.

Leonard had come to her in the night and she could not shake him off. "In sickness and in health," he had whispered on the pillow, using (of all things) the Norse. An absurd dream. For a while he became her father, scolding, hurtful, and then he was himself again.

"Two will be as one," he had whispered.

Swimming in drink, she had answered. Failed at the bank. Our boy under the sod, and death do us part, Leonard. *Death do us part.* She'd carried the phrase in the pocket of her mind, worn smooth with repetition. It had sustained her, had got her free of him and carried her clear to Nome, an amulet against the forces of doubt for what she had done, walking out on her man. And then she'd gone and lost herself to building a business, looking for birds, and talking nonsense with pretty fellas. Wasn't it just like Leonard to do that—come at her the moment she let down her guard.

Esther pulled a sheet of bond from the desk, halved it with a crease, and lettered "Back at Noon" on the face of it. Pulling up her hood, she stepped out into the rain and glanced down toward Front Street. She had taken to scanning the faces for Nate's in the off chance he'd returned early and was already coming along to the offices, but no.

She turned up toward Third, where Mr. Thurl had moved his livery business. She would pass word to him before going to the Alaska Commercial Company store to write up the Cape Nome Company's order, supposing that her own clients, leaving for the Outside, were busy at the work of shedding possessions and could well show up ahead of her, taking Thurl unawares and possibly (very likely) getting rebuffed; the man couldn't smell rank opportunity when you put it under his nose and told him to breathe in.

Steadman was a river of mud, axle-deep in places. Esther kept to the narrow boardwalk and paused in doorways to let others pass. The tail end of the mining season loomed and prices were coming down. There was nothing left to her beach delivery business. Storms had put an end to the big plants and then cleared the beach of all but the most stubborn miners. She'd told Thurl that if he put up a storehouse they could go into trading surplus—sure as snow melts there'd be another stampede, and what-all the miners were walking away from today would be in fancy demand by spring. He'd gone out and bought two lots on Third, and now, in addition to his stables tent and the dog lot behind it, he had put up a fine wood-frame storehouse half paid for by Esther and roofed with salvaged steel drums he'd cut open and nailed more or less flat. You cannot make a round barrel lie wholly flat and she did not care for the rumply look of it on a building she owned a half of, or how the rain puddled brown with rust, but Thurl was a man proud of his economies and she was quiet on them unless it was money to speak out.

When she reached the end of the block the mud on Second was impassable and she was forced to walk half a block west and cross in front of the Plantation Hotel and then fight the crowds back toward Steadman on the north boardwalk. She felt better now that she was out and moving, lost to other things, like how to handle Thurl on the matter of his reindeer hides. The man could get fixed on a thing firmer than a taproot in hardpan. She was not involved with the hides and had tried to turn him away from trading them because of the time and space they took up, the smell of it, and who's to say about lice. "Miners' surplus pays nothing until spring," he'd said. "Where's your winter money? Hides is winter money."

"The winter money's dogs," she'd said.

"Hides and dogs," he'd said.

The smell of it brought her Leonard and his wolving. She'd put her foot down. "The building's half mine, Mr. Thurl. There'll be no hides on my half."

"Suit yourself, then."

Her wording had been a mistake. What she'd meant was that she owned a half interest in the building and had equal say in how it was used, but she was not going to correct herself to Thurl. He knew what she'd meant but went on ahead and set up on his half anyway, with vats for the rendering and racks for drying. She'd told herself to get on with buying up the miners' surplus and filling the building faster than his Eskimos were doing their skinning, but it nettled her. Not just the distraction of it or the mess, but losing the argument. The idea of his having his own business on his side and him and her sharing the surplus business on her side. The fact was (it came to her now) she would be in her rights to charge him rent for using half their building for his hides.

She stopped at Third and Steadman, thoroughly taken by this new idea. She intended to cross, and it was a moment before she noticed the commotion in the intersection. A fellow in a fox hat sat a balky white horse under the downpouring rain, beating its rump with a quirt. The horse was an ivory-colored gelding, haughty and erect, picking its legs like a high-stepper, but it was frothy at the mouth and had mud to its withers. Esther stepped into the street and when she reached the rider she spoke up. "For pity's sake, it's all gumbo below here! Go and stable the horse and use your own God-given feet for a change! See, look—Thurl's Livery, just up there. He'll have room."

The fellow tipped his hat to her, pursing his lips prissily, and then dug his heels at the animal, forcing it ahead into the mire. He had been aboard the *Miss Madden*. He was the man people were calling King McKenzie. High and almighty even back then, when you could see how high the hat but never guessed how long the reach.

She pressed up Third. Beyond the sign that proclaimed "Thurl's Livery & Sale" hung a new one: "Miner's Quality Surplus, Carleton Thurl Proprietor, Outfits Bought and Sold." She slipped around back to look at the dogs, which were sodden and filthy, lying in the mud or in empty drums that Thurl had put around for kennels. Each dog was chained to an iron stake. Before Thurl had gotten the dog lot organized he'd put them all together in one pen, and inside of an hour three of them had gotten their throats ripped out by the biggest malamute, which was two hundred dollars' profit spilled in blood. The man was strange to dogs. Up until that moment she'd had no idea. She'd had to ask Eskimo Tom to come set him straight on how to do them. The main thing was keeping them apart.

She went through the stables to the storehouse, where she found him hammering up more shelves. "I see we are up to twenty-three dogs. I owe Boy Tom some money."

"Miss Crummey." Thurl got down off a ladder and dug his snuff out of an overall pocket.

It was dark in the storehouse and when her eyes adjusted she saw he had a hundred or more raw hides piled along the back wall, twice what he'd had two days ago.

He put a pinch under his lip. "Got your tins," he said.

"So I see." Some 142 cases of tinned fruits and vegetables that had lost their labels. They took up two entire shelves. She had paid two cents a tin with the notion of turning them around to one of the hotel dining rooms or grocers for three cents.

"What about 'em, then?" he said. "Can't be left in here to freeze."

He was wet through and muddy. Made her skin clammy to look at him. He would do a brisker trade if he kept himself neater, but she was not going to be the one to say it. She made it a point not to get personal with Thurl, who had contrary ideas, having tried to slide his hand up her skirt one day. When she swatted it away he'd said, "Could do worse than me, miss." "I already have done, Mr. Thurl, and I am still married to the man." They each had left it at that. She could see in the way he groomed and gentled the horses that he would not be unpleasing to be with, but she did not need it or wish for their business to snag on a burr of something personal.

"I came by to tell you about the Brooklyn Gold Company."

"Don't know it." He shoved at his lip with a knuckle.

"Mr. Isaacs? The little Jew from New York?"

He shook his head.

"One of my best clients. He's offered us his whole outfit. I bought the five tents, stoves, and wood floors all for three dollars, and his workshops for twenty-five." She paused, thinking he might nod at the terms she'd worked. He stood impassive. "So, it's a good thing you are building shelves."

"That's it?"

She took her rain hood off and refastened her hair. "He asked a hundred and fifty dollars for his pump and piping. He was dug in over it. Said it cost him Balaam's ass in shipping charges to get it up here, he was not taking it home."

Thurl frowned. "We already agreed on no heavy equipment."

"So I said! I said, 'Sorry, but we do not deal in machines.' What next but he gets all sniffy. 'Take the whole blankity-blank outfit or nothing!' "

"They all of 'em think they're doing us a favor," Thurl said.

"Said I would think about it, and then I went over to the Pioneer warehouse and talked to Mr. Larsson, who said unless it was designed to pump froze water he wouldn't have any call for it until next spring and couldn't go higher than fifty dollars. So I went back to Isaacs and counted him out forty-five in greenbacks. He called me an angel of God."

Thurl nodded. "What about them tins? Was a mistake, your buying those. You don't know if it's a plum or an okra, are you making a pudding or a soup, bejesus."

Annoyed her that he begrudged the slightest compliment over her terms with Isaacs. Would be hell-fires at the North Pole the day he ever made terms like that. She spoke slowly, as to a foreigner. "You open your tins and then, after you see what's inside, you decide your menu. It is all good food. Every one of them."

"Who's taking 'em?"

She glanced at his hides and back at the piles of tins, looking for an answer, and then came out with it. "I tried North American

Transportation and Trading Company, but guess what? NAT&TCo's already got fifty cases of their own selling for a dollar a hundred."

Thurl harrumphed.

She'd been kicking herself over it. "Would the dogs eat it?"

"Oh, hell, yes, if that's what I slop 'em."

"All right, then," she said. "Also, I talked to the Mongollon people. They have an interesting hospital outfit. I offered ten dollars. They want a hundred and said they'd sit on it. If they bring it up, you can pay ten for it, not more than fifteen. If they bring their buckboard and harnesses, you can give them another ten, but I told them we would not take the horses."

"I will take what they bring me, up until your half is filled, but then I am going to have to turn it away."

"Well, fine!" she said, hot now. "And I will take a hundred dollars rent every month for my share of the hide business."

Thurl looked dumbstruck. "It's my business."

"The rent's for the building. I own a half."

Thurl spat to one side and his left eye twitched. He had a face like a baked potato, and it had gone red. "Am not paying rent for a building I own. You take a share of the hide business if you want it, but don't come looking for rent money."

Oh, for pity's sake. She looked him up and down. Taproot in clay hardpan. Most worthless piece of dead wood she'd ever thought to do business with. "All right, then."

SHE WENT AROUND to the Post Office and called at the back door and gave Inspector Crum a list of the men whose mail she would no longer accept. From the Post Office she went on down to the Alaska Commercial Company store, where she wrote up the

Major's order: two cases of navy beans, and a hundred pounds each of potatoes, beans, flour, lard, bacon, powdered eggs, and salted meat to be delivered to CNCo at Five Above on Anvil Creek.

It was well after noon when she got back to the offices. No Nate, not that she thought he would be. She warmed a tin of beans and sat to Lena's desk to eat it, and wrote the letter she had been composing in her mind for weeks.

Dear Father,
As you will have heard I went up to Nome in Alaska with some honest people and now I can say I have had a good delivery business this summer. A man from Minneapolis called Butler is going out on the Ohio *tomorrow and has promised to carry $750 for me to put in the Northwest Bank of Minneapolis payable to you at the bank in Moorhead. This does not make up for the loss that you have had from Leonard and me. I do not ask forgiveness or try to buy it with money but send this to you for my own satisfaction knowing I have gone on to make a new life. I do not ask your approval. Ask Mama to put bottle gentians on the headstone.*
Your loving daughter,
Esther

She would even accounts with Rugnel. It would take time, but that was one thing she could do.

Two days later there came an envelope in Constance's handwriting, a letter that Esther had given up watching for.

Ballard Mill, Washington
United States
July 30, 1900

Dear Sister,
We did worry when you did not come to us as we were expecting until we got your second letter saying you had stayed in Alaska. Maybe you are coming to us now and this will cross at sea. I did not write because I did not think you would be there for my letter to reach you to tell you Leonard came the middle of June and I told him without lying that you were gone to Nome. He said he would find you. I thought when he gets all the way up to that place and learns you are already gone maybe he will give up looking. If you are reading this letter you are still in Alaska and if he has not found you then truly he did not go there and that matter is over at last.

We have had a season of hard work. Houses here are springing up faster than new wheat. Gunnar runs the mill night and day and still they cannot get enough lumber. If you come, there is work.

Mother writes with nothing but worries for you. Pa and the boys are all right. I told her you had work with some people and then would come here. She writes every week to ask are you here yet. I tell her you are one to have your own mind about things and to let it set.

I was in the family condition again but I lost it.
Ever your loving sister,
Constance

She went out onto the beach in her oilskins despite the wind and walked west in the direction she had always gone. She gazed past the great barge hoping to catch sight of a steamer from the west. The beach was all but desolate, the sea gray and mean. She was no longer the horsewoman in the cream lamb's wool. All had changed. No longer the taker of orders, the bringer of mail and green-goods sitting high at the back of the little delivery boat. Where were all her customers? She leaned into the wind and felt the bite of sand in her face. Wind blown from clear across Russia. Norse wind, she supposed. The sand it carried stung like wheat from the thresher but this was no kind of harvest. Her men were gone, mostly broke. She had come expecting nothing and made a business. But what was that, in the end? She would walk away from it for a home. She thought of her pa receiving the money. Would make him mad, her sending it and him with no way to refuse it.

The great barge *Skookum* lay in the roadstead low in the distance. Already the first week of September. Such a vast cargo toward so late in the season, and too rough to land it.

She told herself Leonard would've come by now. Constance had misjudged him. But she knew better. He had gone clear to Ballard for her. Wouldn't stop there.

It was the knowing he was coming but not knowing when that she could not abide. Like he had the power over her without even being there.

Maybe he had to get work first to earn the passage.

Maybe he was coming the slow way. Which would be what?

She looked at the *Skookum* again, seeing the barge clearly for the first time. Fifty-two days out from Seattle, the newspaper had said. Plus a week at anchor. Maybe he was right there.

She wasn't going to wait around to find out. Lena had gone to Council with Plug and had invited Essie to come; now she thought she might consider going up there until the shipping was closed. If he didn't come by then, she could return to Nome for the winter.

Leaving her business was something to think about. She supposed she could trust it to Thurl. He was not quick but he was honest. She was almost done buying surplus anyhow, and if there was empty space, he'd fill it with hides and pay her a cut. The business was no reason to stay. There was only one reason she came to: Nate.

NATE BOOKED FROM Teller on the sidewheeler *Sadie*, a wretched passage second only to his voyage out. He landed through the surf at midnight and hiked up to the CNCo offices at Ten Steadman, where he managed to let himself in without waking the Major. He ate half a package of crackers with smoked kippers, skinned his new birds, and then stretched out on the floor before the stove and gave himself up to hard sleep.

After mere minutes, it seemed, the Major was standing over him, dressed in his campaign suit.

"Thought we might have to blow reveille over you."

"Oh, hell." Nate cleared his throat and sorted out his whereabouts. "It's morning?"

"Twenty past six already." This voice was Sprague's, who sat at Lena's desk with a fork, eating pork and beans directly out of the tin.

"Look here," Palmer said. "I've brought you coffee and breakfast. Tell us about the Bluestone, and then I have a few things we had best get at."

Nate sat to the coffee without shaving, feeling deep gratitude for the encouragement of stimulants. "Gold Run looks rich enough, but the titles are a complete mess. Everything's been jumped several times, and Wooley's Number Three Below doesn't exist. What's this?"

Palmer said, "You like grits and redeye gravy? Found 'em the other day at Mrs. Powell's and they are the damnedest. Went over special for you. Fried ham and fried apples."

Nate dug in. The food was bitter and mealy but he was hungry enough it didn't matter.

"What about the cheap creeks?" Sprague asked.

"Farrington's a lucky creek maybe, but there isn't anything with a clear title that you'd want to go hauling an outfit in to develop. Maybe this time next year it'll be through the courts and you could buy a claim with some sense it'd still be yours when you went to clean up."

Palmer sighed. "Same all over. McKenzie's been named receiver for all the Lindeberg and Wild Goose claims on Anvil. The Swedes asked Judge Noyes to appoint us. I went and talked to Noyes."

"McKenzie's got the judge in his pocket is what people are saying," Nate said. "They're calling him King McKenzie."

Sprague snickered at the term, stabbing a hunk of beef.

"The day you left, Noyes made me receiver on Number Four at Hungry Creek," Palmer said.

Nate quit eating. That was news.

"We struck the beach camp and I sent Bill with the men and a couple of wagonloads of tents and equipment up to Hungry Creek. You can be glad it wasn't you. They had just a god-awful tundra crossing from Penny River. Had to unload the wagons twenty times. Twice they had to take the wagons apart to get them out of the mud."

"But you got set up and running?" Nate asked Sprague.

Sprague nodded without looking up from his project. "For what good it did us."

"After three days on the claim, out comes Bill, tells me there is absolutely no gold in it."

"Worthless," Sprague said.

"What about Five Above on Anvil?" Nate asked.

"Bill went up there on your report and made a deal with Hultberg to run our crew on his claim under contract through the end of the season. Bill's got the men moving the whole outfit over to Anvil right now."

"Under contract?"

"Hultberg will cover our costs and book the profits. It pays wages, keeps our outfit busy, and gives us a chance to see what's there."

"We're not buying the lay, then?"

"Still overpriced," Sprague said, scraping the last of the beef from the corners of the tin. "Smart money waits."

"Meanwhile, Bill's been talking to McKenzie and bought us a half interest in Number Nineteen Above on Ophir. Didn't have time to go all the way up there and prospect it. McKenzie told him take it or leave it, and Bill said we ought to do it."

Sprague looked up from his distraction. "Your King McKenzie happens to be the only man in town that knows what's solid anymore."

Palmer added, "I need you to get up there and find out what we bought. If it looks good, I'd like you to stay awhile and oversee it."

Sprague and McKenzie. A couple of princes. The last two men in Nome that Nate would choose to trade with, and here he was, woken up minion to both.

Nor could he muster a shiny enthusiasm for the destination. Ophir Creek was at Council. A hundred-mile trip. Three days up, a few days looking at business, maybe two days back if he caught a steamer right. Nate gave the Major a smile that he hoped looked sincere. "All this mushing costs us time. Five Above on Anvil's probably the best thing available. Train ride up the hill behind town."

"If it proves up, we'll buy it," Sprague said, and waved his hand: end of conversation.

Nate gave up on the grits. Could have used a good dose of pancakes and eggs. "Where's the company bunking?"

"I leased the shop next door and we put some cots in," Palmer said. "Sundy brought your things to town."

"Miss Crummey?"

"She's moved into Miss Walton's room at the boardinghouse. I asked if she could take over here, too, but wouldn't you know she doesn't type. She agreed to handle the mail until I get somebody."

"Take over?"

"Oh. How long have you been gone?" Palmer scowled. "I let Miss Walton go with her friend Jefferson up to the Council District. I tried to talk her out of it, but it's what she wanted and I am not going to stand in her way. Maybe she'll be back in a couple of days. Would suit me. But look—"

"Where are the men?"

"Moving the outfit over to Anvil. Bill and I are on our way up there right now. Look," Palmer said. He cleared his throat. "Ah, we got word that Bill's centrifugal pump is here. On that big barge that came in while you were gone. The *Skookum*. See if you can get four bits on the dollar, will you? Oh, and this—" Palmer disappeared into the back room.

Nate looked at Sprague. The mythical goddamned pump, finally skulking into view.

Sprague smiled. "Can't say that your fancy dredge proved to be anything we needed to hurry our shipment for, can you?" He held Nate's gaze.

Palmer came back into the room. "Got you something." He unrolled a polar bear pelt that covered half the floor. "Compliments of the shareholders. Bill and I each felt the need of one, and thought we could do worse than to get one for you."

Nate's face burned as he ran his fingers through the beast. Small compensation, knowing that a good bit of the money they'd lost was Sprague's. Sometimes capital earns what it deserves. The fur under the guard hairs was thick and woolly. Polar bear was a rich man's ornament at Nome, the Major's way of smoothing things over. Not that he minded having one. Particularly the part of it that was bought out of Sprague's pocket.

AFTER PALMER AND Sprague left for the Anvil train, Nate stepped next door to find his possessions, cursing the turn of things. He sorted through what he would need for the trip and then stepped back into the office, thinking Essie might be there. She was not. He left the office, dropped his clothes at the laundry, and bought a bath, which was deep and hot, easing the pains in his muscles. He dressed and returned, certain she would be there, but the office was empty. He supposed she was around town filling orders or something.

He went to the waterfront and hired a gig out to the *Skookum* to see about the pump. The great barge squatted low in the water two miles out, and he smelled the cattle half a mile to leeward despite the wind. The swells ran ten feet, making for a queasy ride. When the gig pulled alongside, he had a devil catching the ladder and got dunked to his thighs climbing aboard. The captain directed a deck-hand to take him below and show him the pump in its crate. Scrawny fellow with a nasty limp, wore an undertaker's suit and called Nate "friend," maybe some kind of Quaker except that he asked after the women at Nome: Were they all of them good-time girls or had he met some that were the clean-cut, straight-up kind? Did he hear if any of them might've struck it lucky at all?

It was Sprague's damned pump, no question. The smell of the animal urine made his nose burn and he got off as soon as he could. Put the pump in storage until spring, take it up to Anvil, or sell it to one of the big outfits in need of a high-duty pump on one of the creek claims. Couldn't give it away this close to freeze-up.

He went back to Steadman to change, and this time she was there.

"You are a worry, Nate."

"Essie!" He went to her in two strides and pulled her into his arms, found her willing mouth. "My God, I was thinking about you the whole time I was gone! See what I got!" He turned to get his collecting box.

She didn't move. "I have been watching for you. There's been word."

"What's that, then?" He looked back and noticed that she seemed reduced by something.

"Of my husband." She spilled the news in a whisper, knowing she could not stop the slow spreading stain of it. "Coming to Nome."

He sagged into a chair. "Oh, hell!" Not that he'd been ignorant of another man's claim. Not ignorant so much as feeling free to disregard it, given the distance. Given Essie's break from the marriage. He shook his head in disbelief. "What'll you do?"

"Go someplace, I'm thinking."

"Not stay and have it out? No, you're right. Do you think?"

She shook her head.

"Coming clear up to Nome?"

"It's not your worry. I just thought—well, you'd want to know about it."

"I'll say! This hits me, too! I've gone around the bend for you, Essie, and don't think otherwise. When, though?"

"How to know? He's already come into my dreams. Not far off is my guess."

"Look. I have to mush up to Council to prospect a claim on

Ophir. Come along with me." It's what he'd been thinking all morning but feared he lacked the powers to put over.

She turned aside and said nothing, uncertain how he meant it.

He went to her. "Look at me. I'm saying come with me, Essie."

"And then?"

"What does it matter? We'll go out."

"Out where?"

"I'll take you home with me."

Here was a thing said in brave spirit but with no sense. "You are quick to offer, forgetting I have carried your mail these past months."

He pressed his nose into her hair. "I have had no chance to tell you something which you have first rights to know. I have ended my connection to Miss Wilder."

More news. She wondered was it true. She pushed him back a little to see his eyes.

"I knew for certain in the Bluestone. You've lit a fire in me, Essie. I had to square things and wrote to tell her." His eyes looked away, deferring to Lily's privacy.

She was stopped a moment by his declaration, then seized it. "Lena and Plug are at Dogtail Creek," she said. "I was thinking we could go there."

"Dogtail's good. I can do my work at Ophir, and we'll lay some kind of a plan." The sudden turn of things! He was eager to pull together what they'd need for the journey before either of them found a reason to quash it. "Come have a look, though." He turned for his box. "I got my phalarope!"

THAT NIGHT THE storm that had been blowing up for ten days wound itself into a piping seventy-five-mile-an-hour southeaster that kept anyone from leaving Nome. By nine-thirty the next morning towering waves had cleared the beaches and stove in the buildings along the south side of Front Street. The sea rolled in across the sand spit and lifted buildings from River Street and swept them two blocks west. The schooner *Harriet* came ashore west of Lane's Derrick. The sloop *Catherine Sudden* wrecked on the sand spit. The barge *York* and schooner *Zenith* came ashore by the railroad depot. The *Merwin*, the *Nome City*, the *Fortune Hunter*, and the *Lady George* all came ashore, great failed hulks with their spars snapped, sails snatched away, cabins dashed, screws driven against the sand. The wind howled and the tide turned and the sea rose higher yet, plucking the hulk of the schooner *Jessie*, lost the year before, right off the bottom and delivering her up against the pilings of the NAT&TCo derrick. While men who could lash down their buildings did so, the sand spit itself was swept away, followed close on by the Hotel Baltimore.

A crowd formed along Front Street to watch the ravenous waves eat away their town. Nate and Esther came out to witness it. A man said it was the kind of storm you see once in a lifetime. Others murmured true enough, and one fellow said, "Especially for those that's drounding." The ships of the roadstead had all put to sea, the smaller ones seeking the shelter of the Snake or Sledge Island—all but the great barge *Skookum*, which was too heavy a burden for the *Holyoke* to pull against the gale. She was doomed, it was plain for all to see, and when her anchors began to drag, the little tug *America* and the launch *Tophat* steamed out from the mouth of the Snake and pushed valiantly at her stern, but very quickly the bow of the barge skewed off to port and exposed the smaller boats to the storm's full fury. They bobbed on the crests and vanished in the troughs. A roar went out to them from shore, but the crowd's outpouring was lost on the wind, nor could it save them, for the gay little *Tophat* broached and rolled, then the dogged tug *America* did the same, and down they went in turn, gone from sight, all hands perished, the crowd stunned to silence.

By eleven A.M. the *Skookum* had reached the shallows at the center of town, broadside to the breakers, having rammed a smaller barge that had beached ahead of her. Everyone safe on shore who was not occupied securing his possessions came as close as he dared to watch the mammoth barge pound her spine not fifty feet off and utterly helpless. It was not just the vessel herself that made for spectacle, but her four hundred head of cattle, her million and a half feet of lumber, all the storied cargo she'd borne the three thousand miles from Seattle, risking the open sea, only to meet disaster at Nome. The waves broke over her deck and her crew clung to the davits atop the deckhouse appealing to the crowd on shore with their arms, gesturing at the smaller barge, suggesting some sort of a rescue. Word passed among those ashore that to play at the thing while the sea was up was foolhardy, but a handful who thought otherwise scavenged several large timbers out of the debris and struggled to fashion a catwalk from shore to the smaller barge, where, presumably, they would lay up another to the larger vessel, but the heaving of the wrecks threw off the timbers and the sweep of water pushed the men back to higher ground.

LEONARD STOOD ON the deckhouse with Billy and judged his luck.

"Wait until the sea settles!" he shouted. It was all he could think to do. The land was so close, but the roiling chaos in the short distance between would swallow a man.

Gawkers had gathered ashore and Leonard's eyes lit on one who surely looked like Essie but it was too hard to see, and she stood with a man. His eyes worked the shifting crowd and came back to this pair. Could not be his Essie, but all the same it surely could be.

It was four-fifteen when a resounding crack split the air and the barge slumped at either end. Her back was broken.

"Tide's turning," Billy cried.

They watched and waited and found it was true, the high tide turned toward ebb and the fury abated slightly. Billy and Leonard and the others of the *Skookum* pulled a heavy plank from the shifting load and now they pushed this off the cargo deck, using their weight to cantilever it out until they could lower the far end onto the smaller barge. At this development a great mutual cheer rose from those ashore and those aboard the giant barge. A man ashore threw a rope, which was caught and quickly tied off at either end to make a lifeline. The *Skookum* and the smaller barge rose and fell and jostled with the crashing surf but not so treacherously now, and the pull of solid land was irresistible.

Billy turned and shouted, "Going to do the honors!" and then grabbed ahold of the lifeline.

Leonard clapped him on the back, urging him on. Billy was the nimblest among them and the right one to show it could be done. He tested the plank with his weight. It rose and fell uneasily but it was fixed firmly at the near end, so he gave a heave and started out onto it. He wasn't halfway along when the smaller barge shifted right and Leonard hollered, "Squat down!" Billy was standing too tall and swiped at the lifeline to catch his balance, and when the plank swung back to the left he fell off it, straight down and out of sight.

Leonard grabbed a line and threw an end over the side and leaned out to see; Billy surfaced.

"Git the rope! Git the rope!"

Billy struggled and grabbed ahold, and then the next breaker came in and heaved the *Skookum* up and Billy slid under. When she came down, she came down hard and Billy was gone. The end of the line washed free.

The people of the *Skookum* stared down for five minutes to see him come up and catch the line, but Billy never did. Someone said he could've found a pocket, might yet be coming out, you don't know how long, but sure as they had eyes they could see the boy was gone.

But Leonard had seen how to do it now. He tied a rope around his waist and looped it around the lifeline and then took his chance, scooting across in a half crouch and sliding on his rump at the last. He gained the smaller barge, and then, despite his gimpy leg, scrambled across it and leapt off into the surf. Three men jumped down to his aid and the crowd reached out and pulled him right up onto solid land. Next thing he knew, there he stood in the middle of Front Street.

He had arrived.

20

They got off at dawn. He carried his side-by-side, his new bearskin, the woolen and rubber blankets, tent, skiff, and personal effects. She had traded her lamb's wool coat for a deer-hide parka and supplemented her kit with two suits of winter underwear, a chamois undervest, two new short skirts of heavy duck, two flannel blouses, moose-hide mittens, and a new long flannel nightdress. She brought the handbag with the frayed clasp that she'd carried from Perley, a good friend for travel, home to a hundred and one small necessities for the trail and whatever kind of a life she was going to find at Dogtail.

They rode east on horseback, following the edge of the world above the angry sea. Nate had argued for waiting until the storms settled and booking ship passage as far as Cheenik, eighty miles east, but Esther had insisted they get away immediately, so she took three horses from Thurl, saddled two and packed their gear onto the third, and they left town, passing the roadhouse at Fort Davis and crossing the Nome River, heading east on the tundra barrens under a raw sky. They traveled side by side, for all appearances man and wife, speaking little, leaving the talking to the wind that worked through their coats and bullied their hats and the horses' manes. They were neither of them certain of their enterprise and the weight of it in the other's hand, thinking only to press into it, trust themselves to events and the simple fact of it, the two of them making their way toward a place that was fixed and had a name, but a destination that was nothing if not uncertain.

She had two stories she wanted to tell him, the beginning of her marriage and the end of it, but she didn't know how to get at it and kept silent. They rounded the headland called Cape Nome by midmorning. Beyond it, where the landscape perished again in a sweep of flatness, they found a log inn set low above the surf, its roof anchored by sod. It was the Cape Nome roadhouse. They turned in, found seats near the smoky fire, and took what food was offered, fish soup and coffee. They were the only travelers heading out; the others were returning from the outlying creeks, coming in for the season and glad of the fact.

From Cape Nome the beach became a narrow spit that ran for miles, the barrier rim of an estuary called Safety Sound. A hundred yards to the right was the piling sea, a hundred yards to the left a vast lagoon, dark with sheltering birds. Nate hollered out their Latin names to her, *Branta bernicla, Aythya marila, Somateria mollissima*, but she barely took notice. The lightness that had blossomed between them was dulled by a heaviness now. He whistled as he rode and kept mostly to himself, offering a word now and then on the passing landscape to let her know he was not put off.

They rode past Eskimo camps, where the skin boats were turned over and the dogs huddled against the wind, rousing only their heads to howl at the passing horses. After six o'clock, with the sun sinking, they gained the roadhouse at Port Safety, a lone refuge standing square above the windswept spit. It was a warm shelter that smelled of cinnamon and had the embrace of home to it, the log walls softened with reindeer hides, gingham curtains in the windows, rugs on the floors. The innkeeper was a stout-hearted Welsh woman by the name of Pennington. She had two shy daughters and a season's worth of tales about disasters that had befallen her patrons, and these she offered up for entertainment as she put food on the table, and as she sat herself down, and as she made quick work of her own meal, pausing in her recounting only to swallow a bite, or to admonish one of the girls on her company manners, or to let the effect of a tale's unexpected conclusion sink in. There were three lodgers besides Nate and Esther, and all were captivated, for Mrs. Pennington was a woman of generous spirit in a stinting land.

There was her account of the two shey-faced puddens who pulled up to her lodge on an ice floe last fall and stepped off to have themselves a hot meal. Seems the men had hiked nine miles over the frozen channel from the mainland to Sledge Island the day before, and when they turned to go back, the ice broke up and carried them thirty-two miles clear to Safety Sound for breakfast.

There was the lodger with the game leg who borrowed her Peterborough canoe to go to Solomon. The other guests bade him off and then watched in agony as a gale swept down and drove him to sea and certain death. One of them took the sad task of setting off by foot for Nome the next day to tell the man's widow of her loss; when finally he knocked at her door, it was the dead fellow himself that answered. He'd been blown forty miles west to King Island and was ferried back home by the Eskimos in time to catch the news while it was still fresh.

The diners applauded, and before the hostess got into her next account Esther asked, "Where's your own husband, then?"

"Oh, hell," the innkeeper barked. "Went to the outhouse to do his business and the hogs ate him."

The innkeeper's daughters gave up their half of the mother's bed for Esther, wrapping themselves on the floor in a pair of musk-ox pelts. Nate bedded with a tall drink of water from South Dakota named Severson, who delivered a two-hour exegesis on the six patentable contraptions he had devised during the course of that season's gold-digging.

On the second day, they crossed the mouth of Safety Sound by ferry and rode the horses downshore ten miles to the west bank of the Solomon River. Esther hadn't ridden so much in years. She closed her eyes and let her mind wander free. The innkeeper's stories came back to her, and from these she pondered the odd place of chance in a life. The chance, for example, that she might not have gotten Constance's letter timely like she did. The chance of the Norgaard boy's dying on the thresher and her and Leonard noticing each other because of it. The chance that her life wasn't over yet, as she had been supposing it was. That there was something more for her. Something better even than what she had imagined.

From Solomon they pressed on for Topkok, another fourteen miles. The more beach they put between themselves and Nome the easier the silence lay between them, now interspersed with recollections of the tidy roadhouse at Port Safety and speculations on what they might find at Council City. Between these snippets stretched long periods of Esther's being lost within herself.

At Topkok fortune smiled, for they met the little steam schooner

Elk as she was calling in on her run to Cheenik. They put the horses into the service of two miners who were glad for the use of them to Nome, booked deck passage, and found space on a bench in the *Elk*'s saloon.

It was a spare cabin with half a dozen other travelers. The wet-wool smell of a steam radiator filled the space with a cloying warmth. They sat with their backs to the bulkhead, looking forward out her curved windows and listening to the soft gabble of conversation as the *Elk* cast off her moorings. Night rose in the form of a damp blackness beyond the windowpanes. She was glad to be off the horse. Too tired to fear for drowning, glad to feel the thrum of the solitary steam piston pushing them east through the troubled sea. East and away.

"Maybe not my business, but I would like to know it," Nate said.

She turned and looked at him. He was leaning against the bulkhead, and his eyes were friendly on her. She settled into her story.

THE BEGINNING AND the end of it were caught in a photograph made the day of their wedding.

"Her pa had hired a portrait man from Fossum's out of Fargo." Came a long pause, the *Elk* sluing and plowing on. He didn't ask whose pa, so she went on like this, story-telling about somebody she knew once.

"They're all of them lined up outside her pa's house, in the snow. The bride's in her ma's ma's wedding dress. The groom's in his rented suit. There's the bride's family. The neighbors. Thirty or more, and they're cold, because it's November and there's early snow on the ground and the Fossum's man won't let them wear overcoats for a wedding picture, but it takes him a dog's age to get his camera ready, so everybody's gripped by the shivers and thinking they're going to come out blurry being as they can't stand still."

"It's a winter wedding?"

"The bride's in a certain condition. There's no time to wait."

"Ah."

"Well, it happens."

"Of course. But, she's happy?"

Here, another pause. "She has made her terms. She doesn't think about being happy."

"She's in love, though?"

She let the question pass. "The Fossum's man can't get settled and he finally asks her pa can the boys bring him out a hay wagon, all he's seeing is the line of us hanging there between snow and sky. Her brothers go and get the wagon, and he sets his camera up on it so he can look down and get the fields in the background. That's why, when the picture comes back, way off in the distance over the new husband's shoulder, there's the Pederson house."

"Which is?"

"The two's new farm."

"A happy accident!"

"No, wait. The husband has an Indian friend, a boy, who came and brought a jug, and in the picture he's holding up the jug in a kind of salute."

"Bully. It's an occasion."

"But, see, what I'm saying is, everything's there in the picture: The bride, who has a baby inside her but you cannot see it, and in the end it's gone. The groom, who is in a suit he'll never be able to own. The farm where the marriage will run its course. And the whiskey that ruins it."

SOFTLY, SHE TOLD it to him. How the flood had come up in the night. How she had waded in its waters but not seen what was right before her, meaning what the flood was bringing them and what it was washing away.

Brought the snake up beside them.

Brought the stink of decay into their life.

Washed away forty acres of their land, you could say, and the chance to make something of the farm, which is to say it brought them Leonard's mischief with Strand. Cut her and her pa apart. Brought her up against Leonard, and lit the fire of his hunger.

THE MUD LAY three inches thick on the land and inside of the house after the water was gone. It was the silty kind, fine and sticky, that pulls your boot off your foot two or three times a day when you're just minding your own business trying to get your farm back in place, and then skids the other foot out from under you, bringing you down onto your rump, soiling your clothes, and leaving you bruised. Everything you try to do is a wrestling match against your own place, land you used to know every bump and hollow of like the inside of your mouth and now it is possessed by a layer of pure orneriness and every inch of it comes to you strange.

They scraped the mud out of the house first, each shovel of it being too heavy to move farther than the edge of the porch so that they'd had to let it pile up like dung where her tulips used to be. Then they'd worked clearing the fields, dragging every sort of thing imaginable to the fence lines and piling it up into great heaps: punky king cottonwoods, broken boards, wet hay, bedding, ladies' dresses, a couple of drowned hogs, all of it the kind of stinking mess that was too wet to be burned off and had to be buried or left in a heap to fester its own way into the ground. Meanwhile, weedy sucker trees sprang up so fast you couldn't get ahead of them.

After the flood, the air stayed basementy and wet for weeks and the mold came in on it, ran green up the insides and outsides of the house and barn. She'd had to open the walls of her chicken house and scrape out the wet sawdust and the ash and try to get the insides to dry out and then find fresh fill and put on new lath and tarpaper, which Flint at the feed store sold her on credit. Still the mold got in there, too. Hot sunshine was what they needed, and it seemed to her whenever she raised her eyes from her work that the sun beat down all around but on their own farm. Seemed like the sixty acres they still owned stayed dank and shady.

By the middle of June the roads were bordered with wild roses and scarlet-eyed daisies. You could see the flood had mostly been good for the soil. The wind played with the wheat in their neighbors' fields, thick as thatch, but their own wheat was thick in some places and mangy in others. She couldn't tell if some of the seed Leonard bought with Strand's money was bad or if it was the mold or something else. They were going to get only half a crop. The realization put her in a mood and she stayed away from talking with her pa as long as she could, knowing he could see it for himself, they were going to earn enough to put food on the table, but not enough to pay their share of the mortgage.

"Any damned fool can grow wheat this year," Rugnel said to her when she finally found the nerve to see him. "Your farm's going to cost me twenty-five or fifty cents an acre out of my own pocket. Why is that?"

"I will send Leonard over to earn out what it's costing you."

"I don't want that man in my fields. Find a way to make your own farm pay."

She told Leonard what her pa had said. Thought he ought to know how things sat.

That was the first week you could see for certain it was going to be a big wheat year. It was the same week (she later learned) that a man from one of the flour mills in Minneapolis came through peddling futures contracts. Essie was gone to Perley with her eggs when he knocked. He was twenty-two or twenty-three years old, ramrod-straight there on Leonard's own back porch, bone buttons on a charcoal business suit. Had a boy's face on him, polished cheeks, a briefcase, and a shine on his shoes. He was a strange sight to Leonard, and he said a strange thing. Said he'd come to offer Leonard terms on his next two years' crops, guaranteed at seventy cents a bushel come hell or high water, sign now or take your chances in the fall when all the other farmers are dumping their own wheat onto the market and driving the price down for everybody.

The young buck was a talker. "You might be thinking wheat brought ninety cents in 1890," he said with a dip of his head to show he knew it, too. "You'd be right as rain, but that was nine years ago, not so many growers. What did it bring in '95? Brought fifty cents. Starvation wages. Now, why was that? Call it the science of economics. Call it supply and demand. Fancy words that mean the same dang thing: there's just too many farmers making too much wheat. Look around, see it yourself."

Leonard looked beyond the man to his buggy in the driveway, trying to size him up. Leonard was not used to having his business solicited. The man was traveling alone. Had a nice-looking rig. Seemed to be in the chips.

"I can see what you're thinking," the man said. "You're thinking, How come this ringer from the city's offering seventy cents if wheat's going to be cheap as dirt by harvest? Let me tell you why.

It's because we got a great big mill. We got contracts for labor. We got contracts for shipping. We got buyers for the product. What we don't know is our cost of raw wheat, and it's worth a pretty penny to us to lock that in today. Take it or leave it, and no hard feelings either way to an honest man like yourself."

To do better than your neighbors, don't do everything just like they do it. This was the truism that came to Leonard. Thought also passed through his mind to say he wanted to think it over, come back tomorrow, which would give himself a chance to argue it with Essie, but why do that when he couldn't put it to her half as convincing, and the idea of even trying to exhausted him. Suffering Virgin could not persuade Essie what was right, she didn't think of it first.

Leonard leaned against the porch post. "You been to see Mr. Strand, then?" He gestured toward his neighbor's place.

"Yes, indeed. And I can see he's a heck of a farmer, no argument there. He's just set in the old ways, if you know what I mean," the man said politely. "Sometimes it's the younger ones like yourself that are more open to the new ways."

Leonard nodded. Fella knew pretty well where things stood. In any case, how far wrong could you go? Suppose he did not come back at harvest to make good? You'd sell your wheat alongside everybody else, same as if you did not sign up. But the fellow looked all right. The kind that knew how to spend money to make money. Who would you rather do business with? Leonard took the man's pen, put the contract up against the post, and signed it.

He did not tell Essie, who would only get her back up. It was better to wait a couple of months until talk turned from bumper crops to flooded markets and collapsed prices. Tell her then, and it would come as a happy turn, for a change. God knows they could stand it. He hid the contract in the eaves. It was only a piece of paper, but how it bucked him up to have it. Her pa would have to eat his words.

Wheat that fall brought $1.12 a bushel, except for Leonard's, which was locked in at seventy cents.

"HE WAS NOT the only one in the county to fall for it, Essie." Mrs. Loqueshear was up to her forearms in soapy water washing bread pans.

Esther sat at the pastry table with her head in her hands. "Leonard's anybody's sitting duck. Some slick-talking dollar bill from Minneapolis catches him in his jug, next thing you know it's cost us two hundred and forty dollars."

Mrs. L shook her head. "Can't get past himself in a hallway without tripping himself in the other direction."

"Don't see why I stay."

"Sure you do."

"No, I really don't."

"One," Mrs. L said, "you got to raise your boy, period. Two, boy's got to have a daddy, period. So you got to stay, and that means you got to break his jug."

"So you say."

Mrs. L stopped her work. "Listen to me."

"Listening."

"Don't spread your legs unless he gives it up. His jug or his trout. You got to use one against the other."

Esther looked away, finding the idea distasteful. "I suppose."

"He's like a dog, Essie. He's going to test you. You just got to hold him to it or you won't have a prayer of breaking him."

When she got home, she laid it out. "What stands between us making it and going under's one thing, and you know what it is."

"What stands between us making it's a long list of misery called a farm."

"What stands between us is your jug. You want us to be a family, you quit your jug."

"Oh, hell, I can quit my jug whenever I want to."

"Then do it."

"You're just kicking at my jug instead of taking any of the blame on yourself."

"Leonard, I have made a decision. You want to have your rights with me in the marital way, show me you can quit your jug."

"Fine," he said. She still had her dander up over the wheat contract. Expected him to roll over dead and give her the last word on it, never mind that she would've done the same damned thing if she'd of been standing on the porch and him carrying eggs to market. Just made her madder if he tried to give her his side of it. So there was a new rule in the house.

He saluted the new rule, not quitting the jug but playing along that he wasn't going to have any you-know-what until the cows came home, and seeing as they did not have cows, he supposed that was it for life.

He could wait out a pissy mood. She was going to miss it, too.

She steered well clear of him, kept her distance in the bed at night. He so much as put a hand on her fanny, saying, "Time comes every cow needs milking," she took her blanket into the boy's cubby. Inside of a week he was itchy as hell and she would not budge. He went down to the Indian's and drowned his sorry self in the jug two days while he pissed over the damned situation between them. Then he let his head clear and went back home.

"All right. I'm going to quit the jug."

"All right," she said. She didn't know whether to kiss him or get mad for giving word he had no intention to keep. And wasn't it a big old bullnose of a thing he brought to bed that night and pressed at her with no preliminaries, not so much as a kiss before it pushed itself in and went a-swimming up inside of her, like to have split her in half, how strong it made him now he was quitting his weakness all for her, and suddenly she wanted it so bad the flush raced through her and she went all rutty down there and let the F-word come out in a tight squealy cry, and she was swept over by the waves of rut, again and again. When she finally let loose of him, it was knowing she had lost herself. She lay back, floating with the feeling, and asked him was everything all right, wondering did he hear what she'd uttered and think she was dirty for it. He let out his air like a boiler blowing down. Said he would have to go again just to be sure, give him a half an hour to be ready.

Next morning when he came down for his breakfast she was humming.

This was an unexpected sweet time. He was so pink with giving up whiskey he could not get enough of her or of strutting around the house and the yard, taking care of things he saw that needed doing, jumping to the kitchen to do her chores. She came in one day to find he had blacked the rusted stove, and when she fired it to cook their supper it smelled the house of scorched tar.

In eight days he could not any longer deny his thirst. He went for the jug in the barn three days running, little sips just to keep him on an even keel and quit the shaking, but it wasn't as much as he needed after so long a time, and after two weeks of giving it up for her he finally gave himself over to it at the Indian's place, just one whole jug to slake his thirst for real, and it laid him out for two days.

She wasn't humming when he got home, but she wasn't ripping into him, either. He knew the price of it well enough. She would not let him at her until he'd been a full two weeks without the jug, and then she took him back, but not in the same way, at least not for her, because every time he took her she was all inside of her head. Thinking, He is not so much strong as needy, and isn't needy the same as weak.

That was their winter. The hunger year. No money to live off and him half starved between two demons. The stretches he was sober and they were together and he was sweet-acting and eager to help whatever she was working at, there was the gnaw of knowing he would stand it only so long.

Privation went through the house like a draft. With the granary empty there were no rats. Everything feeds on something, and they were not surprised to hear the snake grow restless in the wall. So it was, one day in March when Leonard was denied the comfort of his wife and feeling warm to his jug, that the snake became a problem.

ESTHER HAD GONE to Perley with her eggs. She did not take Gabe, who had a little fever, but asked Leonard to look after him. Leonard was off the back porch, knocking apart elm logs with his ax, taking his spunk out on a twisty grain that didn't give until you whacked it three or four times. It was one of those cold mornings that makes a fool of spring, low clouds that look like snow coming, ground still locked in ice. He was propping up a log when he paused, listening to their boy whimpering upstairs at his nap. The boy would likely settle down, so he split another handful of logs, fifteen or twenty minutes, then stopped to have a nip and wipe off the sweat, and there was the sound of it still. Boy awhimpering, but louder.

Leonard parked his ax and went into the kitchen and dipped a rag in sugar water. Sometimes he dipped a rag in whiskey and sugar, did the trick neatly, but this morning he did not know how soon the boy's mother might get home. It was not a trick he cared to get discovered at. He went up the stairs with the sugar rag, wondering if the fever was worse or the boy lost his blanket, and when he looked inside of the cubby he could not make out what he was seeing for a second, then when he did, he got one good goddamned jolt. The boy's stunty leg had grown fat under the blanket in the space of one hour. Leonard jerked back the blanket to see how, and there was the snake coming partway out of the wall, fat with his boy's stunty leg down its throat, swallowed clear up to the top of the thigh, its mouth wide as a mason jar, the hood drawn over its eyes like it was finally getting a meal for the first time in months.

He snatched the boy, but the bulk of the snake was inside of the wall yet and refused to give him up. Leonard ran downstairs for the ax and back upstairs to the boy, and when he got there the snake was gone. He swung the ax into the wall and chopped it open three feet along to get at the snake, but the bastard was shrunk away inside and he had no way of knowing where without chopping open the whole goddamned house.

The boy was in a howling fury. His leg was raw and puffy with pinhole bites up one side. Leonard pried around the boy's private parts with his finger, afraid of the worst, but saw no damage in that department, a thing he could hardly bring himself to think. He gave the boy the sugar rag and then went and swapped it for one with whiskey and in a few minutes the boy was quiet and then he fell asleep. While the boy slept, he packed the leg in horse manure to draw out the poison.

After that he asked himself the question that lay at the back of his mind ever since he brought that bastard snake into the house: how to get it out once and for all. Smoke it out was all he could think.

He wrapped the boy in a second blanket and carried him out and set him in the wheelbarrow by the front porch. He would put fire in the walls around the foundation, smoke the inside so thick no snake would suffer it. He went in search of a piece of sheet tin and some tools. Knelt down beside the house and used his hammer to knock a hole in the plaster just above the foundation. Fished around in there with his fingers to feel where the stud went up the wall, then used a big pair of pliers to chew the hole open six or eight inches at the sill plate. Cut a piece of sheet tin and fashioned a little cup and set it inside the wall. Blew on his hands for warmth and studied how it was going to go: little smudge pots.

He worked his way around three sides of the house, and when he had eight holes and eight tin cups, he got up off his knees. The stiffness in his back made him slow as frozen grease. He checked on the boy, who was fretful. There was snow on the boy's blanket and Leonard looked around and realized it had been snowing for some time. He felt the boy's leg and was glad the puffiness and red were much less. He made the boy a fresh rag and looked to see if maybe she was coming. If she came now, he would tell her to hold her damned tongue, whiskey and sugar was good treatment, but she did not come, and he did not plan on telling her everything when she did.

He sorted through his woodpile for ironwood and then built a fire of it in the driveway to make himself some coals. He got a bucket and pumped it half full of water and then stuffed it with straw to soak. When the coals were ready, he shoveled them into his tin cups and covered them with a mat of wet straw. Smoke rose up in thick plumes, coming out the cracks at the eaves. When he had all his pots smoking good, he went back to check on the boy. He was asleep with the whiskey rag in his mouth. There was no fever. Leonard brushed the manure off his leg and shook out the blanket, took the rag and rinsed the whiskey out of it under the pump.

He went around to check his handiwork. Smoke streamed out at the roof peak, the same milky gray as the falling snow. Snake was in no hurry to come out. After half an hour Leonard had to add coals to keep the smoke heavy. He stood on one foot and then the other. Could have smoked an ox in that house by the time the bastard snake came out the kitchen door, slow and easy as you please, and moseying across the frozen yard. Leonard grabbed for his ax, but there was no ax in the woodpile. He bolted upstairs, but quick as he came back down with it he saw the snake had crossed over to the barn, went to lodge inside somewhere. Suited Leonard. He could find a snake in a barn all right. He went around snatching the coals out of the walls, and then he mixed up some mortar and was pasting the holes shut when she came home.

ESTHER PAUSED IN her tale. The night had grown late and the other passengers dozed in odd postures on the hard benches.

"I didn't understand, at first. Gabe lying outside in the wheelbarrow," she said.

Nate pushed his fingers through his hair and let out a long breath. He had hardly moved, listening with an intensity he could feel through his whole body. "That was when the house caught fire?"

"No. He had put out his fires, but I wouldn't go in because it was so smoky. I took Gabe and went to Ma's. Leonard came for us the next morning. He had opened the windows top and bottom for fresh air. Of course, the fire was still inside the walls, but we didn't know it. We went to bed all together, the three of us in Leonard's and my bed, which normally Leonard never let Gabe do. So maybe he had a suspicion." She was past trying to make sense of it. What was done was done. Maybe he suspected there was fire and did not want to say. Maybe he did not. But there was the fact he let the boy share their bed, which was not Leonard's way.

"Sometime in the night Gabe must have fussed, because Leonard moved him into his cubby. I was asleep and didn't know. The fire came into Gabe's room first, through the hole Leonard had chopped. Caught Gabe's blankets and gown and then the whole upstairs was burning. I didn't know where Gabe was, but Leonard grabbed him. We only just got out. I hitched up the horse and we ran to Perley and the doctor cut away Gabe's gown and wrapped him in blankets soaked with liniment. He was burned all below the waist. We took him to Ma's and he and I stayed there. Leonard went home, made a bed for himself in the barn.

"I sent Hjalmer over to check on him and feed the chickens. Hjalmer came back with the stink of the fire on his clothes, saying it was just a black hole where our house used to be, and the snake had eaten my eggs and chicks and put the hens in such a state they wouldn't lay. He went back and got the hens and brought them to Ma's. Pa wrote Carl to come home from college, and Pa and Carl and Hjalmer got Pa's fields and our sixty seeded and dragged. I asked Hjalmer to make sure Leonard had what he needed in the barn, but he said the Indian looked after him fine. After a couple of weeks, Leonard sent word he killed the snake and I could come and we could decide what to do next, but I didn't feel like going over there and just stayed with my boy.

"He lived eight more weeks. He wanted his wood horse by his bed. I didn't tell him it was burned up. I told him we had let another boy use it while he was sick, and he could have it back when he got well. I told him to hold on for his birthday in June. Would have been four. He didn't make it. We gave him a beautiful funeral, and it was the first time since the fire that I saw Leonard. The man from Fossum's came and made a picture. Afterward, I went home with Leonard to see how I felt. Wheat was coming up. I heard the prairie hens, and saw four little foxes in the windbreak. Knew I couldn't stay."

THEY RODE SIDE by side on the bench with their backs against the bulkhead. She was reduced to silence, and after a few minutes the tears ran down her face, but she did not sob over it.

Nate had no words big enough for such a story. He put his arm around her waist and pulled her to him and said, "Thank you."

They both let sleep come, and at some point she pulled up her legs and turned toward him and buried her head in his shoulder and slept hard with the smell of him filling her head.

21

The *Elk* reached Cheenik at dawn. They awoke feeling muffle-headed and stiff, and stepped off the boat into a misting drizzle. He took her by the hand. It was an Eskimo settlement and Swedish mission set on a low-lying peninsula, jutting its chin into Golovin Bay, streaked with the sweet soot of burning seal oil. The log mission and its outbuildings stood squarely above the driftwood huts of the natives, who had their fish drying from lines and racks. The steamship company kept a small freight house at the landing, and a hundred yards beyond that Esther and Nate found a sodden misery of pitched canvas that passed for a tavern, where they managed to get cornmeal gruel and strong coffee. By nine-thirty, feeling revived, they were aboard the little sternwheeler *Nadine* bound northwest across Golovin Bay toward the mudflats and bog that formed the delta of the Fish River, some ten or twelve miles distant, their artery to the interior. Esther and Nate stood together at the bow, braced by the wind.

They nosed into the mouth of the Fish, hardly twice the beam of the boat, the low-lying banks engulfed by what little wake they made. Flights of tundra swans circled and landed in the gauzy middle distance. Twice, as the *Nadine* crept inland, she stuck herself in the mud, and once hung up on a bar as the bog gave way to gravel and willow thickets. They were fully eleven hours out of Cheenik by the time they put ashore at the village of White Mountain. It was a hillside settlement dominated by the Wild Goose Mining Company depot where Mr. Charles D. Lane's men staged equipment for the Council District. Here, Nate contracted for passage upstream with a man named Homer, who would be freighting some of the *Nadine*'s cargo to Council. He was a rotund fellow in a mackinaw and rubber hip boots, captain of the *Mary Lou*, a slender river barge propelled by a five-dog team that had pulled in beside the *Nadine*. A leggy boy named Otto staked the dogs and was already at work helping Homer stage and load cargo. Homer sized up Nate and Esther. "Leave at eight sharp tomorrow morning," he said. "I will load your outfit last, keep it on top in case there's anything your missus needs on the way upriver."

The only advertised lodging was at Goldseeker's Card Room. When they hiked up to inquire, the innkeeper was trying to settle a dispute in the bar but the argument spilled into the foyer and knocked over a chair, startling a rat with half a sausage in its mouth. "By God and Jesus!" Esther said, charging out the door. "Imagine the bedding!"

Nate followed her. "I know what you're saying, but there's no other place. Maybe the upstairs is all right. I could have a look," but now the dispute was out the front door, and Nate and Essie had to step aside for it and for the five spectators who spilled out behind, one of whom pulled a gun and started taking happy potshots at Goldseeker's sign, sending down a rain of splinters and setting off a chorus of dogs throughout town.

Essie hotfooted it down the slope to the waterfront. She sat on their bags and looked to where Homer and Otto were camped on the far side of the freighter. "Guess you'll need to pitch the tent for me."

"Sure I will. It's just that I can't have you tenting by yourself out here is the only problem."

She looked back up at the hotel. The fighters were chasing each other up the street, while two of the spectators jeered them on. She looked over to the boatman's tent. "If Homer had a wife, I could sleep with her, but he has that boy."

"Yes."

She let out a long breath. "Since he takes us for husband and wife, I am willing to go along for appearances, supposing you are as tired as I am."

"I am absolutely spent, Essie."

"All right, then." She was past being modest, and what nobody saw nobody had to know.

They found a reasonably level place ten yards from where Homer and Otto were set up, and she helped unfold and pitch the tent. They worked silently, neither commenting on the thing that was staring wide-eyed back at them: the fact of their making a nest to bed down in together. He laid the rubber blanket for a groundcloth, then the bearskin for mattress and his three wool blankets for bedding. He fished a folding lantern from his knapsack and lit the candle for her.

"I will be back in ten minutes." He made himself busy at the boat for a decent interval. It was a starkly clear night with no moon, growing stone cold as it deepened.

She shivered too much to unfasten her buttons but managed to undress and get into her flannel. She pulled the blankets over her head and steeled her mind against the cold, thinking the tent was bigger than it needed to be, really, but thankfully not so the bearskin; she was not going to get warm if he was planning to be shy at all.

He entered and tied the flaps behind him, took off his boots, extinguished the candle, and undressed, his heart sounding in his temples. His sap was up and he could've made a mess of the place just rolling up against her if he wasn't careful, and he paused in his efforts while he was stark naked beside her, feeling the air on his skin, wondering what had got him into this predicament, half laughing at his sorry extremis and half chattering his teeth, supposing she was already asleep or pretending. He pulled on a nightshirt and fresh woolen stockings and climbed under the blankets. She lay on her side facing away, and he lay facing her, unable to see her in the utter darkness nor hear her breathe. He moved up against her backside and let his arm surround her and felt her lean into his embrace. The full length of his body gave what heat it contained over to her and greedily took for itself the giving warmth of her own, and thus they lay for a moment, his face in her hair, his arm around her, and his hand gripping her arm and pulling her against him. He pushed against her and she let out a gasp and turned her face and he kissed her.

His hand went to her neck, her breasts, down the length of her to the end of her gown and then up inside it, feeling the down of her skin, the proudness of her hip and tautness of her soft belly, the puppyweight of her breasts, and then tracing the line of her spine into the declivity of her buttocks, the soft heat inside of her thigh.

She tugged at his gown, pulling it up so she could feel the shape of him, finally, the hollow and swell of his back and the cording of his ribs and his little stones of nipples, going to the flat of his stomach before letting her fingers ring the part of him she would take inside her.

HE AWOKE TO odd sensations on his face, sparkles of dampness. How was it possible that snow was falling on them? When his eyes focused he saw the tent had been furred with hoarfrost inside. The condensate of their exertions. He rose quietly so as not to disturb her. Outside he found the earth stiffened underfoot and a scrim of ice glazing the river's edge. The cold was delicious. His every sensation felt magnified.

They broke camp without speaking of what had passed between them, for it was beyond putting into words. Nate quietly celebrated the competence of his body, which had grown strong and sinewy. Esther dared not think about it for fear of judging it or putting too much stock in it, finding trouble in either direction. She told herself it was the natural thing, and that it wanted nothing so much as to be tucked away someplace and kept pure. If he spoke of it, she did not trust what she might say, nor did she want to know what he thought. If he wanted more of her, she was not free to give it, and if he wanted less, she could not bear to know it. All she needed to know from him their bodies had already spoken.

THE *MARY LOU* was a shallow-draft flatboat, thirty-five feet by eight, squared fore and aft. A freighter. She had no cabin. The two travelers were invited to stand or to sit on the cargo, as they pleased. Young Otto drove the team up the shore at the end of an eighty-foot towline, loping along beside them in his waders. Homer stood at the stern, fat and stolid with his legs spread, barking commands at Otto and manipulating the rudder through the familiar shallows and rapids. The river was less than a foot deep in places and they were not two miles upstream of White Mountain when they ground to a halt. Homer barked, "Git yerselves into the water and help us off a this bar!"

Nate and Esther pulled on their gumboots, stepped into the river. Otto mushed the team and Homer hollered, "Git her nose out, quick-like!" and Nate and Esther leaned against the bow and pushed her into the swifter current and the barge began to glide upstream again.

From there they walked more than they rode, the exercise warming them. A muddy path of sorts had been trod into the edge of the bank, slippery, soft in places, crossed with roots and undercut by seeps, and where the bank was too steep or gave way to bog they walked in the river shallows, and where the current ran fast they had the firm footing of gravel. She came to prefer the gravel in the faster current, but the speed of the water upset her balance. She took his hand where she felt unsteady, and he led her to solid ground or out of the current and they did not always drop hands when she got there but allowed the intimacy to linger. Council was twenty-five miles north as the river wends. The stream was shot through with salmon and char, and in the shoal water where the fishes' backs were exposed the river would explode with panic just ahead of the dogs' advance.

They hailed two freighters coming downriver with men leaving for the Outside. A man hollered across to them, "Sell you my claim for ten dollars!" and another shouted, "Pay you ten to take mine!"

These barges each had a horse on the stern rather than a dog team, and Esther remarked on the difference.

"Horse is quieter," Homer said, "but he won't eat a fish, and he makes himself perfectly useless in winter."

A third barge suddenly bore down upon them. They were trying to make a turn, with the *Mary Lou* on the left bank and the dogs ahead on the right. Shouts went up and the descending boatman threw his rudder hard over and the four men aboard her grabbed at the *Mary Lou*'s towline and tried to lift it clear of their cargo, but it snagged and dragged the dogs backward into the river and then the boats collided, pushing the *Mary Lou* broadside to the current. Everyone but the two rudder men jumped overboard. There were seven people in the river unhitching the dogs and pushing the barges clear.

"And good day to you, sir!" Homer tipped his hat agreeably to the other boatman as they parted. Esther climbed back aboard, half wet. The sun had broken through the clouds and she had some hope of drying out. Homer said, "He makes you work for your living. You was my wife, you'd've stayed home. Not many gals of a certain class find a need to go on up to Council, and the fact is most of the boys I bring down swear they ain't never agoin' back. Good creeks are all taken and the crooks are up there doing the dirty business on the best claims, no way a fella can pile up an honest fortune anymore. Me and Otto, we got ourselves fixed up proper with a twenty-foot freighter dog sled. Once these rivers are froze up, we'll run the sled direct to Nome once a week. Otherwise, you are here for the duration unless you got dogs and a sled and want to go out overland on the winter trail. Many as try it and don't make it. Fella I knew got hisself stranded last winter had to move in with an Eskimo family, eat raw fish, said nothing ever tasted better in his life, but you ask me, raw fish is for the dogs." Homer took a minute to roll himself a cigarette.

"What's the overland route?"

He struck a match on the seat of his pants. "Summertime, from Nome, you go inland at Solomon, follow the riverbed up to the East Fork, then up that to the pass and down to Horton Creek, then down the Fox River to where it empties out of the hills, and you think you oughta be there but the sorry truth is you got six miles of bog to cross, better have your waders and skeeter netting along. Winter trail's the better bet, inland at Topkok and across the Klokerblok's the way I go, but you want dogs and a sled. Going to Council's something a fella's got to want pretty bad."

Esther got off and walked some with Nate. If Leonard was at Nome and lit out for Council, he would be a while coming.

THEY REACHED THE mouth of a small river and hawed up into it. The Niukluk, which ran down from Council. By late afternoon, in the lowering sun, they were traveling through stands of spruce. To be among trees felt positively rich to Esther and she breathed in the smell of them like a balm.

Where they laid up was called Johnson's Camp, a slippery bank, a muddy clearing, and two rustic cabins free for the use, one being uninhabitable and the other already staked by two boatloads of men traveling out, so the *Mary Lou*'s passengers pitched their tents off to the side. The four of them were wet and cold and they tried to warm themselves before the flames of a spirited fire, wanton with the luxury of so much wood. They ate a meal of corned beef heated in the tin, and talk went around the fire of the men who'd got there first, and those that came later, and those that struck it rich but got jumped.

Homer said, "Many as strike it never enjoy it. Wander off in a blizzard. Run their team through the river ice. Drink themselves dumb and fall asleep on the trail. Met a deader on the Seward trail last winter, sitting plumb upright in front of an unlit fire, his legs crossed injun style, his hinder froze to the ground, and his arms gone missing to the elbows. Wolverine, I suspect."

"You run to Seward?" Nate asked.

"Once I did, yes, sir, for Mr. Charles D. Lane. Last year, and will again, middle of December, take out the mail and his company accounts. Pays a neat one thousand dollars. Nine hunnert thirty-eight miles each direction. Seward stays open, freight ships out, I drive back whatever he's got for Nome. Gives a man to solitude and the old-timer's thermometer, being that your finer grade coal oil freezes at minus fifty-five, your painkiller at minus seventy-two, and your St. Jacob's Oil at minus seventy-five."

The boatman's two passengers listened politely but their minds turned elsewhere, and when it was tactful to do so they excused themselves. They entered the tent together and snubbed their lantern. He pulled her parka off and helped her out of her vest. She reciprocated. He unfastened the buttons of her blouse and freed her breasts, but she and he were both too chilled from the journey to linger thus. So they shed and hung the rest of their clothes and clambered under the blankets. He straddled her on his knees, unfastened her hair, and pulled it down over her shoulders. He bowed to her breasts and felt an answering touch between his legs.

22

By the following noon a frigid headwind bore down out of the north, slowing their advance and causing them to button their coats and snug their chinstraps. Esther's skin was raw from her wet clothes. She searched for Council around every bend, and when it didn't appear she steeled herself for another mile. To their left, a vast bog choked with willows and alder. To their right, a proper riverbank rising into the low hills.

"Last turn," Homer announced, and then indeed the village appeared in the distance on an outside bend of the Niukluk, to their right, backed up by the pine forest and the rising hills. "Otto's and my place is that one between those trees there. The one with the sled hanging on the wall and no smoke coming out the chimney."

Otto and the dogs leapt aboard at the last, and the boatmen poled the barge to a landing at the center of town below the Beach Saloon. Three idlers in the lee of the saloon watched their arrival, standing with their hands in their pockets and no offer to catch a line. Two casually called Homer's name by way of a greeting. Otto made fast to a post, and Homer escorted his passengers up the bank into town.

The street was mud, lined up either side by log buildings that had been thrown up with their bark intact and now looked leprous, slowly peeled by the elements. The largest of these was the North American Transportation and Trading Company store, but the commonest were saloons.

Homer led them directly to a hotel with a sign over the door, "The Westmoreland Arms." He bade them wait out front while he went in for the proprietress. Esther saw him have a word with the woman, and then he beckoned them in. "This is Miss Flora Louise, a breath of feminine industry from the south of Virginia. She will heat you a bath and lay out a dry bed and make you fit company for each other. Otto will bring your freight. If you need anything else, find me at my place; we don't run back to White Mountain for two days." He tipped his hat. "Obliged for the companionship." He was away, then, steaming back down the muddy street for his boat.

Miss Flora Louise was a stately woman well past fifty, her high cheeks rouged and powdered. She showed them her three guest rooms. "Take whichever you like best."

The ceilings were low, but the rough log walls had been dressed up with Persian rugs and gas lamps. Esther paused in the door to a bedroom at the back of the building with white tatted curtains, an eiderdown, and a real porcelain bath. "This one."

Miss Flora Louise looked pleased. "I will light the fire under the cistern and you can draw the bath in an hour, as you like. If you put your clothes outside the door, I will have my girl launder them and hang them in the drying room. Come for supper at six."

THEY LOWERED THEIR bodies into the bath, sure in their nakedness. The water was blessedly warm and sweetened with oil. They sat face to face and explored each other with their hands, seeing each other fully naked for the first time. She was pearl white and bent with a swan's grace. Her dark nipples played at the surface and he touched each with a thumb in fellowship greeting and she laughed. He felt the underparts of her knees, the insides of her thighs, and gripped his hands around the narrow waist of her, pressing his nose into the hollow of her neck and letting the damp fringes of her hair fall over his closed eyes. She lifted herself to let him come beneath and enter her and he filled her with his longing, the water suddenly heaving such that they were forced momentarily to still themselves, until, ever so slowly, he pulled back and pressed deeper, feeling their reciprocations quickening until neither could hold back and they melted in waves of need and release.

They came to supper in fresh clothes, timid of eye contact, but Homer, who joined them, was voluble, putting them at ease. Miss Flora Louise took the head of the table before an oil painting of General Lee sitting his horse, Traveler, at the battle of Fredericksburg. Miss Flora, stationed beneath in the spirit of progeny, cast a beatific smile upon her guests while her girl brought out a Scotch mutton broth, scalloped oysters, Brunswick stew, and nutbreads. They dined on bone china painted in sprays of pink dogwood. The flatware was King's pattern, the goblets Jefferson cups, the wine an endearing French claret having somehow escaped the devastating phylloxera.

They had meant to reach Dogtail the following day, but when Nate climbed out from under the eider to stand naked in the thin light of the false dawn, she moaned and covered her head. "I am not one for creeks today, Mr. Deaton."

"I am sorry, miss, but creeks is writ on your tinnery."

"Yes, but I believe I have used it up."

"What?"

"My tinnery."

"Hardly. I shall check it against my own. My own says creeks today."

"Creeks is tomorrow, maybe. You bring your tinnery under here, I will have a look."

He climbed back under the quilt and slid against her. "See for yourself, then."

She shivered. "Will take a while. Your tinnery is rather a much, sir!"

Afterward she let herself slide back into sleep. Nate lay awake, cupping the length of her, he alone aware of the gathering hours. The daylight beyond their window chased shadow, a sudden snow squall gave over to shafts of brilliance, these in turn were chased by flurries. He should be on about his business, but he shut the company out of mind, giving himself to the sweetness of these hours stolen with Essie. Miss Flora's girl left breakfast at their door. Unbidden, she fired the cistern at noon and gave a gentle rap when the water was hot. She brought tea at three o'clock. Miss Flora herself knocked at six. At six-thirty Nate and Essie emerged, dressed and ravenous for supper.

NEXT DAY THEY set off by foot for Dogtail before noon, carrying Nate's collapsible skiff and all else they reasonably could, leaving the bulk of their outfit at the Westmoreland. The distance was more than seven miles. The first half of this they traveled on the rutted road that ran to Ophir Creek. The sky was cool and bright. They had been able to shuck their gumboots for leather, which rendered them positively nimble. They crossed open tundra, more or less parallel to the Niukluk, which lay off to their west, and after an hour came under the brows of hills.

She had a glow, warmed from within by the presence of him and by the day's journey, joyful in the power of her own legs over the crust of earth, and also, perhaps by reason of the journey, feeling acutely bereaved of her beloved horse, Mister Jones. As much as she let in her feelings of joy, so also came gloom and foreboding, the shadow of her husband.

"When I left him, I knew deep inside he would come for me," she said out of her silence. "But I never imagined there'd be you."

"What did you think there would be?"

"Oh, well. A small life. A tick under my sister's eaves. The companionship of my boy's picture. Work in a mill. Then, well, Leonard again. Him taking a place in the mill or maybe stringing telephone wires. City work."

"You have done far better at Nome."

"I don't know what to make of it."

"You're that kind of a woman, Essie."

"Fiddle."

"You're the kind that a fellow's just got to step back and get out of the way for."

"You can't make judgments based on Nome. No other place is like it. Outside, I could never do it."

"Why not?"

"People don't like it in a female."

He laughed outright at the stupidity of such a thing, knowing it was true as stated. "You've got a head full of brains and your chin's stuck out a mile. What's the matter with me that I adore it?"

"Would come to nettle you."

"Well, suppose you're right, which you most certainly are not."

"Besides . . ."

"What?"

"Oh, you know." She gestured at herself. "I'm a country girl. Suppose I went east, to your Worcester. Everybody would look at me, and how I talk!"

"All you need is that pretty flowered shirtwaist and blue skirt, buy yourself a boater with a long blue ribbon, you will be prettier than any girl in Worcester. Sure, everybody will look. And when you talk, everybody will listen, because you don't spout flowers, you talk like you have something to say. Anybody that says something smart about the way you puncture airs can't tell fool's gold from the real stuff. Why care what they think?"

"I wouldn't know what to do there, either."

"Worcester Motor-Cycle Shops, for starters."

"Oh, I would love to try one!" She grinned at the thought of it.

"We'll put you in charge of selling to ladies. Sidecars, maybe. And I've seen something up here, Essie: those gasoline motors are the way of the future. No fireboxes, no boilers, no feed water. Between the two of us, we could bring the gasoline motor to the American farm! What about that? I offer myself in all my raw potential, Essie, and I take yourself in all the fullness of yours."

She had no answer for that. They walked in silence. When the road turned to the northeast up Ophir Creek, he said, "Up there's where I head tomorrow." He was openly wistful about it. "Why don't you come along? You might like to see what that country looks like. We're going to come into a rich claim up there, get this company solid on its feet before the season's last gasp, come back in the spring with our sleeves rolled up. There'll be work for you, too."

"Don't keep at it, Nate."

He turned to see what was she meaning, but she walked on without him, suddenly offish and flinty when there was no cause.

He caught her arm and stopped her. "What is it?"

Her eyes were wet, and he guessed why.

"Marriage is a contract, Essie. He did not hold up to it. What more could you give than what you already did? He broke the contract and you left. Fair and square. Now I will marry you. We'll do it in Council."

She pulled away and turned from him. "I am not free to do it."

"It's what you want, Essie."

"And what does that make of it?"

She wanted to believe his words, but in what way did Leonard break their contract? It was a question she could not answer. It was she who had done the breaking sure enough now.

He tried not to sound hot, but could not hide it. "You blame yourself for a thing you could not fix in him. Just try to see it, Essie."

"I am trying!"

He left off. A streak of iron up her backside he could not bend. Just stiffened her worse.

In half a mile the hills came up tight on either side of the river, the spot where Homer said to look for the mouth of a creek on the far bank. Just where a creek ought to open to the river she saw smoke rising out of the willows, and a rowboat pulled ashore and turned over.

"That'll be Dogtail," he said.

They unfolded the *Miss Nomer*, bolted her thwarts in place, and launched themselves into the current, skimming across in half a dozen strokes. It was a narrow stretch of river, swift and deep. He felt certain she wanted what he did. He would give her his absence at Ophir to miss him, and then come and press her to go out.

23

The cabin was small, maybe twelve feet by fourteen. They came up on it from the river and hallooed for signs of life, but got no answer. Dogtail Creek was dry, and the building sat a hundred feet above it at the edge of the woods. Esther took a peek inside the door and spotted Lena's comb on the bed and a dress she knew hanging from a peg.

"It's their place, all right."

They hiked farther up the hill to the diggings and Esther climbed the first dump pile and hollered down the hole and got a muffled response. Moments later Plug and Lena climbed up into the light of day, squinty-eyed and filthy but tickled all over to find they had company. They quit their diggings and turned to hospitality, flustering around the cabin lighting the stove, putting on the kettle, carrying Esther's and Nate's gear up from the river, and then excusing themselves to get cleaned up. The visitors wandered down to the river again and idled away a decent interval, not saying what was on their minds, that Esther would be staying and making herself useful but Nate would be moving on to do his business at Ophir.

When they returned to the cabin, the heat of the fire had come up. Esther kicked off her boots and pulled on dry stockings. Jefferson poured tea and Postum and then lifted a board in the floor and rummaged in a hole that served for an icebox.

"This here butt-roast of reindeer's been waiting for an occasion," he announced.

Lena dug a tin of flour out of a crate and he got the can of bacon drippings from the icebox and she set to making biscuits as the talk chased back and forth between Dogtail, Council, and Nome.

The cabin was like the old pioneer houses Esther knew on the prairie, the logs chinked with moss, the door made of knocked-down goods boxes, a floor of unplaned boards, ceiling of pole wood covered with moss. Two small sashes admitted the last light of day. A corner of the room was given over to a bed, nor was it a big one, and the rest went to the Yukon stove, a table, two stools of hewn boards, a dry sink, and tools and stores piled helter-skelter over the floor. The place smelled of tallow, wood smoke, and perspiration. There was an inviting coziness to it despite the clutter and darkness, and Essie was struck with an urge to improve it. Brighten it with fabric. Put up shelves and hooks and get the clutter off the floor.

"What are you finding down your big holes?" Nate asked.

"Froze muck," Jefferson said, deflecting the query with a deftness that Nate recognized. He was into paydirt and didn't care to advertise.

"Go ahead and show it to them," Lena said.

"Never pays a man to talk," Jefferson said, but he put up his palms in agreeable defeat. He moved a box from a corner of the floor, lifted a board, and pulled out a poke. From this he spilled half a dozen small nuggets into Esther's palm.

They were heavy, odd-shaped, and brilliant. Surprisingly smooth and pleasing to the touch. She turned them over and thought how nicely they would weigh in her pocket.

Plug said, "This poke's just shy a pound. Say two hundred'n fifty dollars. We have got us a rich pocket, my lady and me. I have pulled out more'n fourteen thousand already. The paydirt's about twenty feet down. I got three shafts. Two as hit paydirt and one as missed it, where the old streambed meanders. Going to sink a new one down the hill thirty feet, see if I can locate it." He sat back. "We'll drift through the winter, build us a mothering big dump, clean up when the thaw comes. Between the cleanup and what we can get for a lay in the summer stampede, we plan to sail home as fat as politicians next year."

"It's frozen all the way down?" Nate asked.

"Have to set a dang thaw fire in there every night, lay it the length of the tunnel, stack it up two and a half feet. Next day I extend the drift and fill the buckets, and Miss Lena hoists and dumps them. We can get a hundred buckets out. That's as much as we got time and strength for and come out of the hole to wash out a pan every couple of hours to make sure we're still in the paydirt. Go down at six, quit at five, bucksaw logs and lay up the thaw fire, come in to eat and sharpen the pickax, next thing it's morning. Do it solo, they will find you dead one day. Do it with Miss Lena, they will find you dead but happy."

Lena said, "Essie, I'm just so glad you came! Didn't let myself think you would, and here you are! You work the claim with us and we'll cut you in." Mixed with her excitement was a look of curiosity, but she held her tongue.

Esther dismissed the offer.

"It's not a favor, Essie. There's plenty of work, believe me! I would be happy if I could do you a turn for cutting me into the mail business."

"Nate was coming to Ophir for the Major. Thought I would come see what trouble you have got yourself into is all," Esther said.

"How is it with the Cape Nome Company, then?" Plug asked.

"We are getting toward the end of our wick. Counting on a deal that our Mr. Sprague has hatched up here on Ophir Creek."

Lena invited Essie to share her bed and sent Plug out to the tent with Nate, and that night Essie caught Lena up on the news from her sister and why she'd come.

"I will go back to Nome once shipping's shut and no sign of Leonard."

"You and your fella can camp here as long as you like."

Essie lay quiet awhile. "Guess I have got myself into a pickle."

"I'm glad of it. I like him."

NATE STRUCK THE tent after breakfast and Esther walked him to the river, where a mist rose in the frigid air. The days were grown short, the sunrise reluctant.

"I will be up at Ophir or down at Council until I get my business done," he said. "I will call back soon as I get a chance."

She watched as he loaded the *Miss Nomer*, pushed off, and struck his course, his eyes on her as he rowed into the mist. If Leonard did not call at Nome before the end of shipping, she would take that as his decision not to come for her. She watched Nate collapse the boat at the far shore and lash it to his pack. She wondered would he still want her if she were free to say yes. He hoisted his load and turned to look, and she caught his gaze with a small wave and then he was gone and she climbed for the little log house.

OVER THE NEXT days while Lena and Plug dug their gold Esther built herself a bed. She put up hooks and shelves, separated the food stores from the dry goods and tools, and assigned order to the storage of each. She swept the floor now that it had been revealed, washed the windows, emptied the ashes from the stove, and sorted the kindling from the fire logs. She nailed a red blanket to the ridgepole along one hem and to the top of the wall along the opposite hem. It billowed gaily when the door was opened and, more usefully, caught the bits of moss and dirt that filtered down from the ceiling.

Lena and Plug welcomed her wholly into the life of Dogtail Creek, but they wore a particular respect and kindness toward each other that heightened her solitariness, a feeling she had not minded at Nome among the men, but what had felt like independence in one place quickly came to resemble loneliness in another.

Council City
Territory of Alaska
September 21, 1900

Major F. S. Palmer
Cape Nome Mining Company
10 Steadman Avenue
Nome City
Territory of Alaska

Dear Major,
I went to #19 above on Ophir and represented the company's interests to Mr. McGrath, prepared to take over the claim and determine our needs for men and equipment to capitalize fully on the asset next season. McGrath received me with a shotgun across his arm and an un-Christian invitation to remove myself to a hot place in the lower latitudes. I showed him Mr. Sprague's

receipt for the claim, and McGrath replied that the papers were false and bade me inform Mr. Sprague that he can go to the hot place as well, so far as Mr. McG is concerned. (Perhaps you will relay the message.)

I went directly to McKenzie's lawyer in Council, who said he had been expecting me. In such cases where ownership of a claim is in dispute he advises bringing the matter before the court and seeing the claim assigned to a receiver. I replied, "You mean assigned to McKenzie," to which he rejoined, "If that should be the case Mr. McKenzie has his hands full and would look favorably upon assigning the receivership to a third party," such as CNCo, "in exchange for a consideration." I asked what the consideration might be, and he, without hesitation, said half of the profits. I pointed out that Mr. Sprague had already paid $50,000 for the company's share in the claim, and the lawyer replied that I had correct information in that regard, "are there any other questions?"

I have it on local authority that the claim is amply well proven and Mr. McGrath is not of a mind to sell, which leaves us in a delicate position. McGrath's claim would seem to be the answer to our prayers. Having paid for a legitimate interest, we have no recourse but the court. However, to go before Judge Noyes is to play directly into Mr. McKenzie's thievery. Please advise how you wish the matter prosecuted at this end.

Sincerely,

Nate

He folded the letter into the envelope and sealed it before he could tamper with it further. It was his third draft, which he hoped put the matter squarely into the Major's lap, with Sprague's culpability palpable. He had edited out the sentence "I am left wondering whose pocket our $50,000 has lined," judging it more useful to let the Major arrive at this question unprompted.

Whatever the truth, the Major would sort it out. Nate looked forward to his explanation. He posted the letter, trying to dampen his venomous thoughts of Sprague. He figured to hear back in four or five days.

He had borrowed the use of a horse from Miss Flora Louise, which he now saddled and rode out of Council for Dogtail.

THE MOMENT HIS feet touched solid ground in Nome, Leonard supposed he'd got as far as he needed to get. He'd gone straight to the Post Office the next morning and asked if they had an address for her. Short clerk sorting the mail said, "Ask at Ten Steadman or Thurl's Livery."

"Esther Crummey," Leonard had said again, making sure.

"Yes, sir. Know her well."

He limped briskly in the direction of Steadman, light in his step, feeling warm toward this place, Nome, a regular city, the place where his wife had set herself up and he would fit into it, whatever she had going. He could hardly wait to see her face when she found he'd come. He was slightly giddy in his stomach with expectation, and when he passed a barbershop the notion came upon him to clean up some first, so he stopped and bought a haircut and a shave. The barber told him where there was a laundry up the street, but Leonard had nothing else to change into, so he did the next best thing, buying some gardenia water and sprinkling it over his clothes. He stood at a mirror and pushed his fingers through his short hair, and then stepped out to Front Street and went on to Steadman.

He thought he was looking for a rooming house, but Ten Steadman turned out to be an office for something called Cape Nome Company. He hoped it was the right place and knocked. The door was pulled open by a tall, soft-looking goat who looked surprised to have a caller.

"Yes, sir?"

"Begging your pardon, friend, if I am at the wrong door, but I am looking for a Mrs. Crummey."

The goat gave him a long queer look. "Who, again?"

"Esther Crummey." Leonard looked at the street number and thought the man at the Post Office may have meant to say one-ten instead of ten, a damned nuisance, but then the goat stuck out his hand.

"Of course. Don't believe we have met. I am Major Palmer."

Leonard brightened and stepped inside. "Leonard Crummey. Husband." He looked to see if she was there, but the goat seemed to be alone. It sure enough was a business office.

"Mr. Crummey. Indeed. Well, I am delighted to make your acquaintance, and sore as a boil to say you have missed her, sir. She has flown the coop."

"Back soon, though?"

"Oh, no, no. Left town completely."

Disaster lay in wait at the back of Leonard's mind. It was a thing he courted, terrible thoughts that he played out in his head to shore himself up against the unexpected, but this news was a blow to the body. Twenty, thirty times during his journey he'd asked himself, What's the worst thing, here? and always the answer wasn't what condition he might find her in or what she was up to, it was that she might not want him, or, worse, that he was too late and she had come and gone already, him never to catch her, a chase he'd failed more than once in his sleep, seeking, seeking, and her on the far side of some hill, racing ahead, just past hearing.

He had to drop his bag and sit a minute. He felt his possibilities draining away. He tried to smile at Palmer like the news did not count for much. He felt Palmer studying him. The man seemed uneasy, and Leonard thought something didn't feel right. He began to wonder what Essie would be doing in a place like this Cape Nome Company, and for a moment he guessed maybe she had joined herself in some way to this man standing here, but that was not like her and he cast the idea out of his head. "You're sure it was her," he said.

"Esther Crummey."

"From Minnesota?"

"Yes, sir. Sorry."

"Back to the States, then?"

Palmer paused and sucked on his lip. "If you ask me where she is at this moment, I would have to say I do not know. Damned unpleasant news for you, sir, I am sure of it. Nobody likes to pass bad news, but I will say it was a pleasure to make your acquaintance and I want to say more than that, sir, but, well—what I want to say, sir, is good luck to you!" He held the door open and showed Leonard out.

Something about it was off. Leonard went up Steadman. He had a chill on him now and felt the weight of his journey in his bones. Captain Folsom had paid off his wages and got him a bunk at a rooming house until he could arrange return passage to Seattle, which he had no intention of making, but the wages in his pocket meant he could eat.

He went in search of the livery stable. He should have started at the livery stable. He had intended to start at all the livery stables, but then somebody had suggested he start at the Post Office, and when the little snipe at the Post Office had mentioned a livery stable, well, he should have gone there first, which he would've done if he'd've known the Steadman place was not a rooming house but some kind of a company.

When he found Thurl's Livery he stepped inside and approached a man who was bent over a pile of skins. Did not trouble to introduce himself but simply said, "Looking for Esther Crummey."

The man looked up. "Gone up to the Council District. You have an outfit to sell, I can do the business."

"Council District?"

"Dogtail Creek. I am her partner, if you want to do business, else I am occupied."

"What's the business?"

The fella looked at him. "Dogs. Hides. Miner's salvage. Livery. What're you wanting?"

"Where's this Dogtail in the Council District at?"

Thurl was expressionless. He shook his head, seeming never to have thought to wonder himself. "East a good bit is what I heard."

"Obliged." Leonard backed out. He turned into the nearest saloon to get directions.

HE GOT HIMSELF a wore-out paint and a camp kit cheap as dirt and set out that afternoon, but he was slow making the hundred miles to Council City. Wind whipped in off the sea and he had to kick the animal to make it go. In the second day, when he turned inland at Solomon, every hill he came to he had to get off the horse and lead it over. Every creek crossing or pothole he came to, the horse sank its nose in the water and tried to drown itself.

There was not much to Council but he was never gladder to reach a place. It was the morning of his fourth day out of Nome. He stopped to get a hot meal and ask where Dogtail was at, and then he got back on the horse before it could lie down and die and he rode on up the river a few miles until he reckoned he was close. He found a shallows to ford. The idea had struck him to make her out before he showed himself. See what kind of arrangement she had got herself into. He walked the horse around the flank of a low mountain into the trees, unloaded his kit, and let the horse loose to fend for itself. Then he set off by foot up a slope through the trees.

He was not fit for it even without his kit, which he carried with him expecting he would need it to spend the night up there once he got the lay of things. Every fifty yards he had to rest. He was sweated through and after a few minutes' sitting on his kit he had to pick up and climb again or he came all over in chills. He favored his gimpy side, which made his other hip tired working up a steep slope such as this. When he'd got himself some height, he circled around behind where Dogtail should be and scouted it. Spotted smoke below right away. He dropped his kit and worked his way down the draw into the trees and marked where the smoke rose from. A log cabin, set at the edge of the trees. Above it were dirt piles and holes he recognized for mine diggings.

He found a place to sit and watch from. Seemed unlikely this would be Essie way out here, but if it was, he doubted she would be alone. Thinking maybe she wasn't alone made him uneasy, and he came on to shivering from his damp clothes, half hoping he would see her and half hoping he would not. When a Negress climbed up out of the mine hole he looked twice and knew he was at the wrong place and felt himself go half limp with the relief of it, but annoyed just the same. He was rousing himself to go ask the Negress where in Sam Hill Dogtail was at when a white woman stepped out of the cabin and shut herself into the privy. Leonard sat himself back down. She looked like she could've been Essie's sister. Thought he might just wait on it until she was finished. He edged closer, still in the shadows, and when she came out she hollered something up at the Negress. That voice.

His heart pounded but he didn't even let himself start to breathe until she was gone inside the cabin.

Well, wasn't he one wily bastard. He edged back into the deep of the woods and climbed uphill through the trees a good bit. Needed to give himself a day or so to make sense of things. He poked around until he turned up a nice little hole to camp in. He retrieved his kit and hauled it down to his spot without noticing the weight of it, he was so busy trying to guess at what she was up to.

His stomach brought him back to the here and now. He went up a few paces and searched back and forth in the woods until he found a rabbit run. He cut the limbs off a sapling, got a wire out of his kit, fashioned a loop, bent the sapling, set a trigger, put some pine litter over it. Went back to his hole and settled in. When the sun was gone he let himself make a little cookfire and eat what was left of his beans. After that he slept hard. Woke up only once, when he heard the snare spring.

He camped there three nights, going down by day to lie in the woods wrapped in a blanket, content to watch his wife, think through his plan. She was his lodestar. She was his true north, the planet he steered by, and just seeing her industry filled him with quiet well-being. His little daytime nest was not a hundred yards from her door, easy to see if she looked for it, but easier to miss.

The gold business was treating her good. He could tell by the way she carried herself, how she dived into her work. Looked to be in one of her humming periods, pink-cheeked and full of ideas. Favorable for a happy greeting once he showed his head. Just the same, it paid to have a plan to offer her. The Perley Feed Mill was what he'd been thinking. He'd be good at it, and right in the middle of town where everybody'd see. He wanted to start over, get them a healthy boy to raise up, but he had to be careful going near that subject. Feed mill was a good idea, though.

No question but she was in charge, here, either. Imagine Essie with her own nigger and a graybeard to do her work. She was more like him than he would've let himself guess. He couldn't wait to tell it to Daigneault.

But something it was that kept him from walking right out of the woods and into her yard.

What'd he think she might do, bolt again? Not damned likely, way the hell out here. Bolt to where?

Maybe it was his animal sense made him wary. He argued with it: She'd not be running off somewhere when she had a mine going here, Mister Stupid. She'd be relieved to see him. Surely needed the help, and Lord knows she could stand the company of her own kind. Probably already sent for him, and he wasn't home to get the letter.

He was about talked into showing himself but there comes another fellow, oaring across the river in a little rowboat. *Who's he, then?*

SHE SAW SOMETHING on her blanket when she came in from the woodpile. It was a little blood-colored moccasin. Her heart quit in her chest. She dumped her armload of logs into the wood box and went straight to her bed and plucked it up and thrust her fingers into it to feel of the lining, bringing the toe to her nose and rubbing the leather's richness between her fingers. Was the shoe she'd saved for Gabe's stunty foot to grow into.

She had to sit down. Her hand trembled as she brushed the shoe against her cheek, which was already wet with tears. She pressed the softness of it to her upper lip. There was the scent of Leonard but she could still catch the new-shoe smell on the inside of it, and a wisp of the excitement she'd felt at the time, the secret thing she and her ma had done, buying these shoes. The promise of Gabe's growing into it.

She went to the door and looked out. "Leonard?"

She'd thought the shoe was lost in the fire, but here it was.

"Leonard?" She scanned the woods but he didn't walk out.

What did it mean, his bringing this?

She carried a chair out and sat with the moccasin in her lap, facing the woods where he could see her. She closed her eyes against the bright sun and her mind raced backward while she waited. They had rescued almost nothing. Leonard had gone back for the boy's half a horse, but too late. By then the house was too far gone. They had precious few things to mind losing, but the moccasin was one she'd sorrowed after the most.

She heard a noise from the river and stood and looked to see him coming, but it wasn't Leonard, it was Nate.

"Essie!"

Nate strode up and bent to kiss her, but she turned her cheek to him.

"What is it?" Her eyes were red.

She tugged him into the cabin and he followed, alarmed.

"Tell me."

She shut the door. "Leonard's come."

"Hell and damnation! Where?"

"I don't know. He left this for me. It was our boy's."

"Oh, Essie. This is the worst."

"You should go, Nate. I will talk to him and then come to Council for you."

"No. Pack your stuff. We can take the skiff out. Run all the way to White Mountain or Cheenik, catch the Elk or another. We'll beat him to Nome and be two or three days out for Seattle ahead of him. Unless he's got a riverboat, he can't catch us. Has he got a boat?"

"Don't know."

"I didn't see a boat. He could help himself to one in town, though. Look," he said, landing on a different plan—

She ran her fingers around his neck and shook her head. "I've got to stay and talk it through with him. He'll follow me anywhere I chase to."

"Where is he now?"

"Camped somewhere is my guess. I'll know when he's ready to tell me, which I think he is."

"Damn! Damn! Damn! Well. Here's what we'll do. I'll stay, you have it out with him, and then we'll go. No skulking away. You tell him how things stand, and I'll be right here if he gets hot about it. We'll get Plug up out of the mine. He won't try anything with the both of us right here!"

"He'll be trying to sugar me back, Nate. He doesn't know about you, don't you see? Leonard and I can talk about what lies between him and me, and that's that. If it's him against you, no telling what he'll do, but he's just not going to take it. No, you go on to Council. Give me time with him. Might take a day or two. I'll come to you."

"You sure?"

"I'm certain there's no other way."

He looked away, finding his terms with it. "I came to tell you my own news. The Ophir claim's a swindle Sprague's hatched with McKenzie. Seems the company's on the ropes."

She could hardly hear his news for worrying over Leonard's coming between them. She reached up and gave him a kiss and tugged his ears. "I will come in the next day or two. Promise."

A SHADOW FELL at the door, and when she turned to see why, it was Leonard.

"Oh," she said.

"Who's the fella with the rowboat?" Thought he'd test her.

He was thinner than she'd ever known him, his eyes sunk in his face. Had his muskrat jug on a string like it was a part of him. "He's with the company that hired me."

"Thought maybe you'd got yourself a gentleman caller," he joked.

She looked ripe as a plum. Filled him with a sense of goodwill, wanting to do for her. He nodded and sniffed. "I come in, then?"

"Seems you already did."

"Before now? Didn't want to catch you by surprise. I thought you should know I was coming."

"Poor Gabe's shoe?"

He scratched his head and hitched his trousers. "It was in my pocket after the fire so I saved it. Something to remember him."

She looked at the floor. She had never known him to do such a thing, but it did not mean she could forgive him all the rest, and she did not want him to think she would.

"I was surprised when I came to put it on your bed, though."

"How?"

He scowled. "Are you sleeping with your nigger, Essie?"

"Hush your voice, and you want to watch your language, Leonard."

"Goddamn it, Essie. There's only two beds in here."

"I sleep alone, Leonard."

"Aw, damn it to hell! You mean that nigger and that old coot're sharing a bed in your cabin?"

She paused. "It's them are letting me stay in their cabin."

He turned and went outside and cursed and came back inside. "Their cabin?"

"It's their claim, Leonard. Their cabin. They are friends of mine. When they come up out of their diggings you can meet them yourself."

"No thankee, Ess."

"All right, but get your soddy self right on outside, because this place belongs to them and I won't have you talking like that in here."

They both stepped out, him saying, "I've come for you, anyhow, Essie."

Words she'd heard in her head since getting the letter from Constance. Being forewarned did not make it easier to hear them. She looked around for a place where they could settle things, but there was nowhere exactly to sit, so they went down the path toward the river. It was a cold day and the sun was fast sliding back of the hill. His leg gave him a jerky walk and he was nothing to look at, like he'd been on rations of sawdust, wearing clothes somebody'd maybe once been buried in. They sat on the bottom of Jefferson's overturned rowboat, feeling the cold air off the river.

"I've come to help close out your business interests," he said. "Take your capital back to the States."

Bees swarmed inside her chest and she shook her head and said, "You know what, Leonard?" digging inside herself for a way to tell him no. Now was the time to set it straight if ever she was going to, and she recalled her words to Nate, that she could talk to Leonard about what lay between them and settle it, but now she couldn't find a way to start. She saw he was hungry and needful, and fought to assure herself that he was stronger than he looked or how did he get clear to Dogtail?

"Ess, I got something more to show you." He fished his jug from its pouch and unscrewed the lid.

She shied from it, but he pushed it toward her.

It was not the best light, but she saw the whiskey was turned cloudy and resinous. "What?"

"Look close." He raised it up.

She bent to see and caught a whiff of sweet rot. There was something in there she could not make out, like some piece of a beak and flesh. "Get it away. What in God's name, Leonard?"

"That bastard snake, Essie. I chopped its head off, stuck it in my jug. Haven't had a lick since. Thirst comes over me, I undo this lid and look the devil in the eye and I know why I quit it. I quit it to get you back, and there's no place I don't take my jug, keep me in mind of what I got to do. And I done it."

The thought of it and the smell and seeing the scud made her head go light. She avoided his gaze and looked out at the light fading on the river, and then up toward the mines to see if maybe Lena or Plug was coming out, but they were nowhere in sight, still burrowing at their gold, and here she sat, alone and unbeknownst you could say, wrestling with the advent of her husband.

He had quit his jug. She wondered was it true. Snakehead was proof, you had to say. Was something she wouldn't have guessed.

NATE STEPPED OUT of the Council Post Office and paused at the edge of the street to read the letter.

10 Steadman Avenue
Nome City
Territory of Alaska
September 24, 1900

Mr. Nate Deaton
Council City
Territory of Alaska

Dear Nate,
I shall never knowingly ask you to do something contrary to your morals. Hultberg sold #5 Anvil out from under us. Either 19 Ophir bears fruit, or we are skunked. If we could reel the money back like fish bait we would, but we can no sooner retrieve Bill's payment than we can retrieve the monies we spent on your beach dredge. One bad judgment does not repair another, but this one is Bill's mistake. I leave it in your hands whether we are to make good on it. If there were time, I would send Bill up to do his own dirty work.

The doctor, Sunderhauf, and the others join me in sending their wishes for your success. Be prompt. I have confirmed us on the C. D. Lane, sailing on the 2nd. In all likelihood the last boat out.

March toward the guns.

L. H. Palmer

No damned surprise. He tucked the letter back in its envelope, as low and sour as he could ever remember.

SHE HAD PROMISED Leonard she would make it back to the cabin by dusk, but she had been longer with Nate than she had planned. What she'd said came as a surprise to him and she could see the hurt. She had steeled herself for it and hadn't wanted to stay—every minute with Nate would eat at her certainty—but she was capable of this, because it was the only thing she could see to do.

She had found him in the parlor at the Westmoreland.

He took her into his room and closed the door.

"I have to take him back," she said right away.

"Of course you don't."

Suddenly exhausted, she said, "I can't explain it. Just know I have to do it. I am married to the man."

He looked at her long without words, and she had to turn her gaze. She looked down at her hands and wondered what to do with them, then crossed her right to lie on top of her left, cover her wedding band.

She thought he might be angry with her, but she could see he was not.

He took her in his arms. "Sweet Essie. I will say what you already know and cannot see for the storm you are in. Your marriage was a mistake. You told me yourself."

"Then the mistake was half mine."

"You did the right thing when you left him. If you take him back, you make the mistake again. It's no good. You can see it yourself."

"I owe it."

"Marriage is not a debt, Essie. It is a thing you build together, slowly, like a house. But if the house you see in your mind is not what he sees, you've got to move out."

"Leonard's quit his jug and changed himself. I owe it to find out how much. And what about you? How can you be certain that I am the one for you? You think it, all the way up here in Alaska, but will you feel it once you go home to your own true world?"

He steered her to the bed and they sat together and she wiped her eyes and blew her nose.

"I do know, Essie."

She nodded and folded her handkerchief in her fingers and looked vacantly at the floor. "I have made him seem impossible, but there were good things he did, and they have been coming back to me. I never told you about the half a wood horse he made Gabe and how I didn't see the good of it."

THE BOY WAS three, moving every which way around the house by scootching sidewise on his normal hand and foot. She had said to Leonard couldn't he make a kind of chair with wheels the boy could push around in. Would be more normal-looking, wouldn't wear out his clothes on the one side. Leonard watched the boy but did not say yes or no, so she was surprised one evening that January when he came in from the barn with a little wooden horse. It had a pair of wheels on the right side, but stunty legs on the left, meaning it would not stand upright. He had painted it a chestnut red and put a loop of one of her real horsehair mecates on it for reins. "Looks just like my Mister Jones!" she said. He set it on the parlor floor and let the boy look.

Esther could hardly believe it, Leonard going to the trouble. "Will be a beauty when you get it done," she said.

"*Is* done," he said.

"Legs're only on one side, though."

"Opposite side as the boy's, Essie," he said. "Watch the way he crabs around. He's a go-getter. My idea is, he and the horse together have enough legs to stand on. If I put four legs on the horse, boy's only going to sit and push it. This way he's got to stand and walk on the good leg."

"Sweet Jesus, Leonard!" Was a harebrained idea. Put her off that he would even think it up.

"Well, I made it and I am going to try it." Leonard picked Gabe up and put the boy's good hand onto a handle at the horse's mane. "Throw your shorty over the saddle like this," and he set the boy up onto the saddle and held him upright while he showed him how to walk it forward. Then he let go.

The boy fell over, hit his head on the floor, let loose the howling furies.

Esther jumped and pulled the thing off him. "He trusted you. You want to have your fun, go have it with somebody your own size."

"Don't be preaching at me, woman! Got to give the boy a chance to fall. How's he going to learn it?"

"You add two legs on the other side or chop it up for the fire, but don't bring it back inside like this." She took the wailing child and stormed out the door, went to her chicken house, let Leonard think about it. Made her mad as a cat afire. She set to cleaning the roosting boxes, give him a chance to think it over.

The boy took only two days to learn it, and the moment he did, the two-legged horse was how he got around anymore. Esther carried it along everyplace she took him, showed off her boy and what his daddy had dreamed up. At the Perley bakery Gabe was all over the place, in front of the counter and in back, through the kitchen and the storeroom. "He's half a that horse," Mrs. L said to Esther.

The next summer, when the boy was more grown, Leonard made the horse's legs longer and Gabe got around anywhere he could make the two wheels roll. Leonard took to calling his son Stunts. The first time Essie heard him say it, she snatched his sleeve and turned him to rights. "Don't! Just because he likes his half a horse, he is not your trick dog."

"It's not Stunts for tricks. It's for two stunty limbs."

"Never let me hear you say it again."

He pushed his face up to hers. "You are not the first and the last word on what's right for our boy. Stunts is what other boys'll call him, or close, and if he calls it himself, he's going to be stronger. You make a fuss, this boy's going to know you don't think he's up to it."

Within a week Gabe was calling himself Stunts, and anybody who wanted the prize of his grin called him the same. The name couldn't have fit him better than a buckskin jacket, or pleased him more.

SHE FINISHED THE story and let it sit. In all the things she'd told about Leonard, she'd never thought to tell this. The red shoe had brought the story with it, tucked inside, surprising as the smell of new leather.

"I have got to be on my way," she said.

Nate pressed her hand to his face. He'd had her so short a time. He tried to recall the world before Essie and could not.

He stood and pulled her to him. "Damn it to hell, Essie! I can't let you go! We can both leave from here now! We've got all we need!"

She pushed away, her jaw set.

He wanted to steal her. Supposing he did, though, wouldn't that kill the thing about her he most loved? If he let her go, what was the chance he'd find her again? "Nobody's like you, Essie."

She tried to smile. "I am one of your birds."

He fastened the top button of her coat and straightened her scarf. "You are my only one." If he gave himself another minute he wasn't going to let her go. "I'll take you to the crossing."

She shook her head. "Leonard's waiting outside of town." This was not true, but she could not say goodbye and cling to the back of him seven miles by horse.

She kissed him sweet but short.

"What are you doing about Ophir, Nate?"

He touched the down of her jaw. "Why, I'm turning my back on it," he said, forcing an ironic smile. "What else can I do and live with myself?"

SNOW HAD BEGUN to fall, swirling up in gusts where the hills crowded the river and pushed the weather along. She reached the crossing after dark, finding Plug's rowboat where she'd left it, now under a blanket of white. She raised her eyes toward the far bank and made out a flickering light through the falling snow. Leonard had lit a fire to mark the crossing for her. She would pull for the light, and he would be waiting.

ESSIE WASN'T HALF an hour gone from the Westmoreland before Nate had his things packed and his account settled. He stood below the Beach Saloon at the river's edge in the falling snow and fitted the little skiff's thwarts into place. He probably should have waited for daylight but felt gripped by the need for distance. The buildings of the village ghosted behind him through the scrim of evening, the street empty, all sentient beings sanely before the hearth or the saloonkeeper's bar. He loaded his gear fore and aft for balance, glanced back at the town in all its dreariness, and shoved off, taking two broad steps through the shallows and climbing over the transom.

He figured to make Johnson's Camp in a couple of hours and lay up for the night. He could scarcely believe he was on his way out, and with precious little time to make Nome before the ship sailed. The snow on the banks gave a gray felt edge to the slice of watery blackness running south, defining his course through the rising dark. Not an hour earlier he'd thought to be wintering over with her, and look at him now.

He could not bring himself to the subject of Essie. What he felt for her decision. Bullheaded and plain wrong. And yet, by God, how he loved her better for it. Abiding.

24

Esther asked Lena privately to take Leonard into the mine for wages, and Lena made the offer at breakfast.

"Got a gimpy leg," was all Leonard said in answer, meaning he could've stood to make a week or two in wages if she hadn't seen fit to be born a nigger.

When Lena and Plug went into the diggings Esther said, "You do Lena the decency of accepting."

He gave her a look like what was she drinking.

Esther was sewing a border onto a muslin curtain to keep her hands busy and her mind off Nate. If he was turning his back on Nineteen Ophir, she guessed he was soon going out or already on the river.

"Going to be here awhile," she said to Leonard. "You got to do something."

Idea of it wore like grit under his eyelid. "I love to be back beside of you, Essie, but the two of us are mules at different ends of the wagon sometimes."

She took a stitch.

"Past is past, Essie."

"And what?"

"And what I'm saying is, number one, I think we got to start on a fresh foot."

She could not look up. Wasn't going to trust her voice.

"Number two, I have an idea."

"What?"

"Sell the business at Nome and get up a business at Perley. I was thinking maybe buy the feed mill."

"Where'd that come from?"

"Well, think. People got to feed their animals come hell or high water. Believe I could do a passable job running a feed mill."

"Is it for sale?"

"All I'm saying is, we got to throw in together on something."

"We got time to talk about it. Can't go out till spring."

"Number three, let's you and me scoot back to Nome. Things to do, maybe pick up some kind of work or keep from going bone-crazy in two square feet of cabin."

"Nothing at Nome to hurry us," she said. "Here we've got company and ways to be useful."

"Too damned close here." The four had been sleeping uneasily under one roof.

"Why not put up a lean-to at the back?"

"Good idea." He gave her a sly look.

"Now, what's that supposed to mean?"

He lowered his voice. "Relations, for Christmas' sake."

"I'm going to need a little time before I am ready for relations."

"Damn it to hell, Essie, what a long goddamned trip back to a fella's wife. How long?"

"I will say when I'm ready."

He knew what she was doing. Testing his jug. He had got control of that, but if she needed to see for herself, he would find the patience somewhere.

WITH HER HELP he cut the logs and they put up the room against the back wall of the cabin, and then she sent Leonard to Council for a sheet-iron stove. The space was small but fit for Esther and Leonard to sleep in. The four of them still shared meals in the main cabin, and Leonard went to work in the drift mine. Lena gave him the pick and shovel, and Plug showed him how to do it.

"Dig to the bedrock, then check to see how it slopes. The old streambed'll follow the lowest bedrock, so you drift with the slope. Miss Lena will help you load it, and then she'll bucket it out."

The tunnel was about fifteen feet long, tall enough to stand in. Leonard moved his jug around to hang down his backside and swung the pick into what was thawed by the night fire, and then he and Lena shoveled it into Plug's wheelbarrow. He ferried the load to the bottom of the shaft and dumped it into a pair of buckets while she climbed up the ladder to the windlass. Plug had rigged a long rope with two pigtail hooks twenty-five feet apart so he could fill both buckets and go back to work while she winched up the first, taking the slack out of the line to the second, which came up next. So while she raised and dumped the buckets, Leonard went back at the gravel with the pick. Plug had gone down the hill to where he was getting a start sinking his next shaft.

The drift was cold to work in and dark as a tar barrel except for the glow of their candles. They went down before daylight and came up after dark like animals. Was day after day of picking and hauling gravel, but he had to admit his darkie boss worked like she was born to it and kept him hopping. She teased him one day, "The way you swing a pick, I'd a swore you were a colored boy."

Leonard made no reply; didn't know what she meant by it.

"Colored boy knows how to swing a pick like nobody else," she said.

He didn't mind her saying so. "You tell it to Essie."

At night he rubbed liniment on his leg and hoped Essie was seeing him work himself to death to get back his marital right and privilege.

One day when Plug was on the pick and Leonard was bucketing he caught a glint of something in a bucketload he dumped, and he got off the crib and dug around with his fingers. Lo and behold, there was a piece of gold the size of cherry stone. Put it in his pocket.

That night he pressed his need against Essie's backside and whispered, "Time's come."

She turned over to face him. "Not yet," she said. But she reached down there and took him up under her gown in her hand and helped his need.

Way she did that brought him his Auntie Willa, and God and Jesus didn't he feel himself messing all over everything. He put his face against her breast, breathing hard. Made him dizzy weak and strong, was sorry only it came so fast. Felt a damp surprise on his cheek.

"You don't know how bad I needed it, Ess; got you way up on your snakebit titty."

She hushed him. It was her secret that her left breast went leaky every time she thought of Nate that way.

She cupped his head against her breast. Would have been the wrong thing to turn Leonard away, but it was the wrong thing to turn Nate away like she did. How could a person know between two wrong things?

THE DAYS GOT colder. The river froze, all but the fastest part of the channel. The snow came. The cabin grew smaller.

The four of them living together was like working a folding puzzle. If someone needed to get to the stove to light a smoke or a lantern, the others shied to one side to let him pass. They remade the furniture to do double duty or swing out of the way. Plug and Lena's bed became a bench, with the tick and blankets shoved beneath during the day. The eating table could be pulled up to the bench, and the two stools opposite. The kitchen corner was curtained off for a washroom between quitting the mine and supper.

The stove in Leonard and Esther's bedroom burned red-hot, warming the small space quickly even on the coldest nights. They had to shed their clothes to their long johns, crack the door, and climb into their bed under a single layer of blankets, but come two in the morning the pine was burnt out, the room was below freezing, and one of them had to get out and rekindle it while the other scrounged blankets off the floor. Thirty minutes later the room glowed with the heat of the stove and they were pitching blankets on the floor again.

It snowed every day for four days running, the wind roaring in the spruce tops, and on the morning of the fourth day, after the others had gone down into the diggings, Esther heard the barking of a dog team and stepped out the front door to look. She recognized the dogs before she knew the driver, who pulled up in front of the cabin, bundled in a moose-hide parka.

"Morning, missus!"

"Hey, Homer. You come in and get warm."

"No, ma'am. On my way to Nome. Heard your mister went out, and Miss Flora Louise asked me to check on you."

Essie glanced up to the dump pile at the mine to make sure Leonard was not hearing this. She stepped out to the sled and spoke quietly.

"Thank you, Homer. You tell Miss Flora Louise I am fine." She hesitated. "Tell her my husband's come."

Homer nodded. "So she heard. Wanted me to tell you something more."

"What's that?"

"If you want to pass your wait at the Westmoreland, you come and be her guest and companion."

Esther was taken aback. "My wait?"

"She didn't know, but in case."

"You tell her I am fine and I will call in when I get to Council."

"All right, then. I am off for Nome. You get out of the cold."

The dogs squealed and watched Homer's every gesture, and the moment he gave the signal and cried, "Mush!" they bolted ahead. He swung them in a wide circle, flew down the trail he'd cut coming up, and disappeared in a swirl of snow.

WHEN LEONARD WASN'T digging or bucketing or setting braces in the tunnel, he was raising the log cribbing above the dump pile or going out after firewood. It took half a cord a night to thaw the mine and heat the cabin. They had taken all the dead trees in easy reach and had started mixing green wood into the fire, and now when he went down the mine shaft in the morning the stink of it was so bad he could hardly get a breath. The sappy wood smoldered and burned cool and didn't thaw half the dirt they needed and then it left smoldering log ends that had to be bucketed out before they could get to work.

During the third week after he'd started in the diggings, he said to Lena, "Going to take the day off of mining and get us some dry wood." He gave her a look to say tell me otherwise, but she said, "Better borrow Plug's snowshoes."

He headed south beyond the trails they'd already beat, going slow on account of his leg, but wasn't it fine just to be out of the hole for a change and to see the stinty sunlight. He found a nice tall deadhead a dozen paces past where they'd been wood-gathering and sawed it down. Limbed and sectioned it and then went on, finding two more in thirty feet, which he dropped, limbed, cut, and piled.

Essie was different in a way he could not put his finger on. He felt she was looking for something more from him, and he could not see what. The whole day he spent on wood-gathering he also spent on the question of squaring the yoke between them.

Later that night, as they lay in bed, he whispered, "I am not against trying to get another boy."

She did not answer.

"When you're ready."

She said, "All right."

"And Ess?"

"What?"

"What if he was called Rugnel? Help some to knit us back to your pa."

She rolled over, laced her hand into his.

He tried to go to sleep, but could not. He knew what he was after now. It was a thing you do not go after by the shortest path, but one you work your way up to. Like bothering to hunt up the dead trees for the dry wood instead of taking whatever's closest. Took longer but paid you back. Being married was the same. You had to think past the easy thing and find the one that would work. He wondered if the same thought had likely been on her mind all along and he had not been quick enough to see it. You both want it but you don't say the thing for fear of jinxing it.

MIDDLE OF THE night at the end of October Leonard woke to a red light flooding in through the window.

"My God!" he cried, and ran to pull open the door.

Essie came right behind. They fully thought to see the woods in flames, but it was not the trees, it was curtains of fire in the sky. Northern lights.

"All of heaven's burning," Leonard said. "Come out with me, Essie, and let's watch it."

They pulled on boots and parkas. He led her down the path toward the landing, their feet squeaking in the snow. The cold burned their lungs and put a catch in their breathing. Everything was gone to red—sky and forest, landing and river. They stood arm in arm, in awe of the spectacle. Out at the center of the channel, only two-days frozen, the bare ice shimmered like a streak of fire licking up the river itself.

"It's a sign, Essie. I want us to get a boy. I'm done with drink. I've proved myself to you."

She knew he had, but now she knew something else for certain that she had only guessed before.

He turned to her and she grasped his head in her hands and put her face near to his and gently said, "Oh, Leonard."

"Tonight, you mean?"

She shook her head. "No."

"Goddamn it! I'm your husband, Essie. When?"

"Leonard. Listen. You have to listen. A baby's growing inside of me already."

He jerked his head away.

She tried to choke off the tears that were coming now. "Got a baby growing inside of me, Leonard. I am so sorry."

He stumbled toward the river and turned his face up to the sky and let out an animal kind of wail. She went to him and tried to put her arm around him but he threw it off.

"Who was it? That Major Palmer? That mug you got yourself into business with?"

Felt himself dying. His Essie. He could not breathe.

"Was a foolish thing I did, Leonard. The father is gone away." She wanted to say more. She could have tried to make him think the child was his, but it was a little late for that, nor could she say it and look him in the eye. She hoped with time he could see it as an honest mistake and learn to live with what she'd done and agree to raise the child with her. He would need some time to come around to that, if he could come to it at all, but they had a whole winter ahead and she hoped that maybe he could.

Leonard slumped against Plug's rowboat and stared across the river at the world in blazes. She came and sat beside him, put her head on his shoulder. "We can go slow, maybe work it out."

He moved away. He could not bear to feel the touch of her. "Why don't you go on back inside?"

"I can't leave you out here."

"Well, I can't go in there, Essie, so I guess you got to leave me here."

"Turn to me, Leonard."

He refused. He was not going to see in her eyes what she did, or what she was asking of him now.

She sat as near to him as he would let her and wept softly. "This thing happened. It was a mistake."

He gazed blindly over the river, feeling their future drain away. The sky shimmered and wavered like a breeze on lit coals, one part of the sky running hotter and then another, the shimmer caught by the bare ice of the river, making the ice look hot so that you could not be certain what you were seeing. Put a chill through him.

Time passed. Was it minutes or an hour? The woods were utterly quiet and he turned to see whether Essie had gone, and sure enough.

He pulled out his jug. The ring of the metal cap was the voice of an old friend. He raised the rim to his lips, and whiskey thick as syrup burned his pipes.

Heard his name called. It was Plug. Leonard ignored him, and Plug came down to the landing. "Come inside, Leonard. You won't last out here."

"Go to hell and take your nigger."

Plug tried to coax him.

Leonard felt the whiskey spread through his gut and into his head and limbs. Longed for the Indian there beside him; had nobody to raise his sorrow to. Who'd have guessed, seed of another man inside of her?

His throat was thick and he hawked up some clabber and spit it to the side and wiped his mouth on his sleeve and looked back toward Plug, but the man just turned around and walked away. Leonard would've done the same. Who'd want this problem walking in the door?

The frozen gash of river shimmered like the heat was all beneath it, the water itself running molten under the ice. Could almost believe it was true. He got himself up off the boat, decided to go out and see, but it was tricky to get his balance and he stumbled sideways, caught himself on a sapling. The sky went in a circle. He held the sapling with one hand and tipped up the jug and drank down the last of the whiskey. It no longer burned but filled him with strength. Snake head bumped his lip and he dumped it out on the snow.

"You old bastard."

He went out onto the river and tried to jump a little, test the ice, but there was snow on it and he lost his balance and fell down.

He heard Essie call his name. Got to his feet and put a foot in front of the other and found if he walked sideways on the ice he could stay up eight or ten yards. When he fell, he flopped back and watched the sky turn. When the cold crept through his parka, he got up again. Crabbed his way toward the heat of the flames.

WHEN PLUG CAME back alone, Esther was not surprised. She knew Leonard would want to hole up someplace, lick his wounds, but there was no place to hole up out there. She had to get him inside, and after fifteen minutes she pulled on her parka and went back down to the landing to bring him up, but when she got there he was gone.

"Leonard!"

She looked out onto the river itself and thought she maybe saw a shadow in the snow, but the light played tricks and he was smarter than to try the ice like that.

"Leonard?" she yelled at the river. Nothing.

She knelt down and felt for him under the rowboat. She tried to peer into the woods, and that's when she saw him. He was about twenty feet in, leaning against a tree.

"God in heaven, Leonard! I was sick to death!" She went over and reached to take ahold of him but found she was talking to a snag that was fallen against another tree.

She recoiled, felt the rush of relief vanish and the fear seep back. She returned to the landing and squinted out on the river again. The only reason he'd cross might be to try and make Council. She could see something out there, maybe. Maybe not, but not so large a shape as Leonard would've made. The night was dead quiet.

It came to her there must be someplace he'd camped in the woods before he'd revealed himself. She went back up the bank to his snowshoe trail and turned to follow it, studying the snow to try and see where he might have gone off the trail. There was no moon and the dark and shadow of the forest moved with the northern lights and was hard to read. She heard Plug and Lena calling to Leonard from up the hillside, checking the mines. The woods were stilled with a cold that knifed through a person. No living thing stirred. *I will hike to find you*, she told him. *No matter how far, Leonard. But you got to tell me which way to go.*

No word or sign came.

She returned to the landing. She squinted again at the river. She could make out nothing. Nor could she think of another place to search, so she turned and climbed the path to the cabin.

The three of them sat indoors with strong coffee until the sky began to lighten, and then she went back to the river alone and looked to the far side. Her eye caught on a thing in the middle.

25

He lay half caught in the ice. His feet were below it and his head and shoulders above, his face turned up to the sky. The ice had thickened to three inches or more in the night.

"For the love of God," Esther said.

His boots and socks had washed away and his white feet wobbled in the current as if they were swimming him someplace.

She leaned down and touched her hand to his cheek, which was stone-cold, and then she tugged at his open parka and tried to pull it shut, but the material was stuck fast to the ice. "Well, damnation!" She got down on her knees and gripped the fabric with both hands and yanked it good. The tears were coming now, and she swiped at them with her sleeve because the parka ought to have been buttoned and not left to freeze open like that. Was it too much to ask, let her close his damned jacket? She gave it a fierce jerk, and then again, putting her weight into it, the tears streaming, and a groan came up out of her chest, and she let go of the fabric and rocked back on her heels. The groan rose into a cry. She pulled herself forward, trying to get control—his elbows were jaked outward funny like chicken wings, might be he was lifting off of his backside but gave up, and they looked uncomfortable; she tried to straighten the near arm and get it alongside him but it would not give. "God and Jesus, Leonard, I cannot do it all by myself!" The words came in a high, tight voice that seemed to come out of somebody else. She put her knee against his side and pulled on the arm, crying, "Quit it! I'm trying to help you!"

She was tugged sideways at the shoulder and turned. There was Lena.

"Look at what I have done," Esther cried. "He is cold through! He is gone!"

"Was not your doing, Essie! Was not you! It's what he did himself. You could not have kept him from it."

Esther shook her head, did not want to hear it. "I was not kind. I was not true."

Lena gripped her arm. "Come away, Ess. Plug will free him out of the river."

Esther looked past Lena. The sun was coming up, and there was Plug, silhouetted with his ax.

"No," she said. She got up onto her feet. She tried to dry her eyes and then held out her hand to Plug. "Let me do it."

She stood behind Leonard's head. The gray of the frozen river slowly yellowed in the spreading light. Was empty of promise. Was nothing good that could come. Worst of the night was right there in front of her, and no dawn of a new day could make it otherwise.

She spread her feet and raised the ax high and then she drove it into the ice beside Leonard's shoulder. Chips flew, glistening in the first light. She moved back slightly, raised the ax, and drove it into the ice. She wiped her eyes on her sleeve and found a handkerchief and blew her nose and repositioned herself and raised the ax again. Brought it down.

"Drat! Drat! Drat!" she scolded. "Getting ice chips on his face, Essie!" She bent and brushed them away, had to take off her mitten to get a chip out of the pocket of his eye, and she could see it made no difference, and the knowledge took the strength from her and she dropped the ax and turned to Lena, who took her and held her and wept with her.

SHE AND LENA sat at the fire, unable to put it all together, how it had happened and what it meant. After an hour, Plug came and said a few words to Lena, and the two of them left the cabin. Esther turned to the window and watched them walk down the path together. Shortly they reappeared, working their way up with the frozen body, pulling by the jaked arms and letting the naked feet follow in the snow.

They put him on the floor and talked about what to do, and when they were settled on it, Plug left by snowshoe to get Homer from Council.

Essie cut his clothes away and washed him. He was wasted to scar and gristle, the muscle of his one leg shriveled. The burn made a map of the Perley flood. She could see the ripply waters stretch from side to side, the course of the Red along the bone, and the char that marked the place where her boy had died.

Slowly he thawed. She took the red moccasin from her private things and tucked it in his hands, stiffened by death. She looked at it there for a moment. Then she took it back. She pulled off her wedding band, put it deep inside the moccasin, and tucked the moccasin into his hands again. She had done for him as she was given to know how. Not the wife another woman might have been for him, but the best she had found within herself.

"There's another thing," Essie said to Lena, "but I am not decided on it." She held up his rat.

"He's going to want that."

"You think I should add it?"

Lena nodded.

"So do I." She set the rat with its empty jug beside him. Something from the Indian boy he had been so fond of.

"Well, then." She sewed a blanket around him up to his neck, leaving his face open. She combed his hair for the third time, not getting it right. Did not look like Leonard to have his hair combed, and she reached a hand down and mussed it some.

The day's light was fading. Esther lit candles and the two women got on their knees before him, straightening their dresses, and opened Lena's Bible to the Twenty-third Psalm. They stiffened their backs and began to recite. Green pastures and still waters mixed with the heat of the stove and with the smell of the lye soap in which she had washed him and the smell of the woolen blanket in which she had wrapped him. When the Lord preparest a table before me in the presence of mine enemy she did not understand the meaning and thought of Leonard at the threshing table on the day the Norgaard boy had died and she wondered at the sense of any of it. Gabriel was gone to dwell in the house of the Lord forever, and now Leonard. She wanted to believe, but when they were done reciting, the words didn't seem enough, and she suggested they pray "Our Father," which they did, and the familiar cadences pulled her back to church and the countless Sundays when she had added her voice to the chorus of her neighbors and felt purified by it, no thought then of dead sons and husbands and fatherless babies. It took less than a minute to say the Lord's Prayer, and when they were done, she felt the need of it once more, and they prayed it again. At the end of the second recitation she looked to Lena.

"We've done what's wanted," Lena said.

So Esther picked up her needle and thread and set to sewing the blanket shut over his head.

When he was closed up, she looked at the bundle for a long while. Leonard's force ran strong as oxblood and weak as water and she did not know how to explain it, or how it was possible that last night he had wanted to get a boy and this morning the fire that had burnt within him was out. Years with a man, and still he was strange to her. So many things she had never asked. About his journey to find her. What he did all those times he went to the Indian boy. His life before she knew him, and which of the stories he told were true. Where they would've raised the boy he wanted. A question as simple as what was on his mind. He never told, but now she thought of it, she wasn't sure she had asked.

Truth was, she could have been a better wife. She had not seen it while she was with him. While she was with him, she had done everything she had known to, but liked to think he could do differently for her. They were the same that way.

She let go a longish sigh. She knew he was past being comfortable or not, but she could not help asking, "Do you think we should pull him outside so he can freeze in a reposed position?"

"Oh," Lena said. She bit her lower lip, shaking her head. "Not sure he would be safe."

"How do you mean?

"Animals."

"Oh, Lord. We will keep him inside, and not run the fire too hot."

THE DOGS CAME up the trail in the morning, with Plug riding in the sled and Homer standing behind on the runners. Plug got out and Esther took his place, settling under a blanket. They loaded her few things and then added the body so that the head rested in her lap. Leonard was gone, and yet here was the weight of him.

She looked up at Lena and Plug, reached both hands to them, and said her goodbyes. Then she told Homer, "Let's go do our business."

He drove the dogs in a wide circle and ran them back east along the river's edge and then south.

It was a clear day, the low sun washing softly over the snow that clung to the spruce boughs and covered the sedges and tussocks and bent the scrub willow. They ran past Council at the edge of the frozen bog and then turned southwest into the forest. In the pines west of the Niukluk, near the Fox River, Homer drove the dogs into a small clearing and there he whistled for them to stop.

He and Esther went to work with his saw and ax. By noon they had laid a crib of logs and filled it with tinder and kindling and sticks. Atop of this they built a rough bed. They lifted the body onto it, and then they stopped to rest. Homer lit a small cookfire and boiled coffee and they ate ham and biscuits and chocolate and gazed up at Leonard, closed in his blanket on the log bed.

Over the next hour they gathered more fuel, piling it teepee style, covering the body.

When she was satisfied, Homer kindled it.

The flames licked hungrily through the dry pine and gathered to a roar. Homer continued to gather wood, while Esther tended the fire, adding fuel to be certain of their objective. Ashes to ashes. There was no seeing the body, just a great leaping fire and knowing that the shell of Leonard—and all that either of them once thought to have from the other—lay within it being consumed. Two forces against each other trying for a thing neither could say or obtain.

By nine o'clock the fire had burned down to heaped coals and the little clearing was swallowed by night. She stood before the embers and felt the last of his heat. The clearing was quiet. Snowy meadow. Dark trees at the edges. She thought of him sinking into the soil here, and felt it was right. She waited for other thoughts. She had hoped the heaviness might lift, but it did not. A greater knowledge ought to come of such waste or what was the point of it? She stood patiently. Nothing came but questions. What had she thought she was giving in marriage? How could a knot as fixed as Leonard become, finally, only the mosses and grasses?

THEY PACKED THE sled and turned for the winter trail, running out onto the open tundra under a starlit sky. Homer's dogs trotted eagerly. By now she knew their names: Emik, Suniak, Cheenuk, Auboon, and Tingle. They pulled with their tails curled over their backs and their ears pointed forward, and a breeze blew up and drove the surface snow before them in a flowing stream, the whiteness braiding and crossing the trail, running ahead, chased by the dogs. The creak of the runners and the wisps of snow in her face took her back to her pa's sleigh, crossing the fields after vespers at the Kirkebo church, and she thought how little Gabe liked a cutter on a deep night, and then she remembered Gabe was gone, and so, too, Leonard, and the surprise of it kicked her.

She had lived her life against him, steered by the force of him. Now he was nowhere, and she was adrift. Weightless as the ash he'd burned down to. Left without a thing to push against.

EARLY THE FOLLOWING evening they reached Nome. She watched the familiar storefronts and offices pass, shuttered and dark, coming home to a city that had fallen dormant and showed no warmth for her return. The sled traveled all but unnoticed, accentuating her solitude, sparking a hesitation in her breast, a reluctance to be left there alone. She was between a finished life and one yet to be undertaken, and for a moment she despaired of the effort.

Homer saw her safely into her quarters and then went respectfully on his way. The spare little room was as she'd left it, but the privacy of it came to her now as the greatest of luxuries. She went from nightstand to shelf to coat hook touching her few possessions, bringing back the time of Nate, the skittish supposable days before the sadness of Leonard. She found an extra blanket and tucked herself in and gazed at the darkened ceiling, sustained by the promise of her child, resolving to find her way and do it bravely.

In the dark of morning Esther stepped out for Thurl's to look in on her business and settle up what she was owed for the dogs. Nome was transformed—the mouth of the Snake was frozen, the sea itself had grown solid and still. Only a few holdovers prowled the city.

The idea had crossed her mind to go look in at Ten Steadman, but then she thought better of that, not wanting to see the office dark and empty. She came up Third to find a new sign: "Thurl's Hides: Quality Reindeer & Exotic." She slipped around back to check on the dogs, but the dog lot was empty, as well it should have been. She cut through the stables to the storehouse, where she found him heating his lunch on the fire.

Thurl looked up. "You are back."

He had changed. He wore newish clothes and had slicked his hair with pomade. She sensed the advent of a lady friend. "You have sold all the dogs, then?"

"Yes. Someone came asking for you."

She thought for a flicker. "That was my husband." She did not feel up to the whole story. "How did we come out, then, or have you spent yourself entirely on the hides?"

"One of the company men. Wondered were you coming back from Council. I said I would be the last to know, having heard not one word by mail or raised the scent of your intentions from the air currents, while being left to run the whole business by myself as I seen fit." He brushed something off his sleeve and dared her to argue. "The dogs paid what we'd expected, plus some. Let me tell you about the hides, though."

She hoped the lady friend wasn't one of the sporting girls. "Which company was the caller from, Mr. Thurl?"

"He didn't see fit to say. First, we sold twenty-five of the reindeers to Alaska Commercial Company. All I did was go in and ask did they need any hides by any chance, and the fella says, 'Horse hide? Cow hide?' and I say—"

"Excuse me. Something I need to go see about." She walked out of the storehouse and turned left for Steadman, thinking what a fool if she hadn't gone to the company's offices and there he sat, but she found the place was locked and the windows boarded.

She turned back up Steadman, gripped by an appetite and hoping to find Mrs. Powell's Kitchen open. Against odds, it was. She ordered breakfast despite the hour, past noon. When the eggs came, she stabbed the yolks and watched them settle into their toast foundation, letting her mind lie quiet for a change. She could have stayed at Dogtail, but that was Lena's life and no place Essie cared to cling to.

THE SKY SNOWED almost daily. The snow was shoveled from the boardwalks into the streets, the streets rising on the snowpack so you had to look up to see the occasional passing dog team or horse and sleigh. The cold and dark settled over Nome like affliction. She buoyed her spirits the best she knew how. She made a project of snipping tail and mane hairs from the few horses remaining around town. These she cleaned and sorted, laying the strands out on her bed. She worked in the light of a lantern, hitching a belt which she meant as a Christmas gift for Thurl. Turned out his friend was the restaurant lady, Mrs. Powell, which explained the kitchen's staying open past close of shipping.

Else she walked. She was getting large, and had begun to parade like a goose with her shoulders thrown back. Her route took her down Third to West E, down to River Street, and over the footbridge to the frozen sea to gaze up the silent beach. Then back to River Street, up Front to Steadman, quiet as a cemetery, and back to her room. She took her meals at Mrs. Powell's, in the company of Thurl and his lady friend. She settled with Thurl, who had done better on the hides than she cared to admit, and then she pulled together her few things, and wrote what she had been meaning to say to her friend.

The Le George
Nome, Alaska
December 19, 1900

Dear Mrs. L,
Leonard came to work in one of the gold mines for wages but was kilt from an accident on the river. I cannot believe he is gone. Whom God hath raised up, having loosed the pains of death.

I write because you knew me before Leonard, and now I start again, thinking who was that girl?

This letter and I will go out overland, but strike in different directions considering I must continue to the East and settle a question, supposing I can even find the man involved. I am doing all right and will bring something to show you come Summer.

Ever your friend,
Essie

The next morning, with the thermometer at minus twenty-five, she stood in the front room of the residence with her belongings, watching down the street for Homer. Shortly, he and the team came chasing ahead of a scut of snow and pulled to a stop out front, the dogs in a state of high eagerness. The sled was laden with the Wild Goose Company's ledgers, mail sacks, provisions for the travelers and dogs, a pair of snowshoes lashed at the back, and a white bearskin tied in a roll where she'd thought to ride.

She did not have much to add. Homer only questioned one box. "Feels empty."

"A boater, and don't go crushing it. Got it half-price at the millinery. Spent most of a day poking around Nome for somebody to open the store and take my money. Not sure you've got room for me, though."

He loosed a twine and unfurled the bearskin over the sled's rails, patting it down at the center to make a place. "Your mister left this to be posted, and I thought you might as well use it."

Homer's surprise took her breath away. The bed she had twice lain upon was now to carry her away. She eased herself into the fur, catching her sleeve on the edge of something—a tag, pinned and lettered in a careful hand: Worcester Motor-Cycle Shops, One Locust Street, Worcester, Massachusetts, USA.

She knew to point for Worcester, but hadn't expected to be packaged and labeled for the trip.

"Ready?"

She smiled yes, but how could she possibly say? You give yourself to a thing, and then you hang on.

At Homer's signal, the team leapt forward and the sled pulled away. She tugged the pelt around her as he drove out Front Street, east beyond the edge of town, past the roadhouse at Fort Davis and across the Nome River, the air sharp against her face. They pressed down the coast for Port Safety, Topkuk, and Cheenik, where they would pick up the trail for Seward. There was the creak of the sled, the yip and squeal of the dogs, running at the edge of the world, above the frozen sea.

AUTHOR'S NOTE

My grandfather, Ned Brown, joined the stampede to Nome in 1900 as engineer for the Cape Nome Hydraulic Mining Company. This novel draws heavily on his diaries and other historical documents. Several names are taken from real people—Lena Walton; Nels Hultberg and the "Three Lucky Swedes"; Alexander McKenzie; Judge Alfred Noyes—but the words and actions of all the characters in the novel are my invention. The crimes perpetrated by Noyes and McKenzie are a matter of public record.

Apologies to the birders of Nome for my having relocated the murre colonies of Bluff and Sledge Island to Sonora Creek, for the convenience of my tale. I have sent Alexander McKenzie to Nome several weeks ahead of history, and delayed the journey of the great barge *Skookum* to Nome by a few weeks, although she founders true to history on September 12, 1900. I have delayed by two years the devastating flood of 1897 on the Red River of the North.

Among the books and Web sites I found helpful, I would particularly recommend these to interested readers:

Butler, Walter P. *The Butler Brothers' Gold Rush: The Nome Album, 1900–1901*. <http://photolab.elmer.uaf.edu/gallery/photos/19640033/butler/index.html>.

Cole, Terrence Michael. *Nome: City of the Golden Beaches*. Alaska Geographic Society, 1984.

Drache, Hiram. *The Challenge of the Prairie*. North Dakota Institute for Regional Studies, Fargo, 1970.

Fitz, Frances Ella. *Lady Sourdough*. Macmillan, New York, 1941.

French, L. H. *Seward's Land of Gold*. Montross, Clarke, and Emmons, New York, 1905.

Grinnell, Joseph. *Gold Hunting in Alaska*. Cook Publishing, 1901.

Johnson, Roy. *Roy Johnson's Red River Valley*, Clarence A. Glasrud, editor. Red River Valley Historical Society, 1982.

Lockley, Fred. *Alaska's First Free Mail Delivery in 1900*. <http://www.postalmuseum.si.edu/gold/lockley.html>.

Lokke, Carl L. *From the Klondike to the Kougarok*. <http://www.naha.stolaf.edu/pubs/nas/volume16/vol16_5.htm>.

McKee, Lanier. *The Land of Nome*. The Grafton Press, New York, 1902.

Murphy, Claire Rudolf, and Jane G. Haigh, *Gold Rush Women*. Alaska Northwest Books, 1997.

Robins, Elizabeth. "Elizabeth Robins at Cape Nome." *Seattle Post Intelligencer*, August 19, 1900.

——. "The Gold Miners of the Frozen North: A Visit to Cape Nome." *Pall Mall* magazine, Vol. 23 (January 1901).

——. "The Very Latest Goldfield in the Arctic Circle, Letter from Miss Elizabeth Robins." *Review of Reviews*, London Edition

(October 1900). For all Robins, see: <http://www.jsu.edu/depart/english/robins/alask/ala00tab.htm>

Woodward, Mary Dodge. *The Checkered Years: A Bonanza Farm Diary, 1884–88*, Mary Boynton Cowdrey, editor. Minnesota Historical Society Press, St. Paul, 1989.

ACKNOWLEDGMENTS

I wish to thank the Carrie McLain Memorial Museum and the Kegoayah Koza Library at Nome; Minnesota Historical Society; Consortium Library of Alaska Pacific University and the University of Alaska at Anchorage; library of the University of Alaska at Fairbanks; James J. Hill Reference Library; the historical societies of Minnesota's Clay and Norman Counties; the St. Paul Public Library; and the Hennepin County (Minnesota) Library. Particular thanks to Laura Samuelson, Venus Lamb, Chris Barker, Mark Peihl, Kathleen Flynn, Eileen McCormack, and Trudi Campbell.

For their help in Alaska, I thank Regina Zimmerman, Lee Zimmerman, Cussie Kauer, Carolyn Reader, Dan Stang, Irene Anderson, Mitch Erickson, Kay Hansen, Ken Shoogukwruk, and Aaron Simon. I wish to acknowledge the important work of George T. Harper and his Blacks in Alaska History Project. Thanks to Tom Gray for taking me up the Fish and Niukluk Rivers and showing me the ruins of the roadhouses and camps inhabited by the writers of the diaries I carried. Thanks to Leigh Hill French III for swapping stories of our grandfathers, and to the late Federal Judge Edward J. Devitt for digging up transcripts of the McKenzie trial for me back when this novel was a mere urge.

For the Minnesota chapters I owe a debt to Suzanne Tjornhom, Ralph Thrane, and Don Linehan, whose family farming histories enrich my story. Many thanks to Donna Loreen Wilson, who responded to a plea posted on a poultry newsgroup and became my witty chicken expert and a vivid reporter of her own growing-up on the northern prairie. Thanks to RJ Mulder and Paul Zoschke on matters of steam-era wheat harvesting.

Regarding ships and shipping, I thank Dana Leonard; Ron Burke, the Puget Sound Maritime Historical Society; the Bayfield (Wisconsin) Maritime Museum; the National Maritime Museum, Greenwich, London; and Donald Smith and Charles Swonger of the SS *Meteor* Maritime Museum.

Thanks to Patrick Irvine for period medical knowledge, Joan Dickert for help with Worcester, and Andrea Lloyd for aerial images of the white spruce forest along the Niukluk River.

I have had the rare fortune to count Liz Darhansoff as my agent and Carol Houck Smith as my editor and I am deeply grateful for their enthusiasm and wisdom.

I thank my wife, Ellen, who helped at every step.

THE FUGITIVE WIFE

Peter C. Brown

READING GROUP GUIDE

THE FUGITIVE WIFE

Peter C. Brown

READING GROUP GUIDE

AN INTERVIEW WITH PETER C. BROWN

What was your inspiration for this story?

My grandfather's diaries from the gold rush to Nome. I never knew him, but I grew up with the artifacts he left behind: a walrus tusk, a seal harpoon, some gold nuggets in a leather poke. As a boy I studied his picture albums, seeing Eskimos posing in front of skin boats and smoky fires, and company men in wall tents wearing fur-ruffed parkas, their rifles hung on the wall, polar bear skins for bedding. I wanted to step into those snapshots.

Where did Essie come from?

Essie was a surprise to me. I had thought it was going to be Nate's story. The business of the big dredge and prospecting the creeks follows my grandfather's experiences. But I'm more interested in what goes on between men and women, how they get themselves into fixes and try to make a life in spite of themselves. So I needed a woman. When I put Essie on the train at Moorhead, I had to nudge her up the aisle and practically shove her into an empty seat among Nate and his associates, hoping to get something going. By the time they set sail from Seattle, she was fast on her way to taking over the novel. Since I'd cast Essie as a Minnesotan, we had some common ground to work with.

How did you research this novel?

I sifted through diaries and letters for language and the daily frustrations of life. I studied hundreds of old photos to see how people dressed and held themselves, the tools they carried, how they lived, the free-for-all at Nome. I went where my characters went, trying to get the smell and feel of the places: At Nome I hired a native to take me up the Fish and Niukluk rivers. In the Red River Valley, I attended a pioneer church and pedaled among the wheat fields and buttonholed oldtimers. I joined local historical societies and spent hours in libraries. Reference books from the period gave me terms for medical diagnoses and treatments, and a period sensibility about the body and its functions. I discovered the power of online usenet groups to correspond with people knowledgeable in arcane fields, like chicken husbandry and shipping in Norton Sound.

There's a lot of machinery in the novel.

Hauling boilers and five-thousand-pound engine blocks into the wilderness is a form of hubris that captures 1900 capitalism for me. And then fitting crates of pieces together, hand-forming the bearings and seals—it takes a certain kind of fussiness and precision. There's a tension in that, something they cannot bully, these guys with their big hands and big ideas.

Why did you put a snake in the story?

The snake came to me as it came to Leonard—a way to show Essie he was man enough for her. The snake became a metaphor for what Leonard brought into their lives that doomed their marriage: his sense of not measuring up, if you will, that turned him to whisky and led him to so many wrong choices. I hadn't realized how repugnant a snake would be for some readers.

Did you know how the story was going to end?

I knew it would be resolved in the interior, at Dogtail Creek. I hoped that if I had three strong characters bent on a collision course, the resolution would present itself when the characters got there, and that plus a little sweat is more or less how it worked out.

What's it about, in your mind?

I'm curious how people know what they want from life, and why striving for a thing can sometimes put it out of reach; how most of us face this lifelong struggle within ourselves between our sense of loss and our sense of hope and possibility. Some people are like Essie and can dig down time and again to find the next possibility. Others are like Leonard and succumb. I identified with both of them.

DISCUSSION QUESTIONS

1. Is Essie idealized by the author, or does she have flaws that make her human?

2. By marrying Leonard Essie figured to get a husband who was a good worker and who was willing to let her direct the business of farming. In a society where farms were left to sons, what other choices were open to her? How were her strengths working against her in this decision?

3. How does Essie's thriving in Alaska change what she wants from life? Will the attributes that make her a business success in Alaska work in her favor when she returns to conventional society? What failings or blind spots might cause Essie difficulty in the future?

4. Was it believable to you that Leonard would go all the way to Alaska to try to win Essie back?

5. In struggling with her decision to take Leonard back, Essie asks herself, "How could a person know between two wrong things?" How might Essie have justified turning Leonard away? What had Leonard done to make himself worthy of another chance? Nate accepts her decision, finding it "bullheaded and plain wrong," and yet he loves her better for it. Was Nate's acceptance a sign of strength or an indication he was unwilling to fight for what he believed?

6. Essie's pregnancy with Nate's child is too much for Leonard to see past in his effort to reclaim his marriage. If Essie had handled the situation differently, is there a chance Leonard might have accepted the child, and the marriage could have succeeded?

7. These characters lived in a different era; how do modern sensibilities affect your understanding or acceptance of their decisions?

8. At the end of the book, Essie embarks on her long journey to Worcester. If she finds Nate, will their relationship likely grow and

deepen? In what ways was Nate a good or a bad match for Essie? Given how the novel ends, what kind of future do you imagine for Essie?

Helen Humphreys	*The Lost Garden*
Erica Jong	*Fanny*
	Shylock's Daughters [not on the website]
	Sappho's Leap
Binnie Kirshenbaum	*Hester Among the Ruins*
Barbara Klein Moss	*Little Edens*
James Lasdun	*The Horned Man*
Karen Latuchie	*The Honey Wall*
Don Lee	*Yellow*
Joan Leegant	*An Hour in Paradise*
Vyvyane Loh	*Breaking the Tongue*
Lisa Michaels	*Grand Ambition*
Lydia Minatoya	*The Strangeness of Beauty*
Tova Mirvis	*The Ladies Auxiliary*
Walter Mosley	*Always Outnumbered, Always Outgunned*
Patrick O'Brian	*The Yellow Admiral**
Jean Rhys	*Wide Sargasso Sea*
Josh Russell	*Yellow Jack*
Kerri Sakamoto	*The Electrical Field*
Gay Salisbury and Laney Salisbury	*The Cruelest Miles*
May Sarton	*Journal of a Solitude**
Susan Fromberg Schaeffer	*Anya*
	Buffalo Afternoon
	The Snow Fox
Jessica Shattuck	*The Hazards of Good Breeding*
Frances Sherwood	*The Book of Splendor*
	Vindication
Joan Silber	*Ideas of Heaven*
Gustaf Sobin	*The Fly-Truffler*
	In Pursuit of a Vanishing Star
Dorothy Allred Solomon	*Daughter of the Saints*
Ted Solotaroff	*Truth Comes in Blows*
Jean Christopher Spaugh	*Something Blue*
Manil Suri	*The Death of Vishnu*

Barry Unsworth	*Losing Nelson*
	Morality Play
	Sacred Hunger
	Songs of the Kings
Brad Watson	*The Heaven of Mercury*

*Available only on the Norton Web site:
www.wwnorton.com/guides